The Whizbang Machine

by Danielle A. Vann

Published by Waldorf Publishing

2140 Hall Johnson Road
#102-345
Grapevine, Texas 76051
www.WaldorfPublishing.com

The Whizbang Machine
The Whizbang Machine Series, Book 1

ISBN: 978-1-943847-92-1
Library of Congress Control Number: 2015957020

Copyright © 2016

Printed in Canada

Dedication

For TCV, forever—4503.

To Erin, thank you for being my muse. A simple photo changed everything.

D, M & C, you are my world.

Chapter 1: Changes

Everything changed the sweltering summer of 2007. Literally everything. I was eight; up until then life on Downhill Lane, on the outskirts of New York City, was well, exceptionally normal. The inner workings of our little house were about as predictable as the golden sunrise peeking its head over the eastern sky. That is until death struck.

"Elizabeth, sweetie?" my mom, Laurel, called from downstairs. "It's almost five o'clock."

I suppose you could say that is when my mundane, little life took an unusual twist.

Black ink smeared across the pristine white page with each push of the space bar. I closed my eyes and listened to the hum of the light blue electric typewriter and the chatter turning over in my mind. There was still so much left to type. I listened for a minute longer and then pressed my fingers down to cradle the keys.

"Lizzy?" Mom called again, "Your grandfather will be here any minute. Are you coming downstairs or not?"

"Yes, Mom, I'm coming," I shouted back.

Click, clack.

This is the story of my family eight years later.

"Elizabeth! Take your fingers off that typewriter right now! Jack will be here any minute. Please come downstairs," Mom whined in a panic.

"Okay, okay, I'm coming."

The machine sighed to sleep with the flip of the red off button. I drew in a deep breath, stuffed Jack's last postcard in my front jean pocket and stood eerily still. *Jack,* I thought. After all this time, he would finally be standing inside my house. The place he used to treasure before the bomb went off in both of our lives. It didn't seem like today would ever come. The lump that has sat in my throat for more than two days somehow grew bigger when I allowed my mind to utter his name.

"E-l-i-z-a-b-e-t-h!"

My mother's tone shook away the heaviness of my memories and propelled me forward. "Okay, okay! I'm coming—relax," I called, thundering down the stairs, "I was working on my English paper I've got to finish before school lets out. Oh, and by the way, my typewriter is smudging the page again. Maybe we can take it to Mr. Sherry's shop tomorrow."

"Or you could use the laptop instead of fighting that archaic heap of junk," she countered.

"It isn't a heap of junk. Besides, there is something romantic about writing on an old typewriter."

"You're fifteen," Mom laughed.

"I'll be sixteen in less than a month," I interjected.

"Still, what do you know about romance? I love that you have an appreciation for old things, particularly typewriters, but I'm tired of spending my hard-earned

2

money to repair that thing. So, maybe, just maybe, it's time to step into the modern age, dear. Now, before Jack arrives, look around. How does the house look, Lizzy?"

Mom's hands waved wildly drawing my attention to the streak-free windows and new houndstooth rug laid at an angle on the foyer tile. Her amber eyes held mine for a moment too long, and that's when it hit me. My mother was just as nervous about seeing Jack as I was. Everything had to be perfect before he arrived. The beds donned freshly ironed linens. The hard oak floors had been scrubbed not once, but twice. She had spent every free moment over the last two weeks scrubbing, fluffing pillows, hanging new curtains, and fixating on the past since Jack's last postcard arrived. Everything was in its place, and for a moment, it was almost as if nothing had changed.

Yet, the fact was that everything had changed. Eight years had ticked away since anyone had laid eyes on Jack Yale. The last time I saw him we were holding hands and sobbing as we laid his son, my father, to rest. It was the darkest day of either of our lives.

"Without my boy Jesse in the world, I've lost my roots," Jack muttered, caressing my tear-stained cheeks inside the Monty Family Funeral Home.

"First Jewel, now Jesse. I'm not sure I can handle the everyday reminders of my life in this city, Elizabeth."

I didn't know what he meant. I was too young to understand. All I knew was three days later, Grandpa Jack packed up and sold Yale's Shelves—a bookstore our family had owned for more than fifty years. He put his house on the market, dropped a few tattered boxes of family heirlooms and the old grandfather clock on our front porch sometime in the dead of night, and left without saying good-bye. We might as well have buried Jack too.

Two long weeks passed before anyone heard from him. When he did write it came in the form of a postcard.

Istanbul, Prague, Transylvania, Paris, you name it; postcards came from all over the world. As time moved forward and life settled into a new pace with my father and grandfather gone, I wanted nothing more than to jump inside one of those three-and-a-half-by-five rectangle postcards and set sail.

"What about life here? What about school?" Mom questioned each time I brought up seeing Jack. No matter what I said there was never a good enough answer that changed her mind. Every conversation ended with the same four dirty little words, "*You are too young.*"

After a while, I stopped asking and resigned myself to the possibility that I may never see my grandfather again. My father, his father, my grandmother were all gone within a few short weeks of each other. It was as if the universe erased that side of my life entirely.

It was a tough pill to swallow. An even tougher one each time a new postcard found its way into the mailbox. It was a harsh reminder that Jack was still alive, yet chose not to be near.

There were plenty of cards too. Four hundred and sixteen to be exact. One for every week since Jack went away. Each glossy card drove me further into my desire to run away and travel the world with him.

The mail lady knew my name by heart. She became accustomed to seeing a new treasure in her delivery sacks.

She even changed her mail route so that her delivery time corresponded with when bus twelve dropped me off at home. Each time a new card arrived, she and I swapped dreams of escaping to the new wondrous place Jack's eyes had seen. The last postcard was as big of a surprise to her as it had been to me. Jack was on his way home.

Mom's hands were busy straightening the same four white candles she has fussed over for the last week. When her eyes fell onto my jeans, she asked, "What's in your pocket?"

"What?" I questioned.

"What's sticking out of your pocket?"

"Oh, it's just Jack's last postcard," I laughed.

Mom reached for the thick cardstock peeking out of my torn jeans. My hand clasped down and shoved it deeper into my pocket. Our heads hit and immediately both began to throb under the pressure.

"Ouch," she groaned.

"Sorry," I replied. "What was I saying?"

"Jack's…" Mom began. Before anything else could be said, her entire body jumped. "Jack! My word, he'll be here any second. Elizabeth, help me put the food on the table," she cried, wheeling around on her heels.

The kitchen smelled of warm homemade buttered biscuits, hot honey, cheese, red grapes, and freshly mulled wine. Scores of biscuits covered the granite island. The odd combination of bites certainly couldn't be called dinner; yet, everything in the spread was one of Grandpa Jack's favorites.

"You know, Mom," I snapped, "Jack has traveled to nearly every corner of the world. I doubt he likes any of this stuff anymore."

"Elizabeth," Mom said, "It doesn't matter how far you go, how much you have seen or felt, there are just some things that remind you of home. Please, don't forget that, honey." She patted my lower back tenderly. "Now, would you please get the crackers from the pantry? The postcard from Jack, what does it say?"

"Nothing much, just that he was coming home. I told you that when it came," I replied. "Here's the crackers."

Mom's face shifted as she grasped my arm, "Promise me you will enjoy this time with him," she whispered.

I nodded hard, not sure what to make of her sudden seriousness. A thin gold ring with two dull rubies shining from her ring finger seemed to be the answer to her unusual behavior. I was certain my eyes were playing tricks on me. Blinking hard, I tried to readjust my vision. Deep inside, I was hoping that when I opened my eyes, the ring wouldn't be there. But, it was. It was a direct center punch to the belly. I had gotten used to seeing her without the small reminder of my father slipped close to her knuckle.

A few months back she woke me from the dead of sleep. She urgently shook me until I sat straight up and thought the house was on fire. It wasn't, but she was a mess. Mom wanted permission to take off her wedding band. Eight years was a long time to live in the shadow of your husband's premature death. The pressure that came with her question nearly stole my breath that night. I mulled it over in between her sighs and did what I knew she would do if it were me needing the advice. I told her it was fine. I wanted her to be happy. On the inside though, I wasn't so sure. It took some time and a gallon of tears, but somewhere close to three a.m. my mother slipped off that band and ended her promise to be forever Jesse's wife. We both cried and snuggled close in my bed until sleep came.

The next morning she placed the ring inside my jewelry box and made me swear I would never lose it. I couldn't imagine ever removing it from its spot, let alone daring to lose that golden reminder of my life before my father's death.

Just thinking about that night, dredging up all the memories of my father passing, and seeing that golden promise on her finger again made the lump in my throat grow ever so slightly. One more inch and I swear I would gag. Grabbing the teapot and spooning three heaps of freshly ground lavender tea leaves into it—careful to stay out of her way—I knew if I didn't speak soon I would be a total mess when Jack arrived.

"Mom," I blurted out. My voice trembling with uncertainty. "Grandpa Jack wrote that he has a very special gift for me when he arrives."

"All those places he has been, I can't imagine what treasures he has brought back. I bet he has something wonderful, Lizzy. I really do."

Three soft knocks followed by five quick beats rang out against the old hardwood door in the foyer.

Mom beamed, "I'd know that old knock anywhere."

Chapter 2: Jack's Back

I hurried to the door. For the first time in eight long years, I smiled. Not the inkling of a smile, but a real smile that curled my toes in my shoes. Something had changed. The air grew lighter; our little house gained a brilliance it had been missing for quite some time. As another rap hit the door, I knew exactly what it was—it was Jack. He was home.

Life was awakened inside my mother too. Her smile gleamed brighter. Her voice reminded me of the singsong melody she used to speak in when I was a small child. All this time I had forgotten that she had lost that piece of herself. After my father passed away, we learned to live with a new sort of happiness. One that was much less fulfilling. I honestly hadn't realized it until this moment arrived, and instantly, I missed the way things used to be.

Without speaking a word, she turned the gold lock. It creaked and moaned under her hand. With one quick swoop, she yanked the door open, nearly busting it off its hinges. The smells of the outside: damp grass, blooming gardenia, and impending rain wafted in and filled our noses.

"Jack," my mom cried.

"Laurel Yale, Laurel, Laurel. You haven't aged a single day since I last saw you, kid," Jack said, wrapping his big arms around her.

"Well, it seems you've gone blind or crazy," she laughed, pulling him deeper into her arms.

"Perhaps a bit of both, my dear."

Despite their laughter, sadness still found a way to leak into the small gap between the three of us. My father was the spitting image of his father. I had waited so long to see him, but seeing Grandpa Jack now was almost too much. I wondered what my father would look like today. Would he still look like his father? Would his hair be grey? Would he look wiser? Would he still sing that old goofy song about red robins on the rooftop when he woke me every morning? Everyone says life isn't fair, but this seemed worse. Tears dripped onto my warm cheeks as Jack turned and rested his brilliant blue eyes on me. The wrinkle between his eyes hardened and then eased.

"And just who are you, young lady?" he questioned.

"Grandpa," I cried, bounding into his arms and burying my face in his rough tweed sports coat. I was unable to contain myself.

"Lizzy-cakes," Jack's voice quivered. His hot breath covered my neck. "Let me take a look at you."

My arms wouldn't budge and were locked in place as I refused to let go. He escaped all those years ago, but I wasn't willing to let him go this time. He gently lifted my chin and leaned in closer.

"My goodness Laurel, she looks just like you did when you first started dating Jesse."

"She's the same age I was when Jesse and I started dating," Laurel replied.

"Wow," Jack whistled. "Where has the time gone? I almost can't get over it." His warm lips crashed onto the top of my head kissing it softly before tousling my hair. "I've lost so much time with you, Lizzy-cakes."

One salty tear hit my neck. As Jack began to wipe it off, another hit, followed by another.

The only sound in the room was the ticking of the antique grandfather clock that used to be proudly displayed next to the mystery section of Yale's Shelves and the soft tears that fell from everyone's eyes. As the clock struck six, our brief silence was broken by Jack's laughter.

"I see that old thing still works."

"It does," Laurel laughed, "it even gives the correct time."

Jack's belly bounced as his laughter exploded.

"What's the point of putting an old clock next to a mystery section if it doesn't mysteriously go off at random times? Boy, I used to get the biggest kick out of that," he hooted.

"Oh, Jack. You're really something! You haven't changed a bit. Let's go in the kitchen and sit down," she motioned. "I bet you're hungry and tired. Where is it you came from this time?"

"Laurel, now don't you make a fuss over me. I do quite well on my own these days."

The smell of the homemade biscuits washed over Jack as we made our way to the table.

The look on his face turned Laurel's mouth into a grin.

"I know they're your favorite," she said, dishing up a hot biscuit and a selection of cheeses onto an antique rose plate.

"Lizzy, your momma always took the best care of your daddy and me. Whipped up warm biscuits anytime we got a craving. Did she tell you that she learned to make these biscuits from my momma?"

"No," I answered.

"It's true. She spent the entire summer next to my mother before she passed. My momma sat on her old broken-down wooden stool and directed your momma's little tail around that kitchen faster than she could move. It was a sight, but she learned. Your daddy knew he would marry her when he saw her elbow deep in flour and lard. I knew instantly there was nothing I could do to stop those two from being in love. So, I didn't. I think they were both just barely fifteen. But when love happens, it just happens."

Jack devoured a biscuit in three bites.

"Hungry, Grandpa?" I laughed.

"Now, now, Lizzy-cakes, one cannot be judged when it comes to biscuits, darling. Besides, there are just some things that remind a person of the best parts of home. Don't you ever forget that, darling."

Mom winked at me. All I could do was grin right back. She was right. Jack visibly eased the minute he smelled those biscuits. It was almost as if he let himself come home. He wasn't visiting, but instead closed the gap in time and rejoined what remained of our little family.

"To answer your question, Laurel, I've spent the last month traveling around Egypt. I started in Giza and made my way as far as the North Sudan. It is one thing to see all those places in the hundreds of books we carried at the store, but it's another thing to breathe the air, to feel the sandy wind on your face, and the dirt between your toes. I cannot tell you how many times I stared up at the wonders of all those pyramids. It was really something. I'll show you pictures later, but first, I want to know what my beautiful ladies have been up to."

"Same old, same old. School, soccer practice, school, repeat," I replied, brushing my hand against my forehead and swooning over the table.

"Poor girl's life is so terrible, Jack," Laurel replied with a wink.

"Well, maybe I can do something to help with that," he said.

"What?" I questioned, straightening in my chair.

"Lizzy, I was going to wait until later this evening to tell you, but I can't wait any longer."

"Jack," Laurel interrupted.

"Laurel, it's fine. It's exciting. Let me tell her."

"If you must," Mom whined.

"In your last letter, you asked why I was coming to visit after all this time away. Well, the truth is your mom has finally agreed to allow you to travel with me this summer. We'll leave in two days, barring you have all of your work turned in, and we will not return until school starts again in August. It's just you and me kid, all summer long, hopping flights and trains and exploring as many countries as we can."

Suddenly the thumping of my heart began pounding loudly in my throat. My head felt dizzy as a peculiar floating sensation came over me. If I didn't know better I was almost certain I levitated off the ground. Jack stood, sliding our first flight voucher across the table. As the stiff paper hit my fingertips, I leapt from my chair.

"No way!" I shouted, bouncing immaturely from foot to foot. "I don't believe it! Are you guys serious?"

Jack stood and interlaced his fingers in mine. Together we carried on like a pair of fifteen-year-old girls, jumping and thrashing about.

"It's the truth!" Jack exclaimed.

"I've waited my whole life for this!"

Mom laughed. "Go ahead, Elizabeth, read what the ticket says. Read it aloud."

My fingers fumbled to open the edge of the paper folder that held our tickets for safekeeping. In bold letters, my name stared back at me: Elizabeth Wright Yale. Along the bottom were a series of nine digits 957247753 with the words US passport printed beside it.

I swallowed hard.

"It says I have a passport. There are like official numbers here," I uttered.

"Yes; remember when I had you sign your driver's education forms?" Mom asked.

My head bounced up and down.

"Well, that was actually your passport application."

"Aren't you tricky?" I laughed. "No wonder you wouldn't let me look at the papers."

"What else does the ticket say, Lizzy?" Jack questioned.

I scanned the entire white oblong ticket trying to absorb all of the information. Our flight was scheduled to leave New York La Guardia Airport in two days. We would fly overnight stopping in Canada to board Royal Airlines. The flight schedule seemed obsessively long. I quickly did the math in my head.

"Twenty-two hours?" I quizzed.

My eyes landed on our final destination: Casablanca, Morocco.

"Wait! Morocco?" I declared. "No way! Wow. That isn't a place I would have ever dreamt of going, but now that we are I feel like I should go study everything there is to know about the place."

Mom and Jack exchanged looks and laughed. He spun me around in a fantastic circle. This man of sixty-nine-and-a-half years glided across our kitchen floor in some sort of odd victory dance. He looked more like a kid than a man who is able to cash in a senior citizen discount on any given day.

"I don't believe it," I whispered.

"Believe it kid, we are off to see the world!" Jack exclaimed.

"There is so much to do!" I shouted. "I've got to pack. I'll need clothes. Wait Mom, I'll need new clothes— summer clothes. Oh! Mom! Wait; there is no way you will be able to spend the entire summer alone without me here. I know better. What will you do while I'm gone?"

My mind shot off into a million directions all at once. I could barely catch my breath. So many emotions pulsed through my body that my face started to burn.

"Whoa, slow down little missy," Mom said. "First things first, there is that little matter of your last English paper you must take care of before you jet-set all summer. I've already talked to your teachers. Your grades are all A's. So, as long as you turn in your English paper tomorrow, you're free to go."

"My paper!" I replied. "Mom, the typewriter!"

"I think you're going to have to use the computer for this one, Lizzy."

"Don't worry kid, your old grandpa Jack will help you get everything handled before we leave. But first, why don't you help an old man bring in his suitcases?"

Chapter 3: Boxes

The light of the day was already escaping the sky. It was an unusual sight for this time of year. The sweet smell of fresh rain still lingered on the front porch. The outside world seemed bigger, more open than it had ever felt before. I straightened my back to stand taller. I wanted to throw my arms open and shout that in two short days I would roll my leather suitcases out our front door and set off on the adventure of a lifetime.

"I still don't believe it," I whispered.

In all my wildest dreams, I wouldn't have imagined that this day would come. That there would be an opportunity to travel and be with Jack again.

Jack's soft hand rested firm on my shoulder from behind. With a slight squeeze, he said, "You ready?"

"Yep," I giggled.

"Thanks for helping your old grandpa, kid. The car is pretty packed."

Jack jogged down the five steps to the brick pathway leading to our driveway. He brushed his hand across the tall clumps of lilacs hanging over the sidewalk. The cool dampness from his hands sprinkled onto the tops of my shoes.

"Remember when we planted those?" I asked.

"Sure do, Lizzy-cakes. I think you were four, maybe five. You picked them out for your mother's birthday. I got you all dressed up in butterfly rain boots, your momma's finest gardening gloves that were ten sizes too big, and tied her baking apron around your waist. We made a fine mess putting those bushes in."

"Yes, we did. I still laugh when I think of Mom's face when she got home from lunch with Daddy. She loved the bushes, but hated the dirt I smashed into the mortar between the bricks."

Jack grasped the driver's side door handle. "It's going to take me weeks to get that clean," Jack mocked, "She was hot when I told her that sometimes a four-year-old needs to live a little. Besides, what was a little dirt going to harm?"

A hastened breeze pushed against our bodies. Jack caught a flash of lightning out of the corner of his eye.

"Guess the storm isn't done with us yet," he said.

I pointed my face to the sky. It was literally cut in half. Clusters of billowing milky-white clouds collided into dark, ominous rainclouds. Only a small fraction of light was left in the heavens. The hum of the streetlights flickering on overhead called out to us.

"I'm not sure how much longer this weather will hold off, Elizabeth," Jack rushed. "We better start moving all this stuff inside. This looks like one heck of a storm."

Jack's rental car was overflowing with shabby brown paper parcels and a load of beat-up suitcases.

"What is all of that?" I gasped.

"What does it look like?" he replied. "Gifts for you and your momma, of course."

A slight whistle blew through my lips, "That is a lot of stuff, Jack," I said amazed. "There must be like seventy-five packages in that backseat."

"Seventy-six," he replied sheepishly. "What do you expect, Lizzy-cakes? I've traveled for eight years. It's been a long time since I've seen you. It looks like a mess now, but you'll see. There are some important things in these packages. Here—catch."

Jack tossed a small case in my direction. I almost caught it, but it slipped through my fingers just before hitting the ground. Mom walked to the passenger side and began to stack a load of smaller boxes onto the damp driveway.

"Take what you can, Elizabeth, but try not to drop anything else."

A worn brown case with stickers mimicking passport stamps dug into my hand and started to swing as I made my way up the brick steps to the porch. The light rain an hour before made the walkway slippery. I slowed my steps to avoid falling. Small slivers of yellow light cast from the porch light and stabbed at my eyes. I struggled to keep the uneven boxes resting in my fingers.

"Mom," I shouted, "Some help over here, please."

Quickly coming to my side, Mom roughly shifted the packages against my chest to help balance the weight, "I'm pretty sure if you drop a box or two, we'll have plenty of other junk to replace it with," she said sarcastically. "Jack," she called over her shoulder, "is it necessary to bring all this stuff inside right now?"

"It's starting to sprinkle again, Laurel. Take it all!"

Thunder cracked in the near distance. Another bolt of hissing lightning skittered across the sky seconds before the heavens opened up and began spilling over us. Mom refused to move.

"Mom, we're getting soaked. Please open the door," I whined.

"Where are we going to put all of this stuff?" she rambled. "How about we open the garage? Wouldn't that be easier?"

"No," Jack called out. "The relics inside cannot be replaced. Everything goes in." He pushed us forward until we burst through the front door.

"Relics," Laurel chomped, "It had better be relics, Jack. I swear I will lose my mind if it is nothing more than a bunch of I heart Egypt t-shirts in here."

"Have some faith, Laurel," Jack replied. "Lizzy-cakes, take that stuff to my room."

I managed to dash upstairs in a few breathless bounds. We carried everything to the guest room directly across the hall from my room. After five soggy trips back and forth, my arms ached, my nose twitched from the dust, and I was freezing from the rain.

When Grandpa Jack announced that he was coming to stay for a few days, Mom went into overdrive. It had been nearly two years since anyone had stayed in the guest bedroom, and even that was only for one night.

Imagine my surprise when I came home to find my mother rolling on a fresh coat of vanilla cream matte paint and obsessing if a new striped navy and cream duvet was the right choice. The room was beautiful when she was finished even if I did miss seeing my great-grandmother's tattered red quilt covering the old poster bed. While it was only a small change, those four freshly painted walls and smooth new sheets meant something to her.

By the time we finished unloading Jack's car, the pristine guest room looked more like a disorganized storage locker than a bedroom. It smelled like one too.

"Jack," Laurel said standing in the doorway clinching her teeth, "please tell me that all of this stuff is not staying here."

"Oh Laurel, of course it is," Jack chuckled.

Her face turned red hot, and she scowled.

"Yikes," I whispered, sinking onto the bed next to my grandfather. "Tread easy old man, it's about to get serious in here."

"Oh, lighten up," Jack replied.

Her scowl deepened as she pursed her lips together. Her hands twisted the silk scarf angrily around her neck—tugging it back and forth in a desperate attempt to not blow a fuse. It was already too late. All of her hard work had been turned into a heap of smelly postal mush in less than an hour.

My hand fell gently on Jack's forearm trying my best to warn him to offer an apology and promise to make it right. But he couldn't help himself. The smirk painted across his face made a mockery of my mother's distress. Patting the bed next to him, Jack laughed, "Come over here, Laurel, let's open this mess together. Wait until you see what I got you."

The tone of his voice visibly grated on her nerves. He had hit her last button. That was the furthest from what she wanted to hear. With a huff, she turned and stormed into the hallway. Jack and I listened to her footsteps as she pounded down each step. There was so much noise it sounded as though a thousand men were trailing her.

"Typical," she screeched. "Who brings a hundred boxes of junk to their daughter-in-law's house and calls it a gift? Get off that bed, Elizabeth Yale. You're soaking wet! That's a new bedspread. So glad you could make the trip home, Jack!"

Grandpa Jack bit his bottom lip and turned to me. "Don't laugh," he whispered, pressing one finger against his lips.

My shoulders rocked up and down as I buried my face in my hands. I knew if she said one more word I would burst from keeping my laughter inside.

"Elizabeth, finish your English paper right now, young lady!"

I couldn't hold it in any longer. Grandpa Jack and I howled so loud I fell to the floor and started rolling around.

"Stop," I cried out. "My stomach—it hurts!"

Jack jumped to his feet and pushed the door closed as to not make her any angrier. As the door hit the frame, she shouted, "Very funny, you two!"

"Nice work," I giggled, standing to survey the damage, "guess you better tell me what is inside all this mess?"

Jack's eyes darted along the collection of different sized cartons and said, "I'm looking for one box in particular." He paused, then pointed, "There. Elizabeth, grab the third box from the top of that far stack against the wall. That should be it."

The saturated boxes were dense and protruded from the wall. My knees dug into the edge of the mattress as I turned sideways and scooted my way down the wall.

"Why did you stack the most important box all the way in the back?" I grunted. My hand beat the top box. "This one?"

"Yes, that's it. Take out the third box from the top. Be careful, it's heavy."

I rocked back on my heels trying to steady myself. The mattress dug deeper into the backs of my knees sending shooting pains down into my feet.

"Ouch," I groaned.

"Do you need help, Lizzy?"

"No," I said, breathing heavy.

"Just be careful. It's really important this box isn't damaged."

An odd tingling sensation pulsed through my hands. I shook them hard, but the feeling wouldn't go away. Suddenly, a part of me didn't want to know what was inside the boxes. The way Jack spoke, his tone; a slight air of mystery hung over the box. I was afraid when I opened the carton I would be disappointed. The other part of me wanted to know what was so impressive that my grandfather decided to lug the gift across the world and personally deliver it. Whatever it was, I was glad it forced Jack back home.

He clapped hard as I struggled to break the box free, "Yes, let's see that box, Lizzy-cakes. I have an interesting story to tell you about what's inside."

The moist carton slipped and roughly bounced against the bed. The tingle pulsing through my hands grew to a sharp stabbing pain. Struggling to break free from the tangle of packages, I accidently dislodged two from their position. I managed to move my feet out of the way before they crashed to the floor, but whatever was inside was definitely broken now.

"Oh, Grandpa Jack, I'm so sorry."

"It's okay. Those boxes weren't that important. Now, come out of there before you create a landslide," Jack joked.

Jack's expression distracted me from the pain in my hands. My eyes wandered across the packages again, and I wondered why this one was so special. After a minute or two, Jack asked, "Are you going to open it or not?"

"I am," I replied slowly. My belly flipped as I dragged the box to the floor. Whatever was inside had suddenly made me tremendously jittery.

"Why don't you open it?" I said slyly, pushing the packaging towards Jack.

"No, you go ahead. It's for you," he said.

I forced myself to touch the box. I convinced myself that a box could do no harm, but as I grabbed at the corners, my body stiffened.

"Jack," I whispered.

My eyes narrowed as the room visibly dimmed.

"It's okay. Everything is just fine," he muttered. "Don't stop now."

His voice was steady and held an air of calmness that I needed. Yet, I still wasn't able to bring myself to fully open the box. A burst of cold air passed between Jack and I. Clearing his throat, he abruptly reached out ready to yank the sealed flaps apart. Anything to speed the process along, but as quickly as he started, he stopped. His hands dangled in mid-air as if being controlled by an invisible puppet string. Jack held them there for a second longer before dropping them and letting them find their way to his front trouser pockets.

"It's yours," he said. "Please Elizabeth, open your gift."

It struck me that perhaps he too had experienced the same unpleasant sensation when he touched the so-called gift, but wisdom told him that if he shared that with me now, I would never find the courage to face whatever this internal tremble was.

Jack's eyes burned and fluttered. His breath quickened and grew labored as he bent over my shoulder and leaned in.

"What's wrong?" I questioned.

"Nothing. I'm waiting. Do you feel anything right now, Elizabeth?" He spoke in a hush.

"A bit scared—maybe—sort of excited. I don't really know. It's just a box. How can a box make me feel this way?"

"Shh, it's okay. Go ahead."

The calm of his voice, that little piece of familiarity I held onto minutes before was gone, replaced now with an iciness that made my stomach turn. His fingers twitched. Something was coming—something big. I searched Jack's brilliant blue eyes, looking for any unspoken answer that may be secretly leaking from him, but nothing came. I ran my hand along the edge of the only corner still intact and stopped.

"Jack," I trembled.

He was far more serious when he answered, "You'll never know if you don't have faith and open the box."

With that, I flushed all the thoughts rushing through my mind out with a heavy exhale, and let my fingers rip at the dampened corners. The box unfolded giving way to reveal a faded tan case with a long black handle. One by one, my fingers caressed the antique dial lock. Next to it was a typewheel, from an old-school typewriter. The letters EWY were secured into position.

A slight grin touched my face. That was a nice touch, I thought. A beautiful nod to my love of typewriters. Bold calligraphy, in a foreign language that I was certain I had never seen before, was etched into the side of the case.

"What does that say?" I questioned.

Jack tapped the case lightly. It sounded hollow.

"Do you have the last postcard I sent you?" Jack asked.

"Of course."

"Go get it."

Hesitating for a moment, peering at the small roll-dial antique gold lock securing the case shut, I stood and pulled the crumpled card from my front pocket. Smoothing the edges against my thigh, I turned it over in my hands a few times.

"Now what?" I questioned.

"There are numbers at the top. A combination. Use it to open the case."

I hadn't noticed the digits scrolled in small red print in the right-hand corner until now. 37-1-14-5-23. I read the combination again, this time more slowly letting each number sink in. 37. 1. 14. 5. 23. I felt as though I should be connected to those numbers, but I couldn't figure out how.

"Go ahead, open it," Jack pushed.

"Why don't you just tell me what it is?" I replied slowly. "What is this all about?"

"I can't explain, Elizabeth," Jack replied, "at least, not yet." His voice turned cold and eerie. "I need to see you open the box first."

"Jack, you're scaring me."

"Open the box, Elizabeth," he urged. "I need to know if the gift is truly meant for you before I can explain how I found it. Or I should say how it found me."

"How it found you?" I rushed. "What are you talking about?"

"Open the box!"

Jack grabbed the postcard off my knee and began to read the combination one number at a time. His voice was so forceful that if I didn't do what I was told to do, I knew there would be a price to pay. What that price was, I didn't know just yet, I just knew it was serious.

I filled my lungs with all the air they could hold, and rolled my index finger along the lock. 37. The numbers clicked into place, and my flesh raised. Tiny patches of hair stood on end.

"Go ahead. One."

Click. 1.

"Fourteen," I muttered, rolling the numbers.

"Two more numbers, Lizzy. Five. Turn the lock to 5."

My lungs throbbed and burned from holding my breath. Exhaling, I flipped the lock into place. 5.

"Are you sure I should open it?" I asked.

Jack nodded his head. The same wrinkle between his eyes creased hard. It took a moment to lock the last number in place, 23. The lock creaked and sprung open. Instinct took over, and I jumped back to protect myself.

I'm not sure what I thought would happen. Maybe I thought whatever was inside would glow like the hundreds of treasure movies I've seen, or a swarm of bees would spiral into the air and begin a buzzing raid, but nothing happened. I was even more confused than before. There was no sound, no odd smells were released, no grandstanding of any sort. I looked back up at Jack.

"Well, are you going to look inside?" he questioned slowly.

"I don't know."

"I think you should, Lizzy."

Slowly lifting the lid, I closed my eyes.

Chapter 4: The Gift

An explosion of thunder rang out inches from the exterior of the guest bedroom. The lights overhead flickered while the house rattled and moaned. The long fingers of the Green Ash tree blew and scratched against the window. My eyes bolted open.

"Jack!" I shook.

A wicked smile stretched across his tanned face. Jack could no longer hide his wild, pent-up intrigue.

"Look down," he urged.

"No!"

"Elizabeth, what are you afraid of?"

"All of this," I muttered. I began to stand. I needed to escape whatever witchery or magic Jack had the ability to conjure up. Scrambling to my feet, he grabbed at my hands.

"Elizabeth," he whispered. "I can feel it. This has to mean something to you. You know it does. I can feel it in the air."

"Let me go," I pushed.

"Look at me," he rushed, pulling our bodies inches from each other. My hands burned.

"Look down. Please, Elizabeth, I have to know."

The sound my body was producing didn't seem natural. The stirring of the storm made the window vibrate once more. Thunder roared as the room hummed from the lightning that followed.

"No!" I shouted.

Turning to flee, my eyes settled on what was inside the box. Laid open, seated in exquisite red plush velvet, was a vintage typewriter unlike any other I had ever seen.

It's thick black steel and copper frame was caked with years of soot and grimy dust. The copper in the spacebar had turned a beautiful patina. The machine clearly spent many long years exposed to the elements and corrosive air. Each large circular key still proudly displayed its assigned letter: A, S, D, F, and so forth. Each letter inked in cream stood out against a black face. The numbers along the top started with two and ended with zero. The number one was missing, yet there seemed to have never been a place for it at all. The blackened paper roller was scratched and rusted with wear. With a turn of the golden knob, four numbers and a colorful logo were revealed. A replica of the machine was embossed in gold and placed in the dead center of the roller. A bronze circle encompassed and guarded the machine. The faces of charging thoroughbreds peered around the circle's curves in gold, red, and black. Their reins were whipping wildly out away from what one would perceive to be their hidden bodies. Along the bottom 18 TYPEWRITER 76 was etched in red. Smaller print once filled the space below. Deep grooves and ragged edges had been scored across the words long ago. The haste of the marks proved whoever damaged the machine had done it with heated malice. Perhaps the words could have been saved some time ago, but as for now, orange rust had set in and spread across the indented lines. The only part my eyes could make out was "The W."

"The W?" I finally spoke. "Wonder what that said?"

"That's my girl. I wondered the same. It seems important, doesn't it? Like someone wanted to cover up the words."

"I suppose. Or, it could have been a child."

"I don't know," Jack answered. "Doesn't seem like a child would take the time to be as thorough and destructive as the person who made these marks. I've tried to come up with a thousand phrases that would start with The W and I keep coming up empty-handed. Are you sure you don't know what it means, Lizzy?"

"How would I know?"

Jack blinked hard, his expression stunned and frozen across his face. "Let me ask you," he said, "would you consider the possibility that you are tied to this old machine?"

My head lopped over. Shaking it back and forth, "No."

The man standing before me wasn't the Jack I remembered. He isn't the man who I've held on a pedestal for the last eight years. The Jack I knew wasn't full of odd codes and mysterious old gifts. He was playful. He adored me. He would never be the man who would invite me into what seemed like a dangerous situation without even the slightest hint of an explanation. The other side of my brain was intrigued. I have always been drawn to old typewriters. But why? I don't remember a particular reason for my affection. It has just always sort of been there. Here before me was the oldest and rarest specimen I have ever seen, yet, I was too afraid to get too close.

"The W?" I uttered again.

Jack pulled a folded yellowing sheet of paper from his wallet. Unfolding the printed picture he knelt to his knees to look me face to face. His joints popped and cracked on the way down.

"See this place?" he asked, pointing to a charming flat white building with vivid blue awnings hanging over small arched windows. The ground leading to the building was a mix of the most stunning turquoise, glazed-sky blue, and gravel-colored cobblestone. A sign hung above the sunshine yellow door that read: Kaas. "Have you ever seen this place before?"

"No," I replied, drawing out the sound of each letter. Narrowing my eyes and focusing them deep into Jack's, "I think it's time you start explaining what this is all about, Jack. You said earlier that this typewriter found you. What *exactly* do you mean?"

Disappointment slumped his shoulders, as he tousled my hair again, "It clearly means nothing, Elizabeth. Think of it as a gift and nothing more. I know how much you love to write on old machines. This is more authentic, like what a real writer should have. Don't worry about how old it is, if it scares you, or where I got it. You clearly don't recognize it like I thought you would."

"I'm sorry," I whispered.

"No, don't be. But it would make my heart happy to see you touch the keys," he urged.

Something wasn't right. He backed down way too easily.

"I don't understand, why are you testing me?" I insisted. "If it's about that place, I've never seen it before. Should I have?" Pointing at the picture still clutched between Jack's fingers, "and as for that machine, there is something strange about it. Something wrong. Whatever it is that you need to know or see I want no part of it. I don't get what you are trying to do, Jack. I think you should leave me alone."

Desperate, Jack wrenched my fingers down to touch the old typewriter. He teetered on the edge of speech. With a slight jerk of his head, he watched and waited. When nothing happened, another push of disappointment hit his face, and he released his grip.

"See, it's fine," he sighed.

My muscles released, spazzing as they let go. Laughter filled the back of my throat and burst through my teeth.

"I thought it was going to bite me or something," I howled.

"I told you nothing would happen," Jack chuckled.

A deeper sense of curiosity got the best of me. Positioning my fingers among the keys, they rested for half a second before the machine screamed to life. Whiz–Whiz–BANG! The ground under us quaked. Jack and I both ducked to avoid being showered with broken glass as a mirror broke free of its nail and tumbled to the ground. Golden sparks popped and sizzled out the machine's base. My fingers burned. I tried to tug them away, but the force pulling at me was too strong.

"Jack!" I shrieked in pain. "Please!" I was certain my hands were going to rip open if the machine didn't let go. My bones ached. They were seconds from snapping in two.

Reverberating noise, followed by an ear-piercing hum, echoed in the small guest room. Sparks shooting from the top of the machine looked like a Roman candle during the Fourth of July. Red flashes, followed by white, then gold, then streams of blue filled our eyes. Whoosh, pop, WHIZ, s-i-z-z-l-e, whoosh, WHIZ–BANG!

My head grew dizzy, and darkness filled my mind. I blinked hard to stay awake. Between the pain and the chaos, my body was shutting down.

"Elizabeth!" Jack cried. His voice sounded miles away.

As the last bit of light drew to a close, my fingers finally released their grip. My body went limp and smashed against the floor. I couldn't get enough breath into my lungs to speak, let alone stay conscious. I fought to hang on.

The noise stopped. The room fell quiet—too quiet.

Jack bent and snatched the case, pulling it closer to my head. The electricity still surging through the typewriter seemed to bolt me back into existence. I kicked and swatted at it. I never wanted to be put under its spell again. Jack's rough hand brushed the tangled mess of hair from my eyes and begged me to open them. When I did, a smile so wide and so mischievous filled my vision, I wanted to punch Jack square in the jaw.

"I wasn't sure," he began, "I thought for a moment I had lost my mind, but that, that proves I haven't. Oh Lizzy-cakes, I cannot even imagine what will come of this machine. What will come from all of this! The dreams. The shopkeeper, Lizzy. It's all real! You are EWY!"

"I, I, I," I stuttered. Scarlet ovals were singed into each of my fingers. The pain was unbearable.

Jack rambled, his words filled my ears, but it was all just white noise. I couldn't understand anything he said. Closing my eyes again, my stomach turned, nauseated.

"Elizabeth. Elizabeth," Jack exclaimed, shaking me hard. "Come on, touch the machine again."

"No!" I screamed. "What is wrong with you? I will never touch that thing again!

"I don't know how you did that, or what secrets you are hiding, but none of this is welcome here! You aren't welcome here. That was a hallucination. Yes, a hallucination. What did you give me? What kind of drug can do that? Some grandfather you are! Get out!"

The anger spewing through my blood carried me to my feet. To acknowledge this growing fear inside me is to let it in—to let it spread its poison into every ounce of my being and grab ahold. I would have none of it. The heavy wooden door exploded against its frame as I stormed away.

Chapter 5: The Merchant

My heart pounded.

"Elizabeth," Mom called from downstairs, "is everything okay?"

I stopped, standing in the doorway of my room. The answer was no. Everything wasn't okay. There is no doubt that if I don't answer it would only take a few seconds for her to traipse up the stairs and pelt me with a truckload of questions.

Somehow, I would have to try to explain the insanity I just witnessed. Try to hide, then rationalize the smell of burnt flesh pouring from my fingertips when she begged for a bedtime hug. Even if I were able to conjure up something close to a half-truth, it wouldn't sound believable, not in a million years.

"I'm fine, Mom. I'm sorry." The anger pulsing inside was working to spill out, and it was hard to keep my voice normal and steady. "I didn't mean to slam the door," I finished.

"Okay honey; sleep well," Mom replied. "Elizabeth, don't forget your English paper. You leave in two days!"

The singsong of her voice annoyed me now. I treasured it a few hours ago—a throwback to our lives before everything was twisted and messed up—but now I wanted no part of it. The truth was I wanted no part of Jack.

Bedsprings sighed as they took on the weight of my thin frame. The few lights remaining on in my room cast menacing shadows on every surface. A small red light glowed on my desk. The old electric typewriter I had switched off hours before was glowing again. I wondered if it too had been possessed.

My head lopped over into my hands. Damp hair fell and cascaded onto my knees. Inside something was keeping me from a full-blown panic attack. My mind reeled with the slightest possibility that perhaps what I had just experienced wasn't a hallucination after all. Jack seemed exceedingly convinced that I should have recognized that peculiar machine and the place in the picture he kept shoving in my face. Still, I couldn't shake the sense of trouble that covered me.

Lying back, I gazed at the hundreds of postcards lining the wall above my headboard. Funny how hours before Jack arrived I treasured each of those pieces of him, but now...

"You should have stayed away," I shouted. Tears erupted from a place I hadn't felt for many years. A place I had closed off when my father passed. It was a terrible mistake for Jack to come home. For the first time too, it forced me to realize that life after my father's death wasn't as horrible as I continued to make it out to be.

Nearly an hour passed, the tears dried, and I was exhausted. Right before sleep found me, a slight knock touched my door. I knew it was Jack.

"Go away," I uttered.

"I brought you some tea, Elizabeth," Jack whispered. "You don't have to talk to me, but at least take the tea to help settle you. I can hear you crying."

"I don't want it. Leave me alone."

Jack pressed his hand to the doorknob and turned.

"Elizabeth," he whispered, slightly cracking the door.

"I said to leave me alone. I don't know what you want, Jack," I growled. "I don't even know who you are anymore. You took off. You left. Now you think you can come back here and demand something from me. It doesn't work that way."

Jack stood stunned. His shoulders clenched up around his neck, and he sighed.

"You're right. It doesn't work that way. If I could take back leaving eight years ago, I would, Elizabeth. I messed up, and there will never be a good enough excuse for my behavior. All I can say is when I was packing, the gravity of leaving you weighed upon me so much I almost didn't go. Yet, I knew I wasn't in a place where I would be good enough to be with you either. Sweetheart, I didn't know how to handle life after your father died. He was my only child. I had just buried his mother months before, and then him. I couldn't handle life anymore. My family was gone."

Jack wept. His body convulsed as his sadness took over.

"No, it wasn't. We were still here. I was eight, Jack. I didn't know how to deal with life without you. Yet, you forced me to. I am your only grandchild," I chomped back.

We gazed at each other for several long moments. Then he turned, and before leaving he looked at me and said, "Elizabeth, I didn't deal with your father's death. I left you and your mom to do it for me. I wasn't trying to leave you. I was trying to leave me. It wasn't right." Hanging his head, he walked away.

The few tears I had left began to fall slowly. Gulping them back inside, unwilling to let my anger and sadness take over once more, I closed my eyes and tried to breathe.

Jack's soft voice filled my ears. "I would never purposefully hurt you. Never. And I've certainly never wanted to make you cry. That's not why I'm here. I love you. My heart is broken, Lizzy."

His heart skipped into his throat. With a deep swallow, Jack paused. Watching for any sign that I was willing to relent in my anger, Jack said, "This, all of this, was how I was going to fix what I've done. What I've done to you and to your mother, but also what I've done to myself. I can't even get this right, kid. Some grandfather I am."

I shook my head and looked at the clock, making no effort to look Jack in the eye.

"While I know you don't owe me a single thing, and I shouldn't be here asking, but would you please let me try to explain what just happened in there, with the machine?"

I opened my mouth ready to formulate some sort of an answer, then closed it again, somehow more confused than ever. Jack put his hand in his pocket and very slowly pulled out the antique typewheel and the picture.

Turning the typewheel over in his hand a few times, Jack pitched it in my direction. The metal ball bounced off the headboard and landed with my initials staring back at me. Even the most skilled pitcher couldn't have made the typewheel land in such a perfect position. The other side of the wheel didn't hold my initials like this one did. I realized right then that there was something, a stronger force, at play.

"Okay," I whispered, nodding and motioning him to take a seat.

"A few months ago, I was in Morocco. At Kaas to be exact," Jack began, handing me the mysterious picture and tapping at the page. "Kaas is a small bakery and café that sits at the edge of a long cobblestone merchant alley. During the warm months, patrons sit outside under oversized umbrellas sipping spiced teas and strongly brewed coffee. I was addicted to these warm syrup pastries that the little old lady behind the counter made by hand each morning. I probably spent the majority of my time in Morocco at Kaas. I was drawn there day after day with no explanation. At first, I thought it had more to do with the little old lady than anything, but it all became clear one Saturday morning."

Jack was speaking, but it was clear his mind wasn't with me. He had transported himself back to that place, to that exact moment he was about to describe. Finally, the truth was coming. I could feel it. Jack's eyes wandered around the room blinking hard as he pulled a deep inhale through his nose.

"And?" I questioned.

"Saturday mornings were different. Before the sun rises, the large town square in front of Kaas fills with vendors. Like our farmer's markets here, but instead of booths, men throw rough, sometimes soiled blankets on the ground, and spill their produce and wares in disorganized heaps. You can buy everything from hats to a loaf of bread inside the square. The sun seems to be the opening bell, because the minute light began to shine on the smallest corner of the market, hundreds upon hundreds of locals descended into the place."

"Music bellows overhead. The way it starts slow draws you in, bringing your senses to life, and then without your permission lulls you into a trance. Unknowingly, people move to the rhythm of the violin and oud."

"What's that, an oud?" I questioned.

"Sort of like a bass and a guitar," Jack replied. "It's enchanting. Between the music and the smells, I swear people aren't even present. They move in eccentric patterns with each striking beat the music plays. Everyone willingly hands over their last penny for freshly brined olives and warmed sweet bread."

"There are weavers set up all throughout the streets. Tiny women push their enormous looms into the square. One rough, brightly dyed wool string is weaved into the next, revealing the most exquisite patterns. You cannot help but stop and watch. When you do, they call out to you in Arabic. But when you don't answer in their language, they quickly ignore you and go back to work. Overwhelmed by the frantic and yet beautiful chaos, I stood still and let these souls move around me. I swear it was almost like a dream."

Jack crossed his arms. His eyes told me he was back with me, as a shudder took over his body.

"So, you bought the typewriter from a vendor?" I questioned slowly.

"Not exactly," he replied. "You see, the longer I held my place in the center of the market the more overwhelmed I became by the kinetic energy spinning all around me. It was unsettling. I made my way back to the edge of the square, to Kaas, and sat outside with a warm cup of coffee. It seemed safer there for some reason."

"Halfway through my second cup of coffee, a woman, maybe Brazilian, caught my attention. Well, she didn't as much as her necklace did. In fact, the more I have thought about it, I don't remember ever seeing her face. I can't tell you the color of her eyes, all I know is she seemed as out of place as I was. When she noticed me staring, she came to my table. She was friendly, spoke excellent English, and mentioned she had purchased her necklace a few days prior from a shop down the alleyway. She was very specific to tell me not to shop at any of the other shops, saying that their merchants were unfriendly and had nothing to offer. I had spent nearly a week staring down that alleyway, but hadn't brought myself to wander through."

"So, did you go?" Elizabeth interrupted.

"I did. I wanted to buy that necklace for you. Yet, I never made it all the way down the alley to that particular shop.

"Why?"

"Well, to be honest, I swear I heard my name being called. Then something caught my eye," Jack replied.

"The typewriter?" I questioned.

"Exactly. The third shop on the left was different. The owner, a man named Aden, must have come from a family with resources. Other shops hung blankets from the ceiling to define their stores, but Aden's place was permanent. There were walls and glass shelves, that sort of thing. He had the typical thing every other shop had: knock-off leathers, pieces of clay pottery, the weaver's blankets, but on the top shelf was the typewriter box laid open exposing the crushed red velvet lining. The first thing that caught my eye was the typewheel hanging from the case."

Jack eyed the wheel now nestled between my fingers.

"To answer the question you are about to ask, yes, your initials were already locked in place, just like they are now," Jack declared.

"What?" I questioned. "Come on Jack, you are messing with me. That isn't true."

"Yes, it is, Elizabeth. I wondered how it was possible too. Perhaps it could be explained away as a coincidence if the typewheel was one letter off or the letters were backwards, maybe YWE or something like that, but they weren't." Jack pointed to the wheel, "They are the same today as they were when I purchased the machine."

"How can that be?" I questioned again.

"That is what I'm still trying to figure out, Elizabeth. That day in the shop, I began asking Aden about the typewriter. Immediately, he became uncomfortable with even the mention of it. He refused to look up when I pointed to the top shelf. He wasn't willing to tell me where it came from, how it landed in his possession, or even how much he wanted for it. He made it abundantly clear, he wasn't willing to depart with the typewriter.

"I pushed, offering to buy it for whatever price he named with no bargaining, but still he resisted. He was talking in code, and kept repeating, 'I made a promise.' I asked him what he meant, but again, he wouldn't say. The last thing he said was he was tasked with finding the machine's rightful owner. Until he could prove that person had come, he could not sell the machine. Honestly, I laughed off his pitch. I thought it was a way to make me pay top dollar, which I was already willing to pay because I swear I felt the machine drawing me in, but no matter how hard I pressed, he wouldn't relent. After an hour, I grew tired of his bizarre rantings and gave up."

"So, you just left?" I asked.

"I did, but not before the weirdest sensation came over me," Jack replied.

"What? What was it?"

"I swear I heard your name. It was a female's voice, a familiar one, but there weren't any women around. In fact, the alleyway was strangely still. The marketplace was booming a few hundred cobblestones away, but where I was standing it was just Aden and me in the shop. I finally chalked it up to my old mind playing tricks on me, and I left."

"If you left, how did you end up with the machine?" I asked.

"Well, that is the interesting part."

The grandfather clock downstairs struck twelve, chiming out low bongs one by one until it called out its final hour. When it finished, Jack smiled.

"I've missed that sound," Jack muttered. "I went back to my hotel. It was mid-afternoon, maybe three or three-thirty. The moment I opened the hotel room door, my body felt limp. My mind was in a fog; I barely remember closing the door. It's been many years since I've experienced exhaustion at that level. Whatever was happening, it was too much. I had no choice but to lie down.

"Once I closed my eyes, I saw myself in the alleyway again. Aden was there. He was speaking to a woman with long jet-black hair. It was stick-straight and unusually shiny. Though she never turned around, I recognized her.

"As she spoke, I listened. I knew it was the Brazilian woman, the one with the necklace. I could tell that it was her voice. The one I heard in the alleyway, the one that said your name.

"I wasn't able to hear all of their conversation. It felt like my ears were being covered and uncovered to allow me to hear only what I was supposed to hear. I watched her bend down, roll the typewheel until your initials were set in place, and then she shook Aden's hand. Men and women do not customarily shake hands in Morocco. In fact, they do not touch each other at all in public, unless married. Even then, it's dicey. So, when she extended her hand I knew they were sealing an agreement.

"Before she released his hand, I heard her say, 'You shall never sell this machine. Not until the rightful owner appears and proves they are worthy.'

"Aden said something in return, but I wasn't able to make out his words. As far as I can tell he asked how he would know the rightful owner when they came, because she replied, 'You will know.'

"Aden appeared to be growing ill the longer her hand rested in his own. I knew I was only watching the two speak, yet, I wasn't really there. Still, I wanted to reach out and break her hold on him. Her hair moved smoothly across her back as she laughed.

"'Break this agreement and the curse will fall upon you and haunt your family as it has haunted the others,' she said.

"She turned and walked down the cobblestone alley, disappearing into the crowd. Right before I woke, your name echoed through the alleyway. The sound waves hit the sides of the concrete walls, bounced, and traveled down to my ears. Whatever that was, however that woman made that happen, it seemed like skilled black magic at its finest."

The skin on my arms raised, and my hair stood on end.

"How would she know my name?" I questioned.

"I don't know," Jack replied.

"It was just a dream. An odd coincidence because Aden wouldn't sell you the typewriter, I'm sure."

"I thought so too until the next morning."

"What happened? What do you mean?" I pushed.

"I dreamt that same dream, the details never faltering, on a loop for hours, waking only once around two a.m. to check the clock. The room was ice-cold, and I could feel someone watching me. I was too afraid to get up and inspect. I'll admit, I pulled the covers up to my nose and hid until sleep found me again. I awoke before the sun came up the next day. It wasn't a simple dream. That much I knew for sure. I grabbed a piece of paper from the bedside table and wrote out in exact detail what had happened."

The bedsprings sighed under Jack as he roughly shifted his body. His discomfort was visible.

"Did you still feel like you were being watched when you woke again?" I asked.

"No, not really. I could feel that something was changing, though. Something bigger was happening to me, and my small mind couldn't comprehend all the details."

"That is how I felt when I opened the typewriter," I whispered.

"I know," Jack said, patting my knee.

"So, what did you do then?"

"I got dressed and slipped out of the dimly lit hotel lobby. I made my way to the square. I thought maybe the answer to all of this could be found there, but when I arrived, it was empty. Kaas wasn't expected to open for hours, but the door was standing open. The smell of fresh pastries drew me over the threshold. For seven days, I had come to the bakery for breakfast and lunch. Every day, without fail, the same little old woman was standing behind the counter making pastries and selling coffee. But not this Sunday morning. Things were different."

A ping of fear passed through me and made my shoulders shake. "I'm afraid to ask why," I whispered.

"Yes," Jack coughed. "The old lady wasn't there. The woman with the long jet-black hair had taken her place. She was standing with her back to the door, humming. It was the same voice—the one from both my dreams and the alleyway the day before.

"The minute my eyes landed on her, my chest began to ache. My arms tingled. I swear I was having a heart attack until her voice started to fill my ears. She was singing in Arabic. The melody hit high, then dropped low. Her voice was as smooth as anything I have ever heard. While I knew she was singing a cappella, I could hear hundreds of instruments strumming in perfect pitch behind me. The music pushing through her lips grew louder and louder until my eardrums ached and pulsed. It was a trance. Her voice was taking over. I stood still, waiting for her to say something, to turn and acknowledge me, but the noise only grew to deafening levels.

I tried to grab on to the meaning of the words she was singing, but I heard only one familiar word: curse. The café grew darker as I fought to stay on my feet, and then suddenly she stopped singing."

Jack labored to breathe as his chest heaved up and down. Sweat formed on his brow. There was no way he could make his body respond this way unless everything he was saying was the complete truth.

"Jack, it's okay, breathe. Slow your breath," I whispered. Laying my hand on his back, I shivered hard. He was freezing. "Did she say anything after she stopped singing?"

Jack's brilliant blue eyes flashed, as though pulling himself out of the memory. "She didn't," he replied. "I bolted through the door, running as fast as my legs would carry me back to the hotel. It was barely six in the morning. The same exhaustion from the day before hit me hard. I called room service to bring coffee, but I must have fallen asleep before they arrived. I lost an entire day. I woke again at nearly midnight. Sunday was gone."

"That's strange. Do you think it was her? I mean, causing you to be so exhausted?"

"It had to be. What else would it be," he questioned.

"I don't know. You said you went back to sleep. Did you see her again? What else happened?"

"Yes, she was there, in my dreams, but, this time, more details came."

The grandfather clock sounded again, this time chiming out one hard bong.

"It's one a.m., Elizabeth. You have school in the morning."

"School!" I nearly shouted, "I have to turn in my English paper by nine tomorrow."

Jack patted my knee. "Why don't you sleep for a few hours, and I'll wake you at five and you can finish it."

"No! I want to know more. What happened in the dream?"

"In the morning, Lizzy-cakes. You must rest," Jack said, patting the goose down pillow.

"Okay," I agreed, "I don't think I have the energy to type a single word right now anyhow. Plus, my fingers still really hurt."

Jack kissed my forehead. "Sleep, my darling." Flipping off the overhead light, my eyes slammed shut. Sweet sleep found me within seconds.

Chapter 6: Dreams

"Come help Daddy, would you?" Jesse Yale called out to his five-year-old daughter.

"Coming, Daddy!" Elizabeth's small voice rang out. "Where are you?"

"Upstairs in the attic," Jesse answered. "It's time to bring down the reindeer and Christmas trees. Come help Daddy, would you?"

The rickety attic ladder barely touched the plush tan carpet lining the upstairs. Elizabeth's small foot hit the bottom rung. The ladder creaked and quivered under the slightest pressure.

"Daddy, I'm scared to climb up by myself. Did you forget I'm only five and three-quarters?" Elizabeth said, giggling.

Jesse peeked his head over the edge of the opening, bracing himself on all fours.

"I didn't forget, sweetheart," his face lighting up with a flawless smile, "Climb to me very carefully. I know you can do it."

Jesse extended his hand ready to pull Elizabeth up as soon as she drew close enough for him to pluck her from the rungs.

"Daddy," Elizabeth said, beginning to make her way to him, "When we get the Christmas tree up, can I help you climb the big ladder outside? I want to hang the Christmas lights on the very tip top of the roof."

The word roof blew through Elizabeth's mouth with a slight whistle, having just lost her bottom tooth days before. The sound made Jesse laugh.

"My toothless wonder, I think we better stick to this ladder for the time being."

"But, I want to help," Elizabeth whined.

"I know you do sweetheart, but if you fell, there isn't any soft carpet outside to help break your fall. You might bump your beautiful little noggin. We don't want that, do we?"

Tripping into the attic, Elizabeth let out a laugh, "Wowie, this is really high, Daddy!"

"Now about the outside lights," she giggled.

"Elizabeth Wright Yale," Jesse said tickling her belly. "Listen to me, I need you to be careful. Keep your feet on this big piece of wood, those are the support beams, and do not step off. It's like a balance beam, okay?"

"Okay, fun!" Elizabeth giggled.

"Now listen, if you step into the lower places, you could fall through the ceiling."

"How? It's so fluffy, I can't fall through," Elizabeth said, running her hands over the yellow insulation.

"It's a trick. It looks fluffy, but it will not hold you. So please, stay on the support beams. We don't want Mommy mad at us for putting holes in her ceiling, now do we?" Jesse asked lovingly.

"No way!" Elizabeth gasped.

"Very good! Now, how about we play a game?"

"Yea, yea, yeah!" she said jumping up and down clapping.

"Careful," Jesse warned, "Let's play I-Spy."

"My favorite! What are we spying?"

"Boxes marked with the words Christmas or those that have a big snowman sticker on them. If you see one, let Daddy know."

"Got it," Elizabeth said, giving Jesse a thumbs-up. "I see one!"

Jesse followed his daughter's gaze and extended his finger, "Yes, you do! Keep it up! You are a super spy!"

Jesse and Elizabeth collected and moved fifteen large moving boxes down to the second-floor landing before Laurel came to check their progress.

"Elizabeth sweetie, I have some warm gingerbread men cookies ready for you to decorate."

"Yum," she said, poking her head out of the attic opening. "I'm going to bite their heads off," she giggled hard.

Amused at her daughter, Laurel exclaimed, "You always do! Be careful honey. I don't want you to fall."

Jesse peeked his head around Elizabeth and smiled, "She's an old pro now. Don't worry hon."

"Mommy, can I help decorate cookies after I finish helping Daddy? We only have two boxes left to find. I'm winning I-Spy!"

"She sure is," Jesse called from deep inside the attic.

"Hey, wait for me. He's cheating Mommy."

"You better get in there and find those two boxes before he does! I'll get all the sprinkles out so you can create a masterpiece when you are done kicking some Daddy tail," she laughed.

"I heard that," Jesse exclaimed.

Laurel hid her mouth with her hand, holding back her laughter.

"You're silly Mommy!" Elizabeth chuckled, turning and bumping a stack of towering boxes. The top box tumbled, knocking Elizabeth into the piles of fluff. The next container teetered, wobbling on the uneven stack's edge. Jesse dove, trying to stop the entire cluster from flattening his daughter. As the box hit, it split, spilling its contents.

"Elizabeth! Jesse! Are you okay?" Laurel shouted from the stairs.

"We're okay! We're both okay," Jesse replied.

A handful of old photo albums lay open. One photo, in particular, held Elizabeth's attention.

"Look, Daddy," she said, picking up a black and white photo of two children holding hands, wild smiles plastered across their faces. Their heads turned up to a night sky. "They look like they are dancing. Their gowns are beautiful. I wish I had one like that."

Jesse peered over Elizabeth's shoulder, intrigued by the photo as well.

"They do, don't they?" he said, taking the picture from his daughter then flipping it over. In heavy graphite, the year 1876 was scrolled in cursive on the back.

"1876," Jesse muttered. "Which book did this come from, sweetie?"

"This one," she said, struggling to pick up the thick book.

"Huh," he replied, "I've never seen it before. Grandpa Jack must have brought this box over when he and Grandma Jewel moved. I wonder who these people are."

Elizabeth tenderly climbed into her father's lap, snuggling deep into his chest, and pulled the book onto both of their legs. Jesse flipped open the album's cover, exposing the initials DBY stamped on the first page.

"D-B-Y," Jesse read, "This must have belonged to my grandfather, David Boyd Yale."

"Who?" Elizabeth asked, "You don't have a grandpa."

"Well, I did. He was Grandpa Jack's Daddy," Jesse explained.

"How come I don't know him?" she questioned, "Where does he live?"

"Oh sweetie, he would have loved you. He was the kindest man. He passed away before you were born."

"I'm sorry, Daddy," Elizabeth said stroking her father's arm.

Jesse muttered to himself, "This doesn't make sense. If this photograph is dated 1876, that means the majority of the pictures in this book are centuries old. I haven't a clue how they got into my attic. Grandpa David wouldn't have been alive in 1876 either so why does the book have his initials."

"Huh?" Elizabeth said trying to keep up with her father's scattered thoughts.

Jesse snickered at himself and said, "I'm just rambling sweetheart. Just ignore me."

Jesse flipped to the next page. Stunning photographs, all in black and white, captured tall brick buildings that soared into the night's sky.

"Look at this one," Elizabeth pointed. "That's bea-ut-ti-ful! Wow-wee! Is that a church?"

He gently yanked the worn photo free from the book, careful not to tear the delicate corners. Stained glass columns artfully twisted up the far side of the building to touch what appeared to be a bell tower. A shiny silver bell hung in the center of a large oval opening. The roof sloped down to meet a white stone facade. A tall iron gate guarded the far western entrance where magnificent statues of Saints and prominent figures stood guard.

"Where is that?" Elizabeth asked.

"I don't know," Jesse answered quietly.

A sign in the far right corner displayed the building's name, but it was in a language that Jesse could not read.

"What does the sign say?" Lizzy asked, pointing.

"I wish I knew," he said, scratching his head, "maybe we should show these to Grandpa Jack."

"Maybe so," Elizabeth nodded. "It sure is beautiful, wherever it is."

"Yes, it sure is," Jesse replied, slipping the photograph back into its slot.

He turned the page, revealing pictures of towering windmills, babbling canals filled with small rowboats, and a celebration, of sorts, in what seemed to be a town square.

"That looks like fun," Elizabeth gasped.

"It does," Jesse replied, flipping to the next page.

This time instead of a collection of old photos, there was only one on the page; it was a black and white eight-by-ten of a woman.

A shudder traced up Elizabeth's spine, shaking her involuntarily, "She's scary, Daddy, turn the page."

Jesse held it there for a moment longer. Staring at her, he was becoming more unsettled with each passing glance.

"Please," Elizabeth cried.

"No, wait Elizabeth," Jesse snapped, roughly trying to tug the photograph from the tarnished picture corners securing it in place. "It's stuck. Why would someone glue this photo in and not bother with the others?"

Elizabeth stared hard into the woman's eyes and began to cry.

"Please Daddy," she whimpered. "She scares me."

* * * *

The scream billowing out of my mouth bolted me straight out of bed. My eyes darted around the room. Gone was the attic, I was safely tucked away in my bed.

"It was only a dream, Elizabeth," I whispered into the dark.

That is when it hit me. I had seen my father.

"Daddy," I choked.

It had been years since he found his way into my dreams. I laid back into the mess of pillows and blankets and turned to look at the clock.1:22 a.m.

"Of course, I've only slept for twenty-two minutes."

I held on to the vision of my father's face and kept the sound of his voice when he said my name close to my heart. It has been so long since I've heard it; I had nearly forgotten how soft and even his tone was.

"I miss you, Daddy," I breathed.

Hot tears sprang from my throat and made their way into my eyes. No matter how hard I tried to fight them from coming, they came.

While I knew there was more to the dream, more to consider than just seeing my father, I pushed the thoughts away. I only wanted to focus on him, but the frightening woman's eyes kept pushing my father's face away.

"No," I cried.

Between the tears and my fear, my eyes grew tired. No matter how hard I fought to stay awake, and not allow my mind to drift away to sleep, it found me once more.

* * * *

Without warning, a series of loud bangs stabbed the air. It took a moment before everything came into focus, but when it did, I was standing in a cobblestone alley in the heart of Casablanca, Morocco. Aden, the merchant, was to my right.

A woman was hunched over a typewriter, my typewriter, twisting my initials into place on the typewheel. Aden paced back and forth, his arms folded across his large chest. His aggression kept growing and dripping off him with each fevered pace.

"I'm dreaming," I shouted. "I want to wake up! This is not real!"

I was fighting to bring myself back to reality, to the safety and comfort of my own bed where I knew my body was resting. I began to scream, but no sound came. My voice was caught in my throat. The woman with the jet-black hair moved forward until she was offensively close; her face just inches from mine.

"Stop," she said simply. "Do not scream, Elizabeth. This is all for you, my dear."

My head wrenched back and forth, trying to force her away, but she would not move. The familiar coal-colored eyes bore into mine.

"Leave me alone. I'm not afraid of you," I stated fiercely.

Wickedness flashed into her eyes.

"Oh darling, yes, you are, and you should be. Now Elizabeth, the typewriter is waiting."

The machine quaked, shooting white sparks out of its roller. Dark, sticky oil oozed out of the side of the typewriter and pooled on the floor around it. Aden was as frightened as I was. Hot smoke sizzled, and with each hot puff, a letter, in perfect typewriter font, floated above the enchanted contraption.

"Go ahead, type," the woman shrieked. "Prove you are worthy!"

Her eyes flared excitedly as she knocked me to the ground, forcing me to hang over the typewriter as it sizzled out of control. The nerves in my hand tingled and jumped.

"Type!" she commanded.

There was no way out. Crouching over the oil, shaking from head to foot, I clumsily slid my fingers onto the keys. Papers began to fly from the roller, whirling overhead, raining down as the familiar clanging called out: Whiz-whiz-BANG!

"I said do it now, child!" she screamed.

The typewriter responded, summoning more power with each screech of her voice. Whiz-whiz, it chugged.

"No," I shouted. "It's too powerful."

"NOW!" she ordered, stepping in front of the machine and sinking to eye level. When our eyes met, she grabbed my hands, forced my fingers to connect with the keys, and she refused to let go. The machine rocked onto its sides, back and forth, with another reign of power and then burst into flames. Darkness swirled in my head and then everything went black.

My body shut down, but my mind did not. From somewhere above the merchant, I floated and watched as the wicked woman tossed an antique gold skeleton key in his direction. The handle hit his palm and sizzled red hot, leaving a smoldering burn mark. One circle over the next intertwined and connected until it formed the sign of infinity. I tried to hold on to her words, listening for what the key would unlock and why she so desperately needed me to touch the dreadful machine, but it was all lost. Darkness took full control of my sensibilities.

* * * *

Sitting up, heaving for air, my eyes flew to the clock. 1:43 a.m. I was alive, conscious, but unsure how much of what I just saw was a vivid nightmare and what was actually a frightening glance into the future. Either way, my stomach was uneasy.

"How can that be?" I muttered. "It feels like I have been asleep for hours."

Pulling the covers from my body, I climbed out of bed. Slipping my robe on and tying my hair in a messy knot on my head, a fierce determination to get to the bottom of the typewriter's mystery built inside my chest.

Snatching a piece of paper from my desk, I marched to the hallway niche where Jack had stashed the typewriter for the night. A warm yellow light stabbed the darkness from under the guest bedroom door. Trying to be quiet, I whispered, "Okay, typewriter," waiting for it to roar to life again, "you clearly have something to say to me. So let's hear it."

The gears began to grind as I rolled the paper through the antique roller. The noise wasn't like other typewriters I've used. It popped instead of rolled.

Waiting for the fireworks show to follow as I ran my fingers across the number keys, I stepped back. My left hand slid against my spine, hiding it as it was badly blackened and burned at the tips from my first unpleasant encounter with the unruly contraption hours before. The once white sheet was covered in muck and dust as it popped up on the front side of the roller. I stepped forward, wiped it clean, and pulled away. Logically I knew it was silly to be afraid of a hunk of metal, but this particular heap defied all logic.

"I need you to be good, typewriter," I sighed. "Please don't hurt me again."

Inhaling every bit of air my lungs could hold, I laid my fingers on the keys. Electricity began to build slowly, "Be nice," I warned harshly.

The first press of the keys sounded as it had before, Whiz, it called out. I heard Jack stirring from his bed. Urgency filled my bones, and I began to type rapidly.

I space Am space Elizabeth space Yale.

The machine responded. Pop, Whiz, sizzle, Whiz, then it stopped.

I waited.

"Go ahead," I said sarcastically.

BANG!

Jack's bedroom door swung open. When it did, the machine began to type on its own.

It's a lie. All of it, a lie. EWY, EWY, EWY, EWY. It's a lie. EWYEWYEWYEWY...

With a whiz and a bang, the machine pounded out the same line repeatedly. Warm sparks of electricity jetted from the contraption. Smoke with letters floating above it filled the small niche. Jack and I stood back in amazement. My head swirled somewhere between the present and the dream that jolted me from my sheets.

"What's a lie?" I roared. "Tell us, please!"

The speed of the machine galloped: It's a lie. All of it, a lie. EWY, but close to the bottom of the page, the last Y in Yale had a strike through it, marking it as though it was correcting a mistake. Still cranking ahead, speeding through the repeated sentence, the keys bounced up and down, flickers flying. It kept pushing, whizzing, banging as the noise hit an all-time high.

"Stop!" Jack shouted. Without thinking, Jack reached towards the machine and placed his fingers squarely on the keys. Everything went dead silent. He turned to me, his hands still dangling amongst the keys, and grinned, "There. I think I got it to stop."

He had, but only for a moment.

Bolts of white embers—hard arcs of power—pulsed out of the keys and through Jack's hands. His body vibrated, shaking madly.

"Let go!" I screamed.

Jack strained, attempting to wrench himself free, but his efforts were useless. The power surging through his body was relentless. Reaching out to help, Jack crudely jerked his arm away. His mouth distorted, trying to push sound through his lips, but he could not speak.

"You're going to kill him!" I yelled, "Stop! Please, please, stop!"

Jack's body seized—that was all it could take. He went limp. His hands released the machine as he crashed to the floor in a heap of shocked bones and burning flesh.

His eyes were open, but Jack was not responding.

Jack!" I shrieked, "Mom! M-o-m, call 9-1-1. Mom! I need help!"

Chapter 7: Things Change

The inside of the ambulance was cold and reeked of harsh disinfectants. The chemicals burned the inside of my nose. Two paramedics took turns forcing life back into Jack's chest. One kept count of each compression by mouthing a song only he could hear. When the song ended and that round of compressions finished, Jack's lungs were filled with breath. The medics switched, and the music began again. Between the wailing of the sirens, the rocking of sharp turns, and the hastened speed, Jack was slipping away.

"This is my fault," I cried. "Grandpa!"

No one had time to console my tears. Jack was minutes from departing this world, his soul barely hanging on. Through squinted eyes, I swear I could see him hovering inches from his body, watching as the world spun out of control.

Stats were called, recorded, and fed to the hospital staff awaiting our arrival.

"He's crashing," one of the medics called.

"Please don't take him," I pled. "If I lose him, if he goes…"

No matter how hard I tried to speak another word, I was stuck on *if I lose him*. I gathered my strength, reached out, and grabbed Jack's leg.

"Listen to me," I began.

"Clear," a medic hollered. "Sweetheart, take your hands off him now. We need to shock his heart. Clear!"

Jack's body jolted.

"Beginning compressions."

"We're almost there, Grandpa. I need you to be strong. Please," I begged, my words barely croaking out.

My eyes slammed shut. My head began to swim, unable to continue to function under this level of stress. I stood, fighting the sleepy urge creeping up my legs.

"Sweetheart, open your eyes. Unbuckle your legs. I need you to be present," the medic instructed.

My eyes opened only a small fraction. The world seemed flat, and I was caught somewhere between reality and begging my soul to slip away with my grandfather's should he not stay.

"Stop," the medic urged, "we've got a pulse. Keep breathing for him. We're almost there."

With that, my mind was able to reel back into the moment, coming alive again instead of hiding in a darkened fog.

"How much longer?" I whimpered.

"Not long, I promise. It's going to be okay, kiddo. His pulse is weak, but it's there. I think we can save him now."

"Hurry," I replied.

"We are. Stay with me. Look into my eyes. This isn't your fault," he stated firmly, "Do you hear me? Your grandfather has had a heart attack. I'm not a betting man, but my guess is he's had a pretty serious one. He needs you to stay strong, okay?"

"Okay. But, please, he's all I've got."

He fixed his attention on me—his eyes narrowing hard, "Can you tell me what he was doing before this happened?" he asked.

Everything went deafeningly quiet in my head. What was I going to say? No one would ever believe me if I said that he was standing at a bewitched typewriter that came to life and shocked him into death's grips. That sounded absurd to even me, and I witnessed it.

The driver shouted back, "We're here."

While everything seemed in fast motion before, now the world around Jack took on warp speed. The rig doors flew open. Three doctors and a slew of nurses stood waiting.

"Sixty-nine-year-old male, named Jack Yale," the medic called, disengaging the gurney's wheel locks to unload Jack's still body. Emerging into the warm breeze, he continued, "Presenting with signs of a heart attack. Unconscious upon our arrival. According to his granddaughter here, Jack got up to get a drink of water. He called out to her, and when she got to him, he was lying on the floor unconscious."

The team worked together to unload Jack's still body. The emergency room double doors slid on their tracks, opening with a gush of blasting air as the front wheels of the stretcher bumped and screeched onto the slick tile floor.

A sea of nurses in colorful scrubs ran to our sides, hoping to solve Jack's plight. Each new member got the same update the medic had given outside the ER doors. The lie sounded worse coming from someone else's mouth, but it was done. The words were gone, and that was the story we—Jack and me—would *have* to continue to tell.

"Put him in trauma four," a nurse directed from behind the desk.

The team swiftly turned, wheeling Jack into the bay. A sea of blue curtains suddenly shifted, sliding across the glass door and sealing the team inside and me out. I stood there in shock.

"Jack!" I shouted. "Grandpa Jack!"

My knees felt incredibly weak and close to giving out.

"Elizabeth!" Mom called out, sprinting towards me. "What's happening? Jack, is he okay?"

"I don't know," I muttered. "They had to restart his heart, Mom." Tears spilled faster than I could catch them. "I, I," I stammered.

"Baby," she said, wrapping her arms around me. "Take a deep breath, please. It's okay. Lizzy, it's all going to be okay. You don't look good honey. We better sit down."

"No, not until someone comes out and tells me if Jack's okay."

"It may be awhile," she whispered.

"So, I'll stand here awhile," I snapped rudely.

"Okay sweetie, okay."

"Clear the hall," a nurse called as another patient in crisis was pushed into the bay next to Jack's. An older woman trailing behind looked as though she too would pass out. I had to avert my eyes so that our heavy burdens would not tangle together in the small hallway.

"I hate hospitals," I declared, stomping my foot.

"We all do, sweetheart," Mom replied.

Careful to keep my words from giving away the heaps of mistruths that had already been misspoken, I kicked at the cold cream and brown speckled tile and whispered, "Mom, I'm sorry."

"For what?" her tone turning sharp.

"For this," I replied.

"Elizabeth!" turning my face to hers, staring deep into my eyes, "You aren't responsible for Jack having a heart attack. Your grandfather is weeks from turning seventy-years-old. Neither of us knows if he has kept up with his health. This isn't your fault. Do you hear me? You have absolutely nothing to be sorry for."

I did, but it didn't change the fact that she had no idea what had actually happened in the small hallway upstairs. Furthermore, I wasn't sure I could ever bring myself to tell her. But, when it comes down to it if Grandpa Jack hadn't brought that ridiculous typewriter and broken his promise to the merchant, then none of this would be happening.

"Elizabeth, answer me. Do you hear me? This isn't your fault."

"Okay," I hesitated.

"Ma'am," the paramedic said, coming out from behind the curtain.

Laurel jumped from the rough wooden bench she had just sunk into, stepping forward to receive whatever information he had to offer.

"The team was able to get your father stable. The doctor should be out in a few minutes to talk to you. You have a very brave kid here," he smiled.

"I do," Laurel replied, turning and flashing a half-smile. "Thank you," extending her hand, "Thank you for saving him. You have no idea…"

"Absolutely," he said, stepping on her words. "Kid, you saved your grandfather. Had you not called 9-1-1 as quickly, well, we would have had a different outcome."

"What's your name?" I asked slowly.

"Sean," he replied.

"Thank you, Sean. I..." My head was filled with everything I needed and wanted to say, but nothing trickled out.

Sean pushed the stretcher forward and headed towards the emergency bay doors with the rest of his team on his heels. He turned one last time to offer a smile and a slight wave goodbye. With that, Mom and I were left to wait. Nurses and staff filtered in and out of the trauma bay for hours, promising someone would be with us in a moment. That moment took nearly all night.

The sun began to rise and push its glorious rays through the sliding glass doors at the end of the hallway. Tired of waiting, of wondering, I jumped to my feet and pressed my ear to the door outside of Grandpa Jack's room. The constant faint beep of machines worked to soothe my nerves.

"What time is it?" I called to my mother. Her head slumped, resting on her chest, as she fought exhaustion.

"It's just after six."

"This is crazy!"

Unwilling to wait a moment more, I yanked the curtain back. Both nurses inside spun around and looked at me. The floor was a mess. Used packages and IV lines were scattered everywhere. In the center of all the chaos was Jack. Lying still, his eyes closed, it didn't seem as if much had changed.

"Sweetie, you are not supposed to be in here right now," A nurse exclaimed, stepping forward to bar me out again.

"We have waited all night. No one has said a single word to us about what is going on. That is my grandfather lying in that bed. I have every right to be in here." My voice shook, growing louder with each word that tumbled from my mouth.

"Young lady, you should learn some manners. Take a seat, now," the nurse commanded hotly, "When the doctor is ready, he'll come and speak to an adult, not a child."

"I need to learn some manners?" I declared. "Right, I'm the only one with the problem. Listen lady, I'm not going anywhere until I know what is going on with my grandfather."

"Quiet down before I call security. You're going to wake the patient."

"The patient?" I screamed. "He isn't just some patient. He's my family."

"For the last time, go and take a seat—*now*," she declared through gritted teeth. She pointed her finger with such authority I questioned if this was a battle worthy of my time. Still, I wasn't able to simply let this go. Nor could I simply back down.

"You sit down. I'm not going anywhere," I retorted, stepping so close the tips of our shoes met.

"Elizabeth," Mom roared, coming to her feet.

"What?" I questioned, laying my eyes upon my mother, "We've waited long enough. They can at least tell us what is going on." Turning my eyes back on the nurse, "How about you show some common courtesy?"

My mom yanked the curtain from my fingers and spun me to face the bench, the entire time apologizing for my actions.

"Don't apologize to her," I hollered.

"Elizabeth, you are being extremely rude."

"And she isn't?"

"I didn't say that. I'm just saying picking a fight isn't necessary nor is it like you."

"We should have Grandpa Jack moved somewhere else. Look at that mess! You cannot tell me they have helped him. They haven't told us what is happening because they don't know," I chomped.

My heart swelled in my chest, pounding and thudding hard. Anger was getting the best of me. It went beyond anger; it was something more significant. Something that I hadn't ever tapped into before. The tension quickly became a firestorm in the emergency room hallway. Neither the nurse nor I was willing to back down.

"Get control of your kid or I'll have security escort you both out," she yelled.

"Give me a break!" I shouted. "Is this how you treat all the patients' families?"

Jack's doctor got wind of our exchange and rushed down the hall, nearly yelling, "Good morning ladies."

The nurse eyed him hard.

"Don't good morning me. Are you about to tell us to give you another minute, or do you finally have time to speak to us?"

"Elizabeth!" Mom hollered, "That's enough! Sit down and shut your mouth. Stop it now, both of you!"

I stopped. Mom's deeply creased forehead and heated tone told me I had gone too far. Tension spilled from every pore in my body. Jack's nurse stepped back, disappearing into the dimly lit room. Her fists were still clenched in tightly wound balls of rage.

"You both should know better. I'm sorry," Laurel said, her words aimed at the good doctor.

"I'm sorry," he began. "We've been exceptionally busy here tonight, as I'm sure you've noticed. I'm Doctor Brooks. You can call me Robert if you would like."

"Laurel Yale."

"Nice to meet you, Mrs. Yale. Listen, your father…"

"Father-in-law," Laurel interpreted.

"Oh," Dr. Brooks smiled, "your father-in-law suffered a heart attack. I have run a battery of tests and cannot quite figure out what would have caused an event this significant. Mr. Yale's blood work proves he is extremely healthy— there are no underlying health issues. At this point, I would say his chances of pulling through this are one-hundred percent."

"Oh, that is great news," Laurel breathed, her hands falling over her heart.

"I do have a pressing question though. When I was examining him, I found burn marks on his fingertips. The wounds appear to be fresh. Was he burned or shocked sometime before he was found unconscious? That may explain the heart attack."

Alarmed, Mom shook her head, and said, "No, not that I'm aware of."

Tucking my hands deep into my sweatshirt pockets, I knew if Dr. Brooks or my mother saw my fingers, the lies I told would begin to unravel.

"Elizabeth, do you know anything? Did Jack get shocked while you were unpacking the boxes?" Mom prodded. "They were soaking wet from the rain. Did he plug something in that perhaps wasn't dry? What happened?"

I shook my head no, unwilling to introduce another lie to the already growing pile.

"Elizabeth, answer the question," Mom pushed.

A deep exhale whistled through my clenched teeth, "No, I mean, not that I know of. I was asleep, how should I know what Jack did?"

The corner of Dr. Brooks' eyes tightened as he focused his scrutiny.

"Are you sure, Elizabeth?" he prodded. "You don't seem altogether certain. No one is in trouble here; I just need to have correct information to treat your grandfather the best I know how."

"I'm sure," I said, shifting roughly on the wooden bench. "All I know is I was sound asleep. I heard a noise then Grandpa Jack called my name. I could tell something was wrong, but by the time I jumped out of bed, Jack was already on the floor. I couldn't get him to respond."

Dr. Brooks crossed his arms over his chest. "Well, perhaps Mr. Yale will be able to fill in the blanks when he wakes. I have a feeling whatever caused the burn marks caused his heart attack. I've given him some heavy medicine to keep him asleep. He is stable now so we'll be moving him to ICU. It's up to the doctors up there as to how long they will keep him under. It could be a few hours. It could be a few days. In the meantime, you are welcome to head to the fourth floor and wait for further updates."

"That's all?" I questioned. "Go upstairs and wait some more?"

"Unfortunately yes," he replied. "The heart is a tricky muscle. We need to give your grandfather some time to heal. We're doing everything we can to help him, but really it's up to his body to do the heavy work right now."

"Thank you doctor," Laurel whispered.

In the last eight years, all I've wanted was Jack. I had given in to the fact that my father would never again walk through our front door. He wouldn't be there for all the big moments that a kid needed their father for. I've held on to the fact that Jack would be there, some way, somehow, and that was now in jeopardy.

"Elizabeth," Mom began, "Let's go upstairs. Maybe you can stretch out and sleep a bit."

Sleep seemed impossible. Everything would be impossible until I knew if my grandfather would come back from this or if the machine had shocked away everything I deeply treasured.

"Elizabeth," Mom questioned, "are you coming?"

My eyes were glued to the blue curtain still barricading Jack inside the trauma bay.

"Elizabeth?"

Without a word, I stood and followed her. Halfway to the elevator, I grabbed her hand.

"Do you think he will be okay?" I whispered. "I mean really okay?"

"I know he will," Mom replied, "it's Jack."

Chapter 8: A Promise

The next forty-eight hours were a nightmare. The waiting, the pacing, the lack of information, all of it started to drive me insanely mad.

Mom began a campaign to take me home, wait for information to come in via telephone, but I refused. I told her she was more than welcome to leave if she wanted, but if it were all the same, I would stay.

The remnants of flavorless hospital eggs and soggy buttered toast were pushed through the double doors of the ICU. Behind them was our saving grace, a nurse dressed in bright pink scrubs.

"Yale family?" she called.

"Yes," I said, jumping to my feet.

Mom stood quickly too, shaking her legs to get the blood pumping again.

"One of you may come back now," she beckoned.

"Just one of us?" Mom asked.

"Yes ma'am. One at a time," she replied.

"Go Elizabeth," she said, pushing her hand against the small of my back.

The intensive care unit was shaped in a perfect horseshoe with the center island acting as the floor's command center. Sliding glass doors lined nearly every inch of the pale pink walls. I couldn't help but peek into the dark rooms. The men and women lying in the beds looked helpless with massive clusters of tubes coming from every orifice of their bodies. Swallowing back the discomfort growing inside of me, I turned my eyes to the floor.

Soft laughter held my ears. Two nurses in the far corner dished meds into small plastic cups, laughing and carrying on. Both appeared completely unaffected by the aura of sickness flowing through this place. It would drive me mad if I were in their shoes.

The unit was at max capacity. Each time a curtain swayed slightly, it reminded me that we were not the only ones in this position. I had convinced myself Jack would be fine, but now walking through the curvature of the horseshoe-shaped hallway, I wasn't so certain.

"Right in here," the nurses said, pulling Jack's door open.

Oxygen, heart monitors, a half-dozen other machines I had no idea what they did lined the wall behind his head. A constant and steady heartbeat pulsed across a nearby monitor. The light clamped over his rough finger glowed a warm red. But all of those things seemed minimal in comparison to the way the IV digging into his vein made me wince.

"Oh, Grandpa Jack," I whispered, the words catching in my throat.

"He's okay," the nurse reminded me, her hand falling to my shoulder. "He can hear you. Just talk to him. He'll wake up. It helps when they hear someone familiar."

"Grandpa Jack," I said once more, slipping my hand in his.

"It's going to take some time for the medicine to wear off. Sweetie, keep trying. I promise he's okay. Just keep talking to him," the nurse smiled.

"Okay," I replied. "I'm here Jack."

The rolling glass door slid across the tracks as Jack's nurse slipped back into the hallway. Where was I going to begin? I owed Jack an apology. Yet, nothing I said could compare to what he was going through.

"I hope you forgive me," I whimpered, "That stupid typewriter, I wish you hadn't brought it here. I wish it hadn't hurt you. I wish…" The floodgates opened. The relentless hours of worry came crashing down on me. "Jack," I wheezed, "I need you to be okay. Please, open your eyes. Jack…"

Those seemed to be the magic words that pulled the sleeping giant from his slumber. Jack's eyes flashed and then eased shut again.

"Jack," I cried. "Can you hear me? Grandpa?"

He tried to peel his eyes open, but they refused to obey. He squeezed my hand before letting go. Bringing his fingers up over his heart and forming the simplest gesture of love that I had ever seen—a beautiful heart shaped from his fingers.

"I love you too," I sobbed.

Jack cleared his throat, trying to bring even the smallest amount of wetness to his pipes, and whispered, "This is no one's fault but my own," he said. His voice was hoarse and dry.

"That isn't true," I replied.

"What happened to me, Elizabeth?"

"You had a heart attack, Grandpa. An incredibly serious heart attack."

"How?" he questioned. "The machine?"

"The machine went wild. I can't shake the images of you being shocked within inches of your life."

Slowly, very slowly, Jack sat up. The blood rushed to his face as he became more aware of his body than he had ever been before. His breath came slow and shallow.

"What day is it?" he asked.

"Wednesday," I replied.

Jack repeated my words and shook his head, "Guess we won't be making that six o'clock flight tonight. What time is it anyways?" Jack asked, struggling to sit up.

The discomfort on his face worried me.

"It's about eleven in the morning, I guess. There isn't a clock in here."

Tilting his face towards the ceiling, Jack flinched, "Oh," he sighed. "Lizzy-cakes, tell me you haven't touched that wicked machine since this little episode of mine."

"I haven't," I replied. "I haven't even been home to touch it. You should know that this wasn't a little episode. You almost died."

"You haven't been home since Saturday night? Didn't you say it is Wednesday?"

"Well, technically it was Sunday when you arrived at the hospital, but no, I haven't left the building since I rode in the ambulance with you. They just now let me in the room to see you."

"Go home, Elizabeth. Get some rest," Jack replied.

"I wasn't going anywhere until you woke."

"You have always been better to me than I am to you, Lizzy. I need you to rest, sweetie. You aren't doing your body any favors running it down while I lie here sleeping."

"I couldn't leave," I muttered.

"What in the world did you tell your mother about all of this? Did you tell her the truth?"

"No. I couldn't, I began to, but I…"

"Good," Jack replied quickly, "Laurel wouldn't understand. She would make this into something it isn't."

"I don't know about that," I replied. "I just couldn't tell her the truth after I lied to everyone else."

"What did you say to the doctors? I better get my story straight before they start asking questions."

"They are going to ask too. The E.R. doctor saw the burns on your fingers. He kept prying, saying it didn't make sense for a man as healthy as you to have a massive heart attack. I played dumb, said I was sleeping and was awoken when you screamed my name. By the time I got to you, you were unconscious in the hallway. I didn't know how you got the burns."

"Good girl," he replied, patting my hand gently.

"You really scared me." My voice cracking at the thought of losing him again. "You almost didn't make it. I mean when they had to restart your heart…"

"Elizabeth," Jack replied. "That wasn't fair for you to have to watch."

"Fair or not," I shook, "I love you, Grandpa Jack. I am sorry for the words I said. I *am* glad you came home."

Stroking my hand again, Jack smiled, "I know, I love you too."

"If you have to know why that machine called my name in Morocco, why it seems to be trying to kill us both when we touch it, if you must uncover what secrets it is hiding, I'll help you. I just don't want to lose you. I promise to help if you promise to stay with me."

Jack choked. Fighting back the emotions springing to his eyes, "I'm not leaving you again, kid. I made that mistake once. I swear I won't do it again—promise."

The sliding glass door moved on its track again, the curtain stirring as it did.

"I thought I heard two voices in here," the nurse said smiling.

"How are we doing, Mr. Yale?" she asked.

"Jack," he replied, "My name is Jack."

"Well Jack, I'm Nurse Erin. Can you rate your pain for me?" Her pen was ready to jot down notes inside Jack's chart.

"I'm swell, Nurse Erin," Jack replied.

Erin tapped the pen against the hard silver case and looked up.

"Really, I'm fine enough to go home. Now be a dear and get a doctor to release me from this joint," Jack smiled.

"Slow down Jack. You've had quite the heart attack, sir. We need to do a few more tests. We'll want to make sure you can get up and around unassisted and free of any heart murmurs or sudden attacks. I hate to be the one to tell you this, but you're sort of stuck with me for the next few days. I'll do my best, but I can't promise you'll be hitting the streets anytime soon. Okay?"

"Fine," Jack puffed his chest out, "You were going to be my favorite, but now…." Jack said with a wink.

"I think we'll do just fine, you and me," she laughed.

Grandpa Jack and I waited for Nurse Erin to run through the mandatory hourly observations and clear the room. Sleep and exhaustion pulled at me. My eyes grew heavy as Jack leaned back and settled in bed.

"I guess the only way for me to get out of here is to do as they say. I better rest, Lizzy-cakes. I would like to see you go home. Sleep in your own bed. Take a shower. You're exhausted, Elizabeth. The circles under your eyes worry me. We can talk more when we both have had some rest."

"Okay," I replied, "but something has been bothering me."

"What is it?" Jack asked.

"After you left my room the other night, I fell asleep quickly. Dad was in my dream. I haven't seen him in my dreams for years, and the more I think about it, it wasn't really a dream, but more like a memory that came to the surface while I was sleeping."

"Really," Jack replied, shifting back to a sitting position, "Then tell me about it."

"I was five. It was the first time he had let me climb into the attic with him. He wanted me to help get the Christmas decorations down. Mom came to tell us about cookies she had ready for me to decorate and when she left I accidently knocked over a stack of boxes. The entire stack tumbled, but one box, in particular, split apart and spilled dozens of photo albums across the attic floor. One had your father's initials on it: DBY. I climbed into dad's lap, and we looked at it together. There were pictures of old buildings, a church, a party in what looked like a town square and…" I stopped speaking.

The minute I thought of the last photograph, the woman's eyes filled me with overwhelming anxiety. Shuddering, I looked up at Jack.

"What? What else was in the book?" he questioned.

"The last page was a photograph of a woman. She had black eyes, as deep as the color of coal. I've never seen eyes that color before. She was terrifying. Dad tried to pull the photo from the album, but it wouldn't come loose."

"Who was she?" he asked.

"I don't know," I replied. "I guess I screamed in the dream when I was slamming the book shut because I woke myself up."

"That's when you got up and went to the typewriter?" Jack questioned.

"No, I tried to go back to sleep. I wanted to stay with my father just a minute longer, but the woman's eyes," my body shook involuntarily, "I don't know. Each time I saw them I grew more and more exhausted. I swear I felt the same way you described feeling when you had to go back to the hotel and sleep in Morocco. I'm exhausted now, but even this seems different than the way that did."

"Interesting," Jack replied, pulling on the oxygen tubes dangling from his nose. "Did you finally go back to sleep? Did you have another dream after that?"

"I did. I was standing inside the marketplace. I watched the lady you described turn my initials on the typewheel. It was as if I was watching what happened before you found the machine, except when the woman saw me she forced my fingers to cradle the keys of the typewriter. The very same machine you bought in Morocco. The devilish thing came to life again, and I passed out. I left my body and began floating over the small shop. I watched as she tossed a golden key towards Aden, the merchant. I tried to hold onto their words, listen to whatever nuggets of knowledge I could grab on to, but I woke up. That is when I grabbed a piece of paper and marched into the hallway where you had put the machine. I wanted to know if what had just happened in my dream would happen while I was awake. But you came out of your room, the machine sparked, you grabbed on to make it stop, and less than five minutes later, we were in the back of an ambulance on the way here."

"Listen to me carefully," Jack said in a hush, "Go home, make sure Laurel isn't around, make her go to the grocery store, come up with any excuse to get her far away from the house, and then go into the attic. Look around. See if the photo album that was in your dream, memory— whatever it was, is still up there. If it is, bring it to me. Don't waste a single second, Elizabeth. I believe your father was trying to tell us something."

"Got it," I replied.

"Elizabeth," Jack said urgently, "Whatever you do, don't touch the machine. Do you understand?"

"Of course."

Chapter 9: Home

Leaving the hospital wasn't nearly as hard as the way I arrived. The sun was warm. The light shining on my skin breathed a sense of peace into my soul. Jack was okay. In the end, he would be just fine. Still, I was filled with buckets of questions. Questions that would take some time to answer—regardless of how long it took—they needed to be solved.

"You okay?" Mom asked. "Did you forget something inside?"

"No," I replied. "The sun feels good on my skin. I haven't felt it in days."

"I know," she replied softly, lifting her arms slightly to take on the beams of light. "I hate hospitals. It feels good to shake off the illness and depression inside this place."

"You should have left, Mom," I replied.

"Not without you, kiddo. When we get home, I think I'll lay down for a bit. Come on, the car's right over here," Mom directed.

I was drained. Every muscle felt like a loose rubber band that would snap under the slightest amount of pressure. After struggling to pull the car door open, I crawled in and collapsed in the backseat. Dread flooded me.

"Mom," I began slowly, "I know you are worn out too, but I have a little problem."

"What is it?" she replied, settling into her seatbelt. Her eyes touched mine in the rear-view mirror.

"It isn't a big deal really, but it is something we need to handle today. Could you possibly run up to the school and collect my things?"

She laughed, "I thought you meant your problem had something to do with Jack. That's not much of a problem, you know. Let's go home and rest for a few hours and then we'll go together."

She shifted the car into drive and pulled out of the spot our car had been sitting in for three days.

"Mom," I whined. "My locker is stuffed full of papers and supplies. The school closes in two hours. Tomorrow morning it closes for good until August. I don't get the same locker every year. The custodian will toss everything."

"Okay, then we'll stop on the way home," she insisted.

I sighed deeply, "Mom, please, you aren't listening. It will take so much longer if I go in. Everyone will ask about Jack. I just want to go home. I've been through a lot. The last thing I want to do is answer a bunch of questions."

"Elizabeth," Mom groaned. Concern drew lines across her forehead. "I've been through a lot too. I'm drained. Does this really have to be handled right this minute?"

"Yes," I replied, unwilling to back down. "It does."

I sensed what was coming. She was on the edge of scolding me, shaming me into letting go of such an unnecessary pursuit and only thinking of myself, but I couldn't give in. I had to get her out of the house. Intentionally ducking deeper into the seat, anything to disrupt the heated stares from the mirror, I changed my approach.

"I know you're exhausted. You haven't left my side since Sunday, and Mom, I really appreciate you for that. I needed you, and you were there—no questions. It's just, I don't think I have the strength to deal with everyone's prodding. You know how those women are up there. If they even sense a trace of drama, they want to sink their teeth into it. The last thing I want to be asked is what happened. Is your grandfather okay? Are you going to be able to travel? They are unrelenting. We'll be there for hours. Please," I said, appealing to her one last time.

"Oh okay, Elizabeth. I think you may be making a bit much out of this, but I'll drop you off at the house and go up to the school, alone. I probably need to go by the grocery store anyhow."

The rest of the car ride home was painfully silent. Mom knew nothing. The day my father died we had made promises to each other. Even sealed each one with a pinky-swear, a hug, and a kiss. She promised she would never leave. I promised always to be truthful. We were a team, Mom and me. The thought of lying to her about what happened to Jack crushed me. I had kept my promise up until now. Another thought hit me: this had just begun. The lies I had told thus far were only a small sampling of the many lies that were yet to come. Before this thing with the typewriter was over, I seriously doubted I would ever be able to keep my mother's trust again. I could feel it.

Mom's mind was on autopilot. She was taking the same route home she did eight years ago when Jesse fell suddenly ill. There was no doubt her mind was unlocking and tripping into those painful memories, that is nothing more than basic human nature, but I could see something else surfacing as she studied my reflection in the mirror.

"Elizabeth," she said, "Are you okay?"

"I think so," I whispered. "Why?"

"You witnessed more than I had ever hoped you would with Jack on the ground and then with what happened in the ambulance. If you need to talk about anything…"

"I said I'm fine."

Mom held her breath, unwilling to push the subject, afraid I would shut her out completely. The car turned onto Downhill Lane and inched into our driveway. I didn't budge.

"Mom," I rushed.

Secrets were sitting on the tip of my tongue. I began to say something—anything to make her feel better—but my inner voice dwindled to nothing.

"Be careful," I said, slamming the car door.

The tightened muscles in my back eased as I took a few steps towards the garage door and waited for it to open. I turned and gave a slight wave. I had never wanted distance between my mother and me, but I knew it was necessary at the moment.

Every light was on in the house. We left in such a rush no one bothered to look after our normal routines. I stood in the foyer and stared up the stairs. The open railing showed the typewriter sitting in the same place Jack almost lost his life.

I was drained, but I couldn't bring myself to go upstairs, at least not yet. I stood there, blinking, trying to push the images of Jack's accident out of my head. Everything was silent until I heard the now familiar pop.

Whiz-whiz-BANG. Whiz-whiz-BANG.

The machine was awake. That is when it sunk in, no matter how much I try, I am no longer in control.

"What—is—it?" I asked aloud. "What do you want from me?"

`History is not right. History is not right. History is not right. EWY. Elizabeth Wright Yale, correct it. Correct it.`

I climbed the stairs, answering the call the contraption was clearly making. As I neared the top, a white blinding flash filled the hallway. The same smoke and letters cascaded up and over the machine disappearing as quickly as they came. Furiously typing, I leaned in close enough to read the words the typewriter was forcing into the air. I refused to touch the confounded thing again, but I had to know what it had to say.

"What does that mean, history isn't right?" I questioned.

The machine went silent. Halfway down the page, I noticed the Y in Yale was once again marked through.

"Why are you marking through the Y?" I asked.

Nothing. No response.

"Agh," I said through clenched teeth. "Enough already. Why don't you answer my questions?"

Several things happened at once: The machine shot out another round of golden sparks and floating smoke letters into the air. As the smoke filled my lungs, a sharp pain flooded through me. My knees knocked together and buckled. I tried to keep my legs from going out from under me, but it was a failed attempt. Tumbling to the floor, I got on all fours and backed away, trying to escape the madness. Papers began to fly from the typewriter where none had existed moments before.

"Stop," I commanded. "Stop! Please!"

A single sheet of paper floated from the machine and landed at my fingertips.

`History is not right. History is not right. History is not right. EWY. EWY. Correct it. Correct it.`

"I get it," I bitterly chomped. "History is not correct, whatever that means."

The wooden railing of the banister was cold under my touch. I struggled to bring myself upright and find solid footing to stand. The typewriter hummed with electricity. Fearful that another round of unwelcomed sparks would fill the hallway, I forced my back against the banister and crept to the other side of the hall never taking my eyes off the machine.

I eyed the attic door. This was my chance. The machine could go wild for all I cared. I had to get into the attic.

A thin tan cord barely hung a foot into the large opening. I jumped, trying my best to grab the line, but I missed. I tried again and failed.

"I need a chair," I whispered.

Struggling to lug the awkward desk chair from my bedroom into the hall, I began to sweat. The width was greater than my reach, but once I pushed it through the door, I rolled the wooden seat directly under the attic. Climbing on the wooden base, my feet slipped, nearly sending me to the ground. I caught myself and reached up, yet, I was too short. Stretching with all my might, my toes ached as my finger grasped the cord. I got it. The door creaked as the springs forced themselves to open. I tried to recall the last time Mom was on the upper floor, but nothing came.

The musty smell of stale boxes and warmed timber hit my nose. The dust wafting down tickled at my senses. I grabbed ahold of the ladder, ready to climb up.

Chapter 10: Jack's Memory

Another round of blood was stolen from Jack's veins while he protested. His vitals were checked for what felt like the two-thousandth time. All seemed to be well, but not well enough to leave. When it was all said and done, he wanted to be left alone. Left to his thoughts and the irritating beep of the machines. Anything was better than the constant intrusion of hospital staff claiming to want to help.

Jack grabbed a small notepad and pen off the wooden tray next to his bed. Lunch had been brought, but the smell of stale bread and watered-down beef broth made his stomach turn. Something was bothering him more than his stomach though—the meaning behind the letters that floated from the typewriter each time it sparked.

Jack closed his eyes and watched as the typewriter first came to life under Elizabeth's hands. Mouthing each of the letters, he tucked them away in his memory the best he could. Then he summoned the memory of the machine sparking in the hallway before trying to take him under. One thing was for sure, the letters that floated from the bewitched contraption were always the same.

"A word scramble," Jack pondered.

He closed his eyes again, and then wrote the string of letters as they appeared:

S, C, H, R, I, J, V, E, N, F, A, B, R, I, E, K, W, B.

He studied each character, then mentally moved them around trying to create a phrase or a series of words that would make sense. Hastily scribbling shiver, nice, rein, a fire, brief, fiber, break, tear, Jack's hand raced across the page.

No matter how he tried to weave the words together, nothing clued him into the mystery as to why *these* are the letters the typewriter continually expels.

Frustrated, Jack tossed the pad at the end of the bed and settled back on the rough mattress. The rustling of the privacy curtains made Jack lift his head to see who was there.

"Jack," Nurse Erin called as she stepped into the room, "how are you doing, my friend?"

"Fine," he replied crudely.

"You sure? You look pretty upset, my friend."

"I'm fine. Thank you for checking. What I am sure of is that you are needed elsewhere. I would like to be alone if that suits you."

"What's this?" Erin asked reaching for the pad.

"An old-fashioned word puzzle," Jack replied, "the kind that we old folks used to do before there were four-hundred channels on the boob-tube. You're probably too young to know what that is."

Erin looked at the page and nodded, "Sort of like a cipher?" she asked.

"Maybe you aren't so bad after all, kid," Jack hooted. "See anything that jumps out at you?"

Each letter slipped off Nurse Erin's tongue as she wrapped the paper with her thumb, "I'm not so certain it's a mess of jumbled letters, Jack," she said, "I mean, I don't think it's a puzzle."

A prick of irritation tingled down Jack's arms, "Of course it is," he replied. "What else would it be?"

Erin gave Jack a withering look as she tossed the pad on his lap, and said, "I've seen that word, *fabriek*, before. It isn't a cipher, Jack."

"Where? Are you sure?" he questioned, bolting straight up in bed.

"Slow down, Jack. Yes, I'm positive," Erin replied, "My parents used to drag my sister and me over to my grandparent's house every Sunday evening for an early dinner. None of the kids was ever allowed to go into the formal dining room. It was strictly off limits. In the far corner of that room sat the most beautiful grandfather clock I had ever seen. That word, *fabriek*, was printed on the bottom in brilliant gold script."

"A clock?" Jack interjected.

"Yes, my grandfather used to say that the clock's gears were made of solid gold. I'm sure he told us kids that so we wouldn't mess with it, but I couldn't help myself. All the gizmos, gears, and wires that made the clock move mesmerized me. The front was solid glass so each time the pendulum struck you could watch as the gears shifted and rolled.

"Every Sunday I crawled under the table stowing myself away from disciplining eyes, stretched out on my belly, and waited for the clock to strike. I would sing out when the clock chimes rang. My grandfather would sneak into the forbidden room, and yank me out from under the table by my feet. Everyone would laugh. I didn't care. I only wanted to watch the clock."

"That *is* a special moment, Nurse Erin," Jack grinned.

"It was."

"May I ask do you know where your grandparents purchased the timepiece?"

"That I don't know. My granddaddy was a military man; he was stationed overseas his entire career. I would assume like most things they owned it came home with them after he left the service."

"I see."

"Why do you ask?"

"I own that very same clock," Jack said slowly.

"Jack," Erin smirked.

"I'm being serious. It's been passed down for many generations. My son, Elizabeth's father Jesse, had a deep affection for the clock too. I owned a bookstore during my prime." Jack said with a wink. "Jesse would walk to the store after school every day. The first thing that boy would do was slither between the brick wall and the grandfather clock and mess with the panel in the back.

I cannot tell you how many nights his mother and I listened to him make up stories about what was stuffed inside the clock." Jack laughed, "He used to dream about a hidden fortune inside that would change all of history."

"Well, did you ever let him open the panel?" Erin asked.

"No, we didn't have the key. By the time the clock came into my hands, the key was missing. I did have a locksmith look at it once, but he said there was no way to create a key that would sync with the mechanism inside the panel. It was the rarest thing he ever saw," Jack laughed.

"That's a shame. You should let him try now," she smiled. "You know, cure his childhood curiosity and all."

"He's gone. Been dead for about eight years now," Jack's eyes fell.

"Oh Jack, I'm so sorry; at least you have Elizabeth. She seems like a fantastic kid."

"She sure is."

"Is there anything else I can get you before I make my rounds?" Erin asked.

"No kid, I'm fine."

Erin slid the door open and began to step into the hallway when Jack called out to her, "Erin, wait."

She turned and smiled, "Yeah, did you think of something you needed?"

"Are you certain you don't know where your grandparents bought the clock?"

"Sorry Jack, I really don't know."

"Did anyone ever tell you what language the word was written in?"

Erin picked up the tablet again, reviewing each letter and marking.

"Well," she replied, "I speak fluent French and Spanish. I cannot recall *fabriek* being a word I have ever seen in either of those languages. I would say it is more likely to be German or Western European."

"Perhaps so," Jack smiled, "Erin, thank you for your help. Listen, it's really important that I get out of this hospital. What are the doctors saying? Is there an end in sight for me?"

Erin sighed, "They cannot figure out what happened, Jack. No one has put a timeframe on your release, but I could ask."

"I would appreciate that, kid. I've got some very important work to see to. The longer this drags out, the more pressing the matter becomes."

Jack settled back into the mattress, his eyes heavy.

"Jack," Erin said softly, "What happened right before you had a heart attack? Perhaps that will help me get you discharged quicker."

Jack raised his eyebrows, "Why do you ask?"

"Because, when you are asleep you keep shouting the same phrase. I have to shut your door so that you do not disturb the other patients."

"And what exactly is it that I am saying?" Jack pressed.

"Whiz-whiz-BANG—whatever that means. You've repeated it at least fifty times a night since you arrived on my floor. I thought it was a bunch of gibberish at first, but now you have me wondering."

"Is that so?" laughed Jack, "Well, Nurse Erin, my dear, sometimes the truth is so unbelievable that it's best to keep it tucked into your pocket."

Chapter 11: The Treasures in the Attic

The attic ladder wobbled as my foot hit the first rung. Every moment of the dream a few nights ago replayed in my head; each step felt the same, but this time, my father wasn't waiting among the rafters. Once inside, I flipped on the overhead light. It was just as I had remembered. Scores of boxes lined the dusty walls, all in neat stacks of five to seven high. The entire attic was full. Halloween, Thanksgiving, and Christmas decorations hung on rusted nails. Some hadn't seen the light of day in more than ten years. An espresso-colored cradle hung in the same place my father placed it many years ago. I stood taking in each detail of the space. It was a time capsule. One side held our present while the other was a visual reminder of my life before my father's death. Those two worlds seemed impossibly far apart.

While I wanted to snoop into each treasure trove, I dutifully began moving the boxes away from the wall with no idea which box I was looking for. Time was limited. Mom would be back from her errands soon, and I had to be out of the attic before the garage door opened.

Staying busy felt good. I knew if I stopped, gave in to the exhaustion, the wild thoughts, and the weight of everything happening around me, I would cave. It's a lot for a fifteen-year-old to deal with.

I worked to clear some space to sit down. My father's words occupied my head, "Stay on the thick pieces of wood, so you do not fall through. Elizabeth, be careful, please."

"I won't fall, Daddy," I whispered. "Stay with me. I have to find these books."

Almost on cue, a mental checklist formed in my mind. Outlined in perfect order were all the details my father had shown me in the dream.

Gingerly, I stepped towards the stack of boxes we first found the albums in more than ten years ago. The order made no sense. One was marked antiques. The one below was stamped with the familiar Yale's Shelves logo. The next had Christmas bulbs printed on the side.

Popping open the box marked antiques the contents were rather disappointing. Inside were half a dozen bubbled milk glass vases, a few tarnished brass candleholders, and an empty picture frame. Quickly stuffing everything back inside, I moved to the next box. The Yale's Shelves carton was crammed full with hardback classics. Ones that Jack must have wanted me to read when he left: *The Three Musketeers*, *Gone with the Wind*, *The Great Gatsby,* and *Robinson Crusoe* were beautifully wrapped in gold tissue paper and cinched with a black bow. I sat the books aside. They had been trapped inside that mildewed eight-by-eight square for long enough. When I had more time, when Mom wasn't watching, I would sneak back in the attic and bring them down. Each classic deserved a shining spot on my bookshelf.

A loud buzzing sounded from below. I waited and listened, frozen in place fearful I had been caught. It took a moment, but I quickly realized the sound was the air conditioning whizzing through the air ducts above my head.

"Get busy Elizabeth," I muttered.

Closing my eyes, I tried to recall what happened after we began moving boxes.

"The box broke when it hit the ground," I said aloud. "I wonder if Dad added the albums to an existing box or if he put everything together in a new one."

This added a layer of complication to the matter. If he added the albums to another box, I would have to search every single carton. I doubt there would be time. There was easily a hundred boxes lined across the far wall. That didn't include the boxes stuffed deep among the rafters above.

Bending as low as I could, I attempted to read each scribble on every box closest to me.

One box, in particular, caught my eye. It once read, Christmas décor, but it was marked through with a heavy marker and labeled: OTHER. The handwriting was my father's.

"That has to be it," I said.

Carefully tiptoeing my way to the stack, the floor screeched and groaned. After a few attempts, I was able to shimmy the box free. It was heavier than I expected. Sweat dripped from my brow into my eyes. I stood, shaking my arms to let the blood circulate.

The sound of the aged packing tape being pulled from its position reverberated off the walls. Once it released, the brown flaps revealed a cluster of what seemed to be useless artifacts and dilapidated linens.

"Agh," I groaned. "This is going to take forever!"

Too impatient to move another box, I went from stack to stack, trying to peek inside each container. An hour passed quickly. I was ready to give in when a heavily scratched black metal box with the words David Boyd Yale Trust and W/B Trust, LTD painted in gold calligraphy in the far corner called to me.

Working my way to the far side of the attic, a wild anticipation sent my hands trembling. In the dream, DBY was stamped on the front of the photo album. If I knew my father at all, this is where he would have stashed the albums.

The metal box was heavy. The handles were thin, too thin to actually bear the weight of its contents. Sliding the container across the insulation, something scraped and dug into the wood below. No matter how I tried to adjust it, it kept catching.

Using my knees as leverage, I pushed with all my might. The box barely made it an inch off the ground, but it was enough to slide my fingers between the metal and wood and feel around amongst the yellow padding. My fingers dug deep, clutching for anything that would make the box catch; a cold piece of metal surfaced.

Pulling the find from the fluff, a small silver key appeared. It looked to be a perfect fit. Years of grime wouldn't allow the key to slip all the way in the lock. Blowing hard into the key hole, dust pushed its way out and into my eyes. Rubbing them hard, I said, "Okay, Mr. Yale, show me what's inside your box," as I slipped the key in. With one quick twist, the box fell open. "You are a smart one, Mr. Jesse Yale." I laughed.

Just as I suspected, Dad had placed a dozen photo albums inside the box and locked them away for safe keeping. Covered in a meticulously spun web, I felt bad destroying such fine work as I pulled each album from the case.

A folded, yellowing sheet of paper with burned edges flew onto my lap as the last book was pulled from the box.

"What do we have here?" I asked.

Inside the folds was a letter, scrolled in a foreign language. I recalled similar vernacular from the photographs in my dream.

I sat the letter aside hoping to translate the words before Mom made her way home. It could be the key that busts the mystery surrounding the typewriter wide open.

 The thick, leather-bound stack was daunting—twelve books high—but each one was so thick that if I were to stand, the mound would hit me at mid-thigh. On the bottom of the stack was the album stamped DBY.

As my fingers graced the bind, the pleasant warmth of the attic gave way to a slight chill. Pulling in a deep calming breath, I traced the tattered corners. Its age was showing. The small piece of the cover that was barely exposed was peeling in multiple places showing the cardboard binding beneath.

Pressing my right shoulder against the stack to secure it from falling, I wrenched the book from the bottom of the stack. My hands trembled. While the album was lovely with the entwining scrollwork that ended at a detailed gold flap lock, I knew what was inside—the photo of the woman with the coal black eyes.

"What secrets are you holding?" I asked while flipping to the first page.

There staring back was a black and white photograph. Two graying men, in dark colored suits, white shirts and tie, and shaggy beards looked upon the man in the forefront. He was different. His suit was lighter, the collar higher, and it was all pulled together with a thinner black tie. Every piece the man wore spoke to the gentleman's dapperness. The hat upon his head was round and an exact match to the coloring and material of his suit. His right hand balanced upon a tall wooden cane. Something about him said that he was a capable man, not lame and in need of assistance; perhaps the cane was more of a prop than anything. Whoever he was, the air about him was so strong it bled off the still frame.

Hidden behind a thin, silver, rounded pair of spectacles, his eyes were all too familiar.

"Who are you?" I asked, "What's your name, sir?"

Directly behind the trio stood a red brick factory that reached into the sky. Black billowing smoke poured from its tall stacks. Softly pulling the photo from its holders, the way I had seen my father do, I flipped it over. August 26, 1876, was written on the back. Two words were messily written next to the year. It took a moment to make out what it said, "Whizbog, no, Whiz—Whizbang Factory?" I guessed. "I think that is what you say, Whizbang Factory. What in the world is that?"

An hour passed while I poured through stacks of black and whites, pulling those of interest to show Grandpa Jack. There was no way I could conceal albums this large from my mother. Nor was I willing to summon a lie worthy of her obsessive questioning as I struggled to the car with a handful of heirloom picture books. I would have to find a way less obvious way to smuggle them into the hospital. Settling on using my backpack to hide away my finds, an explosion of sound filled the attic and set it rattling.

"The garage door!" I panicked.

The effort to clean up was instantaneous. Giving each book a little push, the picture I had been dreading the most—the woman with the coal black eyes—fell from its vellum page and landed directly on top of the neatly piled stacks. It was peculiar, to say the least, but there was not time to think it over.

Angling my head out of the attic opening, straining to get a better look into the foyer, I jerked back. Mom hadn't made it inside just yet. There was still time. My fingers fumbled as they worked to pick up the valuable stack of evidence I collected. Swiping too deep, a shard of wood broke loose from its board, drove its way under my index finger nail, and rested at the nailbed. My finger pulsed; my face burned with the pain. There wasn't time to stop, not yet. The garage door pulled from its frame pushing air through the entire house.

"Elizabeth?" Mom called softly, "Are you awake, honey?"

The rustling of grocery sacks filled the downstairs. I waited until she went back outside to retrieve another round of parcels and swiftly scurried down the ladder two rungs at a time. Halfway down I lost my grip. Without thinking, I let go of the photographs and clung to the side to stop my fall. The old still frames sailed over the banister, raining down to the foyer below.

Mom turned the corner, her hands full of milk and orange juice just in time to watch the first photo land on the cold tile.

"Elizabeth?" she questioned.

She looked up and watched as two dozen more black and whites floated down in a mangled mess, and I was still descending the ladder rather ungracefully.

"What exactly are you doing?" she questioned.

"Um," I stalled, doing my best to act natural, letting whatever came first slip from my lips, spluttering, "I was asleep in my room, and I thought I heard an animal or something scratching upstairs in the attic. It was the craziest sound. You should have heard it!"

"So you decided you would climb up there and check it out?" she barked. "Have you lost your mind? What would you have done if there had been an animal up there?"

She bent, sweeping up the pile of fallen photos, and then marched up the stairs. Her eyes grew more and more irritated as she spied the piles of insulation covering the carpet. Following her gaze, I quickly bent over and plucked the yellow shreds off the floor, "Don't worry, I'll clean it up!"

"I *am* worried," she retorted. "The attic is a dangerous place, Elizabeth. One wrong step and you could have fallen through the ceiling. If you're lucky you'd hit the hallway carpet, but if you step in a few places up there, Elizabeth, you can fall two stories to the foyer. If that happened and I wasn't here…" Her voice trailed off.

"I wasn't thinking, Mom," I rushed. "I'm sorry. I heard something. I was trying to help after sending you to the school. I know how tired you are. I wanted to make at least one thing easy for you," I lied.

"Okay," she exhaled. "I appreciate your sudden willingness to help, but please do not go up there without me being home again."

"I promise," I said, my voice quivering under yet another mistruth.

She turned to hurry back down the stairs, but within a few steps from the bottom, she stopped cold.

"What are these?"

"What are what?" I asked, not knowing exactly what she meant. My back was still bent picking up insulation.

Mom pointed to the pile of photographs in her hands, "These."

My mind went in rapid circles. Grasping for any excuse that would make even the slightest bit of sense, I cleared my throat and went for the obvious, "Looks like an old stack of photos to me," I replied, hedging on sarcasm.

"Elizabeth," she warned.

"Y-e-s," I replied slyly.

"What aren't you saying?" she questioned.

The throat clearing was a dead giveaway. Anytime she has caught me in a lie, it always started with me clearing my throat. Distrust mounted in her eyes and she looked down and flipped the photos over.

"Let's try this, why were they floating from the attic when I walked in, Elizabeth?"

"I accidently dropped them when I was coming down the ladder. It was an accident."

"And just what are you going to do with them?" she asked, stopping on the eerie photo of the woman. "Wow, who is this?"

"I don't know. I was hoping you might know," I pushed. An edge of excitement filled my voice and made her eyes narrow ever so slightly.

"You aren't telling the whole truth, Elizabeth."

"Yes, I am."

"No, you aren't. I can tell when you are lying, young lady. For starters, you cleared your throat when I began questioning you."

"I honestly don't know what you are getting so upset about," I replied as if the obvious was eluding me.

"If you don't know why I'm upset then answer the question: What exactly are you going to do with these photos, and where did they come from?"

"They came from a box in the attic. It's just a bunch of pictures. It isn't like you caught me with something illegal—they are pictures! I was searching for whatever made the noise and found a box of photo albums. I pulled those out to show Grandpa Jack. Are you satisfied now?" I said, tired of the lecture.

"Do not speak to me that way, Elizabeth. I'm not sure what has gotten into you, but you better figure it out. You picked a fight with the nurse at the hospital and now me. I'm only asking you to give me a straight answer," Mom paused. "Besides, Jack is in the hospital, he has no use for old photographs."

"He was telling me about his great-grandparents the other night. When I saw the photo albums in the attic, I pulled a few pictures out. There is absolutely nothing to be upset about."

"There is something to be upset about because I can tell when you are lying. Your eyes are darting all over the room. Your voice is shaking. You are hiding something Elizabeth, which is something you do not usually do. Therefore, the only thing I can guess is that Jack has put you up to something. I knew it was a mistake to allow him back in our lives. We were fine without him here! You've been acting secretive and distant since he arrived."

"He had a heart attack, mother. How secretive and distant could I be in a few days' time?"

Mom stopped listening. Her mind was made up. I was hiding something, and she wasn't going to stand for it.

"Why were you sneaking around in the attic?" she demanded.

"How can I be sneaking around if I live here?"

My defensives were up. Mom was on to the fact that something was happening behind her back. It wasn't fair, not to her, not to me, not to any of us.

"I tell you what, since you feel the need to lie, you can stay in your room until you are ready to come down and tell the truth. Until then, no Jack—no nothing."

"But, we've got to go back up to the hospital," I stammered.

"No," she yelled, speeding down the remaining stairs, "We don't. In fact, when it comes to Jack I don't have to do a single thing."

I stopped myself from saying another word, knowing if I did I would say something I would deeply regret. I wiped the tears falling from my eyes as the sound of the photographs hitting the trash can unnerved me.

"Don't throw them away!" I screamed.

"Go to your room! We're done speaking until you learn to tell the truth!"

Chapter 12: Midnight Travels

I refused to come down for dinner. Whatever my mother had to say wasn't worth hearing. When she tossed the pictures, she crossed the line. Besides, if I had to face her now, I'm sure I would be forced to relay some semblance of the truth. There was only one outcome to being honest right now, more grief. Still, the lies weren't only weighing on me they were beginning to eat at me too.

When the house fell silent, I got up and got myself dressed. The more I thought about everything, the harder it was to stay in this house without Jack. I made a promise to him, and it was one that I wasn't willing to break. The promise I made to my mother so many years ago, to never lie and always be on her team, seemed less important right now.

"Sometimes," I whispered aloud, "you have to be willing to take risks," repeating a line that my father hounded my mother with nearly every day of his existence. It was true. This moment was my risk.

The cheetah print wallet marked with a lime-green E stashed under the bed held the essential key to my escape— my rarely used Metro Transit card. Careful not to make too much noise, I slipped under the white flowing bed skirt and stretched as far as my arms would reach.

"Agh," I exclaimed. "Come—over—here," batting at the billfold.

No matter how hard I strained or overextended my arms, the wallet was just out of reach. Slithering back out, I jumped up and looked around. I needed something to help part the piles of junk I had randomly stuffed under my bed; things I wanted out of my mother's sight. Any other time I would have hauled down the stairs and grabbed the broom to accomplish such a feat, but not tonight.

"A hanger," I exclaimed, roughly pulling the closet door open.

Removing the brown cardboard bar adhered to the brass-toned wire hanger, I tossed the limp tube towards my desk. I missed. Contorting the wire until it was in a near perfect line, I went back in. Somehow, the wallet seemed even further out of reach. Batting at the cheetah print, it twisted and turned until the hanger's loop caught the inside fold and dug in.

"Ha! Gotcha," I exclaimed.

Dust bunnies clung on as I stood and grabbed my phone off the bedside table. The Metro bus schedule was hard to read. It took a few minutes to remember which starting route I would have to jump to make it to the hospital. Once I figured it out, I glanced at the clock. 11:46 p.m. The last bus run ended at 12:15. Service would start again at four a.m. I would have about two hours with Grandpa Jack if I wanted to make it back before Mom's alarm clock blared at 5:30. The station was at least three blocks away. If I was going to make the 12:15, I was going to have to go now.

First things first, I had to get the photos. If my mother was so cruel to toss the remnants of my uneaten dinner on top of nearly one-hundred-and-thirty-year-old photographs, I wasn't sure I would be able to control my anger. Taking a few deep breaths, I slowly opened my bedroom door.

The house was dark, almost too dark. It was unusual that the foyer lamp was off, but it didn't matter, the less light, the better. Despite the darkness, the typewriter, still seated in the small cranny in the hall, caught my eye.

"Shh," I whispered.

Silence.

"Don't make a sound, please," I pleaded. "I need to see Jack."

I felt ridiculous begging an inanimate object to not make a sound, but if the blasted thing roared to life, giving away my grand escape, the night would be over.

"Shh," I begged again.

Silence.

When the coast seemed deadly still, I tiptoed my way to the kitchen. The black and white photographs were perfectly spread across the counter. It seemed that mom had spent some time studying them. My eyes quickly glanced across each one. They were all there.

Grabbing my backpack from the pantry, I unzipped it and turned it upside down. A mass of papers, pens, and junk from my locker spread across the floor, each hitting with far more sound than I had hoped.

When it was empty, I went back to the island. If Mom woke and went for a glass of water as she generally does, she would see the photographs were gone. It wouldn't take but a second for her to climb the stairs and hotly demand the black and whites be returned, but when she found my bed to be empty, things would quickly deteriorate. I shook off the possibility of never seeing daylight again, and with one swoop, I pushed the photos into my backpack.

"This is your risk, Elizabeth," I said to myself.

Turning on my heels, I headed to Mom's office to find her purse. Grabbing a ten from her wallet, I slipped it into my back pocket. I had to have a backup plan in case my Metro card was empty.

"Lying and stealing…" I muttered, "I'm really going to have to make this up to her."

Gently pulling the office door shut, I headed down the hallway to the back door. The glow of the red alarm pad was off. Mom had forgotten to set the alarm too. Perhaps, this *really* was my lucky night.

I hesitated, wondering what Mom would do if she saw me sneaking out. Whatever it was, it couldn't be worse than not getting to Jack. He needed to know I had come back as I promised—I hadn't forgotten him.

And maybe if Jack saw the still frames up close, perhaps something in his memory would come to life. Maybe then, we would have a starting point to why the typewriter so desperately needed history to be corrected— whatever history it is referring to.

I turned my watch over: 11:58.

"Seventeen minutes," I exclaimed.

The handle turned, and I charged through the back door. The cool night air hit my face as I rounded the corner. Sprinting out of the back gate and towards the end of Downhill Lane, I turned and looked at my house. It was as I had left it, dark and still. Mom was none the wiser.

I took off, running all the way to Station 8, my feet pounding hard against the black cement. My shoes squeaked with each hit they made. Dogs howled, whining to be set free to catch an intruder as I zipped by. The air grew denser with each block I ran. Despite the sting catching at my side, I had to keep going.

As I arrived, soaked in sweat and out of breath, the high beams of bus number twelve were pulling in. I grabbed the cool bottle of water I had slid into the outer pocket of the backpack and took a deep chug.

"Hhhh," I breathed.

The street lamp above cast odd shadows on the waiting riders. Each wearily stood with their Metro cards in hand, ready to swipe their fares, and take a seat.

The bus settled with a hissing sigh as the doors folded open. From behind the wheel, the female driver motioned everyone onboard. My foot hit the first step, and she squinted at me, "Wait baby," she said. "How old are you?"

"Sixteen," I lied. Lying was becoming somewhat second nature now and I hated the knock it created each time a new mistruth slipped from my lips.

"It's past curfew, honey. I can't let you on my bus."

"Listen," I plead softly, stepping forward to the top platform, "I'm headed to the hospital. My grandfather is in ICU. He had a heart attack a couple of days ago. I live with him. No one is home, and I'd rather sleep in the hospital than stay alone in an empty house all night. Please, I ran all the way here. It's too scary out there alone."

"I see, baby," she said, looking me over for any sign I may be trying to deceive her.

"Please," I begged.

"Okay, now you listen here. I'm Miss Norma. You sit directly behind me. I want to make sure you get off at the right stop. We won't be there until after 1:30. You hear?"

111

"Yes ma'am," I replied.

"Okay baby, go on and take a seat."

As I was settling in, Norma turned and muttered, "You're sure lucky Mr. Larry called in sick. He would have tossed you off his bus, told you that old sob story didn't make one bit of difference to him. Babies belong at home in bed. Yes, he would."

The rest of the line filed in, swiping their cards and turning sideways to move down the narrow aisle. Each looked at me, noting how out of place I was. The last two passengers, both dressed in light blue scrubs smiled, trying to be friendly.

I smiled back and said, "I'm going to the hospital too," in hopes of easing their questions.

Both nodded and moved along without actually replying.

Norma roughly pulled the silver handle and sealed the doors with a bang; with that the bus suddenly moved forward. Taking the next corner, Norma picked up the microphone to greet each of us and give her obligated memorized announcements.

"Good morning ladies and gentlemen. Welcome to Metro Bus number twelve. I'm Miss Norma. We have eight stops tonight. Sit back and enjoy the ride."

The bus rocked, skidding to a narrow stop as the stoplight unexpectedly turned from yellow to red. Norma mumbled under her breath, just loud enough for the first row to catch her string of obscenities.

"One day this city is going to get these lights right. Yes ma'am, they will," she finished. The bus lights dimmed, and each of us silently settled deeper into our seats.

The warm outside air converged with the cool inside of the bus. An icy, thick fog pushed itself from the top of the picture window and made its way down obstructing my view. Making lazy circles across the large pane, trying to clear a space to peer out, it struck me how oddly still the world was.

Brilliant window displays passed quickly, turning into a beautiful, seamless rainbow of colors. The sidewalks stood as eerily still as the darkened sky. In a few short hours, not a single square inch could be had on those same walkways, but for now, not a soul moved among them. Fog pushed its way across my vision once more, and I turned and closed my eyes.

The rocking of the bus worked to lull me to sleep. The sleep I so desperately needed, but it would have to wait. My mind was too busy. The memories of my father, the ones I had pushed away, were begging for my attention. Mom was angry. Jack was in the hospital. The mounting secrets of the typewriter were working to drive me mad. How the world had flipped so completely upside down in the matter of a few short days was beyond my comprehension.

While my head was swimming, Norma dutifully pulled the bus into each stop. Passengers got off, thanking her with warm regards, but not before eyeing me hard, or at least that is what it felt like. The hum of light chatter filled the bus after each stop was complete. I looked at my watch. 1:15 a.m. Not much further.

I made myself a promise that as soon as the sun rose, I would fix things with Mom. It isn't right to do this to her.

Fifteen minutes passed, and Norma called out to me, "Baby, this is your stop."

Halfway standing to make sure we were arriving at the hospital I had intended, I pulled my backpack off the dirty floor below. I smiled at Norma's warm eyes as she watched my every move from the large rear-view mirror.

"Thank you Miss Norma," I replied. "I really can't thank you enough."

The bus came to a soft stop. Only three people stood, the two men in scrubs and me. We were the last passengers left, it seemed.

The men pushed forward, each clipping their hospital name badges to their shirt pockets, waiting for Norma to fold open the doors.

"You two make sure this baby gets into the hospital, you hear me?"

Each turned and smiled, "Yes ma'am," they replied in unison.

It was with that, Norma pulled the lever, opening the doors. The three of us stepped outside.

Chapter 13: A Family Legacy

The moon cast silver shadows across the half-empty parking lot. The first floor of the hospital was so bright it took my eyes a minute to adjust to the glare. White lights poured out of every window and opening, but the floors directly above that stretched into towers were almost all dark. The sick are all asleep, I thought to myself.

"Who are you here to see?" A voice called out from behind.

Spinning on my heels, I turned to see who was asking. The tall, thin man from the bus quickened his steps to catch mine.

"My grandfather," I replied.

"Hospital visiting hours ended five hours ago. So either you are five hours late or five hours early," the man chuckled.

Trying to match his coolness, I smiled, "I know, story of my life, trust me. It's just that I live with him, my grandfather, that is. He's the only family I have, and he is stuck up there somewhere." I stopped and pointed to the darkened towers, "And I'm, well, stuck out here. Our house was too scary to stay in alone."

"How old are you?"

"Sixteen," I lied again.

"You're brave. I wouldn't have taken the Metro in the middle of the night at sixteen."

"Guess you do what you have to," I replied.

"Guess so. What floor is your grandfather on?"

"The fourth," I replied slowly.

"Which side?" he questioned.

Sighing, "He's in the cardiac intensive care unit," I answered.

He paused outside of the emergency room doors, the same ones that Jack was rushed through days before.

"You couldn't make this easy for me, could you?" he said.

"I'm sorry," I said, trying to understand what he meant.

The doors rolled opened as we stepped forward. The still night air was replaced with a cool, hard blast. The sound of patients moaning and carrying on echoed in the hallways. A slight pressure built inside my head as nurses fitfully raced from every corner of the hospital. I would go mad if I had to be here every day.

"Come with me," the man motioned, "I'll call up to ICU and see who the charge nurse is tonight. You better hope Raymond isn't up there this evening. You'll be sleeping on the waiting room sofa until the unit opens at eight a.m. if he is."

I nodded, "Thanks."

"Sure, I'm Doctor Ben, by the way."

He met my extended hand and smiled, "Elizabeth Yale."

"Nice to meet you. What's your grandfather's name? They're going to ask."

"Jack," I replied.

"Stay here, I'll be right back."

Ben instructed a nurse to keep an eye on me. Whatever she did, she was not to send me into the waiting room. It took a few minutes, but when he returned a gentle smile lit his expression, "You are free to go up. Raymond *is* up there tonight. So, I beg you to be as quiet as humanly possible. I mean crawl if you have to. The entire floor is asleep. He'll have my head if you cause a problem."

"You have my word," I promised.

"Good. Now go past the first set of elevators. Take the second set right after the restrooms. Do not ring the bell. Someone will come out if they aren't waiting by the time you get up there. Got it?"

"Got it, and Dr. Ben, thanks," I smiled.

"You're welcome, Elizabeth Yale," he smiled. "Be quiet!"

"I will!" I yelled, turning back to wave goodbye as I picked up the pace towards the elevator doors. This was my only chance of seeing Jack tonight and the countdown was on to beat mom's alarm clock.

The service elevator arrived first. Stepping inside, the smell of trauma and fresh fluids nearly turned my stomach. Positioning myself in the middle of the contraption, I was unwilling to touch a single surface. As I rose, the arrow above the silver doors ticked away each floor until it shuddered to a stop. A female nurse stood waiting on the other side.

"Elizabeth?" she questioned.

"Yes ma'am."

"Come on in, but *please* be quiet."

The unit was dark with the exception of a few dimmed computer screens and the glow of a television shining through the pulled curtain of room 11 straight ahead.

"Your grandfather is right in there," the nurse pointed, "but, if he is sleeping do not disturb him. You are more than welcome to stay in his room, but he needs his rest."

Nodding at the nurse's instructions, I wedged myself into the narrow opening. Holding the sliding door still as not to move it on its track, I forced myself into Grandpa Jack's room and slowly approached his bedside.

He looked peaceful. His eyes were closed. His silver hair was pushed straight back revealing his relaxed face. He seemed older than I had ever seen him before. The life that normally dances across his face was asleep too, replaced with a grayish tone that looked unwell. Seeing the ease of his relaxed wrinkles and hollow cheeks forced me to face the simplest of facts. I was lucky, we were lucky that Jack pulled through this. At his age, with the force of electricity the typewriter omitted, things really could have been much worse.

I picked up the chair that had been moved back to the wall in my absence and took a seat next to his bedside. Jack's hand lay open, in the perfect position for me to slide my fingers into his. The crooked smile that I've always loved filled Jack's face. Whatever he was dreaming must have been pleasant. The way he looked right then reminded me of the man in the photograph—the handsome man that leaned upon the cane.

I pretended to be oblivious to the intense scrutiny coming from the other side of the privacy curtain. Two nurses leaned in, watching to see if I was going to break their rules. The heat of their piercing eyes began to burn into my neck. After a few seconds, I quietly cleared my throat. The squeak of tennis shoes against the linoleum floor told me that Jack and I were finally alone.

Roughly slipping my backpack off my shoulder, I dropped it on the floor next to my chair. The noise made Jack stir. Deep lines crossed his face as he opened his eyes.

"Lizzy-cakes," he said.

"Hi there."

"Hi yourself," Jack said with a small smile.

"I didn't mean to wake you."

"It's fine. What time is it anyhow?"

"It's about two."

Jack turned towards the window, then back to face me, "Two?" he questioned, "Why is it so dark? Is it storming again?"

"Two a.m.," I replied.

"Why aren't you at home sleeping? Is everything okay? Did something happen to Laurel?" Jack sputtered. The sleepiness still hanging onto his body suddenly evaporated, replaced with the awareness of the time and my unexpected presence.

"Everything is fine. Relax."

His blood pressure shot up. Machines registered his distress.

"Grandpa please, you have to relax. If I cause a problem, they will kick me out of here. Nothing is wrong. Everyone is okay. Mom's mad, that's all. She caught me in the attic."

Jack sighed, relaxing back into the uncomfortable bed.

"How did that go over?"

"I'm here now if that is any indication of how that went over. It's a long story."

"Try me," he replied.

"There isn't much to it. I was coming down from the attic. My foot slipped, and I almost fell. My hands were full of pictures, I let go of them to brace myself, and she came in as they tumbled over the railing. When she asked what I was doing in the attic, and why I had the pictures, she didn't believe me. She said I was lying, which of course I was. We argued, and she sent me to my room. It was really that simple."

"That doesn't make sense. Why would she be that mad about you going into the attic?" A hint of confusion colored his words.

"I told her that I thought I heard a noise coming from up there. When she questioned me about the photos, I got defensive. She took off screaming down the stairs, yelling about how you've put me up to something, and how she shouldn't have let you back in our lives. That's when she banished me to my room. I gladly went and didn't come out until I caught the Metro bus to come here. It was a stupid fight."

"I'm sorry I put you in that position. Did you say you took the Metro?"

"Yes, but it's fine," I replied. "I'm fine. I arrived safely, didn't I?"

"Elizabeth, this could have waited until the morning."

"She wouldn't have let me come tomorrow, Jack, or the day after that or the next. She is angry. This was my one shot to bring you the photos and notes I gathered."

"The Metro isn't safe for a child," he chomped. "You have no idea what some of those people are up to at this time of the night, Elizabeth. Laurel would never forgive me if something happened to you."

He was right, anything could have happened along the way. Perhaps my plan wasn't as brilliant as it seemed, but this was too important to wait.

"I'm sorry. I had to see you," I muttered. Swiveling in the chair, I pulled the snapshots from the backpack and held them up. "Look what I found."

"Were you able to find the album you were looking for?" Jack asked, drawing the long wooden tray to his bedside.

"I was," I replied, laying the pile before him.

"What's this?" he asked, unfolding one of the three sheets of paper I managed to snag from the albums.

"Look at it," I urged.

Jack slowly pulled open the aging letter. Slipping on his reading glasses, I subconsciously held my breath in hopes that he knew what was written in the folds.

"Hmm," he exhaled. Grandpa Jack's brilliant eyes flashed towards mine. "It does look the same, doesn't it?"

"It does. It has to be the same language that's printed on the outside of the typewriter case. I was going to try to do some research on the computer but if Mom came into the office things would have only gotten worse."

Jack tapped at the folded oblong sheets, "Are they all the same?" Jack questioned.

"They are. Everything is written in the same language."

"Take a look at this," Jack said, lobbing a thin white notebook towards me. A string of words and letters were

121

printed across the top and then repeated in a single file down the side.

"See the last part? That starts with an F?" Jack asked.

"Yes. Does that say *fabriek*?" I questioned.

"I believe so. Now look at the letters here." Jack pointed to the wrinkled letter pinched delicately between his fingers.

"Seems to be the same letter patterns," I replied.

"And," he prompted.

"And…" I repeated not sure what else he wanted me to say.

"And, then what does *schrijven fabriek* w.b. mean?" he pushed. "But the bigger question you aren't asking is where those words came from." Jack's voice was almost inaudible. He looked down and then stared hard into my eyes.

"I haven't a clue," I replied, shifting to the edge of my chair.

"How about from the typewriter," Jack insisted.

"What? I don't remember ever seeing a sheet with that word typed on it. It always says the same thing, history is not correct," I mocked.

"That's because it didn't type it, not exactly anyhow. Think about it, Elizabeth." Jack was serious again. "When you first touched the machine, what happened?"

"It shocked me."

"Do you recall the machine doing anything else?"

"It started typing."

"And when it typed did anything come out of the machine?"

"Sparks and smoke," I answered, growing annoyed.

"And letters," Jack replied.

"Oh," I said. Nodding my head, "Yes."

I clenched my jaw together, trying to pull the image of the typewriter sparking wildly under each of our touches. The visual came and there floating above the machine were the letters Jack had written out on the small pad.

"What does it mean?" I breathed.

"I don't know yet. I spent the afternoon trying to figure it out. At first, I thought it was some sort of word scramble until my nurse came in. She saw the notepad at the end of the bed, and said the word *fabriek* was printed on the bottom of a grandfather clock her grandparents owned when she was small. The way she described it, I swear she was describing the clock that is sitting in your entryway."

"Now, that's interesting," I replied. "This may be a stretch, but hear me out. Do you think the clock has anything to do with the typewriter?"

"I thought the same thing, but it seems unlikely. Doesn't it?"

Jack flipped through the heap of old black and whites, scrutinizing each one. The third from the bottom pulled a deep gasp from his lips.

"What? What is it?" I fretted.

"That man," he said. "He…" Jack stopped.

"What? Who is he?"

"I don't know his name, Elizabeth, but this photo used to hang in the bookstore when my father was alive. Remember that big tweed chair that sat in the reading corner?"

"I think so," I said.

"You may not. I got rid of it when you first started to walk. Anyhow, each time my great-grandfather, David…"

I stepped on Jack's words, "David? Wasn't your father's name David too?"

"Yes," Jack smiled, "My dad was David Boyd Yale, the third."

"That would make more sense. In my dream, my father said the albums belonged to his grandfather, which would be your father, David. The photographs clearly predate your father. But, if there were two men with the initials DBY before him it could mean that the albums weren't your father's after all. They could have belonged to my three-times great-grandfather, right?"

"Yes," Jack replied quietly. "That would make the most sense."

Clapping my hands, "Now, we are on to something," I laughed. "I didn't mean to interrupt, go ahead."

"Where was I?" Jack asked.

"Your great-grandfather David…" I let the word David dangle from my lips, hoping Jack would be able to pick his thoughts back up where he left off.

"Yes. When David would come to town he would sit in that old chair and stare at this very photograph."

"Why?"

A deep smirk filled Jack's face. He sat up slowly, leaned forward and mimicked his great-grandfather, "My boy, legend has it, those three men created the greatest invention ever known to history. Man was forever changed." Jack's laughter shook the bed.

"What was it? What was the invention?"

"I'm sorry to disappoint you, but to be honest, I don't ever remember him telling me what the invention was. All I remember is the name of the factory because it sounded like he was making it up. He called it The Whizbang Factory. Of all the ridiculous names for him to pull from the air, he chose that."

"Jack," I gasped, "look at the photo again." I jumped to my feet, my hands flying to the tray. "Look at it!" Tapping my finger against the picture. "Look in the background—look at the factory. What does the sign say?"

Jack grinned and moved my hair away from the tray. Never actually looking down, he said, "He was full of baloney, Elizabeth—a serious jokester. Come on, the Whizbang Factory?"

"Look at the photo," I pushed, drawing it so close to his face he had no choice but to pay attention.

Jack straightened with a jerk. His eyes grew larger with each passing second.

"I guess I never looked at it close enough to see the name written on the sign," his voice slightly quivering. "I would have put money on it that the old man was pulling my leg."

"Jack, think hard. What was the Whizbang Factory? Where is it? Do you think it's still standing somewhere? It all has to be connected."

"Elizabeth, it's been over sixty years since my great-grandfather told me about the factory."

The sliding glass door banged loudly. Both Jack and I jumped at the sound. Expecting to see a nurse, our backs eased until my mom stepped through the curtain. Her arms were folded across her chest in livid disbelief.

Chapter 14: The Truth

"Mom!"

"Elizabeth, what is wrong with you? I wake up to find you missing from your bed. I paced the floor for two hours before I was able to convince myself that you would be stupid enough to try to come here. Yet, here you are! I can barely stand to look at you right now," she shouted.

"Mom," I protested.

"No! It's best if you don't say another word, Elizabeth," she said pointing in my direction. "I will never be able to trust you again."

Her anger surprised me. The fierce venom in her words was so unlike her. I sunk deep into the chair next to Jack and braced myself. There was no bedroom to escape to. No door to slam to prove my resentment. I had pushed too far this time, and I would have to sit in her upset until it dissipated.

"Laurel, listen," Jack began, the heart monitor gulping and skipping beats.

"No, Jack, you listen," Mom replied, "I don't have a clue what you've put my daughter up to, but for once you will listen. It's my turn to talk."

Jack sat silent. The privacy curtains swayed as nurses began to gather, looking in on what was mounting to be a hostile showdown. Mom's eyes spoke volumes.

"Jack, the day you decided to pack up and leave was one of the happiest days of my life. Not because I don't love you because I do. I love all the things about you that I adored in my husband, but one thing I did not want to do after his death was spend my life in constant competition with you. The minute Elizabeth was born, and Jesse laid her in your arms," she choked, "you two made a pact. Somewhere in those moments, you two decided to leave the rest of us out of your little twosome. Once Jesse passed, I knew I would spend my life correcting all the crazy ideas you somehow stuck inside my child's head. I was right too. Look at you two now. You haven't even been here a week, and she is sneaking out of the house and lying to me. That isn't my child, Jack. That is you!"

"Mom," I begged.

"No, Elizabeth, you and I will talk in a moment. This is about Jack and me right now."

"Laurel, I didn't ask Elizabeth to come here."

"But she did, didn't she? She will do anything for you Jack, but you already know that. That's part of the fun, isn't it? Bet you didn't tell her to go up in the attic and dig around either?"

Jack's eyes flew to mine. As indiscreetly as possible, I nodded. It was time for my mother to hear the truth whether she believed us or not.

"I did ask her to go to the attic."

"Why? What could you possibly need up there that you couldn't have asked me to retrieve?"

"That's the thing; I couldn't necessarily describe to you what I needed. Elizabeth knew what she was after."

"Don't speak in circles, Jack. What do you mean Elizabeth knew what she was looking for?"

"Mom," I said standing, "I want you to sit down."

"No," she responded harshly.

"Mom," I whispered, "please. Jack and I aren't ganging up against you; it's just that…"

"It's just that what?"

"You wouldn't believe the truth."

"You haven't even given me a chance to."

I shut down. She was right. Neither of us had even tried to explain. Instead, we buried everything without ever giving her an opportunity to tell us we're deftly crazy. Jack and I looked at one another and silently agreed to let her in on our secret.

"You can trust me, you know," I said, looking into my mother's eyes. "With a few exceptions, I've always told you the truth."

"Have you?" she muttered.

Her words sliced right through my core.

"Yes, as a matter of fact, I have," I sniffed.

I could see Jack starting to waver on whether Mom could handle hearing the truth. His fists were balled; his body was tense. The heart monitor leaped and broke the steady pattern again. The internal dilemma was eating at him.

"Laurel," he said softly, "Ease up on Elizabeth, please. She's a great kid. She's your kid; how could she not be perfect? I know we've, no I've, made some decisions that haven't been all that fair to you and I'm sorry for that. If you promise to listen no matter how absurd what I tell you sounds, I will tell you what is going on. But, you *have* to promise to listen."

Her face softened. The giant puzzle seemed to be coming together for her, as the truth was right on the tip of both of our lips. The thing was the puzzle only had a couple of the corner pieces intact. We were missing a slew of information.

"You see," Jack began, "when I was in Morocco, I stumbled across a typewriter."

"The typewriter that is upstairs?" Mom questioned.

"The very same one, indeed," Jack replied.

Jack wove all the details of the last few days together for her. Questions were asked and answered, and in the end, she sat speechless. After some time, Mom cleared her throat and said, "While none of this sounds plausible, I *do* believe you."

Both Jack and I exhaled at the same time. Neither of us had breathed since Mom had fallen silent.

"I do have one question though," she said softly.

"Do you think Jesse knew about all of this?"

"What do you mean?" Jack pushed. "How would he have possibly known?"

Mom closed her eyes and rubbed her temples.

"What aren't you saying, Laurel?"

"About a month before he passed, Jesse received some strange calls. He never told me the full extent of them. All he said was that a man was inquiring about a factory we supposedly owned. I brushed it off. Thought the man had the wrong Jesse Yale. I asked him to speak to you Jack, but now I know he never did. There was so much going on during that time. He probably didn't want to trouble you. You know how he was."

"What was going on?" I asked.

"He was under a tremendous amount of stress. He had been traveling overseas for work trying to orchestrate the largest merger his company had ever dealt with. Your father was the lead. To top it off, Claire had just died. Your grandfather needed some extra attention. Life was sort of upside down, and everything fell into your father's lap."

"Who is Claire?" I asked.

Jack's eyes fell, "Your grandma, sweetie. No one called her Claire except your mother. She is talking about Grandma Jewel."

"I thought Jewel was her name," I whispered.

"No," Jack laughed. "Your grandmother was named after her grandmother. Your great-grandmother was something. That woman was meaner than a hungry bull. Your grandmother preferred to be called Jewel, after her middle name Julian."

"Then why did you call her Claire, Mom?" I asked.

"I don't know. I thought the name was beautiful, and it suited her well. She never seemed to mind," Mom said winking.

"Laurel," Jack stammered, turning his eyes back in her direction, "Did Jesse ever mention anything else? Maybe about what type of factory the man was inquiring about, where it was, the name—anything?"

Mom shook her head, and said, "Nothing, Jack. There wasn't time. He passed away right after he returned from London. A call came in from the same number the night before he passed. Jesse was irate, told the man never to call him again, and then blocked the number. That was it. Nothing else ever came of it."

"It sounds connected, Jack," I whispered.

"Maybe," he said, scratching his head, "But if that were the case why wouldn't have someone contacted me?"

"Maybe that is just another part of this mystery," I replied.

The three of us sat in silence. The gaps in the information were frustrating. We were no closer to understanding what was going on before Mom arrived, but one thing was certain: we didn't have to mask the truth any longer.

The door gently slipped open, each of us was stirred from our thoughts.

"Good morning," a nurse said.

"Morning," we replied together.

"Mr. Yale, we're going to be moving you in the next thirty minutes. You seem to be doing well, and they have a regular room ready. It's the last step before getting you out of this place," the nurse smiled.

"That is excellent news," Jack replied.

"Someone will be by in a few minutes to start the process."

"What time is it?" Mom asked.

My eyes were heavy. Flipping my watch over, I squinted, "It's six fifteen."

"Elizabeth, I'm taking you home. You need to sleep for a few hours. When you wake, we'll do some research together. We'll try to figure out what The Whizbang Factory was and how it is tied to our family. Jack, you get settled into your room, and we'll be back just after lunch if that sounds okay?"

"It sounds perfect," Jack replied. "Laurel," he reached out grasping her hand, "thank you."

A faint smile filled her face as she said, "You drive me mad, Jack Yale, but I love you."

Chapter 15: What's a Whizbang?

Snuggled deep in the sheets, I beckoned the sandman to come and drag me into dreamland, but he did not oblige. Three questions kept resounding in my head: what was the Whizbang factory, what is the significance of the string of letters that pour from the typewriter, and did my father know more than he let on before his death?

Exhaustion stretched its weary fingers through my mind. The numbness settling in my body was more prevalent in some places than in others. After an hour, my body and all tension within it went limp. A fog pulled me away and into the beginning moments of a vivid dream.

My father grasped my mother's hand and spun her in a lazy circle. Bold, brilliant smiles pushed across both their faces. As the music began, a horrific cry stole the pure moment between them. My eyes flew open. For a second, I did not move. I was certain the cry came from my dream, but when the sound of fear radiated from the hallway again, I leapt towards the bedroom door.

"Elizabeth," Mom screamed.

My heart thudding in my chest, "Mom," I shouted, "What's wrong?"

The all too familiar sound demanded my attention: Whiz-whiz-BANG! Mom had taken the same position I had been in the day before. Her body was jammed as close to the stair rail as possible as she shielded her head from the flying sparks. The typewriter buzzed. Arcs of raw power flew into the hall. The letters flowed from the roller, floating up in perfect form just as Jack had written them: *Schrijven fabriek* W.B. I mouthed the letters to myself as they disappeared as quickly as they appeared.

"Whatever you do, do not touch the machine!" I shouted.

A small pile of laundry surrounded her feet. A pair of socks hung from her left hand.

"I wasn't, I didn't, Elizabeth, I didn't touch the machine!" she cried.

With each word she spoke the machine ramped its glimmers of power higher and higher.

"Shh," I called out to her, tiptoeing as slowly as I possibly could. "Do—not—speak! It's responding to you, Mom."

Careful to not absorb the tremors of power, I cradled my fingers onto the keyboard. Everything went deafeningly quiet, the same way it had in the moments before Jack was almost shocked to death. Readying myself for the burst of shocking insanity, I drew my shoulders close to my chin, slammed my eyes shut, and tightened every muscle. Whispering a countdown, "5—4—3," the typing machine moaned and eased.

"Elizabeth," Mom trembled, "what? Why?"

"I don't know," I whispered back, "Did you touch it? Graze it somehow?"

"No!" she roared. "I was only walking past. I washed a few of Jack's things. I was heading upstairs to put them away for him. That is all, Elizabeth, I swear. What is wrong with that thing?"

"Shh," I urged again. "I believe you. Try to relax."

My fingers still dangled above the keys. Slowly I began: What space is space a space Whizbang space Factory?

The machine roared. Whiz-whiz-BANG! My fingers bounced violently across the keyboard as the machine replied to my query.

The answer is under your fingers. The answers are all under your fingers.

I turned and looked at my mom.

"What does it say?" she asked, still holding her position against the railing.

"It says the answer is under your fingers."

"A factory is under your fingertips?" she questioned.

Trying again: What space is space a space Whizbang?

The answer is at your fingertips. History is not right. History is not right. History is not right. EWY. EWY. Correct it. Correct it. EWY, EWY, EWY.

The last Y yet again had the strike through the middle.

"Now what does it say?" Mom questioned, her voice quivering.

"It says exactly what it keeps saying: History is not right. Correct it. The answer is under my fingertips. It strikes the Y of my initials each time it responds. Maybe it's going to strike me out," I said. "It's not like it didn't try to do that to Grandpa Jack."

Mom and I stared at one another for a moment, as we were both attempting to make sense of the machine's cryptic messages.

"Take your fingers off the machine," Mom instructed.

"Why?"

"Just do it," she replied.

Doing as I was told, I drew my fingers away and put my hands together. My fingers burned as they did each time I had the displeasure of touching the wild contraption.

"Hear me out," Laurel started, "What if the machine isn't being as cryptic as we think? What if the question is actually the answer? The Whizbang machine is what is directly at your fingertips and think about the sound it makes. Doesn't your other typewriter make more of a click, clack, dinging sound rather than whiz-whiz-bang?"

"It can't be that simple, can it?" I muttered.

"Think about it," she urged.

I held my breath, placed my fingers back on the keys and entered: Are space you space a space Whizbang?

Nothing. No response. No electric pushes of power. No wild fireworks displays—nothing.

"It was worth a try," Mom said.

Disappointment covered my face, "I knew it couldn't be that easy," I replied.

"Now what?" I asked.

"Now, why don't we try to translate the letters you found," she urged.

Mom began down the stairs, prattling about something unimportant while an idea formed in the back of my mind. With my eyes blazing into the machine, I stepped forward and quickly pounded out:

If space the space Y space of space my space name space isn't space there, space what space is space my space last space name?

Without the usual ceremonious hiss or unyielding power, the typewriter replied `Elizabeth Wright Royal`.

"Elizabeth Wright Royal?" I questioned.

"What?" Mom questioned, turning and looking back at me. "What did you say?"

"The machine," I croaked. "I asked what my name was if the Y was gone, and it replied Elizabeth Wright Royal."

"Royal?"

"That is what it says, Elizabeth Wright Royal."

I paused for a moment and then a sinking feeling found my stomach. "Do you think," I began to say when the harsh tone of the doorbell startled me. "Gosh," I shouted.

"Who would be here now?" Mom stammered, "Coming..."

The door opened with a jerk, and a familiar figure swaggered into the house.

Chapter 16: Jack's back— Again

"You do know that rational people don't just show up on people's doorsteps when they are supposed to be in the hospital recovering from a heart attack, right?" Mom questioned.

"Nice to see you too," Jack beamed. "How was your nap?"

"Forgive me, but how exactly does one go from you are being moved into another recovery room to you are free to go, Mr. Yale?"

"When Mr. Yale is tired of being poked and prodded. Besides every test has come back completely normal, Laurel."

"I was with you Grandpa Jack," I said, coming down the stairs, "You flat-lined in the ambulance. You definitely had a heart attack. You should be at the hospital until the doctors say it is safe to leave."

"There is a difference between my heart stopping from electric shock and having a massive heart attack, my dears. It isn't as if any of us exactly told the truth about what happened, now did we. If you wish, I can check myself back in, but I figured it would be easier with me here. We have some pressing matters to attend to if I'm not mistaken."

"You are the most stubborn man I've ever met," Mom replied.

"Oh, simmer down. I'm all right. What are my girls up to? Any news?"

"This," I replied, handing Jack the typewriter's last page.

Jack's eyes hardened. "Royal," he read. "Did it say anything else?"

"Just this," I said handing him another sheet of paper. "Look at the top three lines. When I asked what a Whizbang was it replied the answer is under my fingers," I revealed.

"Interesting."

"Are you two hungry?" Mom asked, growing tired of the conversation.

Lunch was eaten in impossible silence, each of us letting our minds wander to what would come next. I repressed my curiosity to go and push my fingers back on the keys upstairs, bombard the contraption with a million more questions. Jack straightened stiffly in his chair as he took his last bite and said, "It's funny what comes back to you if you let it."

He had both of our attentions now. His quick mind was pulling memories to the forefront.

"Elizabeth, remember how I was telling you about great-grandpa David telling me about the Whizbang Factory?"

"Yes, of course."

"In the cab here, I kept thinking about him pulling me on to his knee and telling me about the factory. I think the typewriter is being very literal when it says the answer is under your fingers. I think the typewriter is the Whizbang machine. Remember what he always said about the three men in the photograph?"

"That they invented the greatest invention of all time?" I questioned.

"Yes," Jack smirked. "It stands to reason that it would be the typewriter."

Mom cleared her throat, swallowing the last bite of her turkey and cheese sandwich, and said, "I think the same, the Whizbang machine has to be a typewriter. It's really the only thing that makes sense."

"So, if we know it's the typewriter the mystery is solved," I replied.

"No, not exactly. There is so much more to it than that," Jack said.

"Like why does the machine keep saying that history is wrong, urging you to correct it? Or why does it respond the way it does when you touch it? And the most important of all questions, why does it think your last name is Royal?" Mom urged.

"And that's just the beginning, I believe," Jack replied.

"So then, where do we start?" I sighed.

"That I don't know," Jack replied, "Maybe with the letters you found in the attic."

Mom stood quickly, and softly said, "No, we need to go back into the attic."

Chapter 17: The Box

"What are we looking for up here?" I questioned as the attic ladder springs screeched open for the second time this week.

Grandpa Jack clambered up the slender ladder behind me. His hot, labored breath touched the back of my legs.

"Are you okay?" I asked.

"I'm fine," he huffed.

"Grandpa, Mom and I can handle this if you need to rest," I pushed.

"Elizabeth, I said I'm fine," his deep voice shaking.

His normal cool demeanor was replaced with severe aggravation. I let it go and kept my mouth shut. With the three of us inside the attic, my eyes were just beginning to adjust to pinpricks of light cutting through the darkness when Mom flipped the light switch.

"Okay," she said, "We need to find a box with your father's name on it."

The attic was a mess. Open cartons were scattered everywhere. I hadn't had a chance to fix the mayhem I created when I was looking for the albums. The heat of the day had already pushed the attic's temperature well over a hundred degrees. Sweat instantly poured off the three of us and dampened our collars in a matter of seconds.

"We need to work quickly," Mom urged. "It's too hot up here to stay for too long."

"What does the box look like, Laurel?" Jack asked, wiping sweat from his furrowed brows.

"It's small, bigger than a shoebox, but not too much bigger. I wrote Jesse's name in red marker."

"Where did you put it, Mom?"

"I can't remember, sweetie. I just remember bringing a few boxes of your father's things up here once I had the strength to unpack his suitcase. The box we need was at the top of that stack," Laurel replied. "I wish I could remember where I stuck it, but I was practically sleepwalking after he died. If it hadn't been for you, I probably would have stayed in bed and wallowed in the pain for months. Everything was a haze then. The only thing I remember is what I put inside the box and the fact that I wrote his name in red."

The three of us instantly went to work, spreading out, searching each stack strategically in hopes that the box would show itself quickly. No one spoke while we searched, and time began to drag. I picked my way through the fifth or sixth stack when Grandpa Jack shook his head and grimaced.

"I don't think it's up here. Did you perhaps stick it in a closet downstairs? The heat is stifling," Jack groaned.

"Go downstairs," Mom replied, standing and straightening her clothes. She turned to face us; abruptly her expression shifted. I watched her eyes land directly above my head. Pointing, she smiled, "There!"

A medium box, no bigger than eight-and-a-half-by-eleven, was balanced in a corner of two adjacent rafters.

"I knew it was up here," Mom laughed. Five long strides forward, Laurel reached for the box and plucked it from its resting place. Covered with a layer of dark gray dust Mom scrolled a perfect cursive J along the edge. An excited murmur slipped from her lips as she flipped the top open.

Jack knelt onto one knee, "Now, what is inside that is so particularly important, Laurel?" he snorted.

Mom's hands worked fast, flipping through a pile of aging receipts when she stopped.

"Here," she whispered, holding a long white ticket out to Jack.

"It looks like an airplane ticket," I said, "What is so important about a used airline ticket?"

"The importance is the destination," she replied. "I got to thinking this morning. Two weeks before Claire died your father came home buzzing about the trip of a lifetime. His company's merger was ramping up, and he was invited to join the company's president in London to assist in any legal matters that arose while they were there. Your father was thrilled. Not only was he able to go to London, but he was taking me with him. We both knew if we didn't go then it wasn't likely we would ever have the chance to go again. We both jumped at the opportunity. The tickets came, we began tossing our bags together, and then we got the call from you, Jack."

"Jewel died," he said, his eyes welled with tears as her name slipped from his lips.

"Yes," Mom whispered.

"I guess I've forgotten how she died," I said, slipping my hand into his.

"No, you haven't forgotten, sweetie," Mom said, letting a half-smile fill her beautiful face, "We never told you."

"Why not?"

"We all decided you were too young for us to tell you anything more than she was gone," Jack replied.

His face turned dark. The memories pulling at him were more painful than anything physical he had just been through; as he began to speak, I understood the expressions and felt the same pain settle inside of me.

"Your grandmother had a doctor's appointment in the city. She hadn't been feeling well for nearly a month. She kept complaining about intense pain in her stomach. I urged her to go to the doctor, but she kept refusing. Finally, the pain became too much, so her doctor insisted she come in. The only appointment she could get happened to fall on a day I had a large shipment arriving at the bookstore. I asked her to go alone. It was a mistake, a foolish mistake." Jack's shoulders quivered.

"Jack," Mom uttered.

He nodded grimly and continued, "Jewel hated going into the city alone; she refused to drive, so she took the bus. We both figured she was safer that way.

The physician's building was about four blocks from the nearest bus stop. On the way back, she must have been lost in the news she received. The doctor's office later told me she had cancer. I'm sure she couldn't wrap her mind around what that meant for her, for us, or the fact that I had sent her to hear this information alone. I haven't forgiven myself for that nor do I think I ever will."

Tears streamed down Jack's face. Squeezing his hand, I sunk into his arms.

"I don't know, Elizabeth, maybe she wasn't thinking. Jewel crossed the street without going to the crosswalk. She was hit by a taxi. I still don't understand what would have possessed her to walk into the middle of the street like that," Jack choked.

"My God," I muttered.

"She made it another twenty-four hours, but her injuries were too much for anyone to survive," Mom finished.

"I see why you didn't tell me," I replied.

"It was hard, kid," Jack cried, squeezing my hand. Pain shot through my fingers and into the middle of my back, but I refused to let go. For the first time, I began to understand why Jack left everything and ran after my father passed away. My grandmother's death and then my father's was simply too much too soon.

"Our London trip was about a week away," Mom said, "With all that Jack was going through we couldn't ask him to look after you. He wasn't in the right frame of mind—no one would be. We buried your grandmother and the next day, your father boarded a plane to London alone."

"I ruined your chance to go to London," I hissed.

"Don't be silly," she replied, "The timing was off. Nothing was ruined; things were *just* different."

"I guess I'm still lost as to why we need Jesse's ticket to London," Jack replied.

"Well, that's what came to mind this morning. After Jesse called work to let them know Claire had passed, and I wouldn't be going to London with him, a new set of tickets arrived. I never looked at them, but I noticed that Jesse packed an entirely different wardrobe than what he would have needed while he was in London. I wondered why, but I never questioned him about repacking his suitcase."

"I'm still missing something," Jack said, softly.

"Well, like I told you before, the strange phone calls came in about this time too. The day before he called the office to let them know I wouldn't be going, he received one of those calls in the middle of the night. This morning when I was standing in the closet, I swear I could almost see him bent over his suitcase unpacking and repacking. There was something about the way he did it that made me wonder if he actually went to London."

"Mom," I said shocked. "Dad wasn't the type to lie to you, was he?"

"No," she replied, "not at all. But, if he knew something and didn't have all the information perhaps he wasn't prepared to share it with me or anyone else for that matter."

"With me, you mean," Jack asked.

Mom's fingers traced the outer edges of the voucher. With a deep inhale, she flipped it over. Her lips mashed together, and her head nodded thoughtfully. For a quick second, I saw a vision of my father leaving for this trip eight years ago. He waved goodbye on the porch, in a rush. A large black suitcase hung from his hand as he loaded himself into the car. I called out to him; I asked him where he was going and begged him to stay. As he answered in my vision, I spoke the words aloud, "I have some work to do sweetie. I'll see you when I return. It won't be long…"

Laurel grinned, "That's what he said. I remember it too. Those were the words I kept hearing in my head this morning. That's what made me question whether he really went to London or not. He didn't tell you he had to go to London, just that he had work to do."

"Right," I replied.

"What does the ticket say, Laurel?" Jack gently nudged.

"AMS," she said almost inaudibly, "Amsterdam Airport, Pier E, Gate 3."

That seemed to bother Jack for a second, and then he shifted roughly onto his feet. "It's time to find out what Jesse knew."

"Wait," Mom urged, "there's more."

"What?" Jack asked, his voice falling flat as he sunk back to his knees.

Mom dug into the box and pulled a thin document out. The heading was noted: Eigneschap Daad.

"Can't anything be written in English?" I groaned.

Near the middle of the page, the word Royal stared back at me.

"Look," I demanded. I quickly underlined the word that now seemed to be a major player in this oddly twisted mystery with my finger.

"Royal," Mom read.

"As in the typewriter typed Elizabeth Wright Royal," I said.

"Did you say you got this from Jesse's suitcase?" Jack asked.

"Yes," she nodded. "I didn't know what it was at the time. I tossed it in this box and sealed it away until now."

Jack pulled the sheet from her hand. Reviewing each letter and sentence in hopes that something, anything would be comprehendible, "Euros," he noted.

"Isn't that currency?" I asked.

"Yes," Mom replied.

"I think this is some sort of land document," Jack said. "There seems to be a value given, and it is issued to a man named Edward Y. Royal."

"I think we have our starting point, Jack," Mom supposed.

Silently, Jack slid his feet down onto the attic ladder as it trembled under him.

"Where are you going?" I asked.

"The New York City Public Library," he replied.

Mom looked down at her watch, "There isn't time. They close in less than an hour. We cannot get to Fifth Avenue that quickly, not even by car. It will have to wait until tomorrow."

Chapter 18: Patience and Fortitude

The sun was dreadfully bright as it poured through the closed blinds.

"Five more minutes," I whined though no one was asking.

I was still exhausted. One night of restless sleep in nearly a week wasn't what I had hoped for. More vivid dreams and questions raised when I closed my eyes. I wasn't sure I would ever sleep again without the torment of our quest pulling at my subconscious.

I tugged the faded comforter up to my chin and tried to snuggle in. To my dismay, my mind began to ramble. Five minutes later, I gave in, lobbed myself over until my toes touched the floor and staggered to my closet. Sleep would yet again have to wait despite the fog churning in my head. Pulling on my favorite pair of tattered jeans and a soft navy blue blouse, I felt somewhat ready for whatever the day had to bring. Whatever it was, a substantial amount of anxiety enticed me to give into its angst as I slipped on my shoes. Something big was coming—I could feel it.

I stammered into the hallway, waiting for the sound of frying bacon and the smell of strong black coffee to hit me, but the house was silent. Silent except for the sound of Jack's panting breath reassuring that he had not been stirred from his slumber. I surveyed the typewriter. It too seemed to be sleeping, if an inanimate object could ever do such a thing.

The grandfather clock downstairs rang out seven hard bongs.

"It's only seven," I complained. "I wish I could sleep."

Tiptoeing into Jack's room, I stood at his bedside contemplating whether to wake him. He looked peaceful. Far more peaceful than he had been shoved into the uncomfortable hospital bed. His chest heaved up and down in a beautiful rhythm that made me jealous of his rest. I decided to let him snooze.

An idea stirred within me. As quietly as possible, I slipped down the stairs and into Mom's office closing the double doors behind me. Flipping open the laptop screen, my fingers tingled the way they do each time they hang over the typewriter. We were already in too deep to turn away and yet still so far from receiving any sort of answers that I wasn't sure what to research first.

The black cursor blinked amongst the search bar with the question *where to next* in bold letters above it.

"That's the million-dollar question, now isn't it?" I smirked.

Typing out, *what is a Whizbang*? The search tool circulated while it worked to generate an answer. Two items popped up. One was a definition, and the other was a blue link with a web address: www.whizbangfabriek.com.

"There's that word again," I uttered. "*Fabriek.*"

I clicked on the definition first. A noun: known for noise, speed, or startling effect.

"That sounds about right," I said. "Now, www.whizbangfabriek.com what secrets do you have to reveal?"

Moving the mouse in tiny circles under my fingers, I tried to find the courage to click on the blue link. What if the materials contained in the link is the pendulum that swings the entire mystery wide open? After two long minutes, I let the cursor fall on the link and clicked.

Nervous anticipation filled my bones and set my fingers fidgeting with a dull red pencil. Passing the seconds, I whirled the stumpy number two around my thumb and caught it with my index finger as it made a loop. On the sixth time around, a document filled the screen.

My hope of gathering firm answers was shot down. Scrolled across the monitor was the same unrecognizable language that continues to elude our understanding. I poured over the information, hoping something would jump out, but nothing did. One thing was clear, we had to find a translator—today.

"Lizzy?" a muffled voice called out. "Where are you?"

Standing and pushing through the double office doors, I called out, "In here."

Jack was standing at the top of the stairs. His hair was a matted mess on his head. The fog of sleep hung on him as it had to me an hour before.

"What time is it?" he asked.

"I think it's a bit past eight," I replied.

"The day is getting away from us. Are you ready to go?"

"I am," I laughed. "Are you, old man?"

Yawning deeply, Jack stretched his arms high above his head, "I will be. What are you doing?" he asked.

"Research," I replied.

"Oh," Jack said eagerly.

"Don't get your hopes up. Nothing much came up. A definition and another document in the same unreadable language," I sighed.

"It was worth a try," Jack said. "Give me five minutes to brush my teeth and change. Then we'll be on our way."

I rushed back to Mom's laptop and hit print. There was undoubtedly something more to the words on the screen. As the printer churned, I snatched the warm sheets from the tray and went to pack my things. Five minutes later, Jack was ready to go.

"Think we should wake Mom and see if she wants to tag along?" I asked.

"If she isn't up by now, she probably needs the rest," Jack replied. "We really need to get going, Elizabeth."

"Let's leave her a note then," I said, "I don't want her to worry."

Jack scribbled out our plans while I gathered the rest of the papers we had collected over the last few days. The last item piled on top of the stack was the airline ticket marked AMS. Careful not to bend a single thing, I slipped everything into a manila folder and carefully placed it in my backpack for safekeeping.

"Do you want to drive or take the Metro?" I questioned.

"Definitely the bus. At this time of the day, traffic will be insane."

Forty minutes later, Metro bus number 18 picked us up at the eastbound stop. Jack and I sat silent for the majority of the ride. Both of us were filled with too many questions to engage in small talk. As the bus 18 screeched to a stop, the driver's voice boomed over the loudspeaker.

"One more and then we'll be at our stop," Jack said, nudging my arm.

I smiled. The bus practically emptied within seconds, and with a sudden lurch forward we were on our way.

"Jack," I said softly. "What if we are chasing ghosts? I mean, what if all this stuff ends up being dead ends?"

"Then we will have to figure out where to look next," he replied.

"It's just…" I stopped.

"Elizabeth," he said, "sometimes you just have to take risks."

My father spoke those same words to my mother as she kissed him goodbye the day he boarded the flight to Amsterdam. Neither of us knew then just what he meant; now, however, things make perfect sense. I gave myself this same permission when I ran to Jack. Now, Grandpa Jack was imparting the same wisdom to me. We had to chase the leads, continue to move forward, no matter how uncomfortable it was making me feel.

The bus made a sharp turn coming to a near colliding stop with a taxi at Library Way and 41st.

"This is our stop, Lizzy," he said.

We stood and pushed our way to the rear doors. Warm air blasted our faces as the doors shuttered opened. The streets of New York City were alive. People rushed past in all directions. Locals grasped hot cups of coffee with one hand while their other held their phones to reddened ears. Massive skyscrapers propelled into the crystal blue sky. The combination of cement and glass cast ornate shadows along the sidewalks. My senses were on overload.

The gorgeous patina of the railings nearby reminded me of the typewriter—the reason why we were here. For the very first time in all of my fifteen years, I felt alive—completely uninhibited by my age or circumstances life has thrown at me. With each step, purpose soaked into my feet and up my spine.

Seated into the sidewalk was the wisdom of the world's greatest thinkers. Their brilliance was thrust upon anyone willing to look down at the bronze plaques lining Library Way.

One in particular caught my attention. "...There are only two or three human stories, and they go on repeating themselves as fiercely as if they had never happened before...*Willa Cather, O Pioneers!*"

The words settled into my brain.

"Exactly," I whispered.

All that we had discovered seemed to be on the repeat. We were treading in the footprints of my father, and yet, it would appear as though some of our family history had been buried and erased. We were at the starting point that much I was certain. The words the typewriter had urged echoed once more, "History is not correct. Correct it. Correct it."

My eyes turned upward to soak in the beauty of this magnificent city. My face must have given away the awakening inside of me because Jack leaned over and hugged my shoulder, pacing his steps with mine.

"This city will do that to you, kid," he said.

I wanted to stop, read each nugget of knowledge stamped into the sidewalk, but the foot traffic surged us forward. The two blocks up 41st sped by quickly. Before I knew it, we were standing at the massive crosswalk leading to the New York Public Library.

It was breathtaking.

"We have about fifteen minutes before the doors open," Jack said, looking at his watch.

"It's incredible," I stammered.

"Haven't you been here before?" he asked, watching as a man hit the crosswalk button.

"No."

Jack laughed, "Well, prepare to have your mind blown, Lizzy-cakes. I think I read once that there are over fifty million items right inside those doors."

"You are making that up, Grandpa Jack," I said. "There is no way."

"You don't have to believe me, but it's true. Just wait…"

The crosswalk indicator flashed the white walk sign, and we made our way to the front steps. I have never felt so small—ever. The marvelous marble arches and stone columns stretched high above our heads. While the world around me continued on, people rushing shoulder-to-shoulder, car horns blaring, small talk spoken and carried away with the light breeze, only one thought came to mind.

"Grandpa," I whispered, "This may sound strange, but I feel like our history is suddenly coming to life. That perhaps we are only a small part of a much bigger picture."

The hair rose on Jack's arms and traced down his legs. Gently tapping my shoulder with his rough hands, he said, "That is exactly what is happening, Elizabeth—exactly. See those lions over there?" he questioned, directing my eyes to the two massive carved beasts perched upon grand pillars on either side of the library entrance.

"Yes," I replied.

"They are named Patience and Fortitude, protectors of the mysteries within the library. Think about it—their names represent our path. We must be patient in our desire for the truth. We must follow the leads and know that what is destined to come will in time. We must carry ourselves with fortitude in order to face danger or bear pain if it should come. We must be lions, Elizabeth."

Sinking into the grand marble steps, I repeated Jack's words, "We must be lions."

"Whatever we find, good or bad, promise me you'll never let this moment, these truths be buried again. You must keep them inside you, Elizabeth. We have to keep telling the stories we uncover to your children, to your grandchildren, their grandchildren, whomever you decide, but you must never let them be hidden again. You are the link from our past to our present."

I nodded, silently promising.

"Do you think the pieces of this puzzle will fall into place?" I whispered.

"I believe they already have begun to."

The massive rotating door clicked and began to move.

"It's open," I cried.

Chapter 19: New York City Library

The rotating door made one slow, sweeping loop before opening wide enough to allow us to step forward. The turnstile twisted and dropped us inside. If a place could hold magic, the New York Public Library contains all the magic the world has to offer right inside its foyer. Every detail is spellbinding.

As my feet hit the white marble, my heart swelled and pounded against my chest. Lavish chandeliers hung from the sculpted ceilings. The twin staircases artfully rose and disappeared behind huge walls. A massive world expanded before me. It was unlike anything I had ever seen. I stood gulping it in.

"Wait until you see the Rose Reading Room," Jack laughed, "We need to find a librarian to help us get started. Come along."

I followed him to the Reading Room. Its name was lacking compared to what treasures lay before my eyes. Long oak tables, stained the color of warm, rich honey, stretched for miles. Dozens upon dozens of elegant bronze lamps pushed the perfect white glow onto the table below it. The way the sun burned through the arched windows drew me deeper into the building's enchantment.

"Look up," Jack pointed.

The ceilings soared and swirled into elaborate carvings that crashed into vibrant murals of the billowing clouds in a perfect blue sky. Sometime after entering the Rose Reading Room, I had forgotten to breathe. My sides ached and burned, begging for the smallest wisp of air to be drawn into my lungs. The beauty was nearly too much for me to comprehend.

"May I help you?" an older librarian with wide-rimmed reading glasses hanging from the tip of her nose asked in a hush.

"Yes ma'am," Jack replied, "Where would I start if I were interested in looking up my family history? Is there a particular section of the library that I should be looking for?"

A polite smile grew upon her wrinkled face as she answered, "Yes, sir. You will want to start in Room 121. Room 119 may also be of interest to you, depending on what records you are seeking. May I ask if you are looking for something in particular?"

Jack nodded, "I would like to know where my family migrated from. I'm afraid I don't know much about my ancestry."

"Do you happen to know if your ancestors settled in New York when they arrived or did they spread across America?"

Jack's face turned slightly sour. "I don't know," he sighed. "I'm afraid I don't know much at all." Grandpa Jack took the file folder from my backpack and laid it on the desk. "This is all I have regarding my family's past."

The librarian pushed her glasses onto the bridge of her nose, giving her eyes the power they needed to read. As she did, she stopped on a document poking out from the bottom of the stack. "May I?" she asked respectfully, reaching out to pull it closer.

"Of course," Jack and I said in unison.

"How I wish I could read this elegant beauty," she said wishfully holding one of the few handwritten letters I had stashed among the mix of photographs.

"Do you happen to know which language it is?" Jack questioned.

"I believe I do," she smiled. "It would appear to be written in Old Dutch."

"How do you know?" I pushed.

"My dear, I am the first generation of my family to be born in America. My parents came when they were small. My grandfather was a book dealer."

I turned and looked at Jack. He smiled back. The similarities between the two could erupt into a love story of their own if I pushed hard enough.

She continued, "My grandfather, like his father before him, traveled the world acquiring rare literature. When they settled in their Upper East Side apartment many years ago, my grandmother organized his books by language. The Dutch books were among my favorite to sit with on the large window seat and guess at the words. Please don't ask me why. I am not certain why, but I suppose I was drawn to the beautiful scrolling of their language."

Jack's shoulders were raised close to his chin almost as if he was expecting some earth shattering news to fall from the librarian's mouth.

"Was our family Dutch?" I asked.

"Not that I know of," Jack replied.

Shuffling through the stack laid open in the folder, I pulled the small sheet of paper with the words *schvijven fabriek* printed along the top and sides.

"How about these words? Do you know what they say or mean?" I asked.

Peering over the tops of her glasses, the librarian pulled the paper closer to get a better view, "I'm sorry to say I do not know the meaning of the first word, but the second: *fabriek* means factory. That much I'm certain of."

Jack and I let out a small gasp. That seemed so simple to surmise, yet it had eluded us.

"WB," I stated quietly.

"Whizbang Factory," he replied.

"It would seem that you are already on your way to discovery," she smiled. "If you are in fact interested in finding out more we have two valuable resources available to you. The first is a part-time genealogist employed here at the library. There is a fee for this service, but I do believe she is in today. The other is a language specialist. They may be able to crack the code of some of the information you have in your file."

"Could you point us in the right direction?" Jack urged.

The librarian slowly made her way around the circulation desk. With a slight shake to her hands, she pulled a seaweed green binder from its position and flipped the pages until she found what she was looking for. Squinting at the large antique clock on a nearby wall, she smiled, "You are in luck, Mrs. Howard should be in the Milstein Division. However, I'm afraid our language specialist does not arrive until three p.m. today."

"You could start with Mrs. Howard, and should you need our language expert, Mr. Kaufmann, I'm certain he would be happy to visit with you after three p.m. Would you wish for me to phone Mrs. Howard and let her know you are on your way?"

"Yes," Jack rushed. "Please. That would be very kind of you."

"Certainly, your names please?"

"Jack and this is my granddaughter Elizabeth Yale.

"Hurry on then. You'll want to spend as much time with Mrs. Howard as possible."

Chapter 20: Our Ancestry

A thin woman, dressed in a classically tailored black suit, stood waiting outside the Milstein Division. A tightly bound bun sat square on her head, pulled so tight the corners of her eyes appeared larger than they should.

"Jack and Elizabeth, I presume?" she said, extending her hand. The smoothness of her voice and gentle disposition put me at ease.

"Yes," Jack replied, "Jack Yale."

"Hello, pleased to meet you. I'm Mrs. Sara Howard, board certified Genealogist and part-time Curator here at the New York Public Library. I understand that you are interested in finding out more about your lineage."

"Yes ma'am," I smiled, offering my hand, "Elizabeth Yale."

"Nice to meet you as well, Elizabeth."

"Please come in and let's get started."

Mrs. Howard opened the door to Room 121, "We'll start here."

As we stepped inside, a sobering effect took over. Gone was the opulent beauty of the rooms before, replaced now with rows of large rare volumes and computer screens. While it was lovely in its own right, here we would embark on what felt like the sinister knowledge of our past.

"Please take a seat," Mrs. Howard pointed at two large oak and maroon chairs pressed against an old, worn table. "Exactly what are you here for today?" she asked. "Are you trying to seek information about someone in particular or your entire family as a whole?"

"I suppose, Mrs. Howard, the primary information I would like to know is where my family is from," Jack said, settling into his chair.

"Please call me Sara," she smiled. "If that is the case, the first question I must ask is, do you know if a family tree has ever been drawn, Mr. Yale?"

"Jack," he insisted, "Not that I'm aware of."

"Okay, then that is where we must start. We will go back as far as your knowledge will allow and then we'll turn to our resources to help us travel further down your family line. That will give us a peek into where your family originates from and what life was like once they settled here in the United States."

Drawing a single sheet of eleven by fourteen paper from a neat stack, Mrs. Howard grasped a pen between her fingers and said, "Let's start with you dear," pointing to me. "I'll need your full name, first, middle, and last, and the full names of your parents."

Jack and I filled in the blanks as much as we could. There were my parents and me, Jack and his wife, then Jack's mother and father. We filled in each generation with careful thought and consideration.

"You mentioned a David Boyd Yale, the second, that would indicate there was a first," Sara said.

"Yes," Jack replied. "I was trying to remember his wife's name. It was uncommon, and for some reason, I'm drawing a complete blank. I'm sorry."

"This is enough to get started. Let's first look for birth records for David Boyd Yale, the first."

Sara retrieved her laptop from her desk and accessed secured genealogy files.

"Amelie," Jack blurted out. "David's wife was named Amelie Van Der Berg Yale."

Sara clapped her hands, "Excellent," she delighted. "The last name Van Der Berg is an interesting one. It certainly carries a cultural heritage, so, let's delve into what nationality a name like Van Der Berg would originate. We'll turn to our databases and see if we can find her. If we have records of Amelia, that will link us to the first David Yale in the way of marriage, birth, or even death certificates. Do you know if Amelia would have been living in New York?"

"I believe so," Jack answered, "but again, I'm not entirely sure."

My skin flushed as Sara typed Amelia Van Der Berg Yale into the server. Only one Amelia came up, born at or around December 6, 1852.

"My guess is this is our Amelia as she is the only one," Sara said smirking.

Jack drummed his fingers on the cold table, anxious to see what would appear next. Moments later, a birth certificate appeared on the screen. The odd text and foreign language seemed to be the same as what laid inside the folder on the table.

"Old Dutch?" Jack questioned.

"I'm not certain," Sara said, squinting her eyes trying to make sense of text on the screen, "but, we have a program that translates old documents for us. I'll print this original birth certificate so we can take a closer look at it, and I'll also print the translated version. If you'll excuse me, I'll be right back."

"Certainly," Jack said, standing as Sara left the table.

Jack stirred in his seat, unable to sit still in Sara's absence. His eyes moved rapidly across the words on the computer screen, muttering under his breath.

"Well," Sara said as she approached, "it seems the last name, Van Der Berg, is, in fact, Dutch, Mr. Yale."

"Unbelievable," I laughed.

"Yes, it would appear we have found your four-times-great-grandmother, Elizabeth."

Jack pursed his lips and reached for the translated birth certificate.

"Let's see," he said, "It says Amelia Isabella Van Der Berg was born December 6, 1852, in Leiden, the Netherlands."

Jack looked up. We exchanged long glances before he continued to read. "Her mother's name was Anya Amelia from Leiden and her father was Gavin Crane Van Der Berg."

Sara added Amelia's parents to our already growing family tree.

"What else do we know about Amelia?" I pushed.

"That's it, other than her mother was sixteen when Amelia was born and her father was twenty-six."

"Whoa," I replied.

Sara laughed, "That wouldn't have been uncommon in this time period."

I shook my head, "Still," I whispered, "seems inappropriate."

"By today's standards, yes," Sara replied. "Now, what we want to do is to try to find Amelia on an American census. States collected their own census information. As a whole, census gathering began in 1790 and one has been

collected every ten years since. She would have been
twenty in 1872. We'll use that as our marker, and the
database will pull up any census taken after this year. Let's
see if she had made it to America by then."

With the flick of her wrist, Sara closed Amelia's birth
certificate. Sadness filled me when it vanished from the
screen. It was as if a piece of my four-times-great-
grandmother had vanished too.

Rapidly typing, Sara plugged in Amelia's birth date
and year into the database and hit search. Amelia Van Der
Berg Yale appeared on the screen again, this time with
small, cursive text that was difficult to read. Sara magnified
the screen as Jack and I leaned in, pushing our noses inches
from the monitor.

"There she is," Jack hooted, "And she is already a
Yale."

"Yes," Sara said. "Now look at the column that
indicates children. There are three listed. We go directly
under Amelia's name and find David B. Yale, age 9, and
Garnet Maude Yale, age 8."

"Wait," I said, "The column above says three children
but only two are listed. What does that mean?"

"It could mean a child had already passed before this
data was collected," Sara said soberly.

"Or perhaps she was with child at the time the census
was taken?" Jack asked, hopefully.

"No, Jack. I'm sorry, that wouldn't be the case. Census
information was collected by going door-to-door during
this time. Even if Amelia was pregnant, childbirth was still
considered a very dangerous event for mothers, the census

taker would not have listed she had three children until the third child was born."

"Is there a way to find out what the name of the other child was?" I asked, softly. My heart ached for Amelia. I knew what the loss of my father felt like, I could only imagine that the loss of a child would be far worse.

"There is, but what I find most interesting about this Census is that Amelia is here, and she is listed as married— see that M next to her name indicates such—but what we do not see is David Yale's name listed."

Jack cleared his throat, "Something else is missing too. Amelia's son, David, would have been David Boyd Yale, the second. But he isn't listed that way. He is simply David Boyd Yale."

"That could be as simple as an oversight," Sara said. "If Amelia did not list David as a junior or a second, the census taker would not have added this information among the records."

"Fair enough," Jack replied. "We know there must have been a death of a child because of the three listed next to her name, could we now suspect that her husband David had already passed when this census was taken too?"

Sara pointed to the screen, "I do not believe so. Again we see that M that indicates she is married. The marital status would have been listed with a W for widowed had your great-grandfather already passed."

"Then where are you, Mr. Yale?" I questioned aloud.

"Let's try to find out," Sara replied.

Her fingers bounced wildly on the keyboard again. First, she printed the census document and then switched to the World Vital Statistics Records website.

"Let's find David Yale's birth certificate. Perhaps that will give us more understanding of what was happening between him and Amelia. It could be as simple as she brought the children from the Netherlands before he arrived in the U.S. It would be highly unlikely for a woman to make that voyage without her husband, but it never surprises me what I find buried in family histories."

The cursor flashed as Sara typed David Boyd Yale. Within seconds, a certificate written in Dutch flickered onto the monitor.

"Here we go," Sara replied. "I'm going to grab the sheets off the printer, as well as print the translation to this certificate and the original. I'll be back in a moment."

Jack stood once again as Sara excused herself from the table.

"Jack," I whispered, "Where do you think David was? Don't you find that odd that he wouldn't have come to New York with his family?"

"I do, but maybe Sara can uncover why?" Jack replied.

"This is strange, don't you think?"

"What?" Jack questioned.

"To think that these people are our grandparents. I mean, we are talking about people who lived over a hundred and sixty years ago and without them we wouldn't be here."

"It's exhilarating, really," Jack grinned.

Sara returned, her head was turned down, pouring over the documents in her hands. Something was different about her. The ease of her happy expression was gone, replaced with a sense of foreboding that sent chills down my spine.

"I'm afraid…" Sara began, "that our track has been slightly derailed. While we did find David Boyd Yale the information is different than I would have expected."

Jack drew the document from her fingers and pulled them across the table for both of us to review.

"Daan Boyd Yale, born March 16, 1869, in Leiden, the Netherlands. Mother, Amelia, surname of Van Der Berg and father, Edward Y. Royal." Jack read, his voice growing softer with each word he spoke.

"Daan? Royal?" I questioned. "Does this mean David or Daan had a different father than David Yale?"

Sara nodded, then corrected herself. "Well, I'm not entirely sure. You see, I can attribute the different first name by simply assuming the Census taker made a mistake. As I said before, they collected the information at the door. Workers often wrote what they heard or wrote names phonetically opposed to actual spellings. This is common in many of the census forms I've reviewed. But as far as the listed father, we'll need to do some more digging."

Sara's fingers landed on the keyboard again and began to pound away. Jack stood and pushed his chair back to free himself from its confines. One foot followed the other, and he began to pace in a small line, back and forth, all the while moving his hands as though he was speaking.

"Jack," I shouted. My voice bounced and reverberated off the walls of Room 121.

"Elizabeth," Jack and Sara snapped in unison.

My face reddened, burning deep red heat into my ears. "Sorry," I whispered. I had their attention. My hands tore through the file until I found the documents I was looking for. The first was the Whizbang machine's typing:

Elizabeth Wright Royal, History is not correct. Correct it. Correct it. The second was the land deed, written entirely in Old Dutch, with the name Edward Y. Royal listed.

"Look," I gasped. "Remember what the typewriter wrote."

Jack's eyes pushed onto Sara's face and held there for a moment. He was waiting for the question that would obviously come next: what did I mean by what the typewriter wrote. Sara listened dutifully and did not ask any further questions. She took the paper from my hand and stood to join Jack in his fevered pacing.

"Sara, you have translated the other documents into English. Are you able to scan this one into the computer and tell us what it says? Look here," I pointed, "Look at the name."

"Edward Y. Royal," she read.

"Is there a way to look up Mr. Royal, Sara?" Jack pushed.

"Of course."

The three of us sunk back into our chairs waiting for Sara to make her next move.

"Let's look for a marriage license between Edward and Amelia first."

The door to room 121 creaked open again, and heavy footsteps moved through the large room. Jack was quiet, listening to the pounding of Sara's fingers. I turned to watch as the newcomers settled in at a table next to ours. A truckload of questions began to formulate in my mind.

"Here it is: Edward Y. Royal's birth certificate. Wait," she muttered.

A cold sweat began to drip from Jack's forehead.

"Are you okay?" I pushed.

"Fine," Jack replied. "Hot, but fine. What does it say, Sara? What can you tell us about Edward?"

"It's in Dutch," she replied.

Minutes went by as she pulled and saved document after document. Whatever she was uncovering came with a sizeable amount of evidence. After thirty minutes of near silence, Sara whispered, "There, I'll be right back."

We knew what that meant. She needed to retrieve the latest documents, but she returned quicker than she had during her previous runs. Her face was far more ominous than even an hour before.

"Jack," she said, "I think you're about to learn more about your family than you bargained for."

Without saying another word, Sara slid the translated birth certificate and a stack of other documents to our side of the table. We both gasped.

"Edward Yale Royal. Born April 5, 1850, in The Hague. Mother's name was Valentien Edda De Graff Royal. Father's name: Pascal Lambert Royal, both birth places are listed as The Hague—as in the museum?"

Sara nodded, "I do know there are museums there, but I believe it is more of where the Netherlands' government operates from. That may not have been the case in 1850, but it had to be something fairly prominent during this time too. At least, I would think it would be."

A long silence followed her words.

"Who was this man?" Jack mused.

Chapter 21: Edward Yale Royal

Sara's training as a certified genealogist couldn't help but take over. She snatched the pen from the table and scribbled Edward's parents in a line above David Yale's name, scratching out the name Yale.

"Why did you do that?" I asked. "Those are Edward's parents, not David's."

Sara smiled bleakly, "Please take a look at the other documents."

Jack took the pages in his hands. It was easy to see that his mind was caught somewhere else yet still present enough to follow simple commands. I slid my hands under my thighs, securing them away from the urge to snatch the papers from Jack's grips.

"Come on, Jack," I moaned. "Read it aloud."

"Incredible," he muttered.

An edge of resentment hung on his words. Jack roughly tossed the stack in front of me.

"The first is a birth certificate for Garnet Lise Royal, born in 1870 to Edward and Amelia Royal. Birth place: Leiden," I read, turning to the next page. It too was a birth certificate for Garnet, but this time, it was printed by the United States. "A second birth certificate?" I questioned. "Garnet Lise R. Yale, born in 1870 in Manhattan, New York to David Boyd Yale of Leiden, the Netherlands, and Amelia Isabella Van Der Berg Yale."

"One is clearly a forgery," Sara answered.

The sun shifted in the windows, pushing warm heat over the table and into the space between Sara, Jack, and I. I shivered as the weight of what I just read fully sank in.

"Why?" I said.

My fingers flipped through the rest of the stack with haste. There were two birth certificates for David Boyd Yale, Amelia and Edward's son, double marriage licenses one with Edward's name and one with David Boyd Yale I, and the last document nearly stole my breath.

"Alina Amelia Royal, born in 1872 in Leiden to Edward and Amelia Royal," I read. "But Sara, there is only one birth certificate for her. Why? There are two of each document for everyone else."

"I would assume they didn't need it. Remember the census does not show her name, yet she would have been the last and third child. Again, it leads me to believe she passed away before the family moved to the United States."

"Now what?" Jack pushed.

"We try to figure out which surname is correct. I can only assume that Royal is your family's true last name, and Yale was introduced sometime after they immigrated to America," Sara spoke calmly.

"But why?" Jack spluttered. "Why would they change their last name? It doesn't make sense."

"Are you saying we have three generations of men named after a man that didn't even really exist," I scoffed.

"That's an interesting way to look at it, but yes, it does appear that way."

"What could have possibly happened that was so earth-shattering that someone would need to go to such lengths to hide their identity with new records?" Jack insisted again.

"Not only that, they virtually erased our family history," I replied.

"It only gets deeper, I'm afraid," Sara said, pushing another round of documents over. "Look at immigration records for Edward Y. Royal and then look at Amelia's."

Jack sighed, taking the papers from Sara, "I'm not so sure I want to." Surveying the records, he read, "This record states that Edward arrived at the Port of New York in 1878. He claimed he departed from Norway and is of Irish decent."

"Unreal," I hissed. "What is the truth and what isn't?"

"Oh, it gets better," Jack replied. "Amelia's record also shows she arrived at the Port of New York in 1878 with two small children, names unlisted. It says immigrant states she departed from Norway. Small male child corrected her and listed home as the Netherlands. Immigrant held for questioning. Passed six-hour interrogation, children and woman released under pending investigation."

"A third child wasn't listed as being present here either," I interjected.

"You're right," Sara nodded.

"The hardest part of all of this is not knowing why they would go to such lengths to lie. Amelia was almost caught. Can you imagine how scared she was when they interrogated her for six hours?" I gasped. "Something horrific had to have happened to the Royal family for them to risk everything and start over, at least that seems to be what they did. Right?"

"I would agree with you, Elizabeth," Sara said softly, "This was during a time where so many were fleeing to the "land of golden opportunity." Immigration was taken very seriously. The consequence for arriving under false pretenses was beyond what many wanted to risk. If Amelia had been found guilty of lying to government officials she would have been sent back to her home country without her children and her husband. They would have more than likely taken the children from Edward too."

"If they planned to change their names when they arrived, why wouldn't they have given the last name Yale when they reached immigration?" Jack pondered.

"My guess would be they didn't yet have the documents they needed to prove their identity. They had to show proof of their namesake when they arrived at the feet of America. As to why they chose to change their names and virtually erase their past, well, I believe that is the next set of answers you are looking for."

Jack bowed his head. His eyes flickered another puzzled look in Sara's direction.

"Sara, you've been able to translate every document you've uncovered thus far. If we gave you a document would you be able to render it and provide us with a translated copy?"

"I'm afraid not. My programs are preset to translate only documents pulled from specific databases. I do not have the capability to put a new document in and have it translate the information. I'm very sorry, Jack."

"There is nothing to be sorry for," Jack replied. His eyes landed on the clock near the door. "What time did the librarian say the foreign language specialist arrived for the day, Elizabeth?"

"Mr. Kauffman is his name," Sara answered.

"I think she said three o'clock."

"It's nearly four now," Jack said, standing, "Perhaps we should pay him a visit."

Sara stood, folding her arms roughly across her chest.

"Mrs. Howard, it has been a pleasure. I cannot thank you enough for all the information you have uncovered for us today. It has been a tremendous help."

"It is my pleasure, Jack," she replied warmly. "I hope you find everything you are seeking."

"Me too," I replied, extending my hand to her. "Thank you so very much."

"May we take everything you printed?" Jack questioned.

"Of course, they're yours. Please," Sara insisted. "Mr. Kauffman offices out of the Frederick Lewis Allen Room, 228 E, on the second floor. If you have trouble finding him, come back and I will help you locate him. Don't forget to update me on what you find. I always love to hear how the family history ends."

With warm regards, Jack and I rushed through the doors of Room 121 only slightly wiser than when we stepped in.

Chapter 22: Written Despair

Neither of us knew what to say. Everything we knew of our family was based on a set of forged documents and an incorrect census from a hundred and thirty-five years ago. Jack shook his head hard. I couldn't imagine what was happening in his mind—the hounding questions, the inconceivable truths that were now fables; all of it was up for examination.

"I wonder if my father knew," Jack muttered just loud enough for me to hear. The deception ran deep enough that no one was safe from scrutiny.

Whatever was turning over in his mind created a burst of energy. Grandpa Jack's feet surged, pushing him and me forward. It was clear he wanted answers—now. The sound of our feet echoed against the hard marble floor in a half-jog, half-sprint to find Mr. Kauffman. Only he could give us our next clue.

Students quietly strolled past making their way from one reading room to the next. Heavy volumes clung to their chest slowing their every move. Each time a new patron passed, Jack and I instinctively slowed to keep suspicious eyes at bay. Still, time was of the essence; the library would close at seven, and it was now past four-thirty. We still had hours of work ahead of us.

Jack's lungs wheezed under each hammering step up the broad staircase.

"Come on Elizabeth," Jack panted, "Who knows how long it will take Mr. Kauffman to translate the documents."

If he can translate them," I insisted.

The enormous stone hallways narrowed and darkened at the top of the landing. The ceiling, thick with beautiful carvings, was lower than the main floor. So low, it felt as though it would crash down on top of us at any given moment. While beautiful, things were different up here too.

In perfect emerald green etching, 240 A was fixed on the first wooden door. Jack pointed, and we quickly jogged to the right. Twelve doors down on the left was Room 228 E.

A slight glint filled Jack's eyes. He hesitated, placing his hand on the knob as if he was uncertain if he was ready to force it open, then looked at me hard.

"Grandpa," I blurted out, clearly derailing his train of thought.

"What? Are you okay?"

"On the family tree," I began, pulling the paper Sara had artfully created from the folder in my hands, "Did you notice how young everyone was when they died?"

"No, I guess it didn't occur to me."

"Look at this," I said.

He leaned over my shoulder.

"See. Do the math; David Boyd Yale was thirty-eight when he passed."

"You mean, Edward Royal," he insisted.

"Whatever," I stammered. "Look, at the pattern. It's too consistent to be a coincidence. Edward's son died at age forty. Your great-grandfather died at forty. How old was your dad when he passed?"

Jack's face turned hot, "Forty."

"That gives you the honor of being the longest living male in our family for nearly two hundred years. You've lived twenty-nine years longer than anyone else thus far."

"Your father was twenty-seven when he passed, so the pattern falters when it reaches Jesse," he asserted.

"This is true, but I have a feeling there is a reason for that too," I whispered. "People don't all just die around the same age, Grandpa Jack. It doesn't make sense. It's like they were cursed or something."

Jack laughed at my choice of words. "Curses don't exist, Elizabeth."

"Maybe not, but everyone dying around the same age is highly suspect," I replied.

"Let's treat it as another layer of information we have to figure out, Lizzy-cakes. But first, the letters," he nodded towards the folder in my hands, "Are you ready?"

Clenching my jaw, I frowned, "Guess so."

The combined smell of dust and old books hit my nose as Grandpa Jack pushed the door open. This room was different. Gone were the ornate carvings along every wall. They were replaced with huge vintage maps and thousands upon thousands of books that stretched so far that neither of us could see the end. The overhead chandeliers were dimmed so low it was hard to see beyond the next few feet. Large tables haphazardly placed in the center of the room were filled with dim-lit lamps and opened volumes. Shadows danced in the distance. The room was just dark enough to play tricks on your mind.

"May I help you?" A meek voice called from behind us.

"Hmm," Jack said, his eyes narrowing as he turned to see who had spoken.

"May I help you?" she asked again, stepping out of a dark corner.

"Yes," Jack smiled, "We've been working with Mrs. Howard downstairs. She pointed us in this direction, mentioning Mr. Kauffman may be able to assist us in translating a few documents we have gathered."

"Are we too late?" I asked. "It looks like this section has closed for the night."

"Mr. Yale and Miss Yale?" she asked.

"Yes, ma'am," I replied.

"Sara called to say you were coming. We do begin closing before the rest of the library, but Alfred is in his office expecting you. It's the second door on the right. His name is on the door. Go through the first three stacks on the left. His office is on the back wall. I would turn on some lights for you, but they are controlled on a timer. Please be careful, it's quite dark."

Jack and I both thanked her and slowly made our way through the blackened shelves.

"It's so dark," I whispered.

"This room doesn't have windows," Jack replied.

My leg hit a portable library stool sending a shock of pain throughout my body.

"Ouch," I yelled.

A pointed hush echoed through the vast room.

"Are you okay?" Jack hissed.

"Fine. Just find the office, would you?"

Just beyond the last row of shelving, Jack spotted rays of light pushing their way into the darkness from under a closed office door. Jack knocked softly, hoping our intrusion wouldn't disturb Mr. Kauffman on the other side.

"Enter," a man shouted.

Jack looked gravely at me.

"I said enter," he shouted again.

"Oh, this should be interesting," I replied sarcastically, bending to rub the knot on my leg.

"I'm afraid we have no other choice," Jack hesitated.

He deliberated for a moment longer and finally swept the door open into the bright room. Mr. Kauffman's office was different from the rest of 228 E. Half a dozen frames, all in foreign dialect, lined the wall behind an oversized cherry desk. Beyond that, the space was a cold beige. The walls were missing frames of smiling children captured in a rare moment of bliss alongside their mom and dad. There were no pictures of graduation or Easter—there was nothing to prove that this man had a life outside of the library walls.

It was easy to see why. Hunched over his desk examining an old map with the looking glass in hand, Mr. Kauffman didn't bother even looking up as we entered.

"I said come in," Mr. Kauffman instructed. "Take a seat."

I watched Jack carefully, knowing his temper may explode from Mr. Kauffman's impolite demeanor. With a shake of his head, Jack took the high road and laid his gentleman's charm on thick.

"Thank you, sir," Jack replied, "I'm sorry to bother you, Mr. Kauffman, I see you are busy…"

"Extremely," he barked.

"Yes sir, extremely busy, but, you see we were sent to see you by Mrs. Howard downstairs."

"Need help translating Old Dutch, I hear."

"Indeed, sir, we do."

Mr. Kauffman shifted closer to the scroll, peering deep into the magnifying glass, tapping on a particular location he had apparently been tracking for quite some time. Throttling his hand forward, he opened it and closed it rapidly, "Hand me the blue map pencil now, young lady," he demanded.

"Why should I?" I hissed.

"Now!" he demanded.

Jack stewed in his building annoyance, "Sir," Grandpa Jack began. "That is no way to speak to a young lady."

Mr. Kauffman peered up. His pencil-thin lips were forced together so tightly they were losing color.

"Is this matter significant today, or could we make an appointment for later next week? I'm under a strict deadline. I do not entertain distraction well."

"That much is clear," I chomped.

Jack squeezed my arm, silently scolding me for my returned disrespect. I cleared my throat and nodded. I knew the facts. We needed Mr. Kauffman, no matter how unmannered he was.

"What Elizabeth means to say is I'm afraid this issue is extremely urgent." Jack shifted from one foot to the other, "I don't believe we will require that much of your time."

"Then sit," Mr. Kauffman commanded, and he threw himself into the leather office chair that was resting against the backs of his knees.

Kauffman was a rather small man. So small in fact, he looked as though the pockets of pinched and gathered leather would swallow him at any given moment. His wavy hair was a mess, standing on all ends. He was more mad scientist than the image I had painted in my head of a sophisticated language specialist.

"How many documents do you have?" Kauffman asked.

"Two," Jack replied.

"Fine," Mr. Kauffman said. "However, I must tell you that you have been sorely misled. I do not speak Dutch. The only thing I can do for you is to place each document in my computer and give you a print out of the translations. Each translation and text will come with a fee, of course."

"Of course," Jack nodded, pulling his wallet from his back pocket.

"You should also know that not all Dutch words have an English translation. Whatever will not translate you will be responsible for figuring out—on your own. I cannot guarantee you what is translated is correct either. If you agree, then we may move forward swiftly."

Kauffman eyed the clock.

"Fine," Jack replied, mimicking Kauffman's rough tone.

His face softened. "Forgive me, please. These documents are my life, and I do not often have a chance to work with the public. I do not intend to come off so severe. Now, if you would, may I have the documents?"

Jack took the letters from the folder and handed them over. Smiling, he said, "This is of great importance or we would come back a different day. Again, thank you for your time."

Kauffman nodded and then paused, examining the documents I handed him.

"So," he said, "this first item is a land deed. The word deed here is the same as the French translation. The second appears to be a letter, based on the date on top."

"That much we gathered," Jack answered.

"Give me a moment to scan these documents and prepare a translation. Make yourself comfortable. I'll be back shortly."

Mr. Kauffman yanked the door open and left us sitting inside.

"He's something," Jack stated.

"No kidding," I laughed. "I guess as long as he helps us I don't care how much of a fool he makes of himself."

The clock on the wall struck 5:30. How time was moving so quickly was beyond me. Jack and I sat silently—waiting. We were both fidgeting, trying to pass the time in Mr. Kauffman's absence.

"I think we should let Laurel know we are okay," Jack said quietly.

"She would have called if she was worried," I replied, "She probably found our letter this morning and decided to carry on with the rest of her day. Knowing her, she is probably upstairs tearing through the mess of boxes in your room trying to figure out how to make that disaster look half-decent."

Jack smiled, "We should probably tend to that room when we return."

"Oh, there is no we in that equation," I giggled. Thirty minutes passed with no sign or word from Mr. Kauffman. Jack had had enough of tapping his foot against the carpet and shot up from his chair. The door creaked open as he stepped into the pitch-black room beyond the lit office and began to pace.

"Where is he?" he muttered. "He said it would only take a moment. That was nearly forty minutes ago."

At 6:18, Mr. Kauffman finally returned. Jack was frantic. Each minute that passed pushed him closer to snapping. The library would close in forty-two minutes, and we were still no closer to the answers we needed.

"What did you find?" Jack demanded, following Kauffman in from the dark.

Kauffman rounded his desk and pushed the translations towards us. The first document lying on top was the letter. I leaned into Jack as he sank into his seat. I read along as he did.

Wednesday, February 27, 1878

"In the early dawn, the horizon presents the snow-covered shoreline of this strange new place—New York. Edward calls it the 'promised land,' the place our misfortune and perpetual curse will be halted. The escape of such failings is impossible; it has already stolen my precious child. My soul aches for time to reverse, but alas it will not.

Edward claims that he will find work. He is mad to assume that work is to be had. He has forgotten his hands do not know heavy labor. His mind is exceptional, lest not his hands. Still he alleges to know this daunting task will be our redeeming grace.

Our children are filthy, and their bellies are empty. Food is sparse. The tattered clothes on their backs offer no warmth from the ice that hangs in the air. Had we been five and not four, one of us would have perished during these last five weeks on the open sea. I wonder about David. His lungs are filled, and his voice is harsh. I beg his life to be spared for I will gladly take his place should death come to call. The dead of winter is a cruel beast.

Edward still has the blueprints tucked squarely in his breast pocket. He claims to have heard from a man who is interested in purchasing them. I pray that this is the truth, or our journey here will be for not.

The waters of the New York harbor are barely rippling as we approach. Not even this cargo ship can move the ice tangled with the tide. My heart keeps pounding in my chest as we push forward into the bay. If I forget the words we have rehearsed, I will surely be tossed out and sent home. I would rather die than that.

I would pray for deliverance, but our souls are already gone, lost in death and fire. There is nothing left to spare.

God speed,
Amelia Royal

Amelia's cries of desperation sunk into our bones. Jack and I remained quiet while Mr. Kauffman pushed the other document closer to us so he could return to his work with the map.

A single tear dripped from Jack's cheek and onto the letter.

"That poor woman," he swallowed.

"It seems they had fallen on rather desperate times," Mr. Kauffman replied, spying through the looking glass. "I'm afraid I cannot help much regarding the full meaning of the letter, however. It is horribly obscure."

"We know they made it, Jack. The census tells us so— as does the birth certificates."

"It references a set of blueprints, Elizabeth. I wonder…"

"There is nothing more I can tell you," Mr. Kauffman demanded.

"With all due respect, Mr. Kauffman, your tone is unnecessary. We know the letter's meaning, at least, the vast majority of it, anyhow," I replied harshly. "Of course, we have questions, but sir, they are not directed at you."

"I see," he stated, running his fingers through his frizzed hair.

"If you would turn the other document over, you will see the land deed. It seems it belonged to a Mr. Edward Royal. The deed is for a factory, translated to the Writing Factory once converted to English. It's sealed by the KNB, which stands for the Royal Society of Notaries. The entire document would not translate as I suspected it might not. Old Dutch is somewhat of a lost art, I'm afraid, but it is clear the factory is located in Leiden. I believe that isn't all that far from Amsterdam."

"The Whizbang Factory," both Jack and I replied together.

Mr. Kauffman folded his arms across his wrinkled charcoal suit and said, "There is one more thing you need to know."

Jack looked up, waiting for Mr. Kauffman to continue.

"When I translate a document, our system cross-references other materials we have housed here in the library or libraries within our circulation system looking for similar wording. There was a hit on your documents."

From above our heads came a sharp crackling of the audio speakers coming to life. "Ladies and gentlemen, the New York Public Library will be closing in fifteen minutes. Please collect your items and see a librarian on your floor to return or check out your materials. Thank you for visiting with us today. The library will open again at eight o'clock in the morning." A quick hum followed and then ceased.

I jumped to my feet. "What was the hit? Are there more documents? If so, where are they? We're out of time."

"My dear," Mr. Kauffman laughed. "The number referenced would indicate it is located below the main library floors in our storage tunnels. Unfortunately, no one can be of help to find the file at this moment. You'll need to return tomorrow and request to see this file number."

Kauffman handed Jack a yellow scrap of paper with R79-1365GA written neatly across the top. "I cannot say for sure, but I believe that number is referencing a general affidavit. It was likely published in a newspaper at the time it was executed. You'll certainly want to review it."

"Couldn't you call down and have the document expedited?" Jack questioned.

"No sir, I'm afraid not. There are millions of reference materials and books below us, not to mention more than five hundred thousand microfilm files. The wait time is up

to twelve business days once you have submitted a request
with the West Rose Reading Room's reference librarians.
Our staff collects the weekly requests on Thursday
afternoons. The items are pulled on Friday mornings and
made available to the requester on Friday afternoons."

"Unbelievable," I moaned. "We don't have two
weeks."

"The world doesn't always work on our time frame,
dear," Kauffman laughed.

"Elizabeth," Jack urged, "gather your things. The
library is closing. Mr. Kauffman, thank you for your help."

"It's been a real pleasure," he said, pointing to the door
as he turned his face back down to the vintage scroll.

Jack grabbed my hand and dragged me through the
dark stacks until we found the exit.

"Grandpa Jack," I urged. "We need to go back to the
right to get to the stairs."

"Just follow me. I have an idea."

The deeper we pushed into the hallway, the darker it
grew.

"Where are we going?" I questioned.

"Out the back entrance. We need to be closer to the
West side of Bryant Park."

"What are you talking about?"

"Just be quiet and come with me."

Descending two flights of stairs, taking most two at a
time, we merged into the hum of hushed voices exiting the
library for the night. When the light hit Jack's eyes, I knew
whatever he was conjuring up would be dangerous.

Chapter 23: Into the Tunnels

A warm breeze touched my cheeks as I stepped outside. The south exit of the library, on the rim of Bryant Park, was alive. Enchanting melodies rose over the abundance of blooming trees from the Southwest Porch as a band jammed smooth jazz. Children rushed around their parents' legs as they sat under white umbrellas sucking down overly complicated bistro drinks. One child was so heated in her demands to ride the iconic carousel nested within the park, I couldn't take my eyes off her. There was humor in the way her arms flapped like a wild bird trying to make a point. "I want to ride the big-eared rabbit," she screamed. When her foot slapped the pavement, I averted my eyes and turned my attention back to the vibrant vibe of the park.

Artists and dreamers were peppered throughout the large patches of grass. Some with their eyes turned to the sky watching as the sun began to fade behind the tall glass and steel giants that pushed into the sky. The buildings' mirrored windows cast colorful prisms onto the lush greenery spilling over in every corner. Bryant Park was a world all within its own. A world with a pulse. I relished in the fresh air and the smells of water that flowed in a nearby water fountain. My senses were alive.

"Jack, wow, look at that!" I exclaimed, pointing to a man on stilts twisting balloons into unusual beasts for children below. "Wow," I laughed. "Jack…"

No response. I turned to see what had drawn his attention away, but he had vanished.

"Jack?" I called.

People rushed past, some bumping and moving my unwilling body as panic began to set in.

"Jack!"

My breath caught in my throat.

"Jack?" I called again.

No answer.

Within that moment, the music reached an excruciating decimal in my ears. The happy shrills of excited children nearby swiftly changed to relentless whining that grew to a fever pitch.

"What is going on?" I shouted. "Jack!"

Long tree branches moved in closer. Everything was moving in on me while growing darker by the second. I twisted my head back and forth, shaking away what I knew wasn't real. I struggled to pull even the smallest wisp of air into my lungs.

"Your mind is playing tricks on you, Elizabeth," I said aloud. "Jack!"

"Sweetheart, do you need help? Are you okay? Someone call a medic, I don't think she can breathe!" a lady rushed as she came to my side. "I can help you. Sweetie, try to breathe."

"I'm okay. I'm okay. I've lost my grandfather!" I panicked. Beads of sweat dripped from my face and landed on my shirt.

"I'm sure he's around her somewhere. Let's try to stay calm. I need you to breathe, honey."

The woman slipped her hand over my wrist, clamping down hard as she tried to pull me in the direction of her choosing. The way she pulled and squeezed only made the growing doom inside me worse.

"Let go, please." My words were harsh and so uncharacteristic I surprised myself, but I needed her to release me. "I'm sorry," I said, "I need to find my grandpa."

"Let me help you find a police officer," she smiled, her fingers squeezing tighter.

Wrenching my arm away, "No, let go!" I commanded. "I'm okay. Thank you. I'll find him on my own."

A disparaging look flashed across her pinched face, all the while muttering about the way teenagers disrespect adults these days, pausing long enough to say, "Suit yourself," as she released my wrist from her clutches.

"Jack, where are you?" I called again.

The crowd shifted to the left. The margin was so small I could barely see past a woman pushing a double stroller with sleeping twins. As she drew closer, there in the pinprick of space, I saw Jack.

His feet were dangling over a stone planter. His back was bent as it heaved up and down for air.

"Grandpa Jack, what's wrong?" I hollered. "Jack!"

With the library now closed for the night, park goers were everywhere. People were arriving by the dozens, preparing for the first movie of the season on the west lawn. Forcing my way through the crowd, I sprinted to his side.

"What is it? What's wrong? Is it your heart?" I rushed.

"Sit. I'm fine. I'm old; that's all. Got a little lightheaded," Jack snickered. "Can't an old man sit for a spell?"

"You aren't that old, Jack."

"That isn't what my body is telling me, Lizzy-cakes."

Plopping down next to him, I wrapped my arm around his shoulder. Every ounce of anxiety left my body the minute my flesh touched his back. "We got separated. We have to stick together. I freaked out for a minute."

In typical Jack fashion, he changed the subject, "This place is pretty amazing, huh?"

"Better than Disneyland," I laughed.

"Thought you would like it."

I gave him a few minutes to regain control of his lungs. As his chest slowed significantly with each breath, I asked, "How are you doing?"

He straightened his back, pulled in a deep inhale and stood, "Doing fine now. Let's go."

"Wait," I said, tugging his arm, forcing him back to the planter. "Why did you rush us out of the library like that? We could have gone into the Rose Room and filled out the paperwork for the microfilm. We still had ten minutes," I stated. "Now we have to come back tomorrow and wait an entire week before they pull what we need."

"We don't need anyone to pull the file, Elizabeth."

"Of course we do. How else are we going to get it?"

A flicker of excitement touched Jack's eyes, "We are going to get it ourselves."

I rolled my eyes, laughing at his ridiculous joke, "You cannot be serious!"

Jack stood and merged into the crowd without me. There was a brief hesitation as I let his words sink in and when they did, I jumped to my feet and jogged to catch up.

"What exactly do you mean when you say we are going to get it ourselves?"

"Exactly what I said," he replied.

"Jack!" I shouted, wrenching his arm back, forcing him to turn and look at me. We stopped dead smack in the middle of the crowd. A low murmur of displeasure came from those surrounding us on the sidewalk as everyone was forced to go around. "Have you lost your mind? The library is closing. We are not going back in there. Besides the doors are probably locked by now."

"And?" he questioned.

"And, it means we cannot go in!"

"You mean to tell me the answers you are looking for are possibly under your feet at this very second, and you are going to let a little locked door stop you from getting them?"

"It isn't a little locked door, Jack. It's the New York Public Library's massive locked doors! We go in there when we're not welcomed and the little locked door we will be peering through will have an armed guard on the other side of steel bars."

"Elizabeth, stop being dramatic. Come along."

People had begun to watch our heated interaction. Eyes were peering at us from all directions. Within seconds, a whisper of a rumor touched our ears. People wondered if I was in danger. A police officer started inching closer, watching to see if our conversation was going to escalate to the point where he would have to step in.

"Don't be an idiot, Jack," I complained.

"Calm down, Elizabeth," Jack chomped through clenched teeth, "People are watching. Take my hand."

Jack pulled me deep into his arms and hugged me, loudly announcing, "You are my granddaughter, I will always love you even if you make horribly poor decisions."

His voice carried over the crowd, working to ease people back into their lulls. The officer changed course and let Grandpa Jack and I slip away.

"Yea, it's me making horribly poor decisions," I snapped.

"Enough of the dramatics, we need to get to the far west side," Jack insisted.

"Why?"

"Because dear granddaughter, there is a fire escape to the tunnels disguised as a dedication plaque somewhere over there. We need to find it. It's our way in to get the file."

"The west lawn is blocked," I said motioning. "Do you not see the massive movie screen over there?"

"It's our lucky day, Elizabeth. How much do you want to bet the plaque is behind the screen? Pick up the pace, kid; we're losing time."

"How do you know these things, Jack?" I huffed, marching beside him.

"Your grandmother loved it when I read the newspaper to her in the mornings. We would take our coffee out to the back porch and snuggle together in the old, tiny wicker loveseat. She would watch the birds, lay her head on my lap, and I would read the daily news to her. It must have been the late 1980s when I remember reading that a company dug up the very ground your feet are walking on."

"Why?" I asked, drawing out the word.

"The library was out of storage space. The building itself had already been declared a historical monument, so the red tape to make massive renovations was nearly impossible to get through. When you can't go up, the next best thing to do is to go down. Down into the ground to create a series of underground storage tunnels that hold some of the world's rarest and finest antiquities of literary works—the very same tunnels Mr. Kauffman was alluding to a few minutes ago."

"Jack, come on." I urged. "He said there are millions of books and hundreds of thousands of microfilm down there. We will never find it *if* we could get down there."

"Well, normally I would say you are right," Jack replied, pulling the yellow scrap paper from his back pocket, "but, the old grouch gave us the location if you will recall." The paper flapped in the breeze as Jack wiggled it in my face.

"The tunnels have to be massive to hold that many items. Plus, it's underground. It will be pitch black down there. You seriously think we could find a microfilm in the dark. You've lost your mind, old man!"

"Elizabeth, if anyone knows his way around a stack of books, it's your grandfather. You know the one who owned a bookstore his entire life."

"This is different."

"No, my dear, it's not."

"Jack, if we're caught…"

His hand flew to my face, quickly interrupting my words. He wasn't willing to entertain another thought. I stayed on his trail, continuing to badger him the entire way to the west side of the screening lawn—hoping that something, anything, would register and talk him out of breaking the law and entering the publicly forbidden darkness of the New York Public Library's storage tunnels. My next hope was riding on the fact that we wouldn't be able to find the dedication plaque hiding the fire escape. Visions of police officers snapping handcuffs on our wrists and hauling us away kept filling my mind. I did my best to recoil against the idea of being caught, but it wasn't quite working. My mind reeled to Jack in the hospital bed and the promise I made the night I ran to him. I couldn't go back on my promise. I had done that enough in the last week, but breaking the law wasn't something I had entertained when I made that agreement.

"Jack," I whispered, "What does the fire escape look like?"

"That's my girl. I've only seen a picture of it. All I remember reading is it's hidden as a dedication plaque. I'm sure it has something to do with the restoration of the park, maybe even who the donors were to make it happen. Or at least, that's what most dedications read."

Officers had blocked the lawn, requiring everyone to go through security before being allowed to grab their place for the movie. Jack peered down at his watch.

"7:23. We may not make it back there in time."

"Ma'am," a tall officer motioned, "Your backpack, please."

I followed his commands, dropping my bag on the folding table.

"Do you have anything inside that may poke or hurt me?" the officer questioned.

"No, sir. Well, you may get a paper cut," I laughed. "There's only a few sheets of paper inside. You know, research that I did inside the library." I bit my lip. I was rambling and on the verge of saying too much.

He eyed me hard, "School's out, isn't it?"

"Sure is," I smiled.

"Wish my daughter would do some extra school work during the summer," he laughed, pushing an unsharpened pencil through the file folder and then flipping the backpack over. "Stand still, please." An electronic hand wand traced up and down my body. "You are free to go," he said, motioning me forward. "Enjoy the movie."

"Thanks," I smiled. "Have a good night, officer."

Jack had already made it through and was waiting.

"Now what?" I questioned, coming to his side. "Security is everywhere. There must be three hundred people in that line, and there will be more. The sign says the movie starts at nine. In less than an hour, this place will be crawling with thousands of people, but you think we can somehow inconspicuously bust into some secret tunnel. Jack, you may want to consider your plan is horribly flawed."

"Trust me, will you?"

"I'm trying, but…"

Jack positioned us on the least visible side of the movie screen. We stuck out, isolated by ourselves as people filled the center, closest to the huge screen.

"What are we doing all the way over here?" I questioned. "Shouldn't we be trying to blend in somewhat?"

"I need to see around the screen. The plaque has to be behind it."

"You mean behind the armed police officer?"

"Unfortunately, yes."

"Can we go home now, please?" I begged. "You are begging to be arrested, old man."

Jack stood, pretending to stretch, moving his body in an awkward side bend, hoping for a better look. Despite wanting to run to the nearest bus stop and go home, I stood and followed suit.

"Jack," I pointed. "It's over there. It's nestled in that little clump of trees. See it?"

Jack clapped, "Great job, kiddo! That has to be it. Now, how do we get back there without being seen?"

"The port-a-potty," I stated.

"Brilliant, okay, here's the plan."

Jack formulated a plan that had us both moving in and out of the portable restroom while everyone around busily set up the equipment for the night. Once no one was looking, Jack would slide himself into the bushes behind the plaque and breach the fire escape's door. If all went as planned, he would be in the tunnel in less than two minutes. I was to follow immediately after.

"How exactly do you think you are going to open the door without anyone hearing you?"

"Look, they are about to start testing the sound system. No one will hear a thing," Jack reassured me.

"Someone will hear an alarm going off, don't you think?"

"The library closed less than an hour ago. People are still inside shelving books and preparing for tomorrow. My guess is we have an hour before we have to worry about an alarm."

"Once the lock is broken, won't it show up on the security system that there has been a door opened?" I asked.

"It may, but try not to overthink this, Elizabeth. We'll move quickly, be in and out before anyone even knows anything has been taken. Does your phone have a flashlight?" he asked.

Pulling the phone from my backpack, I handed it to him and said, "We don't have an hour. My phone only has a forty percent charge. By the time you turn the flashlight on it will drain quickly. Without it, we'll be lost down there."

"Then we better hurry," he replied.

We casually made our way to the portable restrooms, as a decorated officer with his hand resting on his holster, nodded in our direction.

"Good evening, sir," Jack nodded.

He nodded back as Jack opened the port-a-potty door and slipped inside. A minute passed, and Jack called to me.

"Are we clear?"

"I think so. No one seems to care we are back here."

The door sprung open, and Grandpa Jack slipped out. Within seconds, he tucked himself inside the prickly bushes protecting the hidden fire escape door.

"Is it back there?" I called out in a whisper.

"It is!" he replied.

Trying to draw as little attention as possible, I slid into the restroom and waited until I heard the faint pop of the steal lock give way. To play it safe, I counted aloud, "One-

Mississippi, two-Mississippi, three." By the time I got to twenty, I pushed the port-a-potty door wide and stepped out. I was alone. The officer was gone, so too were the sound guys.

"Jack," I whispered.

No response. He had successfully made it inside the tunnel.

A few seconds later, my foot hit the first rung of the steel ladder attached to the wall. A warm trail of blood dripped down my leg. The bushes had torn at my skin. There wasn't time to whine about the pain, nor was there time to clean myself up.

"Jack," I whispered again.

"Elizabeth," he called out from deep in the tunnel. "Watch it. Some of the steps are slippery," he said, pointing the phone's flashlight my way.

"How did you get in so quickly?"

"With a knife," Jack replied coolly. "Popped the lock in a matter of seconds," he said, snapping his fingers.

I didn't want to know any more. The more details I knew, the greater time I would likely serve in jail when we were caught. I counted each step as I drew closer to the ground—forty-two in total. When both my feet found the ground, it hit me that I was standing inside the enormous tunnels of the library. We had done it. Without breaking in, I would never have a chance to see this forbidden treasure with my own eyes. A small part, a very small part, of me was thankful I had been brave enough to follow my grandfather underground.

Jack slipped his hand into mine, and we began to move. The tunnel stretched on forever. Massive shelves filled the stone block walls extending to the top of a low-hanging ceiling. Wide water pipes hung between the stacks. Each shelf was jammed so close to the next it was impossible to fully extend your arms. The space was tight—too tight for comfort. I wasn't sure how long I would be able to stay underground without descending into a full-blown panic attack.

"Before we go any further, are you sure this is a good idea?" I questioned.

"We are okay, Lizzy."

"I'm scared," I whispered. "It's too tight down here."

"Don't let go of me. Everything will be okay. Focus on your breath, nothing else. I'll lead the way."

Jack moved us quickly through the stacks. The quicker we moved, the chillier I became. It had to be well below forty degrees, and I couldn't stop twitching.

"It's freezing," I shook, puffing out a warm breath and watching it disappear. "Why is it so cold?"

"They have to keep the materials in good condition. Heat ages paper. Plus, we are underground. If they didn't keep it cold in here, the natural heat could melt the microfilm. I would guess it's only going to get colder the deeper we go. If you get too cold, tell me, okay?"

"Okay," I muttered, my lips chattering.

"Where does the tunnel end?" I asked.

"I don't know," Jack replied. "My guess would be a door leading inside the main library. Here, hold this." Jack passed the phone to me. As it hit my hand, the sound of dozens of approaching footsteps sent a spasm of terror through my body. I yanked Jack's hand hard, ducking into a corner screened by stacks of white boxes.

"Who's coming?" I asked.

"Shh," Jack hushed.

My body trembled with both the cold and the fear of being caught. Neither of us said a word for a full five minutes, listening only for voices to call us from our position, but none did.

"I think it's overhead," Jack whispered. "We need to hurry."

"I'm afraid to move," I breathed. Hot, salty tears burned my cheeks.

"Elizabeth, we are okay. You're okay. I don't think we have much further to go. Please, stand up and come with me. I need you to be brave."

"What were we thinking coming down here?" I groaned, pulling myself to my feet.

The deeper we moved, the lower the ceiling became. Jack led us to the right, hunching low as to not strike his head on the hanging water pipes. A set of five stone stairs led to a small landing and disappeared behind a wall.

"Where does that go?" I asked.

"Up to the next tunnel floor, I would presume."

"There's two floors?" I panicked.

"Relax. We are almost to where we need to be if the numbers stay the same."

A smaller tunnel shot off to the left, ending in what looked like fenced cages with huge padlocks hanging from the doors.

"Is that where they lock up trespassers?" I laughed.

"We're close," he said again. "Relax."

Spider webs stuck to my face. "Oh," I cried. "Get it off. Get it off!"

"What?" Jack demanded.

My fingers clawed at my face. "Spider," I whimpered.

Jack shined the light into my eyes, "It's just a web," he said, losing his patience, "come on, Elizabeth. This is taking longer than it should."

Sixty feet into the tunnel, Jack stopped in front of a tall black steel shelving unit. Large bundles of folded and rolled paper were stacked at the very top. A small white sticker declared the scrolls to be reproductions of Columbus' maps. We were standing before history, reproductions or not.

Halfway down, small metal files were lined neatly across the massive unit. Jack dropped my hand and ran his fingers across the line.

"Point the light over here," he said. "R69."

Jack hunched lower, muttering the code written on the yellow paper, "R79-1365GA."

We both traced the stacks to the ground. The file wasn't there.

"It ends at R79-1361," I whispered. "It has to be on the other side."

Together, we rounded the shelf. The other side was a mirror of the first. The same metal file folders were locked into position, each with their own barcode.

"Here!" I shouted.

The file was lighter than I expected. Pulling harder than necessary, it slipped from my cold hands, bounced off the stone floor, and split open.

"Shhh," Jack urged.

The jarring noise echoed off the walls and rang in my ears. In unison, Jack and I bent down to snatch the case from the ground.

"What's inside?" Jack snapped.

I didn't have time to answer. The sound of a massive door opening jolted fear through my body for the second time. This time, the sound wasn't coming from above us, someone had entered the tunnel.

"Someone down here?" a male's voice called out.

"Run," Jack instructed. "Hurry!"

I pulled my backpack from my shoulder and tossed the metal case inside. Jack jogged us to the left, running as quickly as the darkness would allow. Turning the next corner too quickly, my feet hit a patch of icy condensation. There wasn't time to catch myself. My feet scrambled to find solid footing, but couldn't. I went down with a hard thud.

I couldn't hold the agony ripping through my back and legs, and I screamed.

"Who's there?" the voice called out again.

Heavy boots pounded in our direction.

"We have guests," Jack whispered. "Get up!"

I scrambled to my feet, groaning with each movement. The warmth of my blood once again spilled down my leg. The footsteps were closer now. Jack pulled us down another long stack, weaving our way in and out of the shelves, trying to create a diversion with the sound of our feet.

"Stop!" the man boomed.

We did not halt to his request; our feet struck harder against the stone.

"Security, we have a breach in the tunnels. I need back up," he called over his handheld radio.

"10-4," a female answered. "Officers, security breach in the tunnel. Requesting back up immediately. Staff is below. All assistance is needed. Again, security breach in the archive tunnel."

Jack snapped my arm in another direction. I could see the escape ladder just ahead. I plunged forward releasing his hand. Lunging at the ladder, I hooked my fingers onto the rungs and clung on for dear life. The frosty metal burned my fingers as I pulled my aching body up.

"Thirty-two, thirty-three," I breathed, counting my way to forty-one.

My heart pounded so hard I was afraid it would explode.

Two more voices called out commands to surrender. Jack craned his body up. He was nearly on top of me now.

"Go faster," he pushed.

"Thirty-nine," I trembled.

Thrusting forward, I shoved the steel door open with all my might. Clawing my way out, I scrambled through the rough bushes. I had made it to ground level. Jack was on my heels. When his body was fully on the ground, I turned and kicked the door closed. We were free, at least for a moment.

"Crawl around to the back of the bushes," Jack cried.

Gasping with each new tear of my skin, I slithered on my belly until my backpack got caught.

"Jack," I cried.

With a quick flip of his fingers, he freed me from the imposing twigs. A million thoughts crowded my head. The biggest was how we were going to make it out of the park without been caught, especially now that I had blood running down my legs. The park would be crawling with security in a matter of seconds. "Security breach in the tunnel," resounded in my head.

"Do you think they saw us?" I questioned.

"I don't know," Jack heaved. He was having a hard time catching his breath again.

"We need to stand up, but be careful when you do. Walk towards the port-a-potty. We need to slip through the crowd." His voice trailed off.

Slowly, I dusted myself off and focused on making each step appear as normal as possible. Jack joined me.

"We should try to blend in. Take a seat in the crowd," I said, "I doubt anyone will be looking for us among the masses."

"No, that is more suspicious than us just getting out of here," Jack replied. "Don't do anything crazy, Elizabeth. Just follow me. I need you to act normal."

We rounded the port-a-potty. The crowd had grown by the hundreds since we had disappeared out of sight. A few eyes turned in our direction but quickly returned to the opening credits of the featured picture.

"Walk along the sides and cut through the middle," Jack urged.

I tiptoed my way through the mass of blankets, hands, and feet, ending at the opening we had walked through nearly two hours earlier.

A beefy security guard looked up from his phone and smiled, "Not staying for the movie?"

Jack rested his hand on my shoulder—squeezing to tell me not to speak. "Sadly, not tonight. She tripped and did a number on her legs," Jack said, pointing to the red trail.

"Oh, that looks bad. I'll call first-aid, wait right here."

"No," Jack exclaimed. "I'll take her home. She is allergic to all sorts of medicines and sprays. It's best to let her mother tend to her, but I appreciate the offer."

"Are you sure?" the officer questioned.

"Yes," I replied.

"Okay then, try to have a good night. Be careful, young lady."

With that, we rushed onto the sidewalk.

"We need to get to a bus stop. It doesn't matter which. Anything will do as long as it puts some distance between the library and us," Jack said, tugging me along.

Up ahead, flashlights darted along the backside of the library.

"Clear back here!" a heated voice called.

"Elizabeth, RUN!"

Chapter 24: The Escape

One wrong step nearly ended the chase. Jack stumbled, and his ankle hit the edge of the sidewalk, which forced his body down. His bones crashed against the cement with a painful thud. We were trapped.

Fevered voices moved closer as I scrambled to Jack's sprawled body.

"Get up!"

Every inch of him was limp. He lay dazed and expressionless despite my urgent pleas. We were in trouble—serious trouble. Crouching down over him, I carefully studied every angle and direction of the street. Peering eyes were everywhere. If we're caught, it would be done in a very public way. Guards would be given accolades. All because Jack couldn't wait. I would forever be known as *"that"* girl. That girl who broke into the New York Library's secret tunnels and dared to steal a locked-away file. Anger replaced my fear.

"Jack, please, please…" I chomped.

"Split up! Find them!" Four burly security guards with weighted flashlights and guns hanging from their belts charged at their mark—us.

The mixture of warm blood and paranoia made my head swim. The voices grew louder, drawing closer, and I panicked.

"Help! My grandfather," I screamed.

A street maintenance crew ran to our rescue, pulling Jack up by his shoulders, setting him upright. He was hurt—bad.

"This way," one of the guards called.

"Jack," I choked, bursting into tears.

He reached out, squeezing my hand, and said, "I'm okay. Shh."

Less than fifteen seconds later, another round of terror rippled through my core as a lone guard sprinted by.

"One," Jack muttered so only I could hear.

Jack's head hung against his chest.

"Two."

As the second guard sped past, I understood. There was no way we could have outpaced four healthy, young guards. They were looking for criminals who dared to breach the tunnels. Criminals who would surely be running to make an escape. No one would suspect a little girl and her bleeding grandfather. Despite the blood and pain this part of his plan was brilliant.

"Three."

Well, almost brilliant. With hot, labored breath, a fourth guard ground to a stop inches from Jack's back.

"Excuse me," he said, "Have you seen two people running past here? We had a break-in at the library, and we're looking for them."

Two of the street crew shook their heads, but one of them, who appeared to be in charge, saw the flicker of fear in my eyes. He studied it hard, drawing the guard's attention to me, and then said, "What'd they look like?" before turning his glare away.

The guard rested his hand on his gun while disclosing the only details they had of their suspects—all of which were false.

"Two teen males, both about six feet tall, blonde hair, and wearing black or navy zipped hoodies," he announced.

A glimmer of a smile instantaneously filled my face without my permission.

"You sure?" the crew chief questioned.

I turned my face slightly to hide my excitement. If we could just hold on, this would soon be over.

The guard nodded hard, "Yes sir. We have an eyewitness that saw them coming out of the storage tunnels. She claims one of the teens kicked her square in the back while he was running out of the park."

Our eyes met again. Even if I tried to deny it, the crew chief knew the truth. My face went hot.

"Two teens, you say," the crew chief replied, "Nah, no one like that passed through here that I saw. Better move along."

The guard thanked him and the rest of the crew, then suddenly directed his eyes upon me.

"Kid, the old man okay? Need me to radio in an ambulance? Looks like you are bleeding pretty badly, sir."

The guard sunk to our level and Jack shivered. We were inches away from the very person pursuing us.

"Took a spill. It happens. I'm sure I'll be pretty sore in the morning," Jack smiled, trying to make light of the situation.

"Sir, your head is bleeding. You may have a concussion. Let me help. It takes two seconds to issue a medic call."

"That's kind of you, sir, but really, I'm fine. A little blood isn't going to hurt anything," Jack said, turning his head down. His eyes were darting all over the place under each new lie he told. "You know how bad flesh wounds bleed."

The crew chief studied my face. He was watching every move I made, each wince, and each breath I pulled in my lungs trying to count away the fear.

"I don't mean to tell you your job partner, but you have suspects to catch," the crew chief said, standing and tapping on his shoulder. "I've got a radio right here. If the old man decides to go to the hospital, I'll call it in."

"Thank you," I mouthed.

The guard shook the crew chief's hand, and instructed him to radio in if they saw two teens acting suspiciously.

The chief laughed, "It's New York City, man. The whole city is a suspect then!"

"You got that right," the guard smiled, propelling forward to seek his prey. A thunder of people followed.

"Everyone get back to work!" the chief called out to his crew. "Change the lighting system. It looks like the art exhibit is letting out. We're going to get some heavy foot traffic now."

He bent down, grabbing my shoulders to steady himself on his knees, and looked into my eyes, "Listen, kid," he said, "I did some stupid things as a teen. That's why I'm out here fixing these streets instead in one of the tall buildings making a cool million. You two should get along and not cause any more trouble. You hear?"

I nodded. Jack was woozy and unsteady on his feet as we helped him stand. Despite falling on purpose, he had lost a lot of blood.

"There's a bus stop about three blocks up. Do you think the old man here can make it?" the chief asked.

"We'll be fine," I said offering my hand, "Thank you."

"I mean it, kid. Whatever you've done, don't do it again. It's not worth it," he said, dropping my hand.

"Yes, sir. Let's go, Jack."

The guards were probably a mile ahead of us by now. Still in a hot pursuit of two teenage boys, but that didn't stop me from looking over my shoulder every thirty seconds. We darted in and out of alleyways, using the night as our cloak.

One sharp corner led to the next. Together, Jack and I limped the three blocks to the nearest Metro stop. As we rounded the last alleyway, Bus 43 was parked waiting for passengers to board.

"Jack," I pointed. "Run!"

I bolted forward. Jack limped along trying his best to move faster than an injured snail. It wasn't working. The bus heaved, blowing exhaust as the driver shifted it back in gear and moved the lever to close the back folding doors. I got to the back bumper and hollered to the driver in hopes he would stop, but our chance was gone. The taillights mocked us as they merged into a line of honking taxis.

My body ached. My eyelids were heavier than the pain that was still tugging at my body from the fall in the tunnel. Jack looked worse than I felt.

"Maybe we should grab a taxi," I stammered.

"No, we need to call your mom. I don't want anyone to overhear our conversation. A taxi is too personal."

Six blocks passed slowly in near silence. Neither of us knew what to say to one another. We had made mistakes. Yet, somewhere in the quietness, a pact was crafted. No matter what, neither of us would speak of our narrow escape from the tunnel *ever* again. We would not tell my mother of our misguided adventures, and no matter the circumstances, we would not return to the library—*ever*.

Thirty-five minutes later, we approached a bus stop overflowing with waiting riders.

"Here," Jack said. The edge to his voice was chilling. His pain was starting to get the best of him. "Now, I want you to listen very carefully. We are going to get on this bus. We'll call your mother. We will tell her we've been at the library all day, then stuck around the park until the movie started. We missed the bus that would have dropped us near home. We need her to pick us up. Does that sound like a plan?"

I nodded and then questioned, "And how will we explain your head?"

"Took a tumble down the stone steps. They can really mess a guy up," Jack said coolly. His confidence in the lie was so high I nearly believed it myself.

"She'll push for you to have it looked at, you know."

"Is it really that bad?"

"It's pretty nasty, Jack."

"Stop worrying and let me handle it when the questions come. Do you have the story down? Do you have any questions?"

I smiled but didn't say another word.

Leaning over an elderly man in a wheelchair, Jack asked which bus was next, and where it was headed. The two had a brief conversation, and then Jack thanked him with a firm pat on the back.

"Bus M4," Jack said abruptly. "The man doesn't know where it ends up, but pull it up on your phone."

My hands hit the back pockets of my jeans. They were both empty. Flying to the front, the phone wasn't there either.

"You have it," I blurted out. "You have the phone."

"No, I don't," He paused dramatically. "I handed it to you before you dropped the file and alerted the *entire* New York Public Library we were under their feet."

My face burned, "I don't have it," I said hotly.

"Elizabeth, where is the phone?"

"I—said—I—don't—know!"

"If you dropped it in the tunnel do you know the ramification?" Jack's voice boomed. Awaiting passengers turned and joined our conversation with burning ears.

"Jack," I cried. "Lower your voice."

"No, Elizabeth Yale, where is the phone?"

Slinging the backpack from my shoulder, I dropped to my knees and feverishly dug in the main pocket. My fingers bounced off of the library's metal file. I bitterly pushed it away. If it weren't for that file, we wouldn't be in this mess. The mountain of paperwork we had gathered was crumpled and scattered. I dug deep, but there was no phone. My stomach found its way to my throat.

"So stupid," I ranted under my breath. "How could I be so stupid?"

My heart thumped wildly gaining speed with each passing second. Impatient with Jack, with myself, and frightened at the thought of leaving evidence below in the tunnel, I tugged on the small front zipper. I pulled too hard. The pull snapped off into my hand. I paused long enough to collect myself, and hastily tore at the zipper. It wouldn't budge.

"Is it in there or not?" Jack questioned hard.

He waited for me to say something, but I refused to answer, still trying to rip the zipper open.

"Well," he pushed.

When Jack had had enough, he whipped the knife from his front pocket, flicked it open and slashed an x across the front pocket.

"Jack!" I cried. "That's my backpack!"

"I'll buy you another one," he chomped angrily. With the phone now in his hand, Jack groaned. "There's barely enough juice to call Laurel. We'll ask the driver where the bus stops and then call."

I moved away. This was his fault. All of this was on his shoulders. My mind wandered back to a few nights before when I tossed him out of my room. This part, this side of Jack, is something I deeply despise.

Twenty minutes later, Bus M4 stopped at the curb. The crowd moved at once, pushing into a single file line. We were the last to load. Neither of us had a fare ticket or our Metro cards. Jack pulled two twenties from his wallet and tossed them into the driver's lap, "I'm sure this will suffice," he said. The driver looked up at the bus' camera, then down at the two bills, and motioned for us to take our seats.

Every place was full. The bus smelled of sweat and dirt which made my stomach turn.

"There isn't a place to sit," I muttered.

A woman in the very back called to us, and motioned Jack and I to come and take her seat as she stood and joined another single rider across the aisle.

"Thank you," Jack nodded, stopping to allow me to pass and slide in. I faked a smile and let my body crash against the worn bench. Jack settled in next to me. I pressed my body against the cold metal wall and looked away. I needed some space.

Staring hard outside the window, pressing my forehead against the glass until there was no space between the cold pane and my head, I realized how different the outside world seemed now. The frenzy and excitement I felt for life earlier this morning was suddenly gone. Perhaps it would return, but for now, nothing was as simple and straightforward as it even felt twenty-four hours before. I didn't recognize the girl staring back at me in the window. Everything about her was dark, different—very *different*.

My head fell against the back of the seat as I struggled to keep my eyes open. Jack was on the phone with Mom. Lie after lie trickled from his mouth. I didn't care any longer. I tuned him out. My body, my mind, and even my heart were too tired to care about whatever falsehoods he had conjured up. Nor would I back them up when we finally meet up with her. I was done, at least for now.

Shortly after the bus pulled from the curb, I drifted away.

* * * *

"Elizabeth, what are you reading today, sweet pea?"

"Daddy! You're back!" I cheered, jumping to my feet and grabbing ahold of my father.

"Sure am! Haven't slept in a week, but I'm happy to be home with my girl," Jesse Yale laughed.

"Whatcha reading?" he asked, tousling my hair.

"Grandpa Jack just got a bunch of new books, but you know me I only grabbed one of them, and I have my favorite…"

"*Alice in Wonderland*, of course," Jesse laughed. "What else?"

I giggled. "Now, let's get down to business! Did you bring me anything back from Paris?"

"Well, not from Paris," he said, "But I may have brought you back something from someplace else."

"Tell me, tell me! What is it?" I asked, jumping up and down.

From behind his back came the most beautiful hand-carved doll. Softened straw hair flowed from her wooden head and was delicately tied in small pigtails near her shoulders. Her painted eyes were oddly human while her expression was lost in deep thought. Her soft pink lips pursed together in a little smile that seemed slightly devious.

"Do you like her?" Jesse whispered. "She reminded me of Alice." My father's beautiful blue eyes sparkled, watching the delight I found in my new treasure.

"She is perfect, Daddy," I whispered.

"I'm glad you like her, Elizabeth."

"I love her." I smiled. Her dress, a soft robin blue was made of raw silk and woven lace.

"Look at her legs and arms," Jesse urged. "She's a pegwood doll. See how the joints are carved and then the next piece is sculpted to fit?"

"That's neat," I smiled.

My fingers touched her back. Something rough lay under her clothes. As I was flipping her over to examine it, Grandpa Jack called to us from the front of the store.

"Jesse, Elizabeth?"

"Sounds like we are in trouble," Jesse grinned, "let's see what Grandpa Jack wants."

Together we moved through the tall stacks. The beautiful pegwood doll's legs swung from my fingers, her legs keeping in perfect rhythm with mine. Grandpa Jack called for us again. Jesse turned, and made a face. I snickered, and we continued to make our way to the front of Yale's Shelves. I reached for his untucked blue dress shirt, tugging on it to slow his steps. Not missing a beat, he grabbed my hand and yanked me and the pegwood doll up and onto his back.

"Jesse?" Jack called again.

Jesse answered, "Dad? I'm coming."

A few customers milled around the store. Baskets filled with used paperbacks swung from their hands, each smiling at our father and daughter banter.

"Could you please watch the store for a few hours? I'm exhausted. I haven't slept since your mom…"

Jack stopped.

"Go," Dad insisted. "Me and Lizzy have this old place covered, Dad."

"We sure do!" I giggled. "And Miss Pegwood. You cannot forget her."

"I see Daddy brought you a treasure from overseas," Grandpa Jack smiled.

"Miss Pegwood," I said making her dance over the register.

"Okay, Lizzy and Pegwood, it's time to get down."

Dad gently dropped me to my feet, and I rounded the counter to give Grandpa Jack a hug. "I hope you get some rest."

"Thanks, kiddo. Jesse, two hours, that's all I need. Is that okay?"

"Go Dad, I'll see you when you get back."

Sales were made and the store emptied. Miss Pegwood and I stretched across the floor next to the old reading chairs and opened *Alice in Wonderland* for the hundredth time.

"You know what my favorite part of that story is?" he asked.

"No," I replied, watching as my father walked over to the grandfather clock and pulled it from the wall that led down the mystery section.

"It's when Alice drinks the 'Drink Me' drink, and she shoots high into the sky."

I laughed. "I like that part too. What are you doing, Daddy?"

"Making sure the old clock is working properly. I thought I heard it making a weird sound," he replied.

"Sounds fine to me," I said.

Jesse slipped something out of his pocket and quickly tossed it inside the old timepiece.

"What was that?" I asked.

"Shh, something broke off the back of the clock when I opened it. Don't tell Grandpa Jack," he begged. "So, when Alice grew as tall as a tree, I think I like it so much because her world changed in a matter of seconds. She was small.

Just a girl, right, then all the sudden she was a part of something so much bigger than herself."

I didn't know what he meant. I nodded and turned my eyes back to the book.

* * * *

The sound of the overhead speaker violently pulled me from my slumber. I blinked hard, trying to figure out where I was. Grandpa Jack was still next to me. His hand was holding his injured head.

"Where are we?" I asked in a whisper.

"One more stop, and we'll be at the Grand Central Terminal. Your mom will meet us there."

"Jack," I whispered. "I just remembered something important."

"What?" he said, turning to face me.

"The day my dad returned home from the Netherlands he put something inside the grandfather clock."

"That isn't possible. We've never been able to open the back of the clock, Elizabeth," Jack replied.

"Trust me, he figured out a way."

Chapter 25: The Documents Inside

Mom was waiting when the bus pulled into Grand Central. It was a relief to see her smiling face outside the fogged window. I was safer with her near. As the bus rolled to a stop, I looked at Jack.

"Did you open the file?"

"No, too many eyes," he replied. "We'll wait until we get home."

The bitterness between Jack and I was raw—far too fresh to address. Even thinking about it made my blood rush. In the next few hours, I had to make a game-call—ask myself the same vital question that has been on a constant loop since Jack's arrival: Am I willing to continue with this quest? I've gone back and forth, yet, I continue to allow myself to be sucked into Jack's insanity. A huge part of me just wanted a "normal" life again. Well, as normal as it had been in recent years.

Another thought crept in, would the documents inside the stolen file open our eyes to whatever secrets Edward Royal was hiding? Immediately, my inner voice answered *no*. Even allowing my mind to go there told me I wasn't ready to let go of this chase. This madness, the typewriter, the mystery around our family tree, all of it was driving a thirst for the truth that would never be satisfied until I was able to gulp down the reality of it all. This day would turn into tomorrow, and another day after that, and until I knew the full truth of my family, the wheel would just keep spinning.

"Agh," I groaned aloud.

"What?" Jack asked.

"Nothing," I said, bitterly.

The static of the overhead speakers roared to life, "Ladies and gentlemen, please collect all of your things and exit the bus in a timely manner. This is the last stop for the night. Thank you for riding with Metro. We hope you enjoyed your ride. We look forward to having you back with us tomorrow. Please be safe and have a good night."

Jack stood and allowed me to go down the aisle first. Everyone was dead on their feet. Unloading bus M4 took an impossibly long time, but finally, my feet hit the steps, and I ran to my mother. Pain sizzled throughout my body, but I didn't care. I needed the comfort of my mom's arms.

"Hey," she said, drawing me close, "Long day! I hope you guys were able to pull some great research from the library."

Jack chuckled at her words.

"You can definitely put it that way," I replied.

"Come on guys. Let me drive you home. Have you eaten?" she asked.

"Not a bite all day," I replied.

The streetlights overhead bounced off Jack's head at just the right moment, and mom stopped hard.

"What in the world did you do?" she asked.

"You know me, I cannot walk without tripping over my own feet," Jack smiled. "I fell down the stairs." His face fell, pulling at some hidden emotions to sell his story.

"What?" Mom's eyes met mine, looking for confirmation. I shrugged my shoulders defiantly.

"She was in the bathroom when it happened," Jack answered swiftly, offering a nasty glare in my direction.

"Goodness," Mom said. "You should probably have that looked at, Jack."

"Told you," I mocked.

"It's fine. I am starving though. Maybe we could go through a drive-thru on the way home. I'll buy."

An hour later, the three of us spread out across the dinner table and gulped down greasy cheeseburgers and soggy fries. The warm soda felt good against my dry throat.

"So, tell me about today," Mom said.

"Well," Grandpa Jack began, "it was quite interesting. Where's your backpack, kid?"

"Here," I said, pulling it from the floor and tossing it at him. It landed in a pile of ketchup.

"What happened to it?" Mom asked.

"Oh, Jack decided to cut it open when I accidently broke the zipper," I replied scornfully.

"Her phone was trapped in that pocket. I had to call you. I already told you I would buy you a new one," he bit back.

"And I already told you that I don't want a new one. I want the one you decided to cut a big hole in."

"You two need some sleep," Mom interrupted, worried about the edge of our voices. "Go ahead, Jack, what were you going to show me?"

"This," he said, pulling the family tree from my backpack. "We met with a genealogist today. I think you'll find it quite interesting."

Jack delicately handed the paper over to my mom. His lips twitched as she began to examine the sheet.

"But," she said.

It was clear her mind was spinning, asking the same questions Grandpa Jack and I had pondered many hours before. The way she studied the family tree seemed to unnerve him. He deserved it for all the trouble he had caused.

"I don't…" Mom stuttered. "I mean, it's curious…"

"That our last name changed?" I questioned.

"Yes," she said, dropping the tree on the table. "I mean, why? Was there some sort of mistake?"

I laughed at the word mistake. Jack flinched.

"No," he rushed. "Edward, up at the very top, seems to have changed his last name when he arrived in the United States. We found two sets of birth records for everyone in his family. One set lists everyone as Royal, and the other set names everyone as a Yale. Ain't history grand?" Jack said slapping his knee.

"Why would someone do that?"

"Secrets," I hissed out. "It's funny what having secrets will make a person do."

"Elizabeth," Jack cautioned.

"What?" I asked innocently. "It's the truth, isn't it?"

I would never tell my mother what happened tonight; or that I had willingly been a part of a break-in. Not just a simple break-in either, but one that resulted in the theft of a document from the world's second largest library. I would never name myself as a suspect to anyone, but getting under Jack's skin was worth every minute of watching him squirm.

"What else did you find?" Mom questioned.

Jack filled her in. I sat and listened, only interjecting a few points here and there. When Jack finished speaking, Mom had a spun version of the truth that seemed to satisfy her questions.

The minute Grandpa Jack finished speaking, from out of nowhere, the familiar sizzle called from upstairs.

"The machine," I hissed.

"It's been doing that all day," Mom said. "Guess it has something to say. It's going to have to wait. I'm exhausted. You two have to be tired too."

As Mom stood, patting Jack on the shoulder gently, the grandfather clock struck one a.m. Instantly, my mind flashed back to my father, propped on one knee, tossing something into the back of the clock.

"Shh, don't tell Grandpa Jack," echoed in my mind. My body stiffened.

"What's wrong, Elizabeth?" Mom asked.

"Nothing," I shook. "I'm exhausted too."

The machine popped louder this time.

"Is there a way to turn that darn thing off?" Mom questioned.

"It's not like it has batteries," Jack laughed.

Mom bent down and kissed the top of my head, "Try to sleep, Elizabeth. You're as white as a ghost."

"That's because I've been chasing ghosts," I muttered hotly under my breath.

"What?" she questioned.

"Nothing. Good night, Mom."

She left the kitchen and made her way down the hall to her bedroom, stopping to say, "Jack, if you want, I could put a dressing on your wound. It should probably be covered."

His right hand flew to his head, tracing the self-inflicted gash, and said, "It's fine for tonight. I'll take a quick shower and get it cleaned out. If it's worse in the morning, I'll let you take a look."

"Suit yourself," Mom replied, "Good night you two."

Neither Jack nor I moved from our places at the kitchen table, both waiting until the house fell perfectly silent. When it was, Jack stood and stared at the moon through the bay window.

"I'm sorry, you know," he whispered.

"For what?"

"For taking you down into the tunnels. I'm a terrible example."

"You aren't thinking straight," I replied.

The machine upstairs sizzled louder this time making sure it had our attention. The air in the house began to shift. It was charged with so much electricity the hair on my arms stood on end.

"Think we should find out what it has to say?" Jack asked, still staring out the window.

"I don't know that I care," I said, shaking away the chill filling me.

Jack turned, "You don't want to know? You're going to quit when we are this close?"

"This close to what?" I demanded.

"To finding out why Edward Royal changed his name. Why he left the Netherlands? What secrets he was hiding," Jack pushed.

"That's the problem, Jack. I don't think we'll ever know. That wicked machine keeps repeating the same thing over and over again. I'm pretty sure I know history isn't right by now."

The machine raged. Sparks flew and popped. The longer we resisted, the greater the sound grew. One more round called out. This time, the push was so intense the pressure building inside felt as though the house would implode.

Jack bounced from foot to foot. The electricity was propelling his body to fidget and move. Suddenly, he turned, eyed me carefully, and took off running for the stairs.

"Jack!" I shouted.

It was too late. He was halfway up the staircase.

"Don't touch the machine!" I yelled. My foot hit the first stair.

Whiz-whiz-bang! Whiz-whiz-BANG! The keys bounced on their own, pushing out another round of puzzling messages.

"What is going on?" Mom shouted from the hall.

No one answered. The machine ignited with white radiating power as I rounded the top of the stairs. Mom came rushing towards the bottom landing.

"Don't touch it, Elizabeth," she screamed.

The same letters floated up and away from the machine—*schrijven fabriek*. Those two foreign words were burned into our minds. Jack whispered each letter harshly as they drifted away. Out of nowhere, a burst of red heat burned from the roller bar.

"It's on fire," I shouted.

Flames flickered and danced, forcing more white smoke to pour forth. We all stood watching. My fingers twitched, burning to touch the unyielding intensity of the Whizbang machine. Pop. Sizzle. Whiz-whiz-BANG! My body shook. Bang!

"Elizabeth," Laurel shouted again, her feet pounding up the staircase.

It was too late. I threw my hands on top of the keyboard. The flame vanished with a sudden and unexpected breeze. Mom and Jack looked around, both shaking their heads in disbelief. The messages began to pour out.

Elizabeth Wright Royal Yale. Family secrets are the darkest and most deadly of curses. DEADLY. History is not right. Correct it. Correct it, Elizabeth Royal.

The noise mounted in the small upstairs hallway. So loud, a freight train could have blown through, and no one would have known. Buzzing, whizzing, banging, my head was going to explode.

"What does it say?" mom screamed, her words lost amongst the noise. The only word I could make out was *say*.

My fingers typed rapidly in response: The space tree? That space history? How space do space I space correct space it?

The machine banged.

Until history is corrected the forty year curse remains. Death is upon us.

Pop!

Death? I pounded.

Forty years is all you have once the curse finds its way to you. Death is upon us. Death is upon us. History is not correct. It's yours to fix, Elizabeth Royal. The clock ticks.

The machine went cold under my fingers, falling eerily silent. My heart raced in my chest.

"Death?" I screamed.

"The curse, Elizabeth. You said it earlier in the library. Everyone Mrs. Howard noted on the family tree died young. Either before they turned forty or at forty years old," Jack's body shook violently.

"I'm not forty," I rushed.

Mom's face went ghostly white. Her eyes were hollow and locked into the machine. "It's me," she whispered. "It's me. The death."

"What?" Jack pushed.

"No!" I shouted. "No, absolutely not."

"What?" Jack shouted.

"It's me," she repeated, turning her eyes on him. "It's predicting my death. I'm next."

"What are you saying? Why is it you?" Jack pushed.

I swallowed hard. Mom's words ripped through Jack's head and his eyes closed.

"I won't let it happen, Laurel. I won't. We'll stop this," Jack breathed.

"You only have two weeks," her voice cracked. "I turn forty in two weeks, Jack."

I pulled my fingers away from the machine and lunged at my mother's waist. My head hit her warm shoulder. "It's going to be okay," I said.

"Elizabeth," she muttered.

"Jack," I gasped. "The woman told the merchant that if he sold the machine to the wrong person, the curse would find him as it had the others."

Chills raised on all of our bodies.

"We have to figure out how to stop whatever this is," Jack stammered.

The machine popped suddenly.

We all turned and waited. The softest whiz-whiz-bang sighed from its gears.

`The key holds the answers. The answers are under the key.`

Suddenly, I jerked forward, letting my feet lead me down the stairs.

"Help me," I shouted, grabbing the back of the massive grandfather clock. "I know what he tossed inside!"

"Who? What are you doing?" Mom asked, thundering down the stairs.

"Mom!" I grunted. "This thing must weigh two-hundred pounds. Help me move it!"

Jack rushed to my side, grumbling as he pushed the clock forward. His breath was hot and reeked of greasy fries. Mom grabbed the other side. Together we heaved the clock off the wall, the bottom grating against the tile.

"Oh," the three of us sputtered.

"That was a horrible sound," Mom shook.

"The clock's been moved since your father passed away," Jack said. "It's doubtful that whatever Jesse put inside is still here."

"Maybe," I said through gritted teeth, pulling on the back knob. "It's—stuck—I—can't—pull—it—open."

Twisting, pulling, I dropped to the floor; kneeling with one foot against the clock I finally got the door to release and spring open. Just as I saw in my dream, a shiny object lay right where my father had tossed it so many years ago.

"I'm afraid to look," Mom said.

"Don't be," I answered. The tension easing from my voice. "It's only a key."

I plunked the silver key from its hiding place and closed my fingers over the top.

"May I see it?" Grandpa Jack asked.

Silently, offering my palm out to him, he furrowed his brows hard and said, "That is not a typical key."

"The key holds the answers," Mom repeated.

"No, it's not that easy, trust me, Mom."

"So, now the question is what does the key go to?" Jack said.

We stood in silence. Grandpa Jack turned the key over in his hand a half-dozen times.

"GP," he muttered. "What does GP stand for?"

"Elizabeth," Mom said slowly, "How did you know the key was in the clock?"

"I saw it in a dream," I replied. "I fell asleep on the bus. I watched as Dad tossed something into the back of the clock. When the machine said the answer is under the key, it triggered the memory."

"Did Jesse bring anything back from his trip that needed a key?" Jack asked.

"Not that I remember."

"Think hard."

"I am," she pushed. "I don't remember anything needing a key."

Jack began to pace.

"Let's look at the file, Elizabeth, maybe something inside will clue us in."

"I don't know what file you are talking about, Jack, but I'm going to bed. I can't take any more of this craziness."

"I think that's a good idea, Mom."

Jack moved into the kitchen. I hugged my mother one last time and sent her on her way. When I made my way to the kitchen, Jack had the file open and spread across the table.

"What's inside?" I asked, taking a seat next to him.

"It's just what Mr. Kauffman said would be inside. An affidavit and a receipt of sale. Take a look."

"These sheets are numbered. The affidavit is one through six. The sales receipt is numbered with an eight. Something is missing," I replied.

"Perfect," Jack sighed.

The affidavit was vague at best. The rambling legal speak added up to nothing more than Royal swearing that he was the owner of intelligent property that he was selling for a total of two thousand dollars to a man named C. Lewis.

"That's a pretty penny in 1879," I stammered.

"It's a pretty penny now," Jack laughed.

"I suppose that's what pulled the Royals out of the overwhelming poverty described in Amelia's letter. The census showed they lived in New York and owned the home listed. They wouldn't have been able to buy a house in the condition they arrived in."

"You're right," Jack nodded. "The money would have allowed them to change their names too."

"That too," I replied, "but what does intelligent property mean?"

"It could mean a number of things," Jack replied. "The receipt of sale isn't much help neither, other than offering the buyer's name, C. Lewis."

"Whatever was sold must have been worth it. This C. Lewis character must have had an awful lot of money at his disposal to pay Royal that kind of cash outright."

Jack flipped the metal file over. Attached to the back was an old-fashioned manila library checkout envelope and ruled card.

The envelope read: 7-Day Use. Return To Desk From Which Borrowed. New York Public Library Reference File. This publication is due on the LAST Date stamped below.

The small card inserted in the four-by-four open envelope offered a bit more information. R79-1365GA was typed at the top left corner. Under it was D59. In the center, "New York Sales Records" was printed in small handwriting.

"Why would this be in the library's possession?" I questioned. "It seems more fitting to be in a courthouse than a public library."

"Whatever was sold had to have some sort of historical significance to be locked away in the storage tunnels of the library. Maybe that is what the machine means when it types history is not right. Correct it."

I slipped the card from the envelope and gulped. "Look."

Written on the checkout card were three documents: The General Affidavit, the Sales Receipt, and the Record of Registered Intelligent Property.

"Where is the Record of Registered Intelligent Property?" I questioned.

"It's not in here, but look at the signatures," Jack pointed.

Under the date and "issued to" lines followed a short list of library patrons who had checked out the file.

5-30-1895 Norma Snyder.

10-9-1897 R.B. Westbrook.

12-9-1949 Meyer Jesse Yale.

"That's my father," Jack pointed.

"Look at the following signature," I said as my fingers traced the line.

Florence Vivian Yale was written next.

"My mother?" Jack questioned. "Why would she have checked this file out too?"

"Look at when she checked it out, Jack. That would have been almost twenty years after your father's death. What would have made her revisit this so long after he passed away?"

"I don't know," Jack replied.

"You're absolutely sure she never mentioned a curse or the typewriter?" I questioned. "Anything that made you question what she was talking about, but she never really explained?"

"No," Jack said flatly.

"Then maybe that is why she was looking into it. Maybe she was protecting you, not bringing you into the fold so the curse wouldn't find you too. After all, remember you are the longest living Yale/Royal there is in the past hundred and thirty years."

"My mother was in her late eighties when she passed. It doesn't follow the pattern. Where is the tree?"

"Here," I said, handing over Sara's handy work.

"Just as I thought. None of the wives passed away prematurely. If my mother checked out this file, it means she knew about the typewriter. Perhaps Laurel will be safe from this curse."

"Common sense says the typewriter is talking about Mom. I'm not close to forty. You're past forty. Dad is gone. So who else does that leave?"

I was at a loss. Jack's shoulders grew tighter as we read the next name together.

"Dad," I whispered.

Written in perfect cursive was my father's signature: Jesse Boyd Yale. The checkout date: June 11, 2007.

"It's all right here. He knew more than he ever let on. The ticket to Amsterdam, his name on the file, the photo albums and key; it's all proof. We know he checked in the file two days before he left for the Netherlands, but he didn't return article number seven. Why wouldn't he have made a copy and returned it with the rest of the file?"

"That's saying the article wasn't already missing when he checked it out. But if it was inside, my guess is Jesse needed it. He needed it for something we haven't yet discovered," Grandpa Jack said, sinking into his chair.

The grandfather clock struck three a.m. A bitter and nasty laugh slipped from my lips.

"This is never going to end, you know. All of these clues just keep piling up, but not a single one has led us to a solid answer. We'll never figure this all out, Jack." Quiet rage radiated from every pore of my body.

"You're wrong, Elizabeth. The problem isn't that it will never end, the problem is we are not looking in the right places."

Chapter 26: The Airport

The next morning Mom drove us to LaGuardia with the windows rolled down. The warm summer breeze whipped my hair and rattled the suitcases tossed in the back. The machine sat squarely on my lap locked in its case. It felt safer to touch now that it was hidden away.

Had this trip taken place a week ago I wouldn't be able to contain myself, bubbling over with excitement of what was to come, but now…Now, I keep reminding myself that I *have* to go. There's no other option.

Jack and Mom made small talk as she turned the car onto the highway. It was a parking lot. Jack whined, anxious to get in the air. I didn't mind the delay. It gave me more time to memorize the smallest details of my mother's face.

We looked alike, her and me. Our hair is the same color. We share the same light skin. Her eyes are hazel, where I had gotten my father's baby blues, but other than that, I'm a perfect carbon copy of her. Inhaling the lavender lotion she's worn for as long as I can remember, I locked the smell inside. I wanted to remember it and connect it to her.

Happy images of her and I lying on our backs and watching the stars in the backyard filled my mind. The way she used to toss her head back in sheer happiness when we played hide-and-go-seek made me smile. Then came the way she let me win every bike and foot race I had ever challenged her to. I tucked each of those away as well. My heart was breaking. Each gesture of happiness reminded me that I was about to say goodbye.

"How are you doing back there?" she asked.

Offering an awkward smile, "Swell," I lied.

Her laugh lines creased, pulling into a faint smile that gave way to a slight twinkle in her eye. That marvelous twinkle held my reflection in the rear-view mirror. We both seemed to be silently studying one another.

There were less than two weeks, twelve impossibly short days, until her fortieth birthday. The unsettling notion that I may never see her again unnerved me. I thought I had dealt with my father's passing properly—that I have learned to handle this new life and move on—but all of this has proven that I haven't even begun to touch the surface of my emotions. Nor, could I fathom ever recovering from losing them both, not at this age.

Jack tried to drag me into his endless babble, but I didn't take the bait. I sat quietly, closed my eyes, and concentrated on absolutely nothing. I didn't want to talk about our trip. I didn't want to talk about what purpose it would now serve. Nor did I wish to think about the typewriter seated heavily on my legs. For once, I wanted to let my mind drift into a black abyss.

Forty-five minutes later, our car ground up the ramp to the International departure concourse of New York LaGuardia Airport with about a hundred other cars trailing behind. Freeing myself from the seatbelt, I pushed the passenger door open hard and collapsed into my mom's arms. The waterworks were simply unavoidable for both of us because in the end, this goodbye felt far too permanent.

"It's okay,'" she whispered in my ear. "I'll be okay. You'll be okay."

"But," I wept.

"Shh," Mom whispered into my ear while caressing my cheek, "Don't let your mind go there. I'll be right here when you return. Think about everything you are about to see. You're so lucky, my beautiful girl."

Everything I was about to see was precisely what I was afraid of.

"Please don't worry about me," she smiled. "We'll talk every day. You brought your phone, right?"

I nodded.

"Okay good. I promise, Elizabeth, I'll be okay."

That was a promise she couldn't keep. She could promise to try to remain safe, but what would find her while we were away, none of us actually knew. She hugged me tighter and let my tears fall onto her shirt for a minute and then let go.

"You better get inside if you want to make your flight," she insisted. Her voice was weak and nearly inaudible. We both were having a hard time letting go.

Mom reached over and hugged Jack too. The exchange between them suddenly looked heated. I knew she was demanding he bring me home safely. That if anything ever happened to her or to me, it would be forever his doing. He nodded respectfully and then motioned for me to come along.

If I thought it would do much good, I would slap my foot against the concrete and refuse to go like the little girl in Bryant Park, but I knew it wouldn't change anything.

The alternative to not going was far worse than simply boarding the plane. I had to save my mom.

"Kid," Jack said, motioning me forward again.

He had our bags stacked on the curb. I only brought along a few cases, the most important being the machine. Mom's fingers intertwined with mine as she smiled, "I love you, Elizabeth. You have made me so proud to be your mother. I could never ask for a better kid, ever. I need you to remember that. Okay? I will always be with you, no matter where I am. Got it?"

A wave of nausea hit me. She was not only saying goodbye for now but also for forever.

"Don't," I muttered, wrapping my arms around her waist one last time. I stretched onto my tiptoes, softly kissed her cheek, and then let go. "We, both of us, are going to be fine." I forced myself to repeat those words in my head. The more I said them, the more I would believe them. No matter what, it was time to face what was waiting for Jack and me.

I smiled, wiped the tears from my cheeks, and followed Grandpa Jack through a set of automatic rotating doors. I turned to wave goodbye, but she was already gone. Hundreds of people were pulsing by, and I still felt completely alone.

We checked our bags, keeping the typewriter as our sole carry-on, and made our way through security. By the time we had been x-rayed, and Jack patted down, we walked directly onto our plane. The flight attendant did her usual song and dance: if the aircraft should go down use your chair bottom as a flotation device.

"I'm stating this for the record now, if this plane goes down," I said, leaning into Jack, "I'm not going to pull this seat out to float anywhere. I'm giving you fair warning now. Just let me go."

Jack chuckled. "Let's not be dramatic."

Minutes later, the wheels were up and we rocketed into the sky.

"Jack," I whispered, "I need you to make me a promise."

"What's that?" he said, putting the airline's magazine in his lap.

"I need you to promise me we'll put a stop to this madness. That we'll figure out what this curse is and figure out a way to stop it before…," I stopped. I refused to put into words what was hanging on my tongue. I refused to speak of my mother's possible impending death.

"I won't let her die, Elizabeth," Jack said softly. "I won't. I would have stopped your father too had I known. He never gave me a chance to help. I don't know why, but he didn't. I would have traded places with him in an instant. Everything will be fine. I know it will."

I appreciated his need to soothe the situation, but we both knew the truth. Secrets and lies do not live in coincidence. Stories and circumstances are created to feed their purpose. Jack and I were mere pawns in this game of chasing the ghost that haunts our family's tree. Just like the game of chess, the lies told by our ancestors were the queen in this game. The only way to win was to capture the king, and he was the truth. Yet, it wouldn't be as easy as strategically moving ourselves to the next little black box. Too many players had joined the game over time and muddled up the board. Why my father chose to play this game alone, I wasn't sure I would ever fully understand. Whatever the caller said to my dad before his death had to have been significant to make him leave and risk everything—my mother, his own life, and me. I shuddered at the thought of what Jack and I were about to find. What my father couldn't stop, and then swiftly lost his life to.

My brain grew too tired to hold on for another second. I closed my eyes and didn't wake until Jack shook me as we were landing in Canada. There we jumped onto a Royal Air jetliner and ascended back into the friendly skies.

The typewriter's words echoed in every corner of my mind: history is not right. Correct it. Correct it.

After twenty-two hours in the air, our feet hit Amsterdam soil.

Chapter 27: the Netherlands

When we touched down at Schiphol Airport, it was three p.m. and drizzling. An ominous gray sky lie in wait outside. Dense fog and opaque clouds hugged the ground as perfect droplets pelted the tiny airplane windows and rolled away.

A thick-waisted stewardess gave the local time and weather per usual protocol—first in Dutch, then in German, and finally in English. Her bright red lips were spilling forth so much information it was hard to keep up with her. What I did gather was the rain was nothing compared to the bitter cold waiting for us.

My fingers traced the window's edge. The dreariness outside matched the feelings growing inside me. It seems like a bad omen to arrive under such darkened skies. My emotions were firing on all cylinders, on a pendulum between gloom and doom and pure happiness that we made it this far.

Pricks of green shone through the other side of the haze revealing a lush canopy of green. If we had arrived under the warmth of the sun, there is no doubt that the world outside this tiny window would have been breathtaking. That is when I knew, the Netherlands already had a hold on me, and I hadn't even left my seat. A murmur of low voices pushed forward as passengers made their way down the aisle.

"Coming?" Jack asked, tapping my shoulder.

I smiled and stood, craning my neck so it wouldn't hit the low ceiling. Everyone was eager to deplane. I waited until it was safe to merge into the aisle and move without a fight. A chill ran through my bones as I pulled the typewriter from the overhead compartment. The black handle pulsed with a slight electrical charge. The machine was awake inside its box. A small ping of fear hit me. What would I do if the typewriter went wild amongst the airport crowd? What would I say? Nothing came to mind. I would have to think fast on my feet I suppose, because I had no choice but to move forward. The buzzing grew uncomfortable within seconds.

Jack's eyes swelled wide when our feet hit the terminal. Schiphol was unlike any other airport either of us had ever seen. The typical fluorescent lights beamed down onto highly polished floors. Dozens of high-end shops filled the corridor that stretched and twisted on for what seemed like miles. Amongst the frenzy of lights, products, and passengers bouncing from gate to gate like ping-pong balls were small, brightly colored indoor playgrounds. Each detail introduced pure serenity into the surrounding chaos.

Trees stretched into circular openings in the ceiling that were intended to let the light shine in had it not been so overcast. A handful of people, women and children mostly, convened in seemingly relaxed conversation while propped against fake wooden logs. Two little girls turned in lazy circles under a rainbow of colored light sprinkling over their faces and dancing on the floor. Had we more time I would have given into to the childish whimsy pulling at me to go and play by their sides. I felt alive, alive in a way I had never experienced and quickly knew I would never feel the same again. This was even deeper than what I felt when my feet hit the pavement of Library Way in New York

City. Here, I knew I had finally arrived in the very place I have always belonged. It was both beautiful and unsettling.

Jack read the overhead signs, looking for baggage claim. He swiftly turned and grabbed my hand. I was falling behind.

"Come on," he said. "We need to find our bags."

I let him take the lead, tugging me along as I minded to the details around us. We wrapped ourselves through a dozen small shops. Our noses were delighted with the smell of fresh chocolate and cheese until Jack found a small elevator. The ride down was short, but when the doors rolled open, we stepped into a roaring crowd.

The place was bustling. Families and weary travelers pushed to the right. Others scattered to the left. Jack and I stopped in the center of the madness.

"I think baggage claim is over there," I motioned.

Jack ignored me and turned his attention to the left. Two massive sliding doors ground open, almost as if they were under his command, and revealed the underground train waiting to be unloaded. A large crowd had formed.

As more and more people made their way into the basement, the fury inside the case grew. My fingers burned and pulsed. I couldn't dare place it on the floor—who knew what would happen if I did. There were too many eyes to call the contents in question should the machine decide to call out its familiar cry: whiz-whiz-bang.

My hand burned under the strain as I waited for Jack to make a decision. Eyeing a clock on the wall, I realized I had lost six hours.

"Let's try over there before we get our bags," he said, pointing to a long mahogany counter lettered in solid gold, reading concierge.

At the far end of the desk stood a tall, statuesque blonde-haired, blue-eyed, fair-skinned Dutch boy. He couldn't have been older than twenty. His hair, longer on the top, was smoothed back, despite its slight wave. His blue button-down shirt, stitched with his name, matched his perfect blue eyes. He was textbook beautiful. My cheeks flushed red hot as Jack pushed me forward. When our eyes met, my head began to swim, and I nearly stumbled and fell flat on my face.

"Um," I said, unable to think of my own name.

"Hello," he answered, flashing a brilliant smile.

"Yeah, hi," I replied, flipping my hair around my open fingers and twisting it hard. I looked like an idiot, but I almost didn't care—almost. "Do you speak English?" I asked.

"I do," he replied. "I'm Bas, welcome to Amsterdam."

Without thinking, I slipped the typewriter onto the tall counter. Careful not to nudge anything off the counter, I leaned in.

"Bas," I repeated.

"Yes; may I point you in a particular direction?"

The way he said the word "particular" made me giggle. At the same time, his smile made me anxious.

"Yes Bas," Jack said, stepping forward, annoyed by my inability to simply speak. "We are trying to find a little city called Leiden. Do you happen to know the best way to get there?"

"Oh, you are going to Sleutelstad," he said, clapping his hands together.

I tried to mimic his words, but it came out a jumbled mess. "Sle-ut-e-stad," I stammered.

Bas laughed and winked. My face turned scarlet red. Jack cleared his throat to let me know he was not amused by our little exchange. Then he crudely pulled the typewriter from the countertop and pushed it into my hands.

"Here," he said.

Jack turned and faced Bas, "Leiden, is it the same as whatever you just said?"

"Yes sir, Leiden is referred to as Sleutelstad, the key city. I'm from a little village about forty-eight kilometers from there."

The typewriter popped under my fingers. The sudden jarring made me jump. My eyes flew to the case, waiting for another round of smoke and letters to slide through the case's cracks. As it made another loud pop, it hit me what Bas had just said. Leiden is the key city.

"I'm sorry, Bas, can you repeat that?" I urged. "Did you say the key city?"

Bas nodded respectfully.

"Jack," I rushed, pulling his attention to me. "The key city."

He looked confused.

"The key holds the answers," I whispered through gritted teeth.

It clicked. His eyes danced with excitement.

"Tell me, Bas, why exactly is Leiden called the key city?"

"The coat of arms of Leiden is two red keys." He crossed his fingers, forming an x. You see, if you find your way to St. Peter's church in the city of Leiden, look up. You'll see a white coat of arms with the red keys crossing like this. Some believe those keys open Saint Peter's gates in heaven. Others think they are cursed like the city itself. Leiden has a very interesting history."

"Cursed," I shuttered.

"Your backpack Elizabeth, where is it?"

"Spinning somewhere over on those baggage carousels," I replied harshly. I didn't want to check the bag, but the airline demanded we did. If it were lost, I am not sure what we would do.

"We need to hurry," Jack rushed.

"What is the best way to get to Leiden? Should we rent a car?"

"Take the train," Bas urged. "One should be leaving in about fifteen minutes. I would grab your things," he pointed to the right, "and then make your way to the underground train. Take train six to the train depot. You'll see Leiden on the board. It will take you straight there. Hurry though, this time of day the cars fill quickly. The next train after that doesn't leave until later tonight."

Jack and I thanked him and rushed towards baggage claim.

"Wait," Bas called out. Rounding the counter, he tossed a pile of tourist information in my hands, including a map. "I hope to see you in Leiden." His eyes danced.

"Me too," I whispered, and I set off after Jack.

Chapter 28: Unwelcome Reception

We barely made it onto the train. Settling in, the machine wasn't willing to surrender and continued to push forth its endless buzzing.

"Let's take a seat in the very back," I urged.

Jack followed. He was drained. His hair was disheveled, and his eyes were heavy. I knew I should have been feeling the waves of exhaustion too. Not only from the strain of jet lag, but also from the endless push I've made my body endure in the last week. I forced those thoughts away. I wanted nothing more than to get to work.

Jack collapsed into the seat. Ordering a hot tea, he scattered himself across the four-person table, leaving barely enough room for me. My thoughts were on Bas. Not only on his beauty or the draw I felt to him, but more on the important details he had imparted to us. One: that Leiden is known as the key city and two: that many believe it's cursed.

A light snore touched Jack's lips. He was gone. I pulled the tourist flyers and brochures from my backpack and began to study the information. Each pamphlet was just as boring as the next. Nothing noteworthy jumped out at me to help in our pursuit. The facts were typical—where to eat, what to see, where to stay. I tossed them on the table near Jack's head and watched the small cities flash by outside the huge picture window.

Gabled townhouses and wandering canals in tightly walled towns merged into the flat countryside. Tall, lush grass whipped in the wind. Out among the fields, windmills were strategically placed. Massive blades turned in the wind—slicing the air and moving it along the colored houses.

Minutes later, the most beautiful sight I had ever seen stretched out for miles. I straightened myself in my seat trying to get a better view.

"What is that?" I murmured.

A nearby employee laughed at my amazement. Answering the questions I hadn't intended anyone to hear, "Welcome to Holland," she said. "Those are the flower fields. You are lucky. This is the last week before the harvest."

The ground was carpeted with miles upon miles of bright tulips and daffodils. Perfectly straight lines of yellow merged to pink, then red, then orange, purple, and then the pattern started over.

"It must go on forever," I whispered. Leaning towards the train employee I asked, "Where do people live?"

"Inside the Windmills, dear." She laughed again.

"Amazing."

"Where are you headed?"

"To Leiden," I replied.

"Ahh, beautiful Leiden, dark and yet rich," she said.

"Dark?"

She left my inquiry alone.

"Did you know that is the birthplace to Rembrandt?"

"As in the painter?" I questioned.

"The very one."

"I didn't. Wow! Really?"

"Yes, really. Leiden is rich in history."

She disappeared but returned quickly handing me yet another brochure. I took it politely and tossed it amongst the others. As it landed, the words "notable inhabitants" caught my attention. The list boasted Leiden's most famous and accomplished residents. It began with William II, Count of Holland, who later became the King of Germany, and the list went on. Rembrandt and other painters and engravers were listed, although the rest were not quite as known as Rembrandt, but were noteworthy just the same. Near the bottom was a name I knew, Edward Y. Royal.

The small paper gave away more information than anything we had uncovered. It read, "Edward Y. Royal, Mayor of Leiden, inventor and business owner." I wasn't sure if I should shake Jack awake, catapulting him from his dreams, or keep the information to myself.

"Excuse me," I said to the kind employee who was now clearing cups and napkins from other guests.

"Yes," she smiled.

"This name, Edward Royal, do you know anything about him?" I tapped on the brochure roughly.

Instantly, her face turned cold. Her smile faded as a bubbling of rage swelled from within her.

"Why do you ask about him specifically, dear?" she questioned.

"His name is familiar," I declared. The voice in my head warned me against divulging the fact that Royal was my four-times-great-grandfather.

"Well," she said kindly, "I wouldn't worry too much about him. Leiden certainly has more notable people to focus your attention on."

"Why?"

251

"I'm sorry," she replied.

"Why wouldn't you worry about him? His accomplishments seem to be as notable as the others on this list otherwise he wouldn't be listed here."

"Heed my friendly warning. While Edward Royal is listed as a notable, he was anything but. The secrets surrounding that man, around his family, should be left in the past where they belong. Do you understand?"

I smiled and nodded, unwilling to say another word.

"I do mean what I say, dear. There is no reason to ask another question about Mr. Royal, not to me or anyone else. He's not worth the breath."

I shook Jack hard. His eyes flew open, unhappy to be disturbed.

"What is it?"

"Wake up," I demanded hotly.

"What's wrong?" he asked, pushing himself to a seated position.

"How long until we get off this train?"

"What is it, Elizabeth? What happened while I was sleeping?"

"People hate the Royals here."

Jack scuffled at my words, "And just how did you come to that conclusion?"

I leaned in and whispered the details of my exchange with the train employee. Jack adjusted himself on the berth, looked out the window, and said, "This may be harder than we thought."

Chapter 29: The Red Keys

The second the train ground to a stop at Leiden Centraal Rail and Bus station, Jack and I jumped from our seats and pushed our way to the exit. Daylight would be fading quickly, and time was fading with it. That, and I wanted to be rid of the train employee that hadn't relented in her glares since I inquired about my four-times-great-grandfather.

The Whizbang machine's power was greater than any force it had expelled since finding its way to me. The shock that took Jack down and earned him a few days in the hospital was mounting under my fingers. If I didn't let go soon, I would be in serious trouble.

"Move faster, Grandpa," I urged. My feet flew down the train steps and onto the blue cobblestone platform below.

Tension swelled, and the case began violently vibrating. I couldn't hold on any longer. My fingers sprang open, shaking from the intense voltage rushing through the case. My breath caught in my throat and before I could stop it, the case went crashing to the ground. A single spark shot out casting the smell of burnt plastic into the air. I looked at Jack, horrified.

"Pick it up," he demanded, "before someone sees. *Now!*"

Afraid of the burn, I yanked my jacket over my hand and used it like a glove. Even with the barrier between my flesh and the machine, the heat was almost too much to take.

"I need something that will secure the box to the suitcase," I rushed.

Jack scanned the train platform, roughly tugging at my clothes and said, "Give me your jacket."

In a matter of seconds, the two cases, the suitcase, and the machine were knotted together thanks to my jacket sleeves.

"There," Jack huffed.

His fingers curled slowly together like the legs of a dying spider. His pain was evident. The current wouldn't let up. The machine popped and sighed as it once again protested its entrapment in the case. Whiz-sizzle-whiz-POP. A whipping wind blew through the open platform just in time to catch the machine's BANG and swiftly carry it away. I grimaced. Between the cold, the dampness, and the machine's wild calls a single misstep of the smallest proportion could draw unwanted attention our way. Unwanted attention, not only by the locals but possibly by the authorities. It would be wise for us to find a place to stow the machine away for the night.

"It's angry," Jack whispered.

"I think it knows we're here," I replied.

"It will be dark before we know it. We better get a move on it."

Jack was reading my mind. Passengers trickled off the train by the dozens, each glancing in our direction.

"Anything in those maps tell you how far it is to the center of town?" Jack asked.

"It's not far," I answered. "I think it said it's only one kilometer from here. We could definitely walk."

"We can't get on a bus right now anyhow," Jack insisted, "not with the way the machine is acting. Come along, Elizabeth," he said, steaming ahead.

I hesitated, trying to read Jack's expression as I drew closer to his side. His eyes were tight with worry or pain, or perhaps both, but whatever else was concerning him. Together we rushed past a sea of rental bikes and made our way to the road. As we headed east, the flawless blue and gray cobblestone of the Centraal station turned to red stamped brick sidewalks and dark pavement.

"Have you let Laurel know we have arrived?" Jack answered.

"Not yet," I replied.

"You better call. I'm sure she is starting to worry."

Nodding, I pulled the phone from my backpack. My fingers curled over the edge and powered it on. Three messages flashed across the screen immediately.

LY: *Elizabeth, have you arrived? Is it amazing?*

LY: *Honey, are you okay? Have you arrived in the Netherlands?*

LY: *Lizzy, please call. I'm worried.*

I laughed to myself and quickly pounded out a response.

EY: *Sorry for the delay. All is well. We are in Leiden. It's cold here. Don't worry, please. We are headed to the city center now. Will call when we get settled into a hotel. It will be a while though. Mom, I love you.*

Three little bubbles popped onto the screen. Mom was responding.

LY: *You had me worried. I haven't put my phone down all day. Glad you are both well. Stay warm. Elizabeth, I LOVE you!*

I smiled and tossed the phone into the backpack and kept moving. We trudged through small alleyways, down narrow pebble streets, and over large pedestrian bridges flanking the canals. Buildings were stacked tall and wide, each marked with a different shade and tone—noting where one started and another ended. Thatched rooftops and brightly colored front doors were picturesque and about as alluring as anything I had ever seen. While I loved the thought that my ancestors had traveled these same paths, even if it was more than a hundred years before, I couldn't shake the odd sense of déjà vu once again pulsating through my blood. My heart was beating faster here. Perhaps it's my heart's way of telling me I'm home.

Flickers of sound, somewhat distorted by the roughness of our path, pushed from the machine and billowed in the air. Students, both young and old, fluttered by in easy conversation, some turning to see if their ears were playing tricks on them. As they did, I hummed and made crude instrument noises in hopes of diverting their curiosity.

Fifteen minutes after we arrived in Leiden, we were standing at the entrance of the most prominent landmark in the city, St. Peter's church, the place Bas said was supposedly marked with two red keys.

"Unreal," I gasped, craning my neck to see the gilded spires that pointed directly to the heavens above. Arched windows gave way to centuries-old stone. Angry-faced gargoyles and cherub angels were seated together in what looked like a meeting of good versus evil. Their feet were dangling dangerously over the sharp edges ready to break free from the rock, roar to life, and come tumbling down. Chills prickled down my spine as I studied the entire scene.

Jack smiled at the wonder painted across my face. His eyes had seen thousands of worldly treasures, but this was my first time.

"Do you see the set of keys anywhere?" he asked.

"No, do you?"

"No, maybe they're inside."

Jack approached the large redwood doors and pulled with all his might. They wouldn't budge. "It's locked. The church is closed."

"Do churches ever really close?" I mused.

"Apparently this one does," he replied. "See…" tapping at a sign, "Closed at four. We'll have to wait until tomorrow."

"Step back," I urged, "let's see if we can find the keys somewhere etched in the stone. Maybe it isn't as obvious as we think it should be."

Like the games of I-Spy I played with my father, Jack and I scrutinized every square inch of the cathedral's facade. Nothing. No red crossed keys. No indication of the Royal family's heritage locked in stone.

"Maybe it's on the other side," Jack said.

"Maybe."

Rounding the far eastern side of the church, a street fair was closing down for the evening. Vendors with makeshift tables lined the church's courtyard. One table, in particular, caught my eye.

"Jack!" I cried, slapping his shoulder, and then pointing.

"What?" he jumped.

"Look!"

"What am I looking for? Help your old grandfather out here."

"The dolls. Do you see them? It's like the doll dad brought home right before he passed. Miss Pegwood doll, remember?" I questioned. Another push of déjà vu smacked me hard. "This cannot be an accident."

Dozens of pegwood dolls, each individually handcrafted and designed, lined a table covered with a lavender cloth. A small child, no older than four, stood with her hands behind her back, rocking back and forth on her heels, admiring the unique toys. The vendor, tall, thin, with thick jet-black hair and daunting eyes, motioned for her to touch the table. The girl danced with delight.

I began to move forward, wanting to touch the dolls for myself. Jack clasped his fingers crudely around my arm, and hissed, "Let her play."

"I have to know if he made my doll," I urged, trying to wiggle free.

"And you will know," he said softly, "Let her play first. You're too eager. Still yourself, Elizabeth. You must be discerning with your words or you'll spill too much information."

I tried to calm myself down, but couldn't stand still. My knees bounced up and down while my feet moved from side-to-side. The precious pegwood dolly turned in swooping circles dangling from the mesmerized sweet little girl's arm. My insides pulled at me, begging me to rush over, shove the child away, and work to jump inside the vendor's head. Was he the one who sold my pegwood doll to my father? Did he know where the red keys were? Did my dad mention my name? Could he tell me more about the Royal family? My inner voice was growing so loud I wondered if anyone else could hear it. It was my turn. The little girl needed to hurry along.

"Hold still," Jack insisted.

"I can't," I whispered.

The child's mother joined her at the table, her arms filled with produce and bags of fresh coffee. She bent low, spilling part of her belongings. The child leaped to pick up the fresh tomatoes that hit the ground. While I couldn't hear their crouched exchange, I knew what the mother had asked. The sweet child blushed and pulled the doll tight to her chest. She was taking a pegwood home.

The entire transaction took no more than five minutes to complete, but within those five minutes came a massive piece of our puzzle that I had sorely missed. The pegwood dolls weren't dolls at all, but instead so much more.

The little girl leaned into the vendor whispering something in his ear. Delight stretched across his face. His belly bounced up and down with laughter as the child laid the pegwood back into his hands. Pulling the delicate clothes of raw silk and hand woven lace up to cover the dolls head, the man whittled something into its spine. When he was finished, he produced a key from behind his back and waved it like a wand over the little girl's small shoulders. She giggled with delight. With the doll and the key in her hand, the sweet child wrapped her arms around his legs. His body tensed and his shoulders flinched as his eyes caught mine.

"Thank you," the sweet girl called out while they skipped merrily away.

The enchantment the vendor wore was nothing but a show. His slimy ways quickly resurfaced as he dusted off his pants with a scowl. The very thought of the child's touch upset his being. Tossing the wooden dolls into hard, plastic bins with no regard for their beauty, he looked directly into my eyes once more.

"Jack," I said when I finally allowed myself to speak, "he gave her a key."

"I saw. Lizzy, the key, the one from the grandfather clock, is it in your backpack?"

"Yes," I replied. Immediately digging in the bag, I freed the key from the tangled pages and laid it in Jack's open hand.

"Come with me," he urged.

The vendor made short work of packing away the dolls. I forced myself to slow my steps as we approached. The unknown was getting the best of me.

"Excuse me," Jack said kindly, "do you speak English?"

The vendor turned and smiled, "A little," he answered. His accent was thick but understandable.

"I was hoping you could help us."

"Yes," he replied.

"I couldn't help but notice your dolls," I interpreted.

"I saw you admiring them from afar, dear child. Would you like one?"

"I have one actually. My father was here about eight years ago. He brought home a doll just like this. They're lovely," I added.

"Ah, well, your father would have purchased it from me," he replied. His hand hit his chest with pride. "My family has made these dolls exclusively for many centuries."

"You are the only vendor?" Jack said slowly.

"Yes, sir. They are very special dolls. Go ahead, pick one up, perhaps you need another, dear child."

"What makes them so special?" Jack questioned.

"You see, many have tried to copy our designs but have failed without the power of magic on their side. It's the dolls' purpose that makes them so special," he answered.

"And..."I pushed. "What exactly is that?"

The Whizbang machine buzzed inside its case—a quiet intensity started to build. Jack's eyes flew to mine, a silent warning to hurry my questioning along before the machine ramped out of control.

"Have you ever had a secret that you couldn't tell another living soul?" the vendor asked.

"You have no idea," I laughed.

"Well, the pegwood dolls are not just playthings— pretty little dolls to sit high on a shelf, but instead they are *Geheim Poppens*."

"*Geheim Poppens*?" Jack and I asked in unison.

"G—P," I said slowly. "What does that mean in English?" I pushed.

"Secret dolls," he quickly answered.

Secret dolls, of course, I thought.

261

"My four-times-great-grandfather created the figurines. Secrets become our keepers as much as we become theirs. The *poppens* keep and protect even our darkest troubles." He laughed darkly.

The typewriter called out from its case, this time a bit louder. The vendor eyed me sharply, but I refused to look away or turn towards the machine tied to my suitcase. I kept my eyes focused on him and the line of stacked dolls that remained on the table. My heart raced as the machine popped and whizzed. The man's eyes tightened as they flickered back and forth between the case, Jack, and me. Darkness grew on his face and suddenly he waved his hands in the air. First his right hand, then his left, each swirling in wild, wide circles, then tight, tiny spirals, creating a peculiar rhythm as if he were conjuring up magic. When he was done, an odd sensation took over. Just as I gasped for air, a woman's voice filled the courtyard. Jack's face went ghost white.

His head twisted around, looking for where the singing was coming from.

"The choir must be practicing," the man delighted.

Jack's eyes locked into mine, his body trembled under each push of sound. As the voice reached a fever pitch, my belly began to burn.

Regaining his voice, "How do the dolls work?" Jack pushed.

"It's simple. You pick your *poppen*—one that most represents the child you will be gifting it to. Most children choose a doll that looks most like them or has a connection to something they love."

Alice, I thought. Dad had chosen a dolly he said looked like Alice. I tried to hold on to the information the vendor was saying, but the singing was making my head swim.

"You tell me a secret code or place," the vendor continued, "I whittle that code onto the doll's back; it's the least likely place someone would look for a clue or your hidden treasure, whatever that may be. Then I give you a key. That key locks your secrets away so that no one else may hear or see them unless they are given the key. It's fun for the children." He smiled, "Like a game, you know. It's a curse to know the truth sometimes—it can cost you everything. Can't it?" As he finished speaking, his eyes went cold.

My head pounded. The music grew to a near deafening pitch. The atmosphere outside the church changed; it became heavy with a mixture of beauty and sadness. The lightness I felt when we first arrived was now gone. It was replaced by a severe blackness that was working to take over. Jack gasped for air as the woman's voice hit an unthinkable high note.

"What is that?" I shouted, turning on my heels, stealing a look, "My head!"

In the far corner, barely within sight, a woman cowered. Her dark eyes were swimming in anger as her mouth pushed the most extraordinary sounds beyond her lips. I knew who she was—*the woman* from my dream. The one who forced my hands onto the machine. An alarm sounded within me, and as her voice bounced off the courtyard walls Jack bent over and wrenched in pain.

"Jack," I gasped, spending no time considering how it would make logical sense for her to be here, I shook my head in disbelief. "I… Jack…How? It's the woman."

"My chest," he moaned.

All at once, the music stopped. Silence filled the courtyard and then erupted in applause.

Looking back, struggling to catch another glimpse of the woman, the crowd moved, blocking my view, and when it settled she was gone. I tried to convince myself that it was all in my head. That exhaustion and jet lag had to be getting the best of me, but to my right, Jack was still bent, clutching at his chest while his face was still an incredibly dangerous shade of white. I hesitated and then leaned into Jack, "Please tell me you heard that too?"

"I heard it," he whispered. "She's following us."

"How?"

"I don't know," he gasped, "but he summoned her. I saw him do it. We need to get out of here."

Jack straightened his back and tried to speak. His voice was harsher than usual, but he managed to say, "Is this one of your keys?"

"May I?" the vendor asked, plucking it out of Jack's fingers.

The corner of his mouth turned up in delight, "It is. See here," pointing at the key, "The GP is stamped in the center of the key—*Geheim Poppen*. Do you have the doll, sir?" he asked. "I would like to see it."

"Sadly, I left it at home," I said, lowering my eyes. "I have a feeling her secrets would be very intriguing to you right about now."

Jack's hot hand slapped my wrist, his fingers digging deep and squeezing angrily. "That's quite enough."

Quickly and silently, I lowered my head, looking down at the cobblestone. Jack was right; I needed to shut my mouth. He cleared his throat significantly, and extended his hand, "You have been very helpful," he smiled, taking the key from the vendor's hand despite his reservation in returning it. "The dolls are extremely clever. I wish you the best of luck."

"Tell me," the vendor said, "What does your doll look like? They are all different. No two are ever alike."

"She looks like my favorite book character," I replied with a smile. "Thank you for your help."

"Wouldn't be Alice in Wonderland, would it?" he questioned.

A sudden howl came from the Whizbang machine that made Jack whip around.

"I, I, I..." I sputtered.

The merchant flicked his wrist, threatening to summons the music once more. The machine shot a dark red flare from its box, whizzing and banging so loudly anyone standing witness could not ignore it. Jack's eyes darted around the courtyard.

"I almost forgot," Jack shrilled. His voice so thunderous everyone turned their attention in our direction, quickly forgetting the odd noises firing from the hard case.

The diversion was brilliant.

"One more thing, if you don't mind. Do you happen to know if the church has two red keys etched anywhere?"

The vendor smirked and pointed above his head. "This," he asked.

"Yes," Jack shouted.

The machine hissed and then fell silent. It had gotten its point across. We hadn't yet found what we came for: the red keys.

Hanging directly above the pegwood table was a large coat of arms seated in the center of a red-bricked roof pitch. The entire display couldn't have been more than two feet by two feet, but it was still significant.

The corners of the crest rippled away from the sides, rolled like an ancient scroll. At the top was a weighted and thorny crown cast in perfect white stone. In the center were two red keys, crossed in an x, as Bas the airport concierge said they would be.

"Peter's keys," the vendor smiled. "They are said to open the gates of heaven."

Jack nodded slowly, "The answer lies under the key. Isn't that what the typewriter wrote?"

"Yes," I replied through gritted teeth, "Do you think it meant the dolls?"

"Maybe," he replied.

"Tell me, why are they hung here and not on the front of the church?" Jack asked.

"This was the original entrance," the vendor replied. "That and it is said that Leiden is cursed. Legend has it that the grounds the church sits on played a role in a series of misfortunes placed on our city. As the story is told, more than a hundred years ago, some of the church clergies got together and hung this shield over the door to allow anyone who passed through to be cleansed of the jinx. Like Peter's keys are said to open the gates of heaven, the red keys are said to shelter those who pass."

"Curse," I said rapidly, "What kind of curse? You're the third person who has alluded to a curse on Leiden, but no one has said what it was…what it is?"

The vendor's eyes narrowed. As he shook his head, he said, "And no one will. We do not speak of the curse, my child."

"But…" I stammered.

Wickedness covered the vendor's face as he chanted, "One thousand and forty years the curse will remain until the rightful owner shall turn back the hands of time and correct a Royal mistake. The secret will eat away at those who come to play like a disease," he growled. "Seek the curse and it will find you!"

A blast of cold covered my body. Pop! Sizzle! Bang! The Whizbang machine summoned our attention. A flash of raw white light skittered across the sky. Jack yanked my arms as thunder rolled overhead.

A bone-chilling laugh flew from the vendor's mouth and the music slowly began once more. This time it started as a low hum.

"Let's go!" Jack screamed.

I repeated the sinister words the vendor chanted, "One thousand and forty years the curse will remain until the rightful owner shall turn back the hands of time and correct a Royal mistake. The secret will eat away at those who come to play like a disease."

After the tenth time the words crossed my lips, I was certain I had them locked inside my head. Jack had us moving at a near run, refusing to speak.

"What just happened?" I asked. "Do you think he knows we're tied to the Royals? That woman, the singing; she is here, Jack."

"You aren't tied to the Royals, Elizabeth. You are a Royal," Jack grunted. "We need to find a place to bed down for the night. We need to call Laurel and find out what is whittled into the back of that doll."

"He said a Royal mistake. What did he mean?"

Jack stopped hard and leaned his nose in so close it was nearly touching mine. His hot breath burned my eyes.

"Elizabeth, not another word. Listen to me carefully. We need to be extremely cautious about what is said from now on. The deeper we dig, the more questions we ask, the greater the suspicion will grow around us," Jack warned.

"I know, but Grandpa, we are up against the impossible. We'll never know what secret Dad whispered to the vendor when he bought the pegwood in the first place. I hate to say this, but maybe it's best if we go home."

"Elizabeth, I promise to keep you safe. The only thing we need to do right now is to call your mother. We need to know what was whittled into the back of that doll. If it looks like we are in serious danger, I promise, we'll go home. We're a team, you and me. I promise we'll make our decisions together, but first, the doll."

Chapter 30: 52° 9' 0" N/4° 30' 0" E

The damp, cold wind picked up and pushed Jack's graying hair into his eyes.

"I don't think I can handle the cold much longer," I shivered. My teeth harshly chattered with each new push of wind.

"Keep walking, we'll find a hotel soon."

Jack fidgeted as he led the way, moving us swiftly through the hidden back streets and small courtyards of the city. We were slipping away from the beautiful water, the windmills, and ancient buildings, but most importantly, we moved out of sight of the crowds. Jack's anxiety was getting the best of him. Every few steps, his eyes bolted over his shoulder to make sure the strange vendor hadn't decided to abandon the precious pegwood dolls and take chase after the two of us. Grandpa Jack wanted distance. I wanted a warm, safe place to lie down. The last light of the day was nearly gone now, and within a few minutes of walking, we were deep in the belly of a darkening Leiden.

"Look around," Jack urged. "Do you see them?"

"The keys?" I questioned. "They have been on nearly every building for the last few blocks."

"It's interesting, don't you think?" Jack asked.

"What I think is whatever the Royal family did left a profound mark on this beautiful city."

A nasty ping of guilt found me. Whatever awfulness happened, whatever changed Leiden forever, I was a part of it, even if we didn't want to admit it. Each red key was to help guard against our family's misgivings.

"Or," Jack suggested, "what if whatever happened isn't as bad as we think? Maybe this is more like a bad case of a rumor mill spiraling out of control. One person could have twisted even the smallest detail all those years ago, and a hundred and thirty years later people still believe in some idiotic curse."

"I would agree with you if the Royals hadn't run. How often do people leave everything they own, choose to be penniless, and travel thousands of miles by boat in the dead of winter just to escape a little rumor?"

Muffled footsteps echoed at the far end of the alleyway. Jack panicked and grabbed my arm, "Let's move," he urged. "We'll talk about this later."

Rounding the corner and having emerged from the dark alley, the beauty of Leiden was once again before us. The city lights reflected brightly off the water. It looked like one of the many postcards Jack has sent over the last eight years.

"There is a hotel over there," Jack pointed to the other side of the waterway.

"No, there," I replied.

On the far corner, at the end of the street, stood a quaint three-story building. Its classic red- and white-striped window awnings and brightly painted doors, the color of minty green moss, called my name. Three light blue flags with the name Hotel Nieuw Minerva printed in white hung near each door. Despite occupying a full city block, the inn was inconspicuous. It would be the perfect place to hide in plain sight should the locals become bothered by our prodding. No one ever looks for something in the most obvious of places.

The dwelling was also missing one other important detail. There were no red keys over the entrance. Even though I didn't know why, it felt safer somehow.

The lobby was warm and dim. It smelled of steamed milk and hot espresso. Replicas of classic Rembrandts hung tastefully on the walls, a nod to his birth and time in Leiden. Old keys, each a different shade of red, hung on the wall behind the welcome desk. Jack secured the keys to our suite, and we made our way to the third floor.

The room was beautiful, but there was very little time to take in the overwhelming detail. We needed to call Mom.

"Where's the phone?" Jack questioned.

"It's in the backpack," I replied.

Settling into the small couch nearest the windows, I pulled a soft blanket over my legs and watched the boats float along the canal. Grandpa Jack dialed the phone and put it on speaker. Mom picked up on the first ring, and Jack immediately launched into the story of the vendor and the red keys. When he was done, he left no room for small talk. I zoned in and out of the conversation, my eyes growing more tired by the minute. Jack's hand hastily scribbled notes across a small pad he found on the nightstand. Thirty minutes later, he said goodbye and tossed the pad in my direction.

"52° 9' 0" N/4° 30' 0" E," I read aloud, "What do these numbers mean?" I asked, straightening myself amongst the dense pillows.

"That is what is whittled on the back of the doll," Jack answered. "Weren't you listening?"

"Not really," I answered truthfully.

"It's a location—longitude and latitude. It's the answer to whatever your father whispered to the pegwood vendor."

"Why would he put coordinates on the back of the doll? Why wouldn't he ask the vendor to carve in the actual location?"

Jack busily unpacked my backpack, scattering files and pictures across a small desk in the middle of the suite. Without looking up, he said, "My guess is he wanted you, and only you, to find it wherever this leads. That and I'm sure he had already formed a major distrust of everyone in this city by the time he purchased the doll.

"First thing in the morning, we'll figure out the coordinates. For now, let's order room service and look over the documents we have so far. Maybe the answer is within the files, and we've simply overlooked it since we didn't have all the information."

Two hours went by, and the only thing that we found were more questions and greater confusion.

"I'm tired," I whined.

"It is late, Elizabeth. You should probably sleep. We have another long day ahead of us tomorrow."

"Okay," I replied.

Jack stretched his arms over his head. "I could use a little shut-eye myself."

He tossed the pen in his hand onto the desk and closed the file, standing to gather his things to prepare for bed. Light flickered in the room from the streetlamps below our windows. We both looked around the cozy suite, taking in the loveliness of it all before going for our suitcases. Resting in the corner, my bag and the Whizbang machine were still secured together thanks to my jacket.

The absence of the annoying humming and fiery electricity was nice, yet, unsettling too. Something was off. The machine hadn't pushed its wild frenzy upon us since we left the church's courtyard. My mind reeled with possibilities, questions…why had it become so quiet? Internally, I told myself, *the machine can wait,* and I forced myself to change into my favorite pajamas and find a small section of the oversized bed to settle into. Jack took the couch.

I struggled to keep my mind and body still. My head was clogged with checklists and clues, loose ends and incomplete connections. I tossed and turned. When I had run through the list for the tenth time, my brain switched over to the chilling vendor's voice.

"One thousand and forty years the curse will remain until the rightful owner shall turn back the hands of time and correct a Royal mistake."

My brain moved fast to dissect his words. Royal—that was obvious. He meant Edward. Rightful owner—the lady in Morocco told Aden that he could not release the machine until he found the rightful owner. Jack convinced Aden that someone was me. Now, it seemed that woman had followed us here. The last part of the curse is what had me stumped. The curse will remain until the hands of time are turned back, I whispered.

Think Elizabeth, I commanded, but my mind wouldn't listen. No new ideas came. I was stuck listening to the curse's repeat on an endless loop.

An hour later, I gave up on sleep. Quietly pulling the sheets back, I slipped out of bed and found the typewriter's case. My movement stirred Jack from his slumber.

"What are you doing?" he asked.

"Aren't you the slightest bit curious why the machine has gotten so quiet?"

"Elizabeth, let's wait until the morning. You need to get some sleep."

"Jack," I gawk. "I've been laying in that bed for over an hour. I can't fall asleep."

"Then try another hour," he replied.

A mess of freshly typed papers covered the machine's top. Gone too was the electrical field I had grown accustomed to fearing. A soft yellow light that seemed far more innocent and less powerful pushed out from under the keys.

Jack made me jump as he leaned over my shoulder, "Wow," he muttered. "What do the papers say?"

Uncertain if the new light was a peace offering from the machine or a new level of rigid power, I hesitated.

"Go ahead," Jack urged, "Pick up the papers."

I drew in a deep breath, sucking all the air I could hold inside my chest, stepped closer to the machine, and snatched the papers from the cold heap of metal. Nothing happened. The machine did not respond in the way it had each time before; instead, the light grew in its brilliance.

"How oddly beautiful," Jack whispered.

Dozens of papers filled my hands. Most repeated the same ramblings that had been typed before we left home, but one caught my eye.

History is not correct. Correct it.
Correct it. The secret begins to unravel at
the tomb. 52° 9' 0" N/4° 30' 0" E near the
red keys. Be careful. Eyes are watching.
Secrets will eat you alive.

"A graveyard? The coordinates are to a graveyard,
Elizabeth. They have to be. Look at the word tomb," he
muttered.

"Why? Why would my father be lurking around a
graveyard?" I whispered.

"I don't know," Jack replied. "But there has to be
several cemeteries in this city. Find a phone book, maybe
we can narrow down our options that way."

"We don't need to, Jack. I know where the coordinates
lead. I saw a sign on the way out of the church courtyard. It
says the secret begins to unravel at the tomb near the red
keys. All of the buildings we passed only had one key over
the doorway. The only place I saw with two keys was the
church. We're looking for a tomb somewhere on the church
property."

"Nice catch kid," Jack beamed. "Get dressed in
something warm. If eyes are watching, we better go under
the cloak of night."

Chapter 31: The Tomb

The moon was bloated and suspended low in the night sky. Its brilliant light shined into the quiet hotel lobby and cast eerie shadows on everything it touched. The only light, besides the moon, came from the small check-in desk that was unoccupied.

"Where is everyone?" I whispered to Jack.

"Looks like the hotel is closed for the night, doesn't it?"

Out of nowhere, an employee, dressed in a four-piece gray suit, rushed to our sides as we headed towards the door, "Hello, sir, madam, all okay? May I help you?"

Jack and I both jumped—startled by the sudden intrusion, "Hello," Jack replied, brushing past.

"You need something. You are in the suite, no? I can bring something to your room."

"Yes. No. I mean yes we are in the suite. No, we do not need anything, but thank you. It's kind of you to offer. We'll be back shortly," Jack nodded and pushed the mossy-green door open and motioned me forward.

"Go," he commanded.

The streets of Leiden matched the inside of the hotel. The boat taxis had docked for the night. Restaurants and pubs had pulled their shades and closed their doors. The crowds had gone home; nothing was left on the streets but the cold and a few overhead lamps that were still burning. The further we meandered away from the hotel the more I wrestled with the feeling of being watched. Breathe, I reminded myself. All is well.

The cobblestone road ended at the next corner, with several more footbridges ahead. A group of young college coeds huddled together on the sidewalk, laughing. Each were taking a spin on a bicycle that clearly wasn't theirs. As we drew closer, no one in the group even bothered to look up. Yet, I couldn't shake the sensation of a thousand eyes scrutinizing my every move.

I risked a quick glance over my shoulder as we turned onto the first bridge. Standing in the distance was the bellhop from inside the hotel. With one foot propped against the white facade, he pressed his body against the wall awkwardly. A ring of smoke encircled his head. The darkness cast shadows across his face, but I knew it was him. The suit gave him away.

I turned, trying to shake off the intrusion when I saw a second man approach. The way the man moved struck me as familiar.

Breathe, Elizabeth, breathe, my mind cautioned.

The light shining from the lampposts fell just short of their boots, making it impossible to see either of their faces through the dark screen of obscurity. The bellhop fidgeted nervously. I held their glares for a moment, then whipped my head around and caught Jack's arm, "Without being obvious, look back at the hotel," I said in a dry whisper.

Jack moved a couple of feet and then risked a quick glance over his shoulder, "The two men?" he questioned.

"Yes, the bellhop has been watching us since we left," I replied.

"I can't see their faces."

"Me either, but it looks like the vendor, doesn't it?"

Jack looked forward and then back again, "I don't know, maybe."

"I'm pretty sure it's him," I replied. "Why would he be at the hotel? At our hotel?"

"Who knows, but if it is him, we are safer here than at the hotel. Keep moving and don't look back. Let's find the graveyard and try to figure out what the machine and your father have been trying to tell us. I doubt the men will be waiting for us when we return. It's cold, and I'm exhausted. Let's get a move on it."

Intently listening to our quiet footsteps, I counted each one to soothe the panic running away with my mind. At the foot of the bridge, I rose onto my toes, trying to catch one last glimpse of the two men before we moved out of sight, but they were gone. The front of the church was less than five hundred feet away. Bright lights flooded the holy grounds.

"Which way?" Jack muttered.

"The courtyard is to the right. I bet the graveyard is around back."

Together we hurried past several displays of stone statues and historical markers on the southernmost side of the church until Jack spotted a thick, overgrown pathway.

"Down there," Jack motioned.

I followed reluctantly. The path was thick with brush. Branches blew in the whipping breeze, beating the ground. A small marble marker noted what used to be a clear and easy path to the graveyard beyond the brush. Jack bent low, pushing his way into the small clearing.

"Be careful," he urged. "I can hardly see. Watch your face, some of these bushes have thorns."

"There has to be another way down," I insisted.

"Too late," Jack replied. "This one is away from prying eyes. Remember what the machine said, 'eyes will watch.'"

I sighed, dropping to my belly, and slithered my way into the damp, red muck. Jack held the low-hanging branches back long enough to allow me to slip next to him. When he let go, he lost his footing. The damp dirt gave way and sent Jack tumbling. Clouds of dust blew in my face, unsettled by his fall.

"Grandpa Jack!" I shrieked. "Jack!"

Silence.

"Jack!" That same edge of anxiety bubbled in my belly. "Jack?"

Thorns ripped at my skin—the same skin that was still raw from the bushes at the library. Branches whipped in the brisk breeze, lashing at my face and striking my back almost simultaneously. Everything burned as I clambered out of the path and struggled to my feet. Crosses and statues jetted out from weathered tombs adding a sense of mystery amongst the greenest field my eyes had ever seen. We had stumbled into a city of the dead.

"Jack, where are you?" I whispered hotly. More dust rose from behind while the rocks I had upset on the path continued to roll out and strike at my heels.

"Ouch," I chomped bitterly, "We had to go down that way, didn't we? Jack?"

"Down here," he moaned.

Shuddering at the sudden bleakness in his voice, I answered his call, "Where?"

"Here," Jack painfully waved his arm in the air to draw my attention to him. A dirty combination of sweat, blood, and dampened earth dripped from his limb. I wasn't sure what was more unsettling: the fact that he was bleeding again or that he was sitting against someone's headstone.

"Are you okay?" I asked, making my way to his side.

"I think so," he muttered.

"I'll go for help."

"No," he rushed. "I'll be okay. It's just a few cuts and bruises."

"It always is," I chuckled.

"Nice one," he groaned, pulling himself to a standing position. His back stayed bent, unable or unwilling to straighten it from the pain.

"Jack, are you sure you are okay?"

"Not exactly a hundred percent, kid, but I'm fine. Next time, we find another way around."

"Uh," I replied.

Clusters of sun-bleached tombs stretched out for as far as our eyes could see.

"This place is huge," I sighed.

At the far end of the twisting cemetery sat a small cabin. A warm, dim light glowed in the window.

"Shh," I said, pointing to the window.

"It's probably the groundskeeper's house."

"What exactly are we looking for?" I asked.

"I don't exactly know. Maybe a Royal's grave?" Jack guessed.

We split up, each wandering through different sections of the cemetery. Most of the markers were now too worn to read.

"Here's a Royal," I motioned, bending low to read the full inscription, "Pieter Royal 1660." I jumped back, "He died of the plague."

"That's too old. Keep looking."

"Not a problem," I said, shaking myself clean. Rationally, I knew I couldn't catch the plague from a guy who had been dead for three hundred and fifty-five years, but it still made my skin crawl.

"Here's another: Maria Royal, 1701," I called, this time I forced myself not to read beyond the crypt dweller's name.

"Not that one either," he replied. "It needs to be at least dated in the late 1800s if it has anything to do with Edward."

In the center of the boneyard, an eight-foot-tall rusted scrolling iron gate guarded a marble valet. The once paper white marble that covered the flat tomb had turned yellow with oxidation and time. The elements hadn't been kind to this final resting place. Still, without looking at the name, I instinctively knew this was what we had come for.

"Jack, over here. Hurry!"

As I drew closer, several things struck me. The stone grave was smaller than normal. It had to be that of a child's. Two, the hand-soldered gate was at least a hundred years old, but in the center of the mausoleum was a newer marker with the name Alina Amelia Royal. Born December 7, 1872. Died October 3, 1876.

"Jack, it's her!" I yelled. "I found Edward's third child!"

Jack emerged out of the shadows, his muscles tight as he approached. Patting my back, he hissed, "The headstone…"

"I know," I replied. "It doesn't make sense. Why would someone replace the marker after all this time?"

"And only the marker. The rest appears to be untouched."

Jack studied the gated display. "Her death must have been significant to the city seeing how she occupies the center of the graveyard," he speculated. "There are gravesites of more highly prominent figures tucked away in the corner back there, so why does a—" Jack stopped to do the math, "a four-year-old hold the center spot?"

Jack leaned in as close as the enclosure would allow. His eyes struggled to adjust to the little light that was available. "What is so important about you, little Alina?"

My fingers followed the worn iron, tracing their way to the backside of the grave. The metal bent, stretching upward, creating a gateway to enter Alina's shrine—a locked shrine with a sparkling new padlock.

"Huh," I grunted, flipping the lock up and over. It crashed hard against the gate.

"Elizabeth," Jack jumped.

"Sorry."

Directly above the iron handle, a series of numbers were etched into the rusted iron. 52 ° 9' 0", I read. "Jack, remind me of the coordinates carved into Miss Pegwood?"

He quickly rambled off the sequence. It was a perfect match to the scoring in the gate. Next to the last number was the symbol of the curse: the two red keys.

"Jack," I said in a hush. "You need to see this."

He moved between the graves, refusing to turn his back on the groundkeeper's house in the distance, afraid things might change at any minute. But once he made his way to my side, his body relaxed as he clapped, "You found it!"

"Where's the key?" I asked holding my hand open impatiently. It was all here. The answer lies under the keys. My fingers tapped against the gate. "This is what Dad wanted us to find. There has to be something waiting for us inside the enclosure."

Jack pulled the key from his pocket and laid it in my hand, "Go ahead. You do the honors."

My face twisted at his words. Twinges of unsettling guilt found my middle. This was a child's grave. A child that was my aunt, even if her life was snuffed out at the tender age of four. It wasn't right to disturb her final resting place. I stared at the lock for a moment longer.

"If we are going in, we better go in now," Jack urged.

"I'm not sure this old gate will open. The hinges are badly rusted."

Jack pulled at the door, testing the sturdiness. His feet slipped into the bottom openings. Deep moans sighed as the old man's weight moved the gate back and forth, "Give it a try. I'm pretty sure it will open."

The key, stamped GP, slid into the shiny padlock and popped the lock open. Jack heaved the gate open. The eerie groan of reluctance called out from the unoiled iron. When the high-pitched noise stopped, Jack and I ducked into our ancestor's grave.

"Do you see anything out of the ordinary?" Jack asked.

"Other than the fact that we are standing in a grave?" I replied. "No."

A small round light shot in our direction.

"Get down," Jack tugged.

"Who's out there?" I asked.

"*Wie is er*?" A man's voice yelled in the near distance. "*Wie is er*?"

"What is he saying?" I cried.

"I don't know," Jack pushed. "Be quiet. Do you want to be caught?"

The flash of light drew closer, coming up a nearby hill. Jack and I crouched low, trying to hide behind Alina's tomb. A sudden wind caught the open gate and slammed it shut. The iron barrier trembled, giving away our position. Every fiber of my body shook with fear.

"Who's out there?" the man shouted.

Jack tapped my shoulder, silently pointing to another shiny padlock. I nodded and handed him the key. With the flick of his wrist, the key slid in, popped open the second lock, and within seconds, he jerked the marble tomb open barely wide enough to push me deep inside.

The smell was overwhelming; a mixture of stale death and caged decay filled my nose. A small coffin, no longer than three feet, lay respectfully in the far corner. A wild scream, mixed with unsettling madness and complete horror, was building in the pit of my stomach. My eyes slammed shut as hot, salty tears began to pour. This was far more vile than anything I had ever witnessed. My stomach lurched involuntarily. Jack's hand flew to my mouth and locked the distress inside.

"Open your eyes," Jack pled through clenched teeth.

"No," I sobbed, "no."

"Open them, Elizabeth. I need you to look at the wall."

"Who's out here? *Wie is er?*" called from outside the gate.

Neither Jack nor I moved. His hand covered my face until everything was dead silent again. Once it was safe to speak, Jack peeled his hand from my mouth, "Don't scream," he ordered.

I nodded, unwilling to say a word until we were safely out of the crypt.

Jack crawled to the far wall, snatching a dusty manila folder that had been secured to the wall some time ago.

Curiosity got the best of me, "What is it?"

"It's number 8, it's the missing microfilm from the library file," Jack replied.

"We need to get out of here," I demanded.

Jack slipped out of the mausoleum first; making sure it was safe for us to escape. He waved me forward, one finger over his lips. Crawling forward, sucking in as much fresh air as my lungs could hold, I sighed, "Agh."

"Move quickly," Jack beckoned.

Together we took off running, winding our way through the cemetery, up a small hill, and around the backside of the church. The path we took before was completely unnecessary, it seemed. It didn't matter now. Neither of us stopped running until we veered to a stop in front of the hotel's bright green doors.

"What if the bellhop and vendor are waiting in the lobby?" I panted.

"Then we deal with them," Jack replied.

"Are you ready?" he asked, plucking grass from my hair.

"As ready as I will ever be."

The hotel lobby was once again empty. Even the small desk light at the check-in desk had been extinguished. Jack's shoulders slumped in relief.

"Let's take the stairs," he said.

Our suite was on the far end of the hall, on the right. As we rounded the stairwell, something was off. Our door was standing wide open.

"Did you shut the door when we left?" he stammered.

"You were the last one out," I hissed.

Jack dropped the file, sprinting towards the suite to catch whoever was brave enough to enter our room uninvited. I froze. Jack threw himself into the darkness. Seconds later, he returned to the hallway.

"Elizabeth. Elizabeth," he shook, barely able to breathe or speak. I knew what he was about to say.

"No," I cried, "no."

"It's—gone," Jack said swallowing the words harshly. "The Whizbang machine, it's gone, Elizabeth."

Chapter 32: A Tunney or a Royal?

The faded blue walls of the third floor rapidly began to close in around me. Churning black spots filled my vision as my insides went painfully numb. My mind tried to process what this would mean for us, for my mother. No machine meant there was no way to break the curse. This was a death sentence.

"No," I blubbered, "it can't be. It's in there; it has to be. You didn't look in the right place!" My gut burned as panic took over.

"No, Lizzy, it's gone."

"Why?" I stammered. Tears burst from my eyes. "Why would someone steal the machine?"

"It's valuable," he replied. "I'm sure a machine of that age could be sold for a hefty sum to the right dealer."

"No, it has to be something else. There has to be another reason. That vendor, he had to have known what was inside the case when we were in the church square. It was whizzing and banging when we were talking to him. The woman was singing. Then he recited the curse that was clearly connected to the machine. He was standing out of our hotel when we left. It was him!"

"You are forgetting the machine's little displays at the airport, on the train, and at the train station," Jack muttered. "Didn't you say you had a questionable exchange on the train with an employee too? Any one of those people could have stolen the machine."

"I did have an exchange with a train employee, but it wasn't over the machine. It was about Edward. The typewriter was completely quiet during the train ride."

"The lobby was dark when we came in, right?" I pondered.

"Yes," Jack said slowly, drawing out each letter.

"Why would a bellhop be on the clock until after midnight but then not at his station three hours later? That doesn't make sense. The lights were even off in the lobby."

"You're right."

"He watched us until after we made it over the bridge. He was up to something otherwise why would he have cared if we left? Why would he have taken the time to watch us? Maybe there was more to the plan than just coming into the room and taking the typewriter. It was them, Jack. We left and gave them the perfect opportunity to slip into our room unnoticed and take the machine without a fight."

Grandpa Jack was only partially listening, his eyes locked into a small red light flashing from the ceiling down the hall.

"What's wrong...besides the obvious?" I asked.

"Do you see that?" he pointed.

I followed Jack's vision, coming to rest on the red light.

"The light?" I asked. "What is that?"

Jack bounded down the hall, "I don't know, but I intend to find out," he said, dragging a small chair from the corner.

"Be careful," I whispered in a hush.

Grunting to push the ceiling tile back, Jack wobbled on the slick wooden chair. Pressing with all his might, a small black object fell from its hiding spot in the ceiling. Jack ducked to avoid being hit by the swinging black cable.

"Bingo!" he cried. "We've got them now, Lizzy. The bellhop must have not known that the hallway was equipped with surveillance. As long as this little baby was recording when the intruders busted in, we've got them. What time is it?"

"3:18 a.m.," I replied.

"Come on," he said, stepping off the chair, "We need to think this through."

"What is there to think through?" I chomped, following him to our room. "The machine is gone, and so is my chance to save my mother. Who cares what the video says. It won't bring back the machine."

"That isn't necessarily true. There is only one small catch. We're going to have to do something I didn't want have to do," Jack muttered.

Fifteen minutes later, the Hotel Nieuw Minerva was crawling with the finest from the "Korps Nationale Politie."

Jack and I were separated. Both of us were questioned for over an hour while men in heavy blue coats and thick-soled boots reviewed the surveillance video and dusted for fingerprints.

"Sir, please see," an officer with broken English requested.

Jack and I joined the three officers huddled around a small desk. The video was paused on the moment Jack and I left our room. I did everything I could to still my breath and my heart.

"*Spreekt u Nederlands?*" the officer at the end queried.

"I'm sorry," Jack replied. "We only speak English. We're American."

Jack placed his right hand over his heart as though he was about to recite the pledge. A snicker broke through my teeth.

"What?" he said.

I shook my head, turning my eyes down, trying to hold in a burst of unnecessary laughter being driven by lack of sleep and stress.

The officer nodded with a smile. Neither of the men understood the other. The officer in the middle, who had taken charge since the team arrived, turned in his chair. He sat motionless, studying my face.

"Where are you from in America?" he asked.

His English was flawless.

"New York," I replied.

"I hope to go there one day," he smiled.

"You should," I replied. "It's the most amazing place on earth."

"Yes. Now please, can you tell me where you two were going at this time of night? Why did you leave this hotel after midnight?"

Jack cleared his throat. I knew the lies were already forming in his mind. He was ready for whatever questions we would be asked; it was my job to stand back, listen, and back up his mistruths.

"We arrived in Leiden earlier this evening. One of our bags was lost by the airlines. It's probably still in Canada for all I know, but it was one that held my personal toiletries. We left to see if we could find a store that was still open. I needed a toothbrush and a few other items before bed."

"I see," he replied, writing in a small notepad. "Did you find one? A store open at this hour?"

"No sir," Jack replied, a twitch of anxiety building in his throat.

"Yes. Very good," scribbling more notes. The officer commanded the other to fast-forward the video in Dutch. "Er, stop." "Do you know these men?" he asked, pointing to the screen.

There in plain view were the bellhop, the vendor, and another figure with a dark shawl covering their head and face.

"Yes," Jack replied. "This man," he pointed, "is the bellhop here at the hotel. He tried to stop us from leaving when we left to find a store."

The officer waited for me to add something more to the conversation, but I held silent.

"And this man, have you seen him before?" the officer asked.

"Yes," Jack rushed. "He sells dolls at St. Peter's church. What are they called, Elizabeth?"

"Pegwood dolls," I answered softly. I knew what Jack was doing, establishing distance between the suspects, and us, but I didn't want to be involved.

"Yes, the pegwood dolls. He acted peculiar from the moment we began speaking to him."

"And when you say he was peculiar, what do you mean?"

Jack stiffened at my side. I glanced at his face, but whatever was turning over in his mind was unreadable.

"We made no secret we were tourists. He was trying to frighten us by repeating some legend about a curse after I asked about the red keys over the doorways."

"Hmm, yes." The officer turned, muttering to himself as he wrote, "Tunney's *Vloek*."

I leaned in as he wrote the words and circled them in red ink. Whatever *vloek* was, it was an important part of why the Whizbang machine was missing.

"And what about this third man; did you happen to have contact with him?"

Jack drew closer to the screen, and then paused, "I don't believe that is a man, sir." Jack said, pointing to the screen. "See the necklace? I believe our third thief is a woman."

"Ahh, yes," the officer said. "Interesting."

"It's her," I gulped, rubbing at my eyes; uncertain if they were playing tricks on me. Trying to remain quiet, I whispered, "The necklace, Jack; it's her."

I wasn't quiet enough.

"Who?" the officer questioned. "Do you know this woman?"

"No," Jack insisted, "We don't know her, but we've seen her before. I have reason to believe she followed us here."

"To the hotel?"

"No, here—as in to Leiden," Jack replied, dropping a bombshell that would only lead to more interrogation.

"Ah, *naar voren*," the officer demanded in Dutch. The three spoke exclusively in their native tongue while the video sped forward and then abruptly came to a stop. "Here, what are they carrying out?"

Caught in the moment, I blurted out, "The Whizbang machine."

Jack's body jerked towards me, his head violently moving back and forth, "Elizabeth!"

"Excuse me?" the officer coughed, jumping to his feet. "*Hoe is dat mogelijk*? Impossible! It's been missing for over a hundred years!"

The officer's face and words betrayed the shock of my confession. I had said too much. Silence stretched on as he and the others struggled to look at the picture on the screen and rectify the words I had just spoken. The case was hard to make out in the video, but now everyone in the room knew the cursed Whizbang machine was seated inside, at least, everyone that spoke English.

Another string of heated words flew from his mouth in Dutch. Whatever it was, the other officers sitting next to him spun and stared at us.

I opened my mouth to speak but the officer spoke before I could.

"I don't believe I caught both of your names," the detective said. "Yours, sir?"

"Jack Yale."

"And yours, Miss?"

"Elizabeth Yale."

"I see," he replied, scribbling our identities on the small pad. "I don't believe I introduced myself; I'm detective Diedrick Henry. Now tell me, Mr. and Miss Yale, what is your relation?"

"I'm her grandfather," Jack replied softly, "as I stated before."

"Let me make sure I'm perfectly clear; you arrived here in the Netherlands today, is that correct?"

"Yes," Jack replied.

"And what business do you have in our country?"

"We are here to tend to a family matter," Jack replied.

Detective Henry twisted slightly to see my reaction. "And what matter might that be?" His voice turned low and commanding.

Jack hesitated, "If it is all the same, I do believe that is a private matter, sir."

Detective Henry stepped forward, closing the small gap between him and Jack. "Mr. Yale, you called us here. You were in possession of a piece of valuable stolen property that belongs here in Leiden, and now you would like us to find it for you. Is that correct?"

Jack nodded.

"Well Mr. Yale, without the knowledge of why you are here and how you came to be in ownership of the machine, I'm afraid I will not be able to help you. In fact, I'm thinking I should escort you and your granddaughter to the airport and put you both on a plane back to New York for the trouble you are causing in my city. You can also guarantee that neither of you will ever be allowed in our country again. So once more, let me ask you, what family matter are you here to tend to?"

Jack's eyes darted around the room as two more brawny officers entered the room with blaring radios and guns hanging from their belts.

"May we speak alone?" he asked.

Detective Henry nodded and commanded everyone to leave. As the last officer filtered out, Detective Henry took a seat.

"We're alone now, Mr. Yale. So, I fully expect to hear the truth. How did you come in possession of the Whizbang machine?" he asked coolly.

"I purchased it in Morocco."

"Morocco? And when was this?"

"A few months ago," Jack replied.

"What was it about the machine that caused you to buy it in the first place?" Henry pushed.

"I don't know," Jack replied, "I suppose you can say I felt like it belonged to me. That it had been missing, and I didn't even know it, if that makes sense."

"Then this next question should be easy," Detective Henry said, shifting hard in his chair, "Are you a Royal or a Tunney?"

Jack bit his lip, unable to find his voice to answer the detective's question.

"How about you, Elizabeth, are you a Royal or a Tunney?"

A jolt of fear moved through my veins. I tried to relax the growing panic, but it was too late. My head was swimming with a massive list of "what ifs."

Detective Henry tilted his head and grinned, "Oh, you didn't think anyone would know?" he questioned darkly, "You thought you would come to a foreign country and start asking questions about a centuries-old typewriter and no one would know what you were talking about?" A haunting laugh pulled deep from his belly. "We all know what the Whizbang machine is, but something tells me that you don't know even the half of the story."

"What do you mean?" I questioned.

"That machine is a legend around Leiden—a deeply rooted curse, if you will. Anyone who comes into possession of it is in grave danger. If you felt a pull towards the machine as you allege, I need to know who I'm dealing with."

Jack gulped, still uncertain if Mr. Henry was a friend or a foe. My grandfather promised to keep me safe, but here we were sitting with a man, his gun, and a truckload of dark questions that we were both uncertain whether we should answer or not. My safety exited the room when Jack forced the other officers out.

"I need to know which side you're on, sir," Detective Henry said, tossing his notepad on the table, "Your answer will depend on whether I'm willing to help you."

A flash of hot tears found my eyes, I gulped them back, forcing them to stay up and not run down my cheeks.

"Why would it matter which side we are on?" Jack asked hotly. "Isn't your job to protect everyone?"

"Not when it comes to this matter, sir," Detective Henry replied grimly.

"Perhaps the most important question is for you, detective. What side are you on?" Jack pushed back.

"That isn't up for discussion."

"Well then, neither is ours."

"Mr. Yale, we are done here. Best of luck. Don't get yourself hurt or worse while you are in my country. I would hate to be the one to call your loved ones in the states and tell them your stubbornness lead to your death."

296

The detective closed the laptop, pulled it up to his chest, and walked towards the door.

Jack snarled, fury mounted, and through gritted teeth, he said, "We—are—Royals. Will you help us or not?"

Detective Henry and I stared at Jack in shock. Whatever Henry's problem was with either side of this curse, he seemed to be letting it go.

"Royals," he muttered.

"Yes," I whispered.

"Could you please fill me in on what you meant when you asked if I was on the Tunney side or the Royal side?" Jack asked. "Tunney isn't a name we have heard of."

"Then sir, with all due respect, you know nothing of your family or that blasted typewriter." A peculiar smile touched his face.

"That is why we came here," Jack replied quickly. "To learn. Could you please provide us with any information that may help us uncover the truth behind our family's past?"

"I have a better plan," he replied. "Meet me at eight a.m. on the steps of the university's library. There is someone you both need to meet."

"And the machine? What will happen with the machine?" I asked.

"I'm sending my men to look for the suspects you were able to identify. We'll see what we can turn up. As for the woman, she'll be harder to identify since we do not have a clear picture of her face, but we'll do our best. The biggest concern shouldn't be that we cannot find the machine. Your concern and hopes should be that it isn't in a million pieces when we do find it."

My hands flew in protest, "That cannot happen," I growled. "Please, it's extremely important that does not happen."

"I know it is," he replied. "We'll do our best, but dear child I can make you no promises."

"Detective, thank you," Jack replied.

"You're welcome," he said, opening the door, "neither of you step foot from this room until you leave to meet me. Do you understand? Even if someone knocks on the door and claims to be hotel staff or even one of my men, do not open the door. Do you understand? You should not trust another soul when it comes to this matter."

Jack and I nodded.

"Word spreads quickly here—even at five in the morning. You've put yourself in danger coming here. I need you two to stay put."

"Yes sir, we'll see you in a few hours," Jack replied.

Chapter 33: The Journal

Jack shut the door behind Detective Henry and twisted the lock. As the noise outside the door fell silent Jack turned and looked at me.

"Where is your backpack, Elizabeth," Jack demanded.

"Here," I said heaving it onto the bed. "Why? What are you thinking?"

"Something dawned on me while the detective was talking. Where is the picture of the three men at the factory? The one with the man leaning on the cane."

"I'm sure it's in here," I replied.

"Open the backpack, Elizabeth!" Jack snapped.

"Jack," I barked, "calm down. I am."

I stared at him as I unzipped the zipper slowly. I couldn't comprehend what had changed his mood so rapidly.

"Hurry," he urged.

Pouring the backpack's contents on the bed, Jack dove into the pile, rambling while he dug. Each word grew louder than the next. His intensity hedged on uncontrollable. As he spoke, I tried to grab onto each word he said. Finally, word-by-word everything clicked into place in my head. Jack had remembered a vital piece of the puzzle.

"He's in the picture, isn't he?" I asked.

"Tunney," Jack replied. "I think so." Jack turned and stroked my face anxiously, "Help me find the picture, Lizzy. It has to be in this mess of papers. We brought it, right?"

"Yes," I replied. "I remember putting it in the stack before we left."

My arms swept wide across the peach-colored comforter. The papers scattered, exposing the edge of the worn photograph.

"Here!" I snapped.

The black and white photo that once hung in Yale's shelves stared back at Grandpa Jack and me. The two graying men in dark colored suits and with shaggy beards looked upon the man in the forefront. The much more dapper and sophisticated gentleman leaning upon a cane had to be none other than Edward Y. Royal. Directly behind the trio stood the brick factory known as the Whizbang *Fabriek*. While this was an important discovery, it was the man to the left that held our focus now.

Jack cleared his throat, "There—see," he choked. "I knew it. Look at the handkerchief."

A thin square of grayish fabric hung from the man's breast pocket. The first fold stood erect in its flawless press, but the short side of the triangle lay perfectly over his pocket. Stitched on the flap were the initials GRT.

"GRT," Jack said softly.

"That's Tunney, isn't it?"

"I believe so," Jack replied.

"The detective said we don't know anything about our family, right? What do you want to bet that the R in his initials stands for Royal."

"I would say you are probably dead on," Jack affirmed.

"So if we know that Tunney and Royal were related, or at least that seems to be the most logical explanation, we now need to figure out what role Tunney had when it comes to the Whizbang machine."

"Exactly," Jack asserted.

"Wait," I gasped. "Detective Henry wrote something next to Tunney's name when you were telling him about the merchant trying to scare us. It started with a V, but Grandpa, I can't remember what it was. It was written in Dutch."

I grabbed the small pad on the desk, thinking that I would try to visualize the word and write it out from memory, but as I drew the pad closer, I realized it wasn't the hotel's pad Jack had used when writing the coordinates of the graveyard, but instead Detective Henry's notes.

"Jack," I whispered, "look what Henry left behind."

"Let me see," he said, pulling the pad from my fingers.

Jack began to pace in wide circles, making heavy footprints in the thickly carpeted room. He concentrated all his efforts on making sense of Detective Henry's notes. After close to fifty circles in complete silence, I crept closer to him. Although, his focus was so intense that I doubted he would have even noticed I was following his every step.

"What does it say?" I breathed.

Lost in distracted speculation, Jack made another round through the room, shaking me off his determined pace.

"*Vlock*," he stammered. "That's the word you are trying to think of. Detective Henry wrote *Vlock*. Didn't your mother give you an electronic language translator?"

"She did," I said, snapping my fingers. "I put it in— agh, Jack, I put it in the Whizbang machine's case before we left. You had already taken my luggage to Mom's car so I tossed it inside the case."

"So it's gone," Jack replied, sinking his weight into the small couch in the center of the suite.

"I'm sorry," I replied. "I…"

"It isn't your fault."

"Wait, no, I tossed it on top of my suitcase when I opened the machine. It has to be somewhere in the room."

Jack pulled himself up, joining in my search for the device. A shiny rectangular object in the far corner, half-hidden by the flowing white curtains, caught my eye.

Bolting to the curtains, "Here!" I howled.

Flipping the case open and powering it on, the translator came to life.

"What was the word, spell it?" I motioned to Jack.

"Vlo…" he began.

"Wait."

"What did you miss? V-l-o," Jack repeated.

"No, there's already something written here," I mumbled, walking to the couch, "look."

The translator scrolled four words across the screen repeatedly, *Wacht de schrijfmachine*, Elizabeth.

"*Wacht*," I said, struggling to keep up with the speed of the translator. As the last word scrolled by again, I dropped the device. "It says my name. Jack, why does it say my name?"

The blood drained from my face.

"This is what Detective Henry must have meant when he said we had put ourselves in danger coming here. We need to know what this means," Jack said.

"Go ahead," I muttered. "Push the translation button."

A chime rang out while the device converted the words from Dutch to English.

Jack read each word slowly as they began to scroll across the small screen, "Typewriter is waiting, Elizabeth," he swallowed.

"Is that a threat?" I asked.

"I don't know."

"Type in that other word, the V-l-o whatever it was," I insisted.

Jack followed my command. The same chime rang out while the device converted the word.

"Of course," Jack said harshly. "It means curse."

"Tunney's curse," I said. "Tunney is the one who cursed the Whizbang machine, is that what that means?"

"The file from the graveyard," Jack bellowed, jumping to his feet. "I shoved it in between the mattress when I saw the machine was gone. Help me," Jack grunted, pushing the heavy mattress off its frame.

Together we lifted the bed and Jack pulled the worn file from its safe place. The smell from the tombstone found its way to my nose once again. I closed my eyes and tried to focus on something else, but the smell of centuries-old death was winning. It was something that would never leave me.

"What is it you wanted us to know, Jesse?" Jack mused.

The file was secured with an aging rubber band. The minute Jack tugged at the elastic it disintegrated into a pile of small rubber bits. Dusting them off his lap, he opened the file. Inside was a small blue velvet journal.

"Interesting," he said softly.

The nasty stench of decay was replaced with the sweet smell of cherry tobacco. The edges of the journal were lightly worn, but not enough to clue us to its age.

"I wonder who this belongs to," Jack questioned as he opened the cover.

A small brass key, no longer than three inches, fell from its resting place. Jack picked it up and laid it in his open palm.

"Yet another key," I moaned.

Its handle was round, flat, and hollow in the center. An infinite sign was shaped into the brass where three small ridges met the key's shaft. The words W/B Trust, LTD was stamped in microscopic print.

"W/B Trust, LTD," I read aloud. "I've seen that name before."

"Where?"

"In the attic, when I was looking for the photo albums. It was printed on the metal box dad had moved the albums to after the original carton broke. What do you think W/B Trust, LTD is?"

"If I had to place a bet, I would put my money on the fact that it's a bank," Jack muttered.

"Why?"

"Because the key looks like a vault key—one that would open a safe deposit box. Grab your phone; look up W/B Trust. Let's see if anything comes up."

A quick search proved Jack was right. "It is a bank, or was, I should say. It goes by a different name now."

"Where is it?"

"2312 JG, Leiden, is what is listed," I answered. "It looks to be about three, maybe four, blocks from here."

"Gather everything up. Let's take everything of importance. We need to find out what the key opens," Jack demanded.

"You can't be serious, Jack! Don't you remember what Detective Henry told us? He said not to leave the room until we go and meet him at the university."

"I'm not going to sit around and wait for an officer to instruct me about how I should go about getting answers, Elizabeth. He also said we should trust no one, but him. That's convenient, don't you think?"

"Don't you trust him?"

"I don't trust anyone, including Detective Henry," Jack replied harshly. "Now, gather your things."

"I think we're making a mistake."

"We're wasting time. Get your stuff!"

"What about the journal? Don't you want to read what is inside first?"

"No!" Jack said hotly. "It can wait. We need to get whatever is inside of the lockbox out before someone else does. They know your name, Elizabeth. They have more knowledge than we do. They have the machine. You are worried about danger…all of those things are far more dangerous to me than staying locked up in some hotel room. So, either you gather your things, or you stay here. I'm going to the bank."

"Fine," I mumbled, tossing the backpack over my shoulder, "It's six in the morning; no one is going to be at the bank anyhow, but let's rush there so we can stand around and put ourselves out in the open."

Moments later, Jack and I slipped out of our suite, pounded down the backstairs, and swiftly exited the hotel through the employee service door. We made our way out without a single witness to tell of our departure.

Chapter 34: The Chase

The breeze was crisp as the sun began to shine over the horizon. Leiden was in slow motion, still waking from its slumber. The smell of warm delicacies and freshly brewed coffee wafted into the back alley. I pulled the sweet goodness into my lungs, my belly rumbling in protest of its emptiness.

Jack and I moved quickly, shaking off days' worth of unrelenting exhaustion and what was starting to feel like starvation. The bank, now called Huisman Son and Trust, formally W/B Trust, LTD, was two blocks North of the St. Peter Cathedral. To get there, we would have to pass the courtyard. A part of me wanted to see if the thieves were foolish enough to return to the church after breaking into our room, pilfering through our belongings, and ultimately stealing the Whizbang machine. Another part wanted to steer clear and let the police sort out the mangled mess. If we did cross one or all of their paths, I wasn't sure Jack would be able to keep his head about himself.

Despite the early hour, lights popped on in every direction. Small children dressed in school uniforms trickled out of their homes with sleepy eyes and bed head.

"We better hurry up. The city is waking. We only have fifty-eight minutes before we are supposed to meet Detective Henry," I said in a hush.

Grandpa Jack glanced over at me, adopting a grimace that I could only interpret to mean we had trouble on our hands. St. Peter's was in our line of sight. It was as majestic as it had been the night before, yet I wasn't all that comfortable being back in its presence. There were too many what ifs to be stalking around the cathedral, to be stalking around Leiden, for that matter.

Jack's gray hair whipped in the light breeze as he turned in circles without missing a step. He shook his head, trying to shake whatever was taking over.

I whispered, "What is it? What's wrong?"

"Do you feel that?"

A wave of nausea hit me, "Jack…"

"To your left, nine o'clock."

Vendors had begun setting up their stands for the day. There were dozens more portable booths than the day before. A short, heavy-set woman guarded a table of homemade soaps. Her face hardened when our eyes met. She crossed her arms over her wide belly and analyzed my every move.

"The woman?" I questioned, not turning from her eyes.

"No, further," he whispered. "See the next table?"

At the edge of the fair sat a small wooden table draped in the same lavender cloth as the day before. The precious pegwood dolls were stacked and displayed for tourists to gawk at as they made their rounds. A deep exhale flew through my slightly parted lips.

"Where is he?" I gasped, my eyes darting along the cobblestone anxiously.

"Slowly turn to your right. Don't let him see you looking," Jack instructed.

"We should get out of here," I snorted. "I told you we shouldn't have left the hotel room."

Out of nowhere, a bicyclist rounded a nearby bend too quickly forcing a small crowd to jump out of the way. As the group protested and swiftly shifted, I caught sight of the eerie shadow.

"There," I muttered.

Leaning against a long, winding outdoor bookcase was the pegwood vendor. As our eyes connected, he reeled back, twisted, and busted through dozens of collapsed boxes resting against the bookshelf. He stumbled, regained his balance, and took off running.

"That's who I think it is, right?" I shouted at Jack.

"It is! Where is the machine?" Jack shrieked. "Stop him...thief!"

The streets began to fill with hushed murmurs from all directions as people locked into our distress. Jack rocked on his heels, corrected his course, and took off towards the pegwood vendor.

"Jack!" I screamed. "No!"

"Someone stop him!" Jack hollered, his feet pounding against the cobblestone.

Suddenly, my heart began to pound in my ears. Hot adrenaline pulsed, "Jack!" He refused to stop. My body throttled forward. Each pump of my legs pushed me with greater momentum until my feet fell in line with Jack's.

Tables and people blurred past as my steps became quickened leaps. The thudding in my ears grew louder by the second until I could hardly hear anything at all.

"Stop!" Jack hollered again.

A father and his teenage son entered our pursuit, shouting in Dutch and then English. Jolts of pain shuddered through my body as it absorbed the hammering shock of my feet. The vendor weaved in and out of the crowd, mowing over anyone in his way.

A horrific howl escaped from a woman up ahead as the vendor grabbed at her shoulders and tossed her onto the ground. I surged forward trying to see if she was okay. A tight circle of onlookers filled in around her.

"My shoulder," she wailed.

"Jack," I cried.

"Leave her," Jack shouted breathlessly, "They will make sure she is okay."

The vendor ducked behind a tree, moving completely out of our sight. Jack's breathing was becoming more restricted with each push forward. He careened to a stop.

"Go!" Jack urged. "Go!" bending low to heave in air.

"Where did he go?" I shouted.

Cold air sliced at my hot throat. A flash, a streak of a hunched figure passed quickly to my right. I turned to run over the next pedestrian bridge but stopped as a voice shouted from the far bank.

"Stop! Stop!" a police officer blustered. "*Niet springen*! *Niet springen*! Don't jump!"

Frantically searching, my eyes locked in. The pegwood merchant wobbled, clinging to the top railing of the nearby bridge. His knuckles were turning white as his fingers twisted deeper into the decorative metal. Positioned at the height of the walkway, one small breeze and he would be tossed into the canal water below. Small boats passed leaving small wakes in their path, each barking for him to get down.

"Sir, don't jump!" the officer commanded again. "*Naar beneden*!"

I crept closer, unwilling to look away, unwilling to let him off the hook for his misdeeds.

"Where is the machine?" I called. "Tell me where the machine is!"

He said nothing.

"You coward! Don't you dare jump! Where is the machine!" I screamed.

A monstrous smile swept across his face and then he turned away. He looked down at the canal, released his fingers, and let the wind catch his outspread arms. As his body broke the surface of the water, a tremendous splash forced water over the edge of the banks. Officers shouted to one another in Dutch and began radioing for help. The world around me went into warp speed, and all I could do was stand there in wild disbelief. I waited for him to come up gulping for air, but as the minutes passed by, I gave up hope. He was gone. My knees were weak.

A hot hand hit my shoulder and jerked me out of my daze. Jack looked deep into my eyes, "Are you okay?"

"Where is he?" I breathed.

"Maybe he hit the bottom. I doubt the canal is very deep."

I trembled at that thought. I watched the water's edge, looking for signs of movement. It was dark, muddled with boat oil and sediment. Even if he did survive the jump he may have died from ingesting the water.

"Coward," I screamed, dropping to my knees. "You filthy coward!"

"Sir," a police officer called, galloping closer.

The streets had broken out into sheer chaos. Jack turned to address the man in uniform as he beckoned him to move to the canal's edge.

"Is this what he stole?" the officer pointed in the distance.

Small pieces of machinery began breaking the surface of the cool, black water. First came a space bar, then what appeared to be a backspace button, and then the shift lock.

"No," Jack cried, his head forcing low onto his chest.

I stood in disbelief. "The machine…" I gasped. "It was my only chance—Mom," I cried. Hot tears exploded onto my cheeks. Jack wrapped his sweaty arms around me, pulling me in.

"Shh, it's okay. I promise. We'll stop it. I'll find a way."

"No," I cried. "It's done. We're done."

The officer grabbed a long pole with a net secured to the nearby bridge. Dipping it into the water, he stabbed at something bobbing up and down. After three attempts, he plucked a small silver object from the man-made tide. Dumping it from the net at my feet, I forced myself to look down. The typewheel with the initials EWY stared up at us from the cobblestone.

"Yours?" the officer motioned to the piece.

Jack grabbed the typewheel and closed his hand around it, "Yes sir," he replied.

The officer nodded and turned to walk away. My belly flopped and found its way to my throat. Without warning, I leaned over and spilled hot sickness from my core. Jack grabbed my shoulders, holding me in place.

"It's okay, Elizabeth. Let it go."

"How can it be? The machine is in a million pieces."

Chapter 35: Darkness

It didn't take long for the streets to return to its lull of tranquility. Back to locals and tourists riding their bikes along the outdoor market unaware that a thief may be dead beneath their feet. Officers dredged the canal looking for the merchant's body as I watched.

Silently, I made myself a promise that if they found him, I wouldn't watch the extraction. If he were dead, so be it. I already had enough to work through after being hidden away in a child's crypt. My mind couldn't take much more.

"Mr. and Miss Yale," an unhappy voice called from behind, "I thought I told you two to stay put until you were to meet me at the university," Detective Henry clapped his hands defiantly.

We both turned and greeted Detective Henry's angry tone.

"You did," Jack replied.

"Did I speak in Dutch?" He chomped, "Surely that is the only way you wouldn't have understood my instructions."

"No sir, you didn't," Jack pushed back. "With all due respect, I don't believe now is the time for a reprimand."

"Oh, now's not good for you? Is that what you are saying?" Detective Henry said aggressively. "Neither of you move a muscle. If I find that you have, I'll arrest you both and take you to the justice ministry myself. Do you understand?"

Jack nodded but refused to answer. A muffled voice rang out from a nearby alley entrance.

"I think we have company," Jack whimpered, still standing stiff.

"Where?"

"Behind us. Listen carefully. Does that sound like the woman's voice?"

I tried to grab on to her words, listen to the tone, but it was no use.

"I only heard her singing at the church. The only other time I heard her speak was in my dream and I don't think that can be counted," I said.

Chills raised and spread across Jack's body. "It's her," he hissed. "She's less than a few feet from us."

"Don't turn around, Jack. I don't think Detective Henry is kidding when he says he will arrest us."

"Henry," Jack snapped.

The detective shot Jack a disapproving look, unwilling to leave his conversation with the father and son who helped in our chase. When he was finished, he directed a dive team into the water. "Find him," he shouted. "If he is alive, no one speak to him until I'm present. If he is dead, I'm the first to know. You will clear the area pulling his body. Do you understand?"

The team answered in unison as Henry made his way back to us.

"Come along," he commanded. "We're going to the university."

"Detective Henry," Jack insisted, instinctively reaching for his arm, but let his hand drop before making contact.

"Not now, Mr. Yale, please wait until we get into the car."

"Sir," Jack pushed.

Detective Henry stopped short, "What is it?"

"The woman, the one from the video, I believe she is in the alley."

"Now?"

"Yes sir, I heard her voice."

Henry pulled his phone from his pocket and jammed it up to his ear. His words were heated and fast. Whatever he said, a team of uniformed officers went fleeing into the alley.

"Move," he demanded. "We need to get you out of here."

Following Henry's lead, we moved stealthily through the back corridors of the city until we found his car. Once inside, Henry turned to me and said, "I want you to know the likelihood of the merchant dying is pretty slim. The currents in the canal are next to nothing. If he had hit and perished, my team would have found him immediately. There are small maintenance tunnels leading off the canal channel. My guess that is where he will be found hiding out. If he is injured, we'll get him faster."

"I don't care about him," I replied. "The machine is what I care about. Typewriter parts floated from the bottom. It has to be destroyed somewhere."

"I haven't called my team off from looking for the machine. I won't. We don't know for sure that those were parts belonging to the Whizbang machine."

"He had the typewheel on him," I replied.

Jack intervened, "All that means is he is one of our thieves. It only confirms it. The typewheel wasn't a part of the actual machine. It was only locked onto the case."

"I suppose," I replied, crossing my arms and melting deeper into the seat.

Detective Henry made a hard right turn. The cobblestone roughly bumped under the wheels. I stared out the window as the city flashed by. How a city with such astonishing beauty could have such a dark underbelly is something I will never be able to understand.

Chapter 36: The Royal Room

Fifteen minutes later the three of us descended the steps that lead to the bottom floor of the Leiden University Library. The hallway was slender and poorly lit.

"What's down here?" I asked.

"You are among some of the rarest and finest collections in the entire world, madam," Detective Henry answered. "To your right is the Print Room. It holds the largest collection of portraits in all of the Netherlands, including some of Rembrandt's most prized works."

We walked mid-way down the long hallway when Detective Henry stopped and pointed to the door.

"The Royal Exhibit," Jack questioned, "As in Royal, Royal?"

"One in the same," Henry smirked. "I told you I needed to show you your family's history instead of simply telling you."

Henry pounded out an odd series of knocks—a code of sorts—then stepped back and flashed his badge to the hidden camera in the ceiling.

"If it's an exhibit hall, why can't we just go in?" I asked.

"This room was closed eight years ago after a string of break-ins that lasted about a week. The thief is still at large. In order to protect the collection, the university shut down the room only allowing access to government officials and special guests."

"Eight years ago," Jack mused, turning to look at me.

I acknowledged Jack's words with a slight nod.

Eight years falls into the timing when my father was in Leiden. If he needed something out of the room, he was successful in moving it. That thought brought me back to the bank key still hiding in Jack's front trouser pocket. We had to make it to the old W/B Trust before it closed for the day. Whatever was stolen from the exhibit could very well be in the safe deposit box.

A heavy bolt shifted loudly from the other side of the door. Seconds later, an awkward man, no older than thirty, greeted Detective Henry warmly. They exchanged what seemed to be niceties in Dutch, and then he turned to greet us.

"Hello," he said bowing his head, "It's nice to make your acquaintance. I'm Gustav van Rijn."

"As in Gustav hails from the same line as painter Rembrandt van Rijn," Detective Henry smiled.

"Diedrick never fails to mention that piece of my family's history when introducing me to someone new," Gustav asserted.

Gustav patted Detective Henry on the shoulder. The camaraderie between the men was apparent. "Please," he said, "enough about my family, I understand you would like to learn about your own prominent family, the Royals."

"Yes sir," Jack answered.

"And what are your relations, if you don't mind me asking?"

"He would have been my three-times-great-grandfather. Elizabeth is my granddaughter."

"Oh yes, very well; please, do come in. This is the Royal exhibit hall."

The stone-colored room was massive. Dimly lit glass cases lined the foremost two walls. Behind the glass were newspaper articles, blueprints, and huge chunks of cement and ship wreckage. The center of the room had three large wooden tables displaying heavy microfilm equipment and large clock pieces. The first newspaper hanging in a gilded museum frame proclaimed Edward Y. Royal the new father of Leiden. There were dozens of papers with headlines shouting Royal's good deeds. The second headline read ROYAL TO EMPLOY LEIDEN RESIDENTS ONLY. Then ROYAL PROMISES TO REBUILD AFTER BLAST. ROYAL PROCLAIMED MAYOR.

"I'm really confused now," Jack stammered. "This isn't so much an exhibit about the Royal family as it is about Edward himself. Am I correct?"

"You're somewhat accurate," Mr. van Rijn said. "Your three-times-great-grandfather monumentally changed the city of Leiden for the good."

I wandered around the room, slowly taking in each display. In the far corner of the room, a large sheet of darkened glass lined the wall.

"What's in there?" I asked.

"That is the nerve center for the entire library, Elizabeth," Detective Henry announced. "It was relocated down here after the break-ins resulted both in theft and vandalism. Mr. van Rijn and his team are not only historians but act as chief security for the rare collections that are housed in this basement."

"I suppose this should be obvious," Jack said clearing his throat, "but if Edward was someone who changed the city, why is the Royal family's name so tarnished now?"

"Why don't you take a seat, Mr. Yale," Henry directed.

"Yes," Mr. van Rijn offered. "Elizabeth, you too, if you wish. I believe we should start at the beginning."

The ancient microfilm screen snapped on. A series of black and white articles flashed across the screen until Mr. van Rijn found the one he wanted.

"Let's start here," he smiled. "Days after Edward turned twenty a catastrophe rocked the city of Leiden. A boat, loaded with over thirty-eight thousand pounds of gunpowder was docked in the city harbor. It blew the center of Leiden to smithereens. A hundred and fifty-one people perished in the blast, another two thousand were injured, and more than two hundred homes and businesses were destroyed. While the investigators at the time ruled the blast an accident, rumors flew through the city that Royal's cousin, George Tunney, actually had a hand in the blast."

"Tunney," Jack snapped.

"George," I whispered. We finally had a full name to put with the face in the photograph.

Mild amusement stretched across Detective Henry's face, "That's right; Edward Royal and George Tunney were cousins, first cousins at that. Edward and George's mothers were sisters."

"Why did people think that Tunney had something to do with the blast?" I asked.

"Tunney was attending this university a few months before the blast. From what I understand, he was quite brilliant and had a budding career in engineering and architecture before him. There was another side to Tunney, however. He had a love of destroying things as much as he loved building them. He had been caught trying to burn down a city building after his design was rejected for a new city park. As a part of his punishment, Tunney was expelled from Leiden University and brought up on allegations of arson. Before he could go to trial, the Royal family paid the city a hefty fee to clear George of any wrongdoing. Edward was very public about his stance about George. He believed his cousin was responsible for the blast and attempted arson, but with the windfall now supporting the city, officials looked the other way."

"George was free to go? After possibly killing and wounding that many people?" Jack asked.

"Essentially," Detective Henry replied.

"If Edward was vocal about George's involvement, is that where the curse comes into place?" I asked.

Detective Henry's eyes flashed towards mine. I dug in my backpack and handed him his small notebook that he had left in the hotel room.

"You left it in the room," I said, turning it over.

"And you clearly read it," he countered.

"I did, but only after I thought it was the notebook my grandfather had written on earlier that day. I noticed the word *vloek* on your pad and I looked it up. You wrote Tunney's curse. I wasn't trying to read your investigation notes, sir. But I have to know if this is how this supposed curse came about."

"Not exactly," Mr. van Rijn said. "There's more."

"At the time, Edward was working for his father in their family business. They owned and operated the Royals' *Klok Fabriek*; it was the finest and most sought after clock company in the world during its prime," Henry replied. "In fact, the King of England commissioned Edward's father, Ryker Royal, to build a special clock that to this day still sits in parliament. Ryker was so smitten with his design he duplicated the clock only once. It was for his family home. No one knows if the clock was destroyed, sold, or stashed before the Royals fled the country."

"Are you speaking of large clocks? Like a grandfather clock?" Jack asked.

"Yes sir," Mr. van Rijn said.

The microfilm flashed across the screen until it landed on a newspaper article with a drawing of the clock Ryker created for the King of England. I clapped wildly, "They took it with them to the United States."

"That's impossible," Mr. van Rijn stated soundly. "I've checked every record of the ship the Royals fled on. The clock was not listed as a part of the cargo."

"How do you know this information?" Detective Henry pushed.

"Because it is sitting inside my mother's foyer as we speak," I said.

"You are certain it is the same one in the picture?" van Rijn questioned.

"Quite," Jack interjected.

"Well, that solves that mystery," Henry laughed. "It was believed to have been destroyed after Ryker's death."

"I can assure you it wasn't," Jack replied, "but that still doesn't answer how Tunney put a curse on the Royals. Nor does it explain this mess over the Whizbang machine."

"It will," Henry replied.

Gustavo pushed the machine forward, turning the black knobs until it came to stop on Ryker's obituary. Jack and I leaned forward reading the small print.

"Wait," Jack gasped. "He died of unnatural causes—it says homicide?"

"Like he was murdered?" I asked.

"That's right," Detective Henry said. "Ryker and Edward made George work for them doing grunt work to repay his debt. He felt the work was beneath him, and his aunt's family was being cruel. Rumors swirled when Ryker's home mysteriously went up in flames."

"George set his uncle's house on fire?" I huffed.

"That's what was alleged. Ryker died inside the fire. Edward was devastated. The day after he buried his father, Edward fired George from the factory. He refused to pay him his living wages. Edward had just been appointed as the Mayor of Leiden and knew there would be no legal repercussions if he expelled George in this manner. His hands were also in the pockets of every businessman the city had. He made certain George would not ever work again."

"So what happened to him?" I asked.

"I don't know exactly," Gustavo replied. "Those documents were among those stolen eight years ago, and there are no back-ups. I do know what happened later, but there is a gap in Tunney's whereabouts."

Jack pulled the backpack off the chair and dug for the file retrieved from Alina Royal's grave. Handing the microfilm over to detective Henry, Jack shifted in his chair.

"Where did you get this?" Henry questioned.

"I can't say," Jack answered quickly.

"Would this be a part of the missing documents from this exhibit, Gustavo?" He asked, pushing the flimsy piece of plastic in front of his friend.

Gustavo took the microfilm and studied the corners looking for specific markings, "I don't believe so, but I would have to match the numbers with the log. The numbering system at the bottom seems to be different then the system we employ here."

"But it is stolen nonetheless, isn't it Mr. Yale? Again, I will ask how this stolen property came to be in your possession?"

"There were clues, we followed them, it provided us the microfilm. There is nothing more to explain. Now, could we see what it says? I would like to fill in Tunney's history before you explain the rest," Jack insisted.

Detective Henry bobbed his head up and down giving Gustavo an unspoken green light to scan the microfilm into the machine. We all waited, unsure what we were able to learn.

"With Royal taking the position of Mayor, did he keep his father's factory open?" I questioned.

Detective Henry opened his mouth to answer but stopped as a flashing red light suddenly pulsed overhead. Seconds later, the loud blares of the fire alarm screeched at deafening volumes. Both men jumped to their feet and ran into the security room.

"I don't see a fire on any of the coordinates," Detective Henry shouted over the noise.

"The alarm was pulled on this level. Someone is in the hallway," Gustavo shouted back.

"Elizabeth, Jack, someone knows you are here. There is no evidence of a fire. We need to get you out of here," Detective Henry urged.

Jack zipped and tossed the backpack to me. In one swoop, I threw it on my back, turned, and looked at Detective Henry.

"What do you want us to do?" I barked.

"Take the side exit to the left. It will get you back outside. Go now!" Gustavo yelled. "Go!"

"Wait," Jack roared. "Is the clock factory still standing?"

"It is," Henry shouted. "It's about three miles north, right outside of town. It's mostly in ruins, but some part of the factory still stands. Locals won't go near it. That is where the curse originates. Do not go out there without me, Mr. Yale. Please, it's too risky. Go back to the hotel. I will meet with you later."

Fevered voices came stomping down the stairs. Detective Henry shouted in Dutch as Jack and I slipped out the exit.

Chapter 37: W/B Trust, LTD

Warm buttered toast and hot red currant jam wafted over the table. My belly moaned. Jack sipped black coffee and watched the crowd buzz around the small restaurant. Fresh pastries overflowed at nearly every table but ours.

"I'm starving," I whined.

"The food will be here any minute."

"What's on your mind?" I asked.

"All the unanswered questions; we still don't know about Edward and George," Jack snapped.

"You mean how the curse came about?"

"Or more importantly, how the Whizbang machine came about," Jack replied. "If the Royals owned a clock factory, at what point did they switch over and start producing the Whizbang machine? And what role did George have in the company if he had already been banished for allegedly setting the fire that killed Ryker? We're still missing major pieces of the puzzle."

"Do you think it was the merchant that pulled the fire alarm?" I leaned in and whispered.

"I don't know," Jack replied, "but whoever it was they don't want us finding out the truth. I'm not going to stop until we can connect all the dots."

I nodded, leaning back in my seat casually as the waiter staggered to our table carrying enough food to feed a table of five instead of our small table of two. A cold meat tray was placed in the center, followed by a pile of warm toast and small ramekins of seasonal jams, soft-boiled eggs, oatmeal, a cheese tray, and thinly sliced tomatoes and cucumbers. My eyes grew wide.

"That's some spread," Jack laughed.

"I may have over-ordered."

Jack thanked the waiter who didn't understand English. He stood around waiting for more instruction but soon turned away to help a patron calling for him in Dutch. What should have taken an hour to eat disappeared in less than ten minutes. Jack and I were both famished.

A few minutes later, our table was cleared, Jack had a to-go coffee in hand, and I slipped the backpack back over my shoulder.

"Now what?" I asked, stepping through the café door.

"I think we try to catch a taxi and go to the bank," Jack replied. "It's too dangerous to be on foot right now."

It finally seemed that Jack had clued into the danger we were in and wasn't willing to continue to push the envelope.

"What time is it?" I asked.

"A quarter till noon," he answered.

"Why don't we go back to the hotel and wait for Detective Henry. Maybe we can catch a quick nap, and then when he arrives we'll all go to the bank together?"

Jack looked at me and smirked.

"It was worth a shot," I replied.

"We need to get to a main thoroughfare to get a taxi."

We walked in silence for several blocks. Both Jack and I unconsciously peered over our shoulders with each new alleyway we passed.

"I guess we aren't as far as I thought we were. There's St. Peter's," he said.

"Then the bank should be just a few more blocks after that," I replied.

"Let's slip into the alley and go the back way," Jack instructed. "We don't need a taxi after all."

I followed. The cobblestone was uneven and discolored as we made our pass through the first backstreet. The corridor was narrower than most we had traveled and came to an abrupt end up ahead.

"Jack," I whispered. "It's a dead end."

"No, look," he pointed.

Three small grayish steps lead to another tight path. A blooming vine hung overhead, closing out the sunlight. As quietly as we could, we carefully stepped down into another walkway. Turning left, the path opened into a sensational garden.

"Wow," I whistled.

"It's beautiful," Jack gasped. "But we better get out of here before someone sees us. We need to go east."

Alleyway after alleyway we moved silently through what seemed to be a labyrinth of ill connecting streetways and passageways. Minutes later we were standing before the large oversized golden doors marked Huisman Son and Trust, LLC.

Jack pulled the small gold key from his trouser pocket and handed it to me.

"You do the pleasures this time," he smiled.

Huisman's bank was a thing of beauty. Dozens of striking chandeliers were dripping in ropes of perfectly placed crystals hung at different levels casting colorful illuminations on the stone floor below. Tall banker boxes stained a deep red cherry lined the walls in the far back corner. Tellers and lenders greeted us warmly and motioned towards the crushed velvet ropes with bank patrons already waiting their turns.

Seated deep in the wall was the bank vault, the very reason for our presence. Silver and gold-brushed metal formed the perfect sphere in the middle of the casing. The entire safe stretched at least eight feet high and ten feet wide. Enormous wheels and bars convened together to create the vault's handle. A squatty, heavy-set guard, with one hand on his pistol and the other on his baton, stood in position, ready to attack anyone who dared to breach the massive door. Above his head was a familiar sight: the red double keys.

"*Volgende*," a teller called out.

Jack and I were next, but neither of us moved.

"*Volgende*," she said again, motioning us forward.

A woman behind Jack and I tapped Jack's shoulder and said, "*Klaar, volgende.*"

"I'm sorry," Jack replied, shaking his head.

"I think they are ready for us," I said, pulling at Jack's arm. "Do you speak English?"

The teller smiled politely, lifting one finger to instruct us to wait, and disappeared. The crowd behind us groaned, growing weary.

A few minutes later, a bank manager introduced himself, then asked us to step out of line. "Hello," he said, "May I help you?"

His English was broken, but it was enough to communicate our needs.

"Yes," I replied. "We would like to see the box this key belongs to."

"Ah," the manager puffed, "Do you have, um, how do you say, the, um, paperwork for the box?"

"No sir. It was a gift," I replied.

"I see. Please come, we'll need to see our bank's president for clearance."

"But sir," I said, stopping his advance, "Isn't this a vault key? Couldn't we simply go in downstairs?"

"I'm afraid not, Miss. That key belongs to a different vault. We'll not be able to access it without expressed permission or paperwork."

We moved forward again. Jack and I both thought the same thing—this felt like another trap. Once on the second floor, we were ushered inside a large office marked Huisman President. The manager and the president exchanged rapid words and then the manager left without even a goodbye.

"Hello, I'm Art Berg, President of Huisman Son and Trust. It is a pleasure to meet you…"

"Jack Yale," Jack replied, taking Mr. Berg's extended hand into his own.

"And you," Mr. Berg said.

"Elizabeth Yale."

"Yes, the Yales," he smiled.

"What has brought you to Huisman's today?"

"This," I replied, opening my hand to reveal the small gold key.

"I figured as much," Mr. Berg replied, rounding his desk and opening the middle drawer.

"We would like to see whatever it will open," I said quietly.

"Certainly," he nodded, "but first, please take a seat, you'll need to answer a few questions."

Jack and I took a seat in the large wingback chairs in front of Mr. Berg's desk. Nervousness touched my belly. I was afraid I had eaten too much for whatever was about to come. I also tried to commit Mr. Berg's face to memory. If this man was going to lead us into an impermeable room, I wanted to be able to identify him should he not let us out.

"How did you come into ownership of this key?" Mr. Berg began, opening a large leather-bound bank registry.

"It was a gift," I replied.

"A gift," he replied, looking up.

"And who was the giver?"

"I'm sorry sir, I do not see how this is relevant to us viewing the contents of the box," Jack said, heat began to build in his voice.

"It is extremely relevant, sir. We have been charged with protecting the contents of this particular lockbox. When it was opened eight years ago…"

Jack stood quickly, stepping on Mr. Berg's words, "I'm sorry, did you say the box was opened eight years ago?"

"Yes, sir."

"Was it opened by my son, Jesse Yale?"

"Yes sir, it was. With that knowledge, I can forgo the formalities Mr. Yale put in place at the time he opened the security box. I will need your signature in order to take you into this precise location of the vault. Miss, I will need yours as well. Furthermore, we will need your fingerprints."

"I don't believe that is necessary," Jack replied, unwilling to leave that kind of physical evidence behind.

"There is no other way," Mr. Berg replied.

He opened a large black stamp pad and handed Jack a pen. Jack moved the book closer so he could take a better look at the original owner's signature. It was, in fact, my father's.

"Once I have your autographs and your fingerprints, I will take you to the private vault where I will lock you inside so that you may extract the contents discretely."

I gulped. The idea of being locked inside a metal room didn't suit me well. Just the same, I signed on the dotted line and placed my fingerprints on a long blue card. Mr. Berg smiled and directed us to follow him. The heavy iron of the vault moaned and clicked as the bank president turned the wheel in a precise pattern. After seven spins around, the vault door sprang open.

I wasn't sure what to expect but what was before us wasn't what I had in mind. Gold iron bars greeted us as soon as Mr. Berg opened the steel door. The bank president dug into his pocket, pulling an oversized ring of keys out along with a mangled mess of used tissues and loosely wrapped chewing gum. Swiftly tossing the tissues into a waste basket, he pushed a small, flat key, not too different from the one in my hand, into the iron gate. It swung open with a loud screech. The three of us walked single file to a small, gold staircase, then made our way to a second floor of the vault.

The second floor was filled with long, slender rooms, each containing thousands of individual safe-deposit boxes that stretched from the floor to the ceiling. The unused boxes had small modern keys hanging from their locks. The deeper we proceeded into the vault, the larger the boxes grew. By the time we reached our destination, the boxes were the size of a small moving carton.

"Right in here," Mr. Berg directed.

"Were you here when my father first opened this account?" I questioned.

"Yes, I was," he replied. "I had completely forgotten about this box or the promises I made surrounding it until you arrived, to be honest. I must say, your father was a sensible man if I recall correctly, but it seemed he had been caught up in the demons this city has clung to as the truth for more than a century."

"Do you mean Tunney's curse?" Jack asked.

Mr. Berg swallowed hard, shaking off the words Jack had just spoken.

"Please excuse my frankness, Mr. Yale. I shouldn't have spoken ill of your son."

"No offense taken, but sir, are you speaking of the curse, and what promises did you make Jesse? That information may be vital to us."

"The promise was simple. I vowed to never allow anyone other than a Yale to open the safe-deposit box— that is if someone other than himself should return for the contents."

"Was he expecting someone else to come for whatever he placed inside the box?" I asked.

"Not that I can recall," Mr. Berg replied.

"The curse: is that what you mean by demons?" I pushed.

Mr. Berg waved his hand in the air, working to dismiss the tension forming in our three-man circle. He grinned, and said, "I am nothing more than the president of this fine banking establishment. I meant no disrespect. Jesse, if I may call him by his first name, was clearly on a mission. I believed at the time he was working to dispel the darkness surrounding your family's name, although he never told me such in his own words, mind you. May I ask how is Mr. Yale?"

"He's dead," I said flatly.

"I'm, I'm, very sorry to hear that." he replied in shock. "How, when did he pass?"

"A week after returning home from here," I replied. "And at this point, I am starting to question what actually caused his death to be honest with you, Mr. Berg."

The banker went sheet white, and he began to back away.

"I should check on the banking floor," he rushed. "I will instruct a guard to secure the door. When you are finished, knock three times, and the guard will let you out. This specific door locks from both the inside and the out. Make sure you slide the top lock open in order to be freed. Do you have any other questions?"

"Yes, do you know what is inside the security box?" I called, as he was making his way towards the stairs.

"No, unfortunately, I don't. We uphold the highest privacy standards here at Huisman Son and Trust. Your father was assigned a box and then given a key. The very key you are holding. This is the most private sector of our vault. Patrons are locked inside, as I mentioned. It's the only room in the entire bank that does not have security cameras. Whatever happens in that room is between you and your savior. Shut the door behind you," he called.

Jack's hands trembled as he closed the weighted door, and pushed the lock in place.

"Which box is ours?" I muttered.

"Look at the key," Jack said, "There are small numbers printed on the flat surface that goes inside the lock."

Sure enough, Jack was right. Hammered in tiny print was A14658. I grabbed a nearby stool and climbed on, looking up high first.

"That's weird," I said, "the boxes at the top start with a Z."

"It must be backwards," Jack replied.

Stooping low, in the dead middle of the last row, box A14658 was marked Royal.

"Here it is," I motioned.

Jack peered over my shoulder, "Jesse marked it Royal, not Yale."

We both drew in a deep breath, uncertain what we would find, but whatever it was our curiosity was too piqued not to open the box. My hands trembled, making it difficult to insert the key into the lock. Jack grabbed my hand and helped guide the key in. We turned the lock together and the box popped open.

The inside of the safe-deposit compartment was massive, yet inside sat only two small, neatly folded sheets of paper.

"Why would my father decide to store two small sheets of paper in this massive box?"

"Think about what Mr. Berg said, it's the only place inside the bank that isn't equipped with cameras. Jesse would be able to slip in the bank, secure the documents, and be out the door without anyone really taking notice. Nor would there be video to back up he had been here should someone start asking questions."

"I suppose you are right," I replied.

"Go ahead, take the documents out," Jack said.

Reaching inside the box, I pulled two legal-sized documents from their case. The top document was a plot map of Leiden, showing the points of interest and property ownership. The Royal's stake in Leiden was massive. The entire eastern part of the city held their name. The second sheet was handwritten in Dutch and illegible, but the document behind it was a translation dated May 3, 2007.

"Dad had this document translated while he was here," I replied.

"What does it say?"

"Warranty Deed Record," I began, "This indenture, made this 13th day of April, in the year of our lord, A.D. 1779, Ryker Yale Royal of Leiden, of perfect mind and body, thanks be given, agrees to the sum of 1,000 guilder."

"Guilder?" Jack questioned.

"No idea, but look, Dad handwrote off to the side $23,918.19." I said, pointing.

"That's a whole lot of money in the 1700s," Jack whistled. "Who did Ryker buy the land from?"

"It says Royal agrees to buy one hundred and sixty-three acres of land from Katharina Tunney."

"So the Tunney side had a mass amount of wealth after Ryker purchased the land. But we know that George was bailed out by the Royals when he was accused of blowing up the ship," I said. "I wonder why his own family didn't help him."

"Maybe his side of the family believed he was guilty," Jack surmised. "Is there an address on the sheet? Perhaps the factory sits somewhere on that property."

"2900 RB, Leiden."

"At least we know where we are headed next," Jack grinned. "What about the other document? What is that?"

The paper was different than the Warranty Deed, thinner and easy to tear.

"Be careful," Jack warned as I began to unfold the corners, "That's craft paper. It will rip under the slightest pressure."

As the page unfolded, Jack and I stared in awe.

"It's the Whizbang machine," Jack wheezed.

Someone had gone to great lengths to elaborately measure and sketch in exact detail the Whizbang machine's design. Every part, down to the galloping horses emblem and the type bars, was labeled in dark graphite. Along the bottom was Edward Royal's signature, the one that followed belonged to none other than George Tunney.

"It's the blueprint," I gulped. "It looks like they created the Whizbang machine together."

"There's something else you can take from this too. Look, do you see Edward's middle name?"

"Yale!" I exclaimed.

"Right," Jack said, "That is how he got our last name when he changed his name to David. He simply dropped the Royal."

"That makes sense," I replied.

Jack roughly rammed the security box closed. "Elizabeth, carefully fold the blueprint and the deed together and put them in your backpack. Remember the address listed on the deed."

"2900 RB, Leiden," I announced.

"Good," Jack smiled, "Now the documents."

Jack quickly shifted the upper door lock open and pounded out three heavy-handed knocks as Mr. Berg had instructed. Seconds later, the door pivoted opened, and we were free to go. We followed the quick-footed guard out of the vault and into the lobby. Mr. Berg was standing behind the teller counter watching his employees count obscene amounts of Euros when he caught us streaking by. He gave a quick nod as Jack and I burst through the massive double doors of Huisman Son and Trust.

Chapter 38: The Whizbang Factory

A line of taxis sat in wait outside of the bank. Jack knocked on the third cabbie's window and asked if he spoke English. The man shook his head no, directing us to the car directly behind his. The next driver was outside, leaning against his car reading the morning paper.

"Sir," Jack called, "do you happen to speak English?"

"Yes," he replied without looking up from the funny pages. He chuckled loudly to himself and then folded the paper in half. "Do you need a ride?" he finally asked.

"If you are available," Jack replied.

"Certainly, please hop in," he gestured. "May I take your backpack, young lady?"

"No!" Jack and I answered in unison.

"O-k-a-y," the driver replied, drawing out the word, "just trying to lighten your load."

Once inside the cab, Jack and I put on seatbelts and the driver shifted the car into gear.

"Where may I take you today?" he asked, looking in the rear-view mirror.

Jack patted my leg.

"2900 RB, please."

The driver tapped the breaks, "I'm sorry," he said, shaking his head, "I don't believe I heard you correctly. Where is it you would like to go?"

I repeated myself, a bit louder this time, "2900 RB, please."

"The clock factory?" he questioned.

"The Whizbang factory," Jack answered swiftly.

The driver shook, trembling involuntarily.

"I'm sorry I won't be able to take you all the way there."

"Why not?" Jack questioned.

"It's cursed, you know. People don't go out there. It's not a place for tourists like yourself to wander around. Whatever stories you've heard I'm sure they are nothing compared to the truth. You shouldn't go out there," he said darkly.

"We aren't tourists," Jack replied.

"Then who are you?" he asked.

"We are Royals," I replied.

The driver turned his eyes on the road and refused to speak another word for the remainder of the drive. Jack and I sat quietly too.

He turned the car northbound and drove out of the center of Leiden, past the Centraal rail station in which we first arrived, and out along the water's edges. The drive seemed impossibly long, taking small, dirt unmarked paths that weren't really roads at all. Nearly an hour later, the car skidded to a stop.

"This is as far as I go. Get out," the driver snapped, shifting the car into park.

Jack and I looked around. We were in the middle of nowhere. There wasn't a building or inkling of life anywhere our eyes could see.

"How much further is the factory?" Jack asked.

"A mile or two. Keep heading north. You'll find it," he replied.

"How much do I owe you, sir?"

"Nothing," the driver replied sharply, "I do not want your money."

"It was a long drive," Jack said, pulling a fistful of Euros out of his wallet, "Let me pay you, sir."

"It's blood money," he replied.

"Excuse me?" I questioned.

"One thousand and forty years the curse will remain until the rightful owner shall turn back the hands of time and correct a Royal mistake. Get out!" the driver howled.

Jack stretched as far as his arms would reach, pulled the passenger door handle, and forced the door open with a grunt. Before I could react, Jack pushed me hard, sending me to the ground below. The driver shifted the car into drive as Jack scooted himself across the bench seat. As his right foot hit the ground, the taxi lurched forward sending Jack stumbling. I extended my arms trying to catch him before he hit the ground, but I wasn't quick enough. We both were in a dusty heap. The driver made a sharp U-turn, kicking up dirt and rocks that landed in our eyes and struck our faces. As quickly as he had skidded to a stop, he was gone. Jack and I were still lying on the ground dumbfounded.

"Those were the exact words the pegwood merchant said on the church grounds before he stole the machine," I exclaimed.

"I thought so," Jack whispered.

"Are you okay?" I asked, picking myself up off the ground and reaching out to help Jack.

"Yeah," he replied. "I guess we better get walking, kid."

We dusted ourselves off and headed north as the driver had so rudely instructed. Less than half a mile later, the road narrowed to a single-person footpath. Mother Nature's glory was ablaze along the trail. A deep green canopy expanded over our heads as the trees bent and intermingled their branches with the tree across the way. Hunter green ferns flanked the bottom of the large trees, adding a lushness to the winding path. Pops of yellow daffodils were scattered everywhere. The pathway was magical in a way, and yet, I couldn't help but feel that we were marching our way into a nightmare.

Almost an hour later, the path opened into a majestic clearing. Dense trees surrounded a small pond. In the near distance stood an aging stone cottage with a dark thatched roof.

"Who do you think lives there?" I whispered.

"I don't know," Jack replied, "but I think we better tread carefully here too."

"That can't be the factory, can it? It's too small, right?" I questioned.

"I would think so," Jack said, standing on his tiptoes to look through the dense trees. A few moments of silence passed as we both looked around, when Jack suddenly jumped, "There!"

A red brick factory, four stories tall with a rounded roof was in the clearing. Chimney stacks shot straight into the sky. In its glory days, this place would have been a work of art, but now, over a hundred years later, it was disheveled and unfit for human traffic.

"How do we get back there?" I asked.

"This way," Jack beckoned.

We walked the length of three football fields before we stood before our family's factory.

Jack laughed, "Where is the picture of Edward and George standing in front of this place?"

I slipped my backpack off my shoulder, balanced it on my knee, and dug inside. I quickly found the photo and placed it in Jack's hand.

"Look," he said, "we stopped in almost the same spot the picture was taken."

"The sign is gone," I replied, looking from the photograph to the building.

The bottom floor windows were mostly broken. The work of vandals, no doubt with a curiosity to know if the curse is real or not. The top story was lucky to still be intact. Blue and orange stained glass still held their spots. I closed my eyes and tried to imagine the life that once surrounded this place. Workers fluttering from one place to another, heated black smoke pushing its way through the chimney stacks. I didn't want to open my eyes. The factory felt alive.

"Think we should go in?" I asked.

"Definitely," Jack grinned.

As we began to advance towards the door, a woman called out from behind.

"Hello!" she yelled. "*Stoppen, geen* trespassing!"

Jack and I froze. Neither of us had entertained the idea that someone would be at the factory, not when it has been abandoned for so many years. The woman jogged to Jack and me and stared at us hard. She rapidly reprimanded us for trespassing in Dutch. When she paused long enough to take a breath, Jack stepped forward.

"Madam, do you speak English?"

"Yes, quite well," she replied.

"Ah, very good, hello, I'm sorry if we frightened you. We have an interest in the factory."

"I'm sorry, sir, but the factory is closed. It's not for sale."

"Yes, I see that. Is there someone who I may speak with to allow us to gain entry?" Jack asked.

"Me," she said roughly, "and as I said, it's closed. Now, please, see yourself off my property."

"May I ask your name?" Jack mused.

"Vivian," she replied.

"That's beautiful."

"I'm Jack, and this is my granddaughter Elizabeth. We traveled from America just to see the Whizbang factory."

"Why?" she pushed.

"Research," Jack said rapidly.

"Of what nature?" Vivian replied, folding her arms across her meek chest.

"Well you see, Vivian, we believe our bloodline had ownership in this factory."

The glint in Vivian's eyes disappeared. Her brows furrowed hard as she looked back and forth between Jack and I.

"What is your last name?" she asked in a low voice.

"Yale—our last name is Yale."

"Why don't you come with me? I live in the small cottage up the way. We'll have some tea, and perhaps I can help you with your research," Vivian replied.

"That would be very kind of you," I said.

Chapter 39: Octoker 3, 1876

Vivian was a petite woman, in her late sixties, with graying hair that rivaled Jack's. There was a familiarity to her that I couldn't put my finger on. She and Jack made small talk on the way back to the cottage. I stayed a few steps behind gulping in the lush greenery. My mind kept coming back to the fact that I was walking in the same footsteps my great-grandparents would have walked every day for years. There was something humbling about that fact.

I caught on to the last bit of Vivian and Jack's conversation as she said, "The cottage once belonged to Edward Royal and his family. My family took it over shortly after they fled to the United States."

"And what is your last name?" I asked.

Vivian turned and smiled, "It's Myers dear."

A name neither Jack nor I had heard, "And how are you connected to the factory and these grounds?"

"I am a descendant of the family," she replied. "I live on the grounds to protect our heritage."

Jack guzzled in Vivian's charm and her words. I, on the other hand, felt her answers weren't direct enough. She opened the cottage door and welcomed us inside.

The walls were lavished in library paneling. Every inch of the small home spoke to the opulence of the Royals. Velveteen drapes touched the ceiling and dusted the floor in the seating room, shielding the light from coming in. Piles of books and newspapers were lined across every wall and covered every surface.

"Sorry," she apologized, "we don't get much company out here."

"We?" Jack questioned, looking for signs of another person in the small house.

Vivian laughed, "I can't keep myself from saying we. I lost my husband a few months ago. I'm a lonely widow now."

"I'm sorry for your loss," Jack whispered. "I know how that is."

Vivian smiled a wistful grin, "Please take a seat where you can find one. Move what you need. Now tell me, you said you were doing research about your family. Are you speaking of the Royals?"

"Yes," Jack replied, moving a stack of books and sinking into an antique settee.

"Well, where should I start?" Vivian replied.

"How about when the clock factory turned into the Whizbang factory?" I urged.

"My, you have done your research, haven't you?"

"Well, let's see. Ryker Royal passed away in a fire one month before his son Edward was elected Mayor. Did you know you had a Mayor in your family?"

"We did," Jack grinned.

"Good. Edward was consumed with the town's business. He wasn't much of a businessman, truthfully. He was more of an idea man. Pretty lame in the head, if you ask me. After Ryker's untimely death, Edward didn't come around the factory much. The supervisors did what they could, but business wasn't coming in. Ryker was worth millions. It was passed to Edward seeing how he was the oldest. However, he and his wife, a dreadful woman,

Amelia I believe was her name, they had an affinity for the good life. They spent that money faster than humanly possible. Edward also began supporting the local newspaper. Buying headlines, if you will. Made himself out to be a big hero as he spread rumors and lies around about other parts of his family."

I watched Vivian speak. The way she spoke about Edward raised my heckles. I hung onto every syllable, afraid I may miss a clue. Jack had eased into Vivian's story. He was more relaxed than I had seen him since he first arrived in New York.

Vivian continued, "The story goes that Edward fell in love with the printing press the paper used. He was taken by the confounded thing, truthfully. He spent years fantasizing over making a portable version of the machine."

"Leiden at that time was quickly becoming the center of massive printing for books all across the world. Royal was convinced that if he could create a smaller, portable printing-press-type piece of machinery he would effectively create his own wealth, but in the process he let the clock factory die."

"But he had to have been successful, right? Otherwise, we wouldn't have had the Whizbang machine."

Vivian's eyes narrowed at Jack, "What do you mean we wouldn't have had the machine? Have you seen the machine?"

Jack's body stiffened. He roughly adjusted himself on the couch, "No, no ma'am, I meant figuratively *had* the machine. He wouldn't have reopened the factory as the Whizbang factory is what I meant."

Vivian laughed, "I was a bit confused for a moment. I thought you meant you *had* the machine. It was stolen from the factory during the 3 October Festival in 1876. No one has seen it since."

Jack remained upright as her words sunk in for him as they did for me, October 3, 1876. That was the date listed on Alina's headstone.

"October festival?" I questioned.

"Yes," Vivian coughed. "I should first explain that Edward was successful at designing a smaller version of the printing press. Called it the Whizbang machine after the way it whizzed and banged while the operator typed, but when it went into production, there were glitches. The faults in the system rendered the machine useless. Edward tried to fix it, but like I said before, he was an idea man."

"So then what happened?" Jack pushed.

"Well, Edward had a brilliant cousin known for his brilliant eye in architecture."

"George Tunney," I asked.

"Yes indeed. George was a good man. Smart," she said tapping her temples. "Tunney and Royal were first cousins, but Royal spent most of his time speaking against his own blood and making sure the family glory remained focused on only himself."

I cleared my throat. Vivian's story of Edward and George was vastly different from the one we heard in the Leiden University Library. Vivian stopped and peered over at me.

"I'm sorry, please go on," I smiled.

"Edward went to George and begged for his help. After months of pleading and making extreme promises,

George agreed to fix the flaws in the Whizbang machine's design. The design problems were small, but George didn't let Edward in on such information. He demanded Edward keep his promises. Conditions were laid out. Edward was to pay George a commission, a hefty one of five hundred guilder, and George was to receive a royalty from every machine sold. Furthermore, he was to be given equal glory for the machine's creation. Edward agreed to the conditions and the factory was reopened as the Whizbang *Fabriek*."

"That was on October 3, 1876?" I questioned.

"No," she replied sharply.

"Then what was so special about that date?" *Other than the death of Royal's daughter, Alina,* I thought to myself.

"Royal's machine was an immediate success worldwide. Royal's team reopened the *Klok* factory under the new name and purpose in early August of 1876. Royal's men gathered orders, produced machines in record time, and began sending massive loads of Whizbang machines across the ocean to America. As success came, George and Edward began fighting. Edward hadn't paid George the commission he had promised him. The more George pressed, Edward began claiming he had used the funds as reimbursement for a loan Ryker had spotted him. As you can imagine, that didn't go over well."

"You mean paying back his debt to the city after the gunpowder blew the city apart?" Jack asked.

"Why yes, that is what I mean," Vivian said slowly. Her body language changed. With each push of information, she began to realize we knew more than most.

"George was furious," Vivian added. "He was living in extreme poverty at the time and his family had shunned him for other acts he had been wrongfully accused of. Most of which were lies fed to them by Royal himself. George quickly became Leiden's scapegoat."

"Wasn't there a fire?" I asked a bit too prematurely.

"At the factory?" Vivian asked.

"Yes," she replied. "That happened on October 3."

"Has the building been repaired since the fire?" Jack interpreted. "I didn't see evidence of a fire from the front of the factory."

"No, it hasn't been," Vivian answered. "Attempts have been made; each time a repair has gotten underway it sets off another accident. The factory has actually been ablaze six times. The majority of the damage is inside and on the backside of the building."

"I see," Jack said, "Would you consider that a part of Tunney's curse?"

"I don't believe I mentioned a curse," Vivian responded curtly.

"One of the historians we spoke with did," Jack said quickly, trying to clean up his words.

"My dear," Vivian said coldly, "the curse runs much deeper than that."

Vivian's words pushed a round of chills through my body that touched me so deeply that my bones shook. I swallowed hard, and barely was able to croak out, "What exactly happened on October 3?"

"Leiden has celebrated the third of October since 1574. That was the end of the Spanish siege here. It's two or three days of parades, festivals, historical reenactments, funfair;

you name it, it happens. Except in 1876, Royal made the celebration about him and the Whizbang machine. The townspeople gathered at St. Peter's courtyard."

As Vivian spoke, I let her words paint a vivid picture in my head.

"The town came dressed in their very best. Men in their suits, women in their hats and full-length dresses. This was an affair to remember. Banners hung from nearby rooftops proclaiming October 3 was to be Leiden's Salvation day. The day of the Whizbang machine. Of course, that salvation was to be Edward Royal.

"As the sun set, bands played on a stage Royal had built. Leiden was alive with music. Old gas lamps burned in the square. Children spun on their heels, holding their mothers hands as everyone delighted. It was magical.

"Midway through the celebration three men climbed to the highest peaks of the bell tower of St. Peter's. Royal had them drop fifty Whizbang machines in crates strapped to parachutes. There among the partygoers, with the glow of the gaslights flickering, the Whizbang machines floated from what seemed to be the heavens. The newspaper snapped photos of the enchantment. As people looked on in awe, Royal took to the stage. 'Ladies and Gentlemen, boys and girls, October 3 will always be a day to remember. I have single-handedly created a machine that will revolutionize the world. Fifty Whizbang machines are yours for the grabbing.'"

"The crowd went wild, everyone except George Tunney. People swarmed the floating machines, each wanting one of their very own. Royal had planned this and perfectly positioned himself into the hearts of everyone in Leiden, and he did so without his cousin."

"In the chaos, Tunney slipped away. Whether it is true or not, it's said he took the original Whizbang machine and the blueprints with him."

"The party raged on. Forty minutes after Edward Royal's speech, Royal's right-hand man, a fellow called Ian Hess, ran to his boss' side. Hess, who had been holding down the fort at the factory, reported it had gone up in flames. There wasn't much between the factory and St. Peter's church at the time and from the right angle it was easy to see the red brick facade, even at night. As Edward looked up, he saw the flames shooting into the sky."

"Edward stood in disbelief, watching everything he had go up in smoke. He had planned to give the city of Leiden a new coat of arms that night. One that held two red keys. He had his workers produce two red keys that would accompany the coat of arms. He gave Alina, his four-year-old daughter, the special chore of keeping them safe until he presented them at the party. Amelia ran around frantically through the crowd looking for Alina when Hess realized he had seen the child at the factory moments before the fire broke out. Alina had forgotten the keys in the boiler room where she often played. An older cousin took her back to the factory to retrieve them as to not disturb her parents."

"The blaze burned for hours. Hess wasn't able to get his entire crew out of the building before he went to retrieve Royal. Two days after the fire was started, the last ember burned. The back of the original factory was a complete loss. Royal walked the factory himself identifying bodies. In total, he had lost sixteen men. He found his sweet Alina clutching the red city keys in the boiler room. She too had perished in the fire."

Tears rolled down my cheeks. I closed my eyes trying to understand why the feud between Royal and Tunney had gotten so out of hand.

"And the cousin that brought Alina to the factory?" Jack asked softly.

"She was Tunney's daughter. She made it out without a scratch."

I gasped, "Please tell me she didn't take Alina to the factory knowing her father would do something awful."

"I won't, because I cannot be certain it was Tunney who set the fire. Perhaps it was a terrible coincidence," she said.

"What happened to Tunney?" I asked.

"He was never seen or heard from again," she said.

I sat with the incredible misfortune of knowing Royal and his wife suffered.

"Dear child," Vivian whispered, "You need some tea. Please, let's go into the kitchen."

Jack and I stood and followed Vivian down the small hallway. Dozens of photos in antique frames hung along the wall. One, in particular, caught my eye. I grabbed Jack's wrist and pulled him to a stop.

"Look," I trembled.

In the center of the wall hung a photo of the pegwood merchant and the woman from Morocco. The pair smiled for the camera on their wedding day.

"Jack," I swallowed, "they're married. Vivian is connected to them."

"Don't say a word," he muttered. "We need to get out of here."

Vivian was already in the kitchen banging a teapot against the edge of a metal sink.

As we made our way to the end of the hall, a door stood open enough to see what was kept inside the small room. Lined against every wall, displayed perfectly on long shelves were the pegwood dolls. Jack and I stared, unsure whether to run or to press for more information until Vivian figured out who we really were. Jack pushed his way into the pegwood room as Vivian rounded the corner to find us.

"My dolls," she said darkly.

"They're beautiful," I said turning.

"Yes, they are each rare, please come out of there and join me in the kitchen."

We did as we were told, unwilling to let this be our downfall. Vivian shut the door behind her sealing us out.

"You know, every month for the past few years someone sneaks into the factory and leaves a collection of roses where little Alina passed. They must come in the middle of the night because I've never seen who comes, but they arrive like clockwork. Today is that day. Would you like to go into the factory and see if her delivery has arrived?"

"Really? Who would do that?" I questioned.

Jack cleared his throat and said, "Yes, Vivian, why don't we go see the factory."

She flicked off the gas on the stove, moved the teapot, grabbed a small stack of matches, and turned with a smile, "Shall we?"

A plan began formulating in my head. Jack and I needed to escape from this woman. She was dangerous—too dangerous. A room full of pegwood dolls, the photography of the woman and the merchant, Vivian may claim her last name is Myer, but inside there was no way that her blood wasn't that of a Tunney.

Chapter 40: Trapped

Incredibly, the smell of char still hung in the air after more than a century. Blackened open walls exposed themselves to the eroding elements while pools of water sat on the cold, gray cement. The brick floors above our heads crumbled as we entered, exposing the next story above it and the one after that. The roof rafters, four stories high, dangled in a careful balancing act that could give way to gravity at any moment.

This relic of Dutch history, our history, was in complete shambles. Yet, everything was exactly where it had been the day of the fire. Unfinished Whizbang machines lined rusted production tables. Individual parts lay tarnished, decaying, and scattered along the cement floor. There was beauty in this destruction despite the overwhelming sense of sadness growing in my chest.

Snatching a typewheel off the floor, Jack turned to Vivian, "Why didn't Edward ever clear this place?"

"He never stepped foot inside the factory again. Not after he found Alina. Losing a child does things to a parent, dark things."

Jack lowered his head as he folded his arms roughly across his chest. If anyone could understand his three-times-great-grandfather's pain, it was Jack.

Vivian continued, "Royal hired crews to repair the building, but like I said one repair sparked another catastrophe. The next fix after that only made matters worse. It essentially bankrupted Royal."

"What about the machine? Why didn't he try to create others?" I asked.

"He tried to redesign the machine but continued to come up with the same flaws he begged Tunney to fix in the first place. Tunney was nowhere to be found, and every other person Edward commissioned to help was simply unable to find the flaw. George never shared with another living soul how he fixed the design. It was his way of ensuring that Royal would always need him."

"It didn't work out for either of them, did it?" I muttered.

"What's that?" Jack asked, pointing to a marble pedestal in the middle of a vestibule.

"When the factory was in full swing that pedestal held the original Whizbang machine. Go see for yourself, it was actually locked into place. Tunney had threatened to steal the machine when Edward refused to pay up. After that, Royal installed the locks and hired a team of guards to stand over the machine. It was a twenty-four-hour operation. If you look up, you can see where Royal even had special lighting installed over the device."

"It was Edward's crowning joy," Jack muttered.

"Indeed, it was. I often daydream about what that machine would look like displayed on this pedestal, the lights shining down on its regal beauty…I'm sure it was a stunning sight."

Jack grinned as Vivian let her mind wander away. Suddenly, her eyes flashed cold, and said, "It's been my life's mission to bring the Whizbang machine back to the factory. I will continue to search for the machine until my last breath."

I choked, "Have you ever seen the Whizbang machine in person, Vivian?"

"No, I cannot say that I have. How about you Elizabeth, have you?"

I turned on my heels, unwilling to answer, searching for anything that might change the subject, and hastily said, "What's behind these doors?"

A deep laugh rose in Vivian's throat. My eyes locked into Jack's as he motioned towards the exit. Vivian reached for my arm, digging her sharp fingernails into my skin, and pulled me away from Jack's side, "Edward's office is right down this hall. Come along, it's right this way."

Above the wooden casing surrounding the door was Edward's full name etched in dusty glass: Edward Yale Royal. In the middle of the modest room sat Edward's decaying desk. It was a time capsule to our great-grandfather in his heyday. His circular silver-rimmed glasses lay on top of a leather-bound bookkeeper's ledger. The picture of Edward, George, and the third man we now believed to be Edward's assistant, Ian Hess, standing outside of the Whizbang factory was propped against a gas light. Everything was as Royal left it the night of October 3, 1876.

It's funny how quickly life goes from the simple and routine act of living from day-to-day to completely broken. A part of Edward died on October 3. The factory is living evidence of his despair. The repeat of history—Alina and Edward, my father and Jack—both fathers drowned in their sorrow. The hardest part is not knowing if Edward was ever able to make his way back to living a life that wasn't defined by that specific date on the calendar. Jack had been, but look what it took. The very thought of both men's suffering nearly stole my breath away.

The tears forming in my eyes were washed away as Jack roughly yanked open Edward's small center desk drawer. His face went red as he closed his eyes.

"What is it, Grandpa?"

Jack pulled a silver pen from Edward's desk, rolling it in his palm, back and forth, as Vivian watched but didn't speak a word.

"J.Y.," he whispered.

It belonged to my father.

A sound pulled Vivian's attention away, stepping out of Royal's office and into the hall to investigate. Jack pocketed the pen while her head was turned. Then he pretended to put it back in its place and shut the drawer.

"Why would he have left the pen?" I questioned.

"I don't know," Jack sighed. "I wish the machine was here to ask it a few questions."

"Me too, but it's gone, Jack. Did you hear what she said? It's her mission to bring the machine back to the factory. We have to get out of here."

Jack shook his head as Vivian stepped back inside.

"What was that sound?" I asked.

"I'm not certain. It could have been another round of bricks falling from the upper floors. It's happening more lately. We need to have the roof closed to protect the factory from the elements, but honestly, no one will work on this place anymore. They're too afraid."

"It didn't sound like bricks to me," I replied firmly, "It sounded like the entrance door opening. Did someone come inside?"

"Oh no, of course not, dear. We would hear them moving about if they did. Everything echoes in this old haunt. Now, why don't we continue to look around?"

Vivian directed Jack and me to a large room with heavy steel doors on an overhead roller. An aging plaque noted the space as the boiler room. The very place Alina died. Vivian rolled the doors open only enough to allow us to squeeze inside. The smell of coal and heat hit our noses.

"Please," she motioned.

"You first," I insisted.

The boiler room was exceptionally dark. The only pinprick of light filtering in came from the hall. It was more of a dungeon than a room. If the door were to close, it would be impossible to see.

"Come on," Vivian asserted, "you traveled all this way. You wanted to see the factory. This is the most important part."

She moved forward, stepping into the darkness, "I'll go with you."

Jack and I squeezed our way inside, my backpack catching on the steel frame. Vivian offered to hold it for me, but there was no way I would allow her to get her hands on the materials on my back. I turned sideways and made my way into the boiler room.

"Now then," Vivian said darkly, "this is where poor—sweet—little—Alina—died. Sad little thing. If only she hadn't forgotten the red keys. Want to know something else?"

Jack's body went rigid and stayed absolutely still as Vivian drew closer to the steel door.

"This is where you will die too. Your son especially liked this room. He looked like a scared rat scurrying in the corner as I shut the door on him too. He wasn't a man. He was a baby. Standing in here crying for his daughter and his wife. It was disgusting."

I lurched forward, ready to take her old bones to the ground when from behind her back she pulled four long matches and struck them against the wall. Flames ignited and flickered at the end of the sticks. They crackled, burning off the residual coal from the wall.

"Vivian," Jack choked, "This place will blow."

"I know," she laughed. "Won't that be fun? Well, not for you, but it certainly will be for me!"

Jack tugged hard on my arm and forced my back against the far wall. There was no way out.

"Do not drop those matches, Vivian," Jack screamed.

Another terrifying laugh ripped from her belly.

"You're a lunatic," I screeched.

"Ah, such sweet nothings, dear child. What's the matter, are you afraid you'll die the way Alina did—burnt alive? If you have trouble accepting Alina's death, why don't you consider dying the way Edward did? They're one in the same, you know!"

I gasped. Jack launched himself in her direction.

"Don't," she shouted. "I will drop these matches and boom! The pathetic Royals will be gone once and for all!"

"What do you mean Royal died the same way?" I bellowed.

"Now, there's a piece of the puzzle I bet you haven't figured out yet. Poor Edward. Came back here after fleeing. Thought he would clean up his mess, break George

Tunney's curse. What a shame he had to die. Oh, and that pen you stuffed in your pocket, Jack. Well, I took that from your son. Kept it as a souvenir. I hope you don't mind."

She took the last step outside of the door, and whispered, "Bye, bye," slowly waving. As the steel door rolled closed, she tossed the matches into the center of the room and slammed the door.

"No!" I screamed, "No! Jack!"

Chapter 41: Tunney's Curse

"Elizabeth, give me the backpack!" Jack roared.

The fire danced, growing larger by each passing second. The powdery coal left on the floor fueled its might. I refused to move, mesmerized by the flickers. Jack jerked the backpack off my back and pulled out three large bottles of water.

The stream of liquid only damped the fire slightly. Smoke wafted in the air filling Jack's lungs. He coughed hard, and screamed, "Cover your nose and mouth."

I couldn't move.

"Do it now, Elizabeth!"

My vision grew dark. Pricks of blackness floated in my eyes. My head swarmed with only one image—my mom. I watched as she lifted me from a small bassinet and handed me to my father. I had just been born. A moment later, she and I were standing over my father's grave. This was complete torture. Flashes of our life together came and fled quickly.

Jack turned the backpack upside down and cleared the contents. He swung wildly, beating the battered backpack against the heated flames. It was working.

I watched as I hugged my mother goodbye. How I wished I would have told her how much I loved her. How I have never wished for a different mom, never in a million years. She was absolutely the very best. Her face floated away, replaced with stone cold blackness.

"Elizabeth!" Jack shouted.

My eyes snapped open.

"Give me your jacket—hurry—before the flames return!"

The fire was nothing but a small flicker of embers. Grey smoke covered every inch of the small room, but something deeper occurred to me. I was alive. Ripping my jacket from my shoulders, I tossed it to Jack who smothered the last spark.

Jack collapsed on the ground in a heap of sweat, fear, and exhaustion.

"Are you okay?" he whispered.

"I think so," I sputtered. "Jack, we're trapped."

"I know," he said, burying his head in his hands. "I will get us out somehow."

The unbearable silence lasted for too long. Jack was at a loss and so was I. Suddenly, muffled voices leaked in through the small creaks around the steel door.

"Shh," Jack snapped.

I listened, unable to make out the conversation as it was distorted by the steel barrier, but I counted the voices. There were three. Three people stood on the other side of our trap.

"Let them think we died," Jack slurred low. "Don't make a sound. If they open the door, we bolt. Do you understand?"

"Yes," I whispered.

Jack pulled me forward, creeping to the door's edge. Waiting. Listening. A rough click sounded on the other side. Jack hunched and leaned forward. The voices grew louder and then suddenly vanished. The door remained closed.

"Now what?" I stammered.

"Now we figure out a way out."

Jack paced the floor. His feet kicked up dusty blackness with each pass. I bent low, collecting the backpack's contents that were hastily scattered. The cell phone, while cracked, glowed, pushing a small amount of light into the darkness. I typed in my code, 4-5-0-3, and flipped the tab up and hit the flashlight. The small, round, white light provided just enough illumination to shake away the crushing darkness.

Jack stopped in his tracks and looked at me, "Thank God," he bellowed, "Tell me it isn't almost dead."

"I can't tell. The screen is shattered."

"We'll use it sparingly then."

I stood and shined the light on the steel door. It was nothing more than a flat piece of steel. It was clear it locked from the outside. Jack rocked the panel on its tracks, but the tension of the lock snapped it back into position. Neither of us had the physical strength to bust the industrial lock open. Jack was furious. His hand pounded against the door in a fit of rage.

"Let us out!" he screamed.

The only thing we could do now was sit and wait. Vivian, the merchant…someone would come. Deep down inside I knew they would. Their evilness wouldn't be satisfied until their curiosity over our deaths was suited. It may take time, but they would come. Jack trembled and returned to his incessant pacing.

"This is hopeless!" he shouted.

"No," I snapped. "Someone will come."

Jack remained quiet. I picked up the blue velvet journal we extracted from Alina's grave and opened it. As I propped the light against my chest to help me read the passages a figure on the factory's outer wall caught my attention.

"Jack," I said, pulling myself to my feet.

In the glow of the light, thick shapes emerged under the coal dust.

"Give me my jacket," I urged. "We have to get the dust off the wall! That looks like a part of the Whizbang machine!"

"We're in the factory," Jack barked. "It's probably just a picture."

"What if it's not?" I bit back. "Give me the jacket!"

Jack snapped the charred fabric off the ground and tossed it to me. Hastily smearing the black sediment across the wall, each push revealed another section of the drawing.

"Give me the phone," Jack ordered.

Laying it in his hand, he shined it across the length of the brick. The beam stopped and held on a brush broom leaning against the far corner.

"You're right! Whatever it is covers the entire wall. There's a broom."

Together we worked to expose the hidden brick. Jack pushed the broom while I wiped the wall. Dust and soot flew. Hours passed. Smut and grime covered every inch of our beings. We fluctuated between working in the light and in the darkness. Sweat poured as did our blood from catching our hands and arms against the brick. When the light of day had faded and a new day had surely dawned, the brick was clean.

"Turn on the light," Jack uttered. His voice was scratchy and nearly inaudible.

Typing in the code once more, I pushed the flashlight button. There painted on the brick was a cipher.

Each red brick was assigned a number. The top far left corner of the eight-foot wall was labeled number one. It ended on the far right. Printed on the last brick was 3,855. The first image was that of the grandfather clock. The original grandfather clock. The one that sits in both England's parliament and our shabby foyer on Downhill Lane in New York. The painting of the clock started on brick ten and ended on brick two hundred and ninety-five. The number four was the only number on the clock's face.

In the center, straddled between brick one thousand and brick one thousand and one was an exact replica of the Whizbang machine. Jack and I stared at it hard. There was one glaring difference between the painting and the actual machine. The Royal's trademark of galloping horses and whipping reins was replaced with the number six.

"Four, six," Jack whispered.

On the lower half of the wall was the beginning mark of a skeleton key. The largest of the paintings, the key, stretched from the lowest brick to the ceiling.

"There's not another number," I sighed.

"Oh yes there is," Jack laughed. "See it?"

"No," I insisted.

"Look at the key's opening."

"That's the sign for infinity," I chomped.

"Or it's the number eight," Jack replied.

Jack walked to the clock, pointing, he said, "The number four." He moved to the Whizbang machine, "Six," he said tapping the brick, as he moved to the key. His hand shot straight up, "Eight. It's a code."

My eyes moved across the wall, trying to make sense of the pattern when suddenly they landed on a small dial.

"It's the way out!" I shouted. "It has to be!"

Dropping to my belly, I twisted the dial: 4, 6, 8. Nothing happened. I tried it again, slower this time. 4, 6, 8. Nothing.

"Try it again," Jack cried. "Turn the dial the other way."

I drew a deep breath of air into my lungs and narrowed my focus. I twisted the dial to the left making a full circle then slowly landed on the number four. I rotated the knob to the right, six. Making another full circle around, I positioned the disc on the number eight.

"Push it in," Jack whispered.

The brick parted. Pieces broke loose and crumbled to the ground. I tugged and chipped away at those that remained. When the wall was free of mortar, a steel trapdoor sat open to a long tunnel fitted with small tracks.

"What is this?" I hissed.

Jack's hot breath touched my ear, "The way out."

Slithering on our bellies, we made our way into the tight tunnel. The walls were brittle and flanked with the same blackened soot. Lumps of gray decaying coal dust sat against the edges of the tunnel.

"What do you think these tracks are for?" I asked, as I made my way onto all fours and began crawling.

"My guess is this is how Royal moved the coal into the building. They would have used carts to bring it inside. Someone would be at one end filling the cart, and when it was full, they would have pushed it along these tracks to the boiler room. This has to lead outside."

The tunnel twisted and looped back. Smaller tunnels shot off to the left and the right, but we continued to push forward. My knees burned, scraping against the rough ground, but finally a dead end was within sight.

"There," I pointed, "There's another door."

"Let's hope it's unlocked," Jack pushed.

Slowly, we crawled to the end. We heaved our bodies against the steel.

"Push," Jack strained.

The door moved slightly. I flipped from my hands and knees and placed my back against the door. Using my legs as leverage, I hoisted my weight against the steel. Pain resounded within my body as I went limp. The door barely moved.

"There has to be something against the opening," I cried.

"Let me try," Jack insisted.

I moved, clearing the way for Jack. He ducked, unable to fully sit up.

"I'll push with my back while you push at the top of the door. Maybe we can move it together."

I stood as much as the tunnel walls would allow. My knees were bent. My back rested against the brick above. I laid my hands directly over Jack's shoulders. He gathered his strength and said, "On the count of five. Are you ready?"

"Go," I whispered. A fierce determination to be free of the tightness surrounding me filled my chest.

"One," Jack said, beginning to apply pressure to the door. "Two."

"Three, four, five," I huffed, pushing with all my might.

The door burst open, sending me flying on top of Jack.

"Yes!" I cried as daylight washed away the darkness.

Jack and I climbed out of the tunnel and looked around. We were on the backside of the factory.

"Elizabeth, listen to me," Jack huffed. His blackened soot-covered face was hard to take serious. "We have to get off the property undetected. Follow me and whatever you do, do not say a word!"

I nodded as Jack looked for a way to hide our movement. Without warning, he took off for the woods surrounding the property. We ran without stopping for more than half a mile. Freedom, the open air, even the chill touching my face had never felt so good, but one thing kept pulling at me. Was this really the end? Was I truly willing to go home without the machine, even if it is in pieces? Was I really willing to go home without the curse broken?

That's when it hit me. I skittered to a stop and shouted, "The click!"

Jack stopped short in his tracks, "What click?" he huffed, his chest heaving.

"When we the heard the voices. Vivian said Royal had locks installed to secure the machine. The click!"

I turned on my heels and pounded the ground. My body raced forward. Forward back to the Whizbang Factory.

"Elizabeth—NO!" Jack shrieked. "Stop!"

I was too far-gone. My feet kicked dirt high into the air. Momentum surged me onward to the point I could no longer feel the ground. If I didn't know better I would have thought I had taken flight. My heart hammered in my ears, my focus never moving. I was going back into the factory with or without Jack.

I turned to see if he was following me, but he was nowhere to be seen. Still, my feet galloped on. Rounding the corner, I burst through the front entrance of the Whizbang Factory. Catching a small pool of water, I stumbled, unable to catch myself before my head ricocheted off the hard cold cement.

My belly turned from the pain. I laid on the floor, wet, bleeding, and unable to see through the black dots floating in my vision. A moment passed, and I blinked hard, pushing the pain away.

Before my eyes, on top of the pedestal my four-times-great-grandfather had built, was the Whizbang machine locked in place. It wasn't in a million pieces as the merchant tried to lead us to believe. It was there, returned to its original holding place on the marble.

"Well, well, well," a man's voice called from the factory's doorway. "You're a smart one, Elizabeth Yale. Or should I say Royal?"

I turned, scrambling to my feet. The merchant leaned against the doorway wearing the most wicked smile I had ever seen.

"Don't come near me," I ordered.

"You look like you've seen a ghost. Thought I died when I jumped, did you?" he said slowly stepping forward.

"I mean it, don't come near me!"

"Don't touch the machine and all will be fine."

Slowly backing my way to the pedestal, the machine let out a deafening pop. Whiz-whiz-bang. WHIZ-WHIZ-BANG! Smoke and letters intertwined over the roller and floated to the ceiling. Hot oil seeped from the bottom as I had seen it do in my dreams.

Pop!

A wild buzzing grew louder until I had no choice but to cover my ears.

"Don't touch the machine," the vendor urged. "It's back where it belongs—with my family. You know, the Tunneys."

The Whizbang machine shook violently. Rocking back and forth, it was trying to free itself from the pedestal locks.

One thousand and forty years the curse will remain until the rightful owner shall turn back the hands of time and correct a Royal mistake. The secret will eat away at those who come to play like a disease floated in the air.

The vendor let out a wicked howl and repeated the curse.

"Stop," I shouted. "What does that even mean?"

The machine's violent rocking mounted. The marble pedestal swayed left then right. Fire ignited from the keys.

"No!" I screamed. "Help! It can't catch on fire!"

WHIZ!

"No,"

WHIZ-WHIZ-BANG! White light flashed above our heads. The factory quaked. POP!

"The building is coming down," the merchant shouted.

I turned my back on him. There was only one way to stop this. Letting my fingers dangle over the keys, my body vibrated as the ceiling above began crashing down around me. Bricks fell and slammed into tiny bits at my feet. Lightning flashed and bounced off the open walls.

My fingers hit the keys. Vivian and her daughter, the woman with the dark eyes, rolled the boiler room door open. The steel ground hard against the wheels.

The machine popped with all its might. Fire raged from its body. My flesh burned. The machine held my hands the way it did the first time my fingers found the keys.

"Forty years is all you have once the curse finds its way to you. Death is upon us. Death is upon us," the wicked pair chanted.

"Elizabeth," Jack called.

My body seized. I gulped in air. Hot smoke filled my lungs and set my insides on fire.

"H-e-l-p," I cried.

"Elizabeth," Jack shrieked, "please! Let go! Lizzy!"

"The clock ticks or life falls into reverse," the pair screamed in unison.

`Free me. Free yourself.`

My eyes slammed shut. Each pulse of power sent me closer to the edge of madness. My head swam with a million thoughts. The same visions filled my mind. My mother. My father. My death.

The wind blew pushing my long brown hair into my face. Lightning flashed so close the heat rivaled the fire burning under my fingers. The machine called wildly

WHIZ-WHIZ-BANG! The chanting grew louder. My eyes
flew open and my fingers pressed against the keys.

`You are free`!

The Whizbang machine jumped, snapping from its
locks. Raw electricity pulsed through my core. I closed my
eyes. My body levitated off the ground with the electricity
shooting through the soles of my feet. I tried to yell to Jack,
but my words were caught.

One last push of raw power surged through my body
and everything around me went deafeningly still.

BANG! the machine called.

With one last ferocious shake, everything stopped.
My body crashed to the floor in a hot heap of bones and
raw skin.

"NO, no, no! E-l-i-z-a-b-e-t-h!

Fact or Fiction
Notes and Research from the Author:

This book contains historical facts, events, and figures woven together to create a work of fiction. This chapter is a simple guide to help you discern what is a fact and what is the brainchild of my imagination. You will also find a basic Dutch to English glossary. As a non-Dutch speaker, I hope the translations served me well.

The Glossary:

A combination of words and phrases originally entered into a translator in English and were translated into Dutch. During the writing of this book, I fell in love with the Dutch culture and the language. These are the key words and phrases written throughout *The Whizbang Machine*:

Vloek: Curse
Fabriek: Factory
Schrijven: To write
Klok: Clock
Geheim Poppens: Secret Dolls
Sleutelstad: The Key City
Guilders: Currency used before the Euro was adopted
Spreekt u Nederlands: Speak Dutch?
Naar voren: Forward
Niet springen: Don't jump
Stoppen: Stop
Geen: No

Wie is er: Who is there?
Volgende: Following
Klaar: Ready
Wacht de schrijfmachine: The typewriter is waiting
Hoe is dat mogelijk: How is that possible?

The People:

One month before I was given the pleasure of joining the Waldorf Publishing team, my dear friend, Erin Burkamp snapped a photograph of an old Royal typewriter, seated in a beautiful tan and maroon case, her family had been gifted. Knowing my affinity for antiques, especially those that deal with writing and literary works, she sent me a text one early Sunday morning with the words, "Look at what David's father gave us."

I hadn't yet made my way out of bed. Hearing the familiar chime of my phone, I rolled over wondering who was texting me at such an early hour. As the photo came through, with it came the idea for this book. I sprang from bed and began outlining. Unbeknownst to Erin, that single photo became my muse. In honor of this gift, her oldest daughter became the character of Elizabeth Yale.

Edward Hess founded the Royal Typewriter Company in January 1904 in Brooklyn, New York, with a man named Lewis C. Myers. In March of 1906, the first Royal typewriter, the Royal Standard, was sold. When World War II started, Hess and Myers began exclusively producing wartime needs such as guns, bullets, and necessary components to fighting the war. When the war ended, Royal went back to functioning exclusively as a typewriter company.

Outgoing President G. E. Smith secured exclusive sponsorship of the September 23, 1926, epic championship boxing match between William Harrison "Jack" Dempsey and Gene Tunney. Fifteen million listeners were reported to have tuned in.

On October 9, 1926, Royal produced its one-millionth typewriter. New Royal President, George Edward Smith, bought a Ford-Stout Tri-motor airplane, dubbing it the Royal Air Truck, and had flight crews drop two hundred Royal typewriters in crates attached to parachutes to dealers across the Eastern seaboard. Royal is reported to have delivered over 11,000 typewriters in this manner.

Worldwide demand caused Royal to open a new factory in Leiden, the Netherlands, in 1953.

Hess passed away in Florida in 1941. He was a prolific inventor that held one hundred and forty patents.

Rembrandt Harmenszoon van Rijn was born July 15, 1606, in Leiden, the Dutch Republic, now the Netherlands. He was the ninth child. After attending Latin school, he in fact enrolled and attended Leiden University. Some of his notable collection remains in Amsterdam's Rijksmuseum in The Hague.

How the characters came to be:

Edward Royal was named in honor of Edward Hess and his world-changing invention, the Royal typewriter.

Ian Hess, Edward Royal's assistant, was also a nod to the famed inventor.

George Tunney was named after prizefighter Gene Tunney, whereas **Jack Yale** was a nod to Gene Tunney's rival "Jack" Dempsey.

Fictional curator and historian, **Gustavo van Rijn** is the four-times-great-grandson of artist Rembrandt van Rijn. Gustavo's character was created to establish the rich bloodlines still present in Leiden today.

All other characters were works of fiction.

The Places:

Library Way can be found by approaching the Schwarzman building, the main New York Public Library building, from the east and walking along 41st Street in Manhattan. Library Way was completed in cooperation between the New York Public Library, property owners and commercial tenants along 41st, library organizations, and the New York City Department of Transportation. Quotes from authors and poets are etched in beautiful bronze plaques installed in regular intervals in the sidewalk along 41st leading to and from the Schwarzman building.

The **New York Public Library** is the second largest library in the United States behind the Library of

Congress. It also holds the title of the fourth largest library in the world with nearly fifty-three million items in circulation.

Patience and Fortitude, lion guardians of the library, are world-renowned sculptures proudly seated at the New York Public Library's entrance at Fifth Avenue and 42nd Street in Manhattan. Sculptor Edward Clark Potter was paid $8,000 for modeling the lions and famed sculptors the Piccirilli Brothers crafted the twin lions from Pink Tennessee marble. The brothers were paid $5,000 for their craftsmanship.

The Rose Reading Room, opened May 23, 1911, is located on the third floor of the library, Room 315. The majestic public reading and research space stretches nearly two city blocks. Exquisite old-world architecture meets modern-day technology inside this unique and stunning space. The Rose Reading Room is said to be the home to more than forty thousand reference materials.

The Milstein Division (Room 121) and the **Milstein Division Microform Room** (Room 119) is one of the largest genealogical collections free and open to the public. The emphasis of both collections is on New York City. While the collection is comprised of Naturalization Records, Passenger Lists, Photographic Collections of New York City, Regional Records, African American Resources, and Newspapers dating back as far as 1764, the family historian would find their research best served in other various sections within the library. Nor does the New York Public Library employ a genealogist or language specialist for hire.

Bryant Park has quite a rooted history of its own. In 1775, George Washington's troop raced across the site at the start of the Revolutionary War. A little over eighty-six years later, Union Army troops used the area as an encampment. Bryant Park has been known by many names, Potter's Field, Reservoir Square, to name a few. In 1884, Reservoir Square was renamed to Bryant Park, to honor romantic poet and longtime editor of the *New-York Evening Post*, William Cullen Bryant. Today Bryant Park is home to an Outdoor Reading Room operated by the public library, Le Carrousel, an old-fashioned carousel, which delights small children and adults alike; restaurants, cafés, a stylish hotel, art installations, concerts, and public events.

The **Underground Storage Tunnels of the New York Public Library** do in fact exist. Below the surface of Bryant Park stand 120,000 square feet of storage. The underground facility can accommodate up to 3.2 million books and 500,000 reels of microfilm. The stacks are connected to the main library by a sixty-two-foot-long tunnel. If you are looking for the hidden fire escape that Jack and Elizabeth used to penetrate the tunnels after hours, that too is a real landmark. Standing on the west side of the Bryant Park lawn is the fire escape disguised by a dedication plaque. According to calls to the library, the storage tunnels are not open to the public.

Grand Central Terminal, sometimes referred to as Grand Central Station, located in New York, is a transportation hub famous for its rich history, bustling crowds, fine shopping, and numerous transportation options such as rail, subway, or bus services.

Leiden, the Netherlands, also known as Sleutelstad, the key city, is located on the Old Rhine. Roughly twelve miles from The Hague and twenty-five miles from Amsterdam to its north, Leiden is rich in history not only in the Netherlands but also here in the United States. Pilgrim leader John Robinson along with religious followers fled the volatile political environment in England for Holland, choosing to settle in Leiden in the early 1600s. He established a church near the city center and main church, St. Peter's. Twenty-five members of Robinson's congregation actually sailed on the *Mayflower* and settled in Plymouth. Robinson was expected to make the voyage but died before making the trip. He is buried in St. Peter's church.

Besides this history tied to the United States, Leiden has played other important roles worldwide with many tied to the university. Leiden is also known as the city of books for its role in printing and worldwide distribution of manuscripts. The city has recently started hosting the Leiden International Film Festival, which is quickly becoming the largest of its type.

Leiden University, established in 1575, is the oldest university in the Netherlands. Don't go looking for a Royal exhibit in the basement. You'll be sadly disappointed. The university is famous for developments such as Snell's law, the Leyden jar: a capacitor made from a glass jar, cryogenics, and liquefied helium. Albert Einstein also spent time at Leiden University during the early and middle stages of his career.

St. Peter's Cathedral, the Pieterskerk is a late-Gothic church established first in about 1100. The site held a county chapel. In around 1390, construction began on a new cathedral. It took approximately one hundred and eighty years to build. The building took a hit in the gunpowder explosion of January 12, 1807. It was boarded up and wasn't restored until 1880. Famous dignitaries are buried there, including painter Jan Steen, Leiden professor Herman Boerhaave, and Pilgrim Father, John Robinson. The building is open to the public.

The Red Keys are crossed in an x-shape on the coat of arms in Leiden. Many public buildings do bear the coat and the keys. These keys are believed to belong to the gates of heaven held by St. Peter, for whom the church is named in the city's center. Sleutelstad means the key city.

The Hotel Nieuw Minerva is available for check-in. Look for the room that is modeled after Rembrandt's home. You may find there is some comparison to the third-floor suite Jack and Elizabeth inhabited during their time in Leiden.

Korps Nationale Politie is the law enforcement division of the Netherlands. Detective Henry was not modeled from any of the KNP's officers, detectives, or officials.

Events:

3 Oktober, otherwise known as the 3 October celebration, is the city's biggest and most popular annual festival. The celebration denotes the end of the Spanish siege of 1574. Lasting two to three days, the celebration includes parades, feasts, historical reenactments, and the typical fanfare one is used to seeing at festivals.

1807 Boat Accident: catastrophe struck the city of Leiden on January 12, 1807. A ship loaded with 38,360 pounds of gunpowder exploded in the middle of the city. One hundred and fifty-one people lost their lives, thousands were injured, and more than two hundred homes were destroyed. The space is now the home to a city park, the Van der Werfpark. The dates of the incident were changed to work within the story, and foul play was never considered with the explosion, at least not according to researched documents.

Don't miss the next adventure:

The Whizbang Machine

Tunney's Curse

Epilogue: Tunney's Curse

Forty years is all you have once the curse finds its way to you. Death is upon us. Death is upon us. History is not correct. It's yours to fix, Elizabeth Royal. The clock ticks.

I suppose I should have seen this coming—given a bit more thought and contemplation as to how my life would ultimately come to an end. It was foolish ever to think I could beat the Whizbang machine at its own game.

"Elizabeth, please! What have we done?" Jack Yale cried, violently jarring my shoulders. "E-liz-a-beth! Stay with me!"

My body seized, pulsing with white, hot electric current. The burn nearly stole my breath away.

"Elizabeth, wake up! We need to get out of here!"

Dilapidated bricks tumbled from the caving upper floors of the Whizbang factory, smacking the cement and disintegrating into granules of red clay near my head. The floor shuddered. Shockwaves of ferocious shaking suddenly sent the walls quivering; boards sighed and snapped, each losing their battle to stay intact. Piece by piece it all began to topple down.

"Earthquake!" someone yelled in the near distance.

Earthquake, I thought; *Elizabeth, try to hoist yourself off the floor.*

I couldn't move.

Nearly two hundred years of aging sediment rained down, striking my legs, gashing my face, and filling my nose. I was stuck.

"Elizabeth, please! You cannot leave me!"

Dazed and disoriented, lying in a mangled heap on the damp, cold factory floor, I swallowed hard, trying to gulp back the mounting fear growing inside me and rise to Jack's heated request, but all I swallowed was a thickness that tasted like charred ash. This is what people mean when they say a life hangs in the balance. I pulled in a swig of air, but it barely made it past my throat.

"Someone help me!" Grandpa Jack shouted.

Jack's voice slowly faded away.

"Eliz—"

Fate had twisted in an unfortunate way for Jack and me. The rhythmic thudding inside my chest that I've taken for granted for the past fifteen years suddenly ceased to be. My lungs, burning with unwelcomed grime, fell eerily silent too. I read once in Biology class that when the human body dies, it takes the brain up to six minutes to shut off. That seemed insanely cruel at the time—it seems impossibly wicked now.

I tried to remember how all of this came to be. How my bones ended up pressing into the cold floor, clinging to what was left of my life, and the only thing that I could recall was planting my fingers amongst the keys of the Whizbang machine and feeling my feet break free from the concrete. The only thing that made sense now was that the machine made good on its promise and claimed its latest victim. *All of this was in the name of Tunney's curse*, I thought, *how sad*. Maybe, just maybe this wasn't my end, perhaps I was stuck in a horrific nightmare with no way to escape—this being nothing more than a glimpse of what could possibly come to pass if Grandpa Jack and I didn't end the curse. That's it; it's just a dream. *Hold on, Lizzy, everything will change in a moment.*

When this terrifying hallucination, dream—whatever it is—ends, I'll wake up to the smell of warm coffee and my mom singing downstairs in the kitchen on Downhill Lane. Maybe this has all been a dream—Jack, the machine, maybe it has all been nothing more than a vivid nightmare.

I held still, letting my mind fall silent and listened for anything that would clue me in. Nothing.

"Hello?" I whispered.

My mind shot off in a million directions, everything firing at once. Endless questions pulled at me while insignificant memories played on an endless loop. My past and present careened and converged into one another while my brain relentlessly spun out of control.

"Grandpa Jack!" I whimpered. "Where are you?"

"Elizabeth, look! You missed an Easter egg," my mother giggled. "Hurry up, before someone else gets it!" A large yellow and white gingham basket filled to the brim with colorful eggs swung wildly on my forearm as I turned, smiled, and toddled back towards my mother. I couldn't have been older than two.

My mind turned in circles—Jack, my mom, the machine, the merchant. I was going crazy.

"Jack!"

"Daddy, I bet I can beat you up the hill! On your mark, get set, go!" I shouted. My short legs shot forward, charging headfirst as quickly as I could. I watched as my

father purposefully lagged behind, only pretending to run. I remember this day. I was five. I won the race, and we celebrated with ice cream.

Please, I begged. *Stop. Let me wake up!*

"Elizabeth, darling, you look beautiful. Merry Christmas, my love," Grandpa Jack said. *I was six.*

Each moment that flashed drew me deeper into the unyielding insanity pulling at me. Wrestling against what could only be the final moments before my brain fully stopped, I tried one last time to move, but it was a futile attempt.

"Please," I whined. "I have to save my mother. I need to wake up!" I struggled to get ahold of myself, to breathe in a sense of calm. The pain was starting to fade. I didn't want it to; it was the last connection I had to my body. There was little left but despair.

"Let me ask you a question, sir. What do you know about this supposed curse on Leiden?" my father asked.

"Dad?"

Blinking hard, I watched as my father spoke to the merchant in the courtyard days before his death.

"Curse?" the merchant replied.

"Yeah, I heard someone talking about a curse last night in the small pub just over the next footbridge. Sounded like a bunch of hocus-pocus, if you ask me."

"I assure you that isn't the case, sir," the merchant replied.

"Then what's the story?" Jesse Yale pushed.

My mind bent, switching directions.

No, go back, I have to know what he said, I begged my insides.

Jack and I were standing inside the boiler room. Flashes of the Whizbang machine, the grandfather clock, and the key filled my head. My eyes narrowed their focus on to the key. The eight—the sign of infinity—within the key's handle…my mind laid out each of the keys Jack and I had gathered from our search thus far, none of them held that symbol. This was far from over. I blinked hard, and before me the room shifted. It was on fire.

"Don't, please!" four-year-old Alina Royal begged. "Uncle George," she cried.

"Stop your whining, child," George Tunney screeched. "Get in there. Your father wants to play games—then I'll show him a game."

"Father! What are you doing? Let go of Alina!" Daphny Tunney shrieked.

"Daphny, why are you here? I demand you leave the factory!" Tunney shouted.

"It's on fire, Father! Let go of Alina, please, she's just a baby. This isn't you. You don't want to hurt anyone, Father. Papa, *gelieve*, please."

"Her father has spent years accusing me, destroying my life, our lives, I will do the same to his," George replied.

"Not with his child," she cried.

"Get out or you'll burn too!"

The echoing cries of trapped workers came from behind the barricaded workshop doors. Hands slapped at the wood, banging fiercely, holding out for salvation.

"I won't let this happen, Father! You are not a monster," Daphny squealed.

"A thousand years and forty years the curse will remain…" Tunney began.

Fire raged. Warm timber cracked under the heat. The mountain of coal in the boiler room ignited, setting off a wild explosion.

"Father!"

"Daphny!" Alina cried.

Alina's bright red hair, curled in perfect ringlets, shook as her body trembled. "Please," she cried. Her soft, brown eyes narrowed in fear. "Uncle, I'm sorry. Daddy will fix it. I promise. Please!"

The seams of her heavy, blue silky dress buckled as sparks burned and ate away at the fabric.

"No!" Alina cried.

"Daphny, if you will not leave then get in the boiler room," Tunney screeched.

"No!" Daphny began to slowly back away.

Black smoke encircled their heads; Alina's cries worsened, matching those rising from the workroom.

Daphny stopped cold. She wouldn't let Alina die.

"This isn't the way to fix your troubles with your cousin," Daphny screamed. "Hurt Royal, not all of these innocent people! Not your own family!"

Tunney snatched his daughter's bright blonde hair, twisting it in his fist and yanking her sideways. With one heavy shove, he pushed her body onto the flame-engulfed floor of the boiler room next to his niece. Without a moment's hesitation, Tunney shut and barred the massive door.

No, my mind screamed.

Tunney turned, pausing to taken in his sinful deed. A broad smile stretched across his face, which was red and shadowed by the now raging fire.

"The curse will remain until the rightful owner shall turn back the hands of time and correct a Royal mistake."

He bent down, hoisting the heavy Whizbang machine from the cement floor and tucked it under his arm, turning towards Edward's office. Plucking a wooden pegwood doll hand from his cousin's desk, George started for the door. Hastily, he thrusted his heated words upon those who were being ravaged by the flickering flames.

"One thousand and forty years the curse will remain until the rightful owner shall turn back the hands of time and correct a Royal mistake. The secret will eat away at those who come to play like a disease. No one will outsmart the curse of the Whizbang machine. Long live the Tunney name."

Whiz-whiz-BANG! Everything jolted, shaking with such might, I was confident the earth would split into two.

I gasped, trying to breathe, but my lungs were still. My mind went shockingly blank. Deafening stillness filled me as the blackest darkness took over every corner of my brain. Despair once again filled my soul. The soft, muffled chime of a clock pendulum slowly grew to an outright earsplitting level.

Tick-tock.

Tick-tock.

A white flash filtered in, breaking the darkness. The image of the clock spun into view, its hands twisting rapidly.

Flash.

The Whizbang machine trembled with all of its might, pushing its raw power into my hands somewhere deep in a locked away tunnel.

Flash.

Tick-tock.

The doll hand twitched wildly as if it too were possessed.

Tunney's words slowly filtered through my head once more. I tried to hang onto the words, but everything grew dizzy and clouded again.

Flash.

Please, I begged. *Please, just make it stop! Let me wake up.*

"Elizabeth!"

Turning, my father was standing in a cloud of dust and waist-high rubble.

"Dad?" I shivered.

"What is happening? Have I died?" I asked, trying to pull myself from the hard cement.

"Shh, it's okay, Elizabeth. I need you to listen to me carefully before we run out of time."

"Out of time? Answer my question; have I died? I can't Dad; I have to save Mom!"

"Elizabeth, you're close, but you haven't died yet. You have to make a choice."

Tick-tock.

"What choice? Where are we?"

"We are sort of in-between," Jesse Yale replied.

"In-between what? Like purgatory, is that what you mean?" I questioned. "What about Mom?"

Tick-tock.

Jesse's eyes flew around the room.

"Elizabeth, I need you to know the truth. It's the only way you can possibly stop this curse. Edward wasn't as innocent as you think. Go and find the pegwood factory. Remember the map. Take it with you.

"What map?"

"From the bank. You'll learn more once you find the other factory. Please, Elizabeth, if you don't stop the curse it will wipe everyone out."

"Wipe everyone out?" I questioned. "Hasn't everyone involved around died? Besides Jack and me, of course?"

"No, Elizabeth, the curse has only just begun."

"What?" I demanded. "Then it is impossible to stop!" Tick-tock.

"The pegwoods, Elizabeth—start with the dolls. Find that hand."

My father's arms wrapped around my back, drawing me close into his chest.

"I don't want to leave you again," I cried.

"You aren't, Lizzy. I'm with you."

"What if I can't stop this?"

"You don't have a choice. You have to, Elizabeth."

"I need you to wake up before it's too late."

"Too late?" I quivered.

"Sweetheart, try to breath," Jesse whispered.

The ticking of the clock stopped, replaced with two loud bongs.

"Elizabeth, you must take a breath! NOW!

"I cannot."

"Try!"

One-two-three, air filled my lungs. There was a moment of silence, and then fevered hands hit my chest, pumping at my heart.

"Elizabeth!" Jack whimpered. "Baby, I'm so sorry."

"Dad," I called out.

He was gone.

Flash.

"Elizabeth!"

My mind was caught in between the present and the past. Jack's soft voice filled my ears. He sounded a million miles away. "Lizzyyyyy…"

Flash.

Tunney gently laid the Whizbang machine right outside the smoldering factory door. Tossing the pegwood doll hand on top, he pulled a hammer and a few long steel nails from the back pocket of his trousers and began to seal everyone inside. The fury of his anger was evident with each strike. Each hit sent echoes of those screaming inside the burning factory into the night's air.

He didn't utter another word. Instead, he let his madness drive him to the edge of which he could not return.

"Elizabeth!"

Flash.

My four-times-great-grandfather, Edward Royal, was standing on the stage. "Ladies and gentleman…" he began.

"E-liz-a-beth!" Jack howled, compressing his weight into my chest over and over again. "Please, breath. Please!"

Bong. Bong.

"Make a choice!" my father called. "One more bong and you're here with me forever. I need you to stop the curse. You have to stop Tunney, Elizabeth. He isn't finished yet!"

One last powerful jolt struck my chest. My body quaked—then silence. No earsplitting chiming. No memories on rapid replay. History wasn't correct, it was mine to correct, just like the machine had said echoed in my head. With that a kaleidoscope of colors spun into view, my stomach lurked, propelling my body forward as I pulled in a massive gulp of hot air into my lungs.

"Elizabeth!" Jack panted.

"Ahhhhhh," I shook. I was alive.

Acknowledgments

Thank you to the New York Public Library staff who picked up the phone and listened and answered endless questions.

A million and one thanks to the Waldorf Publishing team. I am so lucky to be a small part of this amazing publishing house. This book would not be possible without Barbara Terry, agent and publisher extraordinaire, who is a true champion of writers, and makes me laugh with her quick wit and honesty. It's a refreshing and beautiful thing. To Beth Stifflemire for all you do. Mark Isaac for creating the vision I had in my head of the perfect cover. To editor Carol McCrow for your sharp eye and encouraging spirit. Words cannot express my gratitude. Thank you for being my village.

To my girls of summer (M, R, T, H), thank you for your friendship, your encouragement, and the love you have shown while I wrote this book and several others. You are the very best.

Lastly and most importantly, to my little family, thank you for your undying enthusiasm even when it meant putting up with late nights and early mornings, a few missed lunches, months of bad take-out, and a few more dirty socks than normal. You are the true stars and my everything.

About the Author

Danielle A. Vann was raised in
Oklahoma City, Oklahoma. She
got her start in writing in the
field of journalism where she
worked as a television news
writer, producer, news reporter,
and evening/morning anchor.

She currently lives in Mansfield,
Texas, with her husband, Todd,
and their three children. While
this is her first published fiction novel, Danielle is the
author of two children's series, ***Gracie Lou and the Bad
Dream Eater*** and ***The Gracie Lou Series***, and ***The Very
Tall Tale of Ranger, the Great Pyrenees and his Adorable
Friend, Miss Keys***, and co-authored ***Building Faith
Through A Carpenter's Hands*** with celebrity carpenter
Brandon Russell.

To learn more, visit www.authordanielleavann.com.